-a Finder's Keepers mystery-

Prologue

Long stringy hair fell forward covering her face. The child wanted no one to see her tears, especially those who taunted her, criticizing her lack of ability to articulate even the simplest words. She hated school but most of all she detested recess. The bullies controlled the yard, waiting for someone to torment.

She settled farther into the corner of the small closet. This had become her safe place. Her solitude, however, left room for the dark thoughts. *You're worthless*, they whispered. *Your mother loathed you. She couldn't stand being near you. That's why she ran off.*

Sarah stared at her feet, wet tracks sliding down her face to the brown muslin dress she wore. She slid a paring knife from her pocket. She turned it over and slowly poked her finger on the sharp blade. Red liquid oozed from the cut. Using her blood, she sketched a line on the bare wall next to her. The appendage found refuge in her mouth.

Her bottom hurt where she sat on the rough-hewn plank floor. She closed her eyes. Images of night time betrayal surfaced. Her eyes flew open again. Pushing the long sleeve to her elbow, she surveyed the scars that decorated her arms. Her father liked to use a hot poker when she didn't meet his expectations. She coated another digit with blood and then began to draw some more. Soon, the stick figures of her mother and brother adorned the wall.

The bell rang. The girl jumped. She yanked her sleeves down to cover the recent wounds. Waiting until nearby foot-steps grew faint; she opened the door an inch at a time. Unde-tected, she crept from her hiding place and scampered to the classroom. She scrambled to her seat as soon as she crossed the threshold.

"Sarah." The loud voice drew everyone's attention. "You're late."

She looked at the voice of authority standing at the front of the room. His scowl sent shivers down her arms. "Sorry, sir." Her thin voice echoed in the silent room of chil-dren, all trained to obey unconditionally. The belt bruised their skin at school and everyone feared the same when they got home afterward. She stared at her desktop, tracing the etched 'stupid' that someone had carved just for her. Hopelessness, not a familiar word, but her sense of a dismal sameness, an aware-ness of never escaping, overwhelmed her.

The day dragged as her teacher taught reading and how to spell from the Bible. Each student had their own book of scriptures, but outside of school, flipping the pages was never permitted. Only the adults in their community could interpret the High German language inside. They made sure all the pas-sages about obedience and, for the women, submission, were read every Sunday. Although she was fluent, she spoke Platt-deutsch with all the other kids walking to and from school.

Today, the passage described love. That puzzled her. Love was what her father said when he visited at night. But the Bible described it as something good, a word seldom spoken in her world. *I wish I was brave enough.*

It wasn't the first time she considered ending her life. *I am worth nothing except to cook and clean for the family. I don't care about the whole lot of them.* The rebellious thought caused a frown to appear on her angular face,

"Sarah, pay attention." He shouted the words, the ven-om dripping from his lips. He'd make sure her father under-stood her failings. Rebuke happened often when she got home.

The girl stood beside her desk to repeat the end of day prayer. Sarah's thin body shivered. Home was a place of dread, a never-ending list of work to do. Supper took a great deal of preparation on the wood heated stove. She was the only one to do it since her mother left.

Her soul hungered for an excuse not to go there. However, her feet shuffled absentmindedly along the one dusty street in their small village. The uncluttered grey walls of the house appeared all too quickly. She saw her father before he detected her tiny frame as she entered through the gate. When he lifted his head, she shuddered. He motioned her toward the house; his angry glare telling her she'd better not be slow with the evening meal.

The child sighed as she pushed the wooden door inward with her foot. Brick walls encompassed four rooms. The larger one contained kitchen furnishings with some open shelves for dishes and staples like flour and salt. Vegetables lay beneath the floor in a root cellar which also stored barrels of preserved meat. The other three were bed chambers, one for her, one for her brother, and one for her father. When her mother left, that room became his alone.

She flexed her shoulders to ease the proverbial ache and tiredness. Exhaustion spoke of little sleep and restless nights. Her bones ached but ... *I gotta get going.* She'd make stew. Her father complained not so much when she cooked that dish. After gathering the supplies she needed, Sarah began by stoking the fire and added a couple of logs. Her arms strained with the weight of the rough wood but there was no one to help.

I wish I had a gun. She emitted a long slow breath. *Nobody cares.* She remembered the weapon she'd seen her father use to hunt wild boar down by the river. It was so long and too heavy. Her reflections tumbled over themselves as she scraped the peel from potatoes and carrots she'd carried upstairs. *God, are you real?* She looked heavenward. *So far away. Is that the heaven the Bible talks about? He doesn't listen either.*

Her stomach rolled around mixing the bile into a bitter reflux. She gagged but nothing came out. She was used to the emptiness but she dreamed of more. Sarah drew in an exasperated breath. Life was about marriage as soon as she turned thirteen and babies after that. The girls in her village worked from sun up to sun down and sometimes long after. The boys were waited upon, favoured as were the men.

She couldn't afford to be sick. But she was anyway. Her head throbbed as she stirred the stew. Stepping away, she set bowls on the table, with cups of milk. In the centre, she placed a loaf of bread baked early that morning before school began. The smell of the simmering food forced her insides to rebel again as if they wanted to expel the stuff before she'd eaten it. She brushed at the lone tear that left a trail down her hot face. *Maybe second grade will be different.*

Chapter One

Jeremy Goodman hummed one of the hymns they'd sung the day before. He and his family attended the same church for most of his life. He walked past Christine's office door. Then he stopped and took a couple of steps backward. He studied his friend's actions for a few minutes but then stuck his head through the open door. "Busy?"

Christine lifted tired eyes in his direction. Her computer screen had drawn her attention all morning. She rubbed the bridge of her nose to relieve the burning sensation from her eyes. "I need a break. Want to share a quick cup of coffee?"

"I'll ask Jenna to make a fresh pot." He continued his trek to the reception area of his small investigative agency. "Jenna." He paused when he saw her red eyes. " Hey, you okay?"

His office assistant turned toward him. Her shoulders slumped. "I will be. Feeling sorry for myself, I guess. The doctor's report wasn't so good this time."

Jeremy walked closer. He wrapped his arms around the distraught woman. "Has the cancer escalated? I thought the chemo treatments were helping."

"I thought so too, but apparently not. He said the tumour grew. All that throwing up for nothing." She shook her head. "Can't dwell on it. What can I do for you? Give me something to take my mind off me."

"Are you sure you're up for it. Christine and I could use a fresh pot of coffee. I could do it myself." His creased forehead gave away the concern he had for his employee. "Jenna if you need some time ...."

"I don't and don't you try to make me take it easy. I've been taking it easy for months now and look where it's got me. From now on I live to the fullest ... no restrictions, Hear?" She grabbed the coffee pot, walked briskly toward the sink in the little kitchen area behind her desk and turned the tap to cold. "I'll bring you each a cup as soon as it's brewed. Won't be long."

Jeremy shook his head and turned back down the short hall toward Christine's office. He walked inside greeted by Chief, Christine's service dog. He reached toward the dog's head and scratched between his ears. "You guarding the home fires, boy?"

"Hah. He's been sleeping all morning. He moves when you walk in. Me he ignores, don't you Chief?" Christine leaned back in her desk chair. "There's a lot on the Internet about those Mennonite villages in Mexico. They're actually not far from the border."

"You doing research on ways to rescue those kids out of there?" He sat in the only other chair in Christine's workspace. "I need to find you more furniture. Some landlord I am," he snickered. "This room needs a woman's touch I think."

"Not this woman. Decorating is not my thing. Just the basics man, just the basics." She crossed her arms over her head giving them a good stretch. "I don't know what to say to Helen. We've ... I've never worked across borders before. I possess a passport but ..."

"Yeah, been thinking a lot about this case. I think we're way over our heads here." His chair squeaked as he turned to Jenna who'd walked through the door. "That didn't take long."

The woman placed two steaming mugs on the desk, the only table top in the room. "You need a small table where you can sit away from that computer once in a while." She turned to leave.

"Wait, Jenna. I have a question for you." Christine wrapped her hands around the hot mug. She inhaled the intense aroma of coffee, an aroma that never ceased to invigorate her. "Do you think Jeremy and I should take on this new case?"

Jenna glanced around for a chair. "Let me drag my chair in here and I'll grab my own coffee. It does smell good."

"I'll do that." Jeremy hopped up and exited the room ahead of the efficient woman. "I'll bring the coffee too."

Jenna sat in the chair he'd vacated. "My legs feel like dead weight these days."

Christine waited for the older woman to continue. She wanted to ask how Jenna felt but decided to wait until the receptionist offered the information. "Another opinion would be helpful. Jeremy and I are vacillating over whether or not to go to Mexico and find Helen's children. She's nearly frantic; seems worried and yet she left her there with a man who is abusive. I guess I wonder how much of her story is true."

"I think caution would be good. It's no small thing she's asking. If the authorities catch you smuggling a child across two borders ..."

"The mother said she would give us papers with permission to bring the children here, but I think she needs to go with us since she's the biological mother." Christine waited while Jeremy wheeled Jenna's chair into the room.

He situated the cushioned chair beside his and left again to get the coffee for his assistant. Once he returned, the conversation continued.

"Jeremy, I was telling Jenna that I think Helen needs to go with us. What do you think?" Christine settled back in her chair and placed her hands on her desk.

"I told Christine that you guys need to use caution. You'll be crossing two borders. Kidnapping children could bring you all kinds of trouble." Jenna took a quick sip of the strong brew in front of her. "Ohhh. Hot."

Jeremy drank from his own mug. "Christine and I have been going back and forth on this one. We need to give this woman our answer soon." He reached toward Chief again as the dog settled down near his right side. "I agree with your assessment about her coming with us, but we still should figure out how to sneak inside that village without causing any questions."

"I need to do more research." Christine hung her head. "Should we be asking God to give us some help here? Does He do that kind of thing?" Christine's faith was so new that she still needed to ask a lot of questions.

Jeremy's awkward glance pleased her. She knew her faith still surprised him. It was gratifying to know that, once in a while, like now, she was a step ahead of him.

He responded. "I'm sorry. I should have suggested that about an hour ago. Jenna, I'd like to begin by praying with you."

"Oh. Please. I can use all the intercessors available." Jenna sighed.

"What's an intercessor?" Christine took another sip of coffee as she waited for Jeremy's insight.

"To begin with, Jesus is our first intercessor. He stands before the Father and intercedes on our behalf. Then there are the people who pray for us. They are called prayer warriors or intercessors. There were many people at church praying for you when you were shot, Christine. Jenna, you know that everyone's had you on their prayer lists. Let's turn these two issues over to the Father." Jeremy bowed his head.

Christine and Jenna did likewise. Jenna began, "Father, you understand the hearts of these two wonderful people. They care for your children so much. There are more questions than answers with regards to the Rempel woman. Would you steer them in the right direction and Father, help them to make wise and safe decisions. In Jesus' name."

Jeremy jumped in with his request for Jenna. "Father, Jenna needs your healing touch. Please give the doctors wisdom in how to treat her cancer so that she can enjoy many long years of remission. Thank you, Lord. Also, I ask for wisdom for Christine and me. If this is not someplace you want us to go, close that door. Thank You for caring for us and for protecting Christine. Keep her safe, Lord. Amen."

Christine remained silent. Jeremy glanced at her and saw her lips move. His heart felt a little warmer than it had a few seconds ago. *Thank you, Father.* He raised his head and reached for Chief, the dog quietly waiting for some attention. His soft fur trembled as Jeremy used his fingers to scratch down to his skin.

Christine lifted her eyes and watched as Chief arched his back a little. "He likes you. That's a good thing too. Otherwise, you wouldn't be able to barge into my office whenever the mood strikes."

"Oh, barge in, is it." Jeremy checked his watch. "Well, I got a call from Sergeant Irving and he wants you and I to come to the station. He wants more clarity about the pictures and the video we took at the judge's hideaway. Do you have time?"

Christine looked at Jenna who was standing in preparation to move her chair back to her desk. "There's a lot more research to do on this Mexican thing but, sure, I can go with you."

Jeremy moved to Jenna's side. "You're not carrying this." He pushed the chair and looked over his shoulder toward Christine as he walked to the door of her office. "Can you be ready in fifteen minutes? Bring Chief. The squad room hasn't had a visit from him for a while. Irving's suggestion."

Christine looked a little sceptical. Jeremy snickered. "Honest." He left just ahead of Jenna. She waved toward Christine and grabbed her empty cup on her way out.

"I'll be right behind you." Christine's voice trailed him into the outer office.

Jeremy glanced at Jenna. *She appears more energized than an hour ago.* "You need to rest regularly now that you've insisted on being at this office every day. Christine did offer to bring a cot into her space where you could lie down when she's not using it. Why don't you take her up on it?"

"Jeremy, you pay me to look after things around here. If I'm napping I'm not pulling my load. I'll take it easy and maybe cut back to three days a week again." She settled herself into the chair Jeremy had arranged behind her desk. "Now, I have some filing to do so scat. You and Christine need to get going."

"We do. We'll be back in an hour or so. If we receive any urgent calls you can take a number and call us, otherwise ...."

"I know. You'll call them when you return."

Jeremy gave her slight shoulder a gentle pat and turned toward the sound of footsteps. The dog's nails clicked on the tile flooring as both he and Christine stepped into the foyer. "Did you make the decision about which vehicle we're taking?"

Jeremy flashed his keys. "Let's go in my truck. I need to stop by Dad's office for a minute after we finish at the cop shop. Is that okay?" He led the way to the door.

Christine waved toward Jenna. "I'm not expecting anyone to call." She followed Jeremy out the door. "A visit with your dad is needed anyway. I want to see if he's booked another appointment with Rompart."

Chapter Two

Christine stared out the window of the truck as it passed pedestrians and other traffic along the busy thoroughfare. The police station was located downtown, right in the centre of the drug and prostitution rich environment of Winnipeg. *I wonder if they located the building here on purpose or if the illegal traffic followed the building.* "Jeremy, you'd think that with so many police leaving and entering this area, the drug dealers and pimps would locate their traffic elsewhere."

"Yeah, the concept always astonished me. They seem to want to hug the walls of this station. But it's been this way for years." He spotted an empty parking space and manoeuvred the large truck into it.

"Did Irving really invite Chief to come with us? I think that man is a closet animal lover." She snickered but sobered when she spotted a young girl staggering down one of the alleyways. She shook her head. *Can't save them all but ...* "Jeremy, I'm going to find out where that alley leads. She stepped off the curb at the back of the truck.

Jeremy looked in the direction she indicated. "What's over there?"

"I don't know, just a hunch." She took a step toward the alley.

"Wait. I'll go with you." Jeremy started to follow.

Christine held her hand toward him. "I think I can handle this. A young girl went in there. I need to check if she's okay. You might scare her off."

Jeremy scowled. "Christine, she could be meeting her pimp, or maybe her drug source. Are you carrying?"

"No." She frowned. "I never thought I'd need it."

"I'm coming. I'll hang back where she won't notice me but I'll be able to watch your back. Okay?"

Christine nodded her head. "I guess I need to carry my gun with me at all times. Come on. Let's go before she disappears."

Jeremy leaned against the truck bed. Christine crossed the street as soon as the next vehicle passed by and entered the alley. She kept her attention ahead of her, but her ears and eyes scanned the doorways she passed. She did feel safer knowing Jeremy was behind her somewhere. The brick walls smelled of urine with a hint of garbage. A bag of refuse rustled when she passed, an indication that some rodent was looking for a free lunch. She shivered. *I hate rats.*

The alleyway was long but turned right at the end, hiding what was up ahead. The girl was nowhere in sight. *I waited too long.* Christine walked a little faster and as she approached the corner, an argument reached her ears.

She scurried toward the damp wall and peered around the corner. Two men held the girl by her arms. Their angry voices were muted so she couldn't make out what they were saying. The girl seemed terrified, though. *How do I handle this?*

Someone tapped her shoulder. Christine jumped and used her elbow to disable whoever was close by. A grunt confirmed she'd connected. She turned around ready to use her arms and legs as defensive weapons. "Jeremy."
She whispered his name a second time. "What are you trying to do, scare me into a psych ward?"

Jeremy pointed toward the scuffle around the corner. "I heard it too and wanted to stop you from barging in unprepared. Why don't we act as if we lost our way after leaving a local bar? Like .... kinda drunk." He draped his arm heavily around her shoulder. "Less go." He hiccoughed for effect.

Christine giggled loudly. "Ahh, Chester, you some kinda ...." She belched. "Oops. **Shorry**." They walked toward the trio as if they'd been up drinking all night. "Where you **takin'** me anyway?"

Jeremy glanced at the thugs holding the girl between them. "You guys live 'round here too? Want a party?" He swallowed as if his stomach was about to erupt.

Christine giggled again. "Hey, girlie. You got some place where we can use the restroom around here. We think we're **losh**." She giggled again and staggered for added effect making Jeremy have to take an extra step to keep from falling over.

The two thugs stared at them for a few seconds and seemed to catch their breath. "Get outta here." The taller of the two recovered first. "Go home and sleep it off."

Christine reefed her shoulder out from under Jeremy large bicep. She staggered toward the two strangers. "Awww. Come on. Less party."

The second creep took his hand off the girl who used the release to her advantage. She yanked her arm out of the other's grasp as well and started to run. Christine took off after her. "Wait. Where's the bathroom?"

She listened as Jeremy continued to engage the two frustrated men. Their patience would eventually wear off but in the meantime, she kept her eyes on the terrified young woman. Once she figured she was out of the attacker's earshot, she tried once again to stop the woman's retreat. "I'm here to help. Stop."

The woman's steps slowed slightly but she continued to move away from her pursuer. Christine tried again. "I ..." She sucked in a deep breath. "want to help" She drew in another breath. "... you." Christine stopped and leaned forward, her legs shaking from the extra exertion.

She lifted her eyes expecting to see a retreating back but instead the woman was looking at her from a few steps ahead. "Why **you** chasin' me? What you want?"

Christine wrinkled her nose. Her thoughts turned to wondering why people needed to urinate in public places but she reasoned that some of them probably didn't have any homes. "I ... We noticed you head into the alley and wanted to help. This doesn't look like any place for a young woman. We watched those thugs follow you in here."

"Taint none of your business." The small framed female began to turn her back. She looked over her shoulder. "I can take care of myself."

Christine would not be apt to describe this person as an adult. She looked to be closer to the age of a teenager. Christine cleared her throat. "I'm sure you can but there were two of them." She took a step closer. "What's your name?"

The woman-child sneered. "I said this is none of your business. Now leave me alone." She ran toward the other end of the alley as if following a light at the end of a tunnel.

Christine began to follow but stopped. She raised her eyes heavenward as if getting a message from God Himself. *You can't help her if she doesn't want your help.* "I know Father but ... she seems so young ... and scared." Her voice came out in a whisper but the one she listened to seemed to boom. *I'm in control.* "Yes Lord." She looked around. *Where is Jeremy?*

Glancing once again toward the path taken by the woman, Christine sighed. Then she retraced her steps to find Jeremy. As she rounded the corner, angry voices filled the rancid air. Jeremy was still trying to convince the hoodlums that he was not a threat to them. Christine began to stagger as she approached on silent feet. "Awww come on honey. Less find some place to party." She hiccoughed.

The thugs growled in her direction. "Listen to your lady friend. Get outta here."

Jeremy took a step toward them menacingly. "I need a drink." He staggered toward Christine and wound his arm across her shoulders again. "Less go find us a drink." He chuckled. The couple turned to head back toward the street. Christine kept her ear peeled for any sign that footsteps followed. There were none.

Jeremy hastened his stagger just a little but once they reached the sidewalk across from the police station, he stopped. "Don't you ever do that again. That could have gone wrong in so many ways. Where's the girl?"

"She didn't want any help so I let her go. After what we learned about the human trafficking trade in this city, I couldn't ignore the situation." Christine began to snicker. "We make a convincing couple of drunks, don't we?" She took a step toward the police cars lining the sidewalk on the opposite side of the street.

"Christine, you were almost killed and we aren't sure who it was who put a hit out on you. It may have been the judge but we have no proof he did it. You have to be more cautious and going into an alley anywhere near here is not a good idea." Jeremy took an extra step to catch up.

She turned to glance behind before stepping onto the sidewalk. "You're right, of course, but at the time ... well, I let my instincts take a backseat to the need. I'll be more careful." She looked at him as his hand grabbed the door handle. "Promise." She flapped her eyelashes in his direction.

Jeremy rolled his eyes. "Oh, brother." Then he moved ahead of her into the cop shop. Approaching the desk sergeant, he asked for Sergeant Bill Irving. "He's expecting us." He nodded toward Christine.

Chapter Three

Bill Irving lifted his head from the stack of paperwork centred on his desk. He spotted Jeremy and Christine as
they entered the front door to the station. *Now for some answers*, he thought. His full six foot four frame rose out of the
chair. *I could use a distraction.*

He walked toward the couple when the receptionist
pointed them in his direction. He waved in acknowledgment
and waited while they slipped through the gate separating the
squad room from their guests. "Hi, Jeremy. Christine. Come
this way."

Irving led them toward a small room, one of the many
used for interrogating prisoners. "How has your day been so
far?"

Jeremy chuckled. "Not as quiet as I would like. Christine had us chasing a working girl through the alley across the
street. At least I think she's a pro."

Sergeant Irving scowled at the woman in front of him.
"Have you forgotten ..."

"I already reminded her that the person who wants to
excise her from this planet may still be out roaming around.
She doesn't listen well." Jeremy practiced his stern look while
he spoke.

Christine sat a little straighter in her chair. "She looked like she needed help. And it turned out she did. What do you think would have happened to her if we ignored our instincts?"

"Heaven forbid." The sergeant cocked his head in their direction. "Oh forget it." Irving reached for the file he'd brought with him. "I need you both to go over these photos you gave me, describe what went on. The judge is denying he killed the kid. His lawyer is trying to get his charges reduced to child endangerment. I want that scumbag to serve every year of a twenty-five-year sentence or more." He pounded his fist on the metal table adding an echo to the room.

Christine's face revealed the astonishment and revulsion churning around her insides. "He most certainly did kill the kid. I saw him and so did Jeremy." She rifled through the 8x10 glossies from the file folder. Grabbing one, she pointed toward a picture of the judge with his hands around the boy's neck. "There. He strangled the boy."

"His lawyer says he was only trying to help the boy breathe, that the child was holding his breath on purpose. Did you hear him say anything to the kid to indicate he was planning on killing him?" Irving leaned back in his chair and looked at Jeremy this time.

"I didn't but ... Sergeant, the judge had an evil look on his face before he did it. He did exactly what he intended to do. He strangled the boy." He lay his hands, palms up, on the surface of the table. "We were helpless to prevent what happened. It was so fast. By the time we shouted at him to stop, the child's limp body was draped over his knee." Jeremy shook his head. "The man deserves everything the law can bring down on him. I wish Canada had a death penalty."

Christine shuddered. "I'll never forget how hopeless I felt. The kid's eyes seemed dead as if the light had gone out of them. But there was definitely a difference after that creep wrapped his hands around his neck." She checked through the pictures again. "Look at this one. I took a picture of the floor below the boy's feet. The judge had just walked in and the boy produced that puddle. He was terrified. How can people live with themselves ... and this disgusting piece of humanity is busy excusing what he did? Death is too good for him. I want the prisoners to find out what he did. They'll look after him."

Jeremy cleared his throat. "Christine." He looked at Sergeant Irving as he placed his hand on Christine's arm. "We'll talk about this later. Bill, anything else we can explain for you?"

"No. I have what I needed. You'll be called as material witnesses."

Christine's eyebrows furrowed, her furious countenance visible to both men. "I can't wait. I want to describe in detail what those two creeps did to that kid. By the way, what charges have been brought against the pastor?"

Irving grimaced. "They are charging him with aiding and abetting but he did much more than that. However, from what you guys told us, we can't prove the rest. We need more victims to come forward. I'll bet he's abused some of the kids from his church but until ..."

"We could go undercover. Attend the services; ingrati- ate ourselves to some of the families. Maybe ..." Christine looked hopefully toward Jeremy. "Couldn't we?"

Jeremy dropped his head and spent a few minutes study- ing his hands. Then he gazed across the table at his business associate. "Christine, what about the Rempel woman?"

"I still haven't decided to take that one yet. I need to do a bunch more research. I can do that and work this case too. Jeremy, that pastor needs to be charged with paedophilia, child porn, and anything else they can lay on him. The sergeant's right. More kids have to step up, if we can find them, and con- vince them to testify. A lot of if's." She stood in preparation for a hasty exit. "Don't churches invite people to a Wednesday night service? That's the day after tomorrow. We could begin to infiltrate the congregation then."

Jeremy slowly rose from his own chair. "We'll let you know what we decide, Bill. Come on, Chief. Let's get this woman out of here before she gets us involved in another case."

Christine strode out of the room with the two men. The animal walked ahead of her with Jeremy, his tail raised high like a flag waving in the breeze. She turned back toward the sergeant. "If there are any other kids hurt by this man, we'll find them. Then we can put this man of the cloth away for a long time."

"Just be careful, Christine. This network is far reaching. We've probably caught some big fish but there are more of them out there, I'm sure. These guys aren't above using force to keep their victims quiet." The Sergeant added a beefy pat to her shoulder. "I wouldn't want you to land in the hospital again."

"Jeremy has my back." She looked at the man waiting for her near the sergeant's desk.

"I heard that. Who's going to watch out for me?" He glanced down at the dog "Maybe you, huh, Chief."

"You guys keep me posted. I'm sure the Crown Prosecutor they've brought in will be getting in touch. I gave him your contact info yesterday." He walked to his **work space** and the stack of paperwork that hadn't diminished any in his absence. "See ya later."

Jeremy waved his goodbye and strode toward the front door. The sergeant shook his head. His hands are full. He snickered. *Life hasn't been simple since she returned to her city of origin.*

Chapter Four

Christine attached Chief's leash as soon as they left the building. She watched Jeremy stride toward his truck. *I wonder why he seems reluctant.* Her steps were slow as she crossed the street. Walking around the back end, she opened the passenger door, guided Chief inside disconnecting his leash as soon as he landed on the front seat, and followed him inside.

Jeremy had already inserted the key into the ignition. She fastened her seatbelt and turned toward him as he steered the vehicle into traffic. "Why are you hesitant about going undercover at the church, Jeremy? I assumed you'd be as anxious to gather evidence against that phony pastor as I am."

Jeremy glanced at her briefly and back at the front window. He cleared his throat to give him some time to form an answer. "Christine, do you remember thinking that maybe now was the time for you to resolve your issues with Rompart and take on the management of your Father's company?
You just had another attempt on your life. Remember?"

"I do. But ..."

"No buts. These creeps are dangerous. They're killers and someone out there wants you dead. We made the assumption that we caught the person who put out a contract on you but what if he is only one? There could be others who wouldn't hesitate to eliminate anyone who comes between them and their addictions." He turned toward the end of town where his Father's office was located.

"I understand that. Anytime I followed the clues to find a kid that's gone missing, I've known the dangers. At least, I'm learning the dangers. I understand the risks but, Jeremy, those kids need us. If that pastor hurt any of the kids in his congregation, they need to see their abuser charged for his offenses. As long as he goes unpunished, they remain under his control, one way or the other. They face their abuser every week." Christine furrowed her brow.

Jeremy took a swift peek in her direction before turning the final corner to his Father's street. "I get that you care about this stuff but Christine, you're no good to anyone laid up in a hospital. We'll check out the church Wednesday night but before then, we'll visit with a friend of mine who has some pretty high tech gadgets that might level the playing field a little. Okay?"

Christine's grin told him she was happy with his change of heart. "In the meantime, I can do more research for the Rempel case. Our home is secure. If anyone does find out where we live, they'll find that breaking in won't be as easy as my other little house was. Besides, the security agency is keeping an eye on things." She turned toward the side window as Jeremy pulled into the parking spot for Goodman and Son. "Did you tell your dad we're coming?"

"Yeah, I called earlier before we left the office. Let's pick his brain about all this too. He might have some insight about Mexico as well." Jeremy turned the engine off and opened his door. "Come on Chief. No need for a leash here."

The dog bounded over the seat. His large paws landed on the edge of the driver's seat and he slid to the ground. His grunt told his friends he'd landed harder than intended as the air left his lungs. Tail raised high; he raced them toward the office door.

Jeremy laughed. He glanced at Christine. "He behaves as if it's been years since he saw Dad. I think they bonded rather well while you were laid up."

Christine chuckled as she walked hurriedly after her animal. "Some service dog. He's all about making friends. That does work well when we rescue a kid, though."

She waited for Jeremy to open the door. "I'm just happy he gets along so well with most people."

Jeremy followed her inside. He waved to Clare, his father's office assistant and fiancée. "Is it okay to go on back?"

Clare nodded her approval and returned to the filing she needed to get done. Jeremy led the way down the short hall to the nicely appointed office of Barkley Goodman, a lawyer for Christine and for Rompart Industries, Christine's legacy from her dad. He knocked on the door at the same time as Chief's bark of welcome.

"Come in." The deep base voice from the interior continued to talk as they strode into his office. The phone was held in the older man's hand. He nodded toward the sofa and chairs as he ended his conversation. "Thanks. We'll talk again tomorrow." Barkley stood. "Hi, you two. Jeremy, I need you to do something for me. Got some time?"

Jeremy looked in Christine's direction and back at his Dad. "How long do you think it'll take?"

Barkley took one of the vacant chairs, crossed his legs, and relaxed into the cushions. "Probably no more than a day or two. I need you to follow someone."

"That should work. We need to visit with Jake Klippenstein to obtain some surveillance equipment and some GPS trackers before Wednesday but that won't take long. I can phone him some details so he'll have the stuff ready when we stop by." He looked toward Christine for confirmation.

She nodded. "I'll be doing research anyway."

Barkley turned toward his client. "What's the research for?"

"I ... We've been asked to travel to Mexico to rescue a little girl and her brother from their abusive father. They live in one of those Mennonite communities down there in the northern part of Mexico where all the drug cartels have been spotted. I need to find out more about the community and try to find a way in and then back to Canada without raising any red flags from the authorities. Piece of cake, right?"

Barkley cleared his throat as if he were about to choke. "This is your lawyer you're talking to. Piece of cake my foot." He glanced at his son. "You're not really considering this, are you?"

"Dad, the mother ..."

"The mother wants you to retrieve them. I think I'd better hear the whole story."

Chapter Five

Barkley Goodman let out a long low breath as he listened to Christine and Jeremy's thoughts about the Helen Rempel case. His response came from his legal training. "Getting across the border may take some doing. The woman should go with you. It isn't kidnapping if she's their mother. But the father might have legally gained full custody since she took off. Anyone will say she abandoned them. The authorities still frown on taking Mexican nationals to another country without the custodial parent's permission."

Christine sighed. "I understand this is not going to be easy, but from what the mother describes, these kids are in grave danger. Most of the men in this village are criminals tied to the drug trade. They mistreat their children and their women. She got out, saving her life with every intention of finding a way to retrieve her children someday. She's come to us. We want to try to help if it is at all possible."

Jeremy interjected, "I've listened to this woman. She's clearly distraught. She lived under this horrendous abuse since the day she was born but somewhere she got the courage to flee. Christine, did she ever tell you where she got the idea that life would be better in Canada? Do they receive visitors from Canada who would tell them about conditions here?"

Christine pursed her lips. Her brow furrowed in concentration. "No, she didn't but you're right. The research I did describes a closed community, segregated from any outside influence. The men may have contact with other Mexicans, but from what I read, the women and children do not." She took a notepad from her purse. "These are some questions I intend to ask Helen when we see her again."

Barkley nodded in assent. "Those aren't the only things you need answers to. Why didn't she take the boy and girl with her if she thought they were being abused? What kind of mother only thinks of herself under those circumstances? I've known women who will put themselves in front of an abuser to protect her kids but running to save herself ... It doesn't make sense."

"I know. There are too many holes in her story." Christine set her notepad down.

Jeremy frowned. "We're judging her culture by ours. People in our country think differently than people from one of those remote villages. Just think about the Amish communities here and in the US. Their ideas are totally foreign to the rest of us and yet they live within our borders. How different must this Mennonite community be living separately in Mexico? Mark down the questions, Christine, but don't assume you know the answers. Keep an open mind." Jeremy stood. "I need to call a man about some surveillance equipment."

As soon as Jeremy left his father's office, Christine turned back to Barkley. "We'll take this one slow. I'll tell you what we decide. I told Helen we'd need her to tell us a whole lot more before we agree to take her case. She's desperate, though. If we won't do it, I expect she'll find someone else who will." Her lips turned up at the corner. "Have you and Clare set a date yet?"

Barkley blinked. His grin quickly spread over his face. "You're as bad as my son. We'll fill you both in as soon as we have something to tell you. For now, we're enjoying the romance." He chuckled. "It's been a while for us. Let's talk about Rompart. Are you ready to proceed?"

Christine stared at the floor for a few seconds and then looked directly into his eyes. "One minute I think I am but I receive another phone call with someone asking for my help to find a missing kid. I hate that there's a need for investigators like me. Kids should be safe, protected from the evil that lurks out there. Notice I called it evil. Before I met Jesus I just thought there were some people who were bad and some good. But now I know that it has a name. I also understand we win in the end but, in the meantime ..."

"Yeah, evil exists, unfortunately. What you do brings hope to people but consider this. Ever thought about using the resources from Rompart to finance a whole slew of investigators to bring home missing kids?" Barkley leaned back and studied the face of his client.

Christine ran a hand over her eyes. She stared back. The revelation was new to her. "I could, couldn't I? Are the assets really extensive enough to do that?"

"Christine, Rompart owns over 300 buildings in this city, some large, some small but all are generating income. Aside from repairs, and acquisitions of new sites, plus several other expenses which you'll understand when you go over the books, Rompart is solvent. As heir to the company, you've been accumulating quite a bit of investment which I've been looking after. Your parents had a will, as I told you, naming you a sole beneficiary. I, as executor, have been the overseer of those assets. If you liquidate some of them, you'd be able to run many cases vicariously through trustworthy detectives."

Christine gulped. "I guess I hadn't thought that far ahead. I always figured it was a one or the other situation. I do want to dig into the trenches at Rompart. My father started that company. I want to carry on what he began but the kids ... the world for them is so frightening. I want to be part of bringing those hypocrites to justice. How can a judge, someone who decides what punishment to hand out when a person is found guilty, do those same things to a little child and then ..." She almost choked on the words. "... act as if he's the one being misjudged." She shook her head. "Anyway, if we can formulate a way I can do both, let's do it."

Jeremy stepped through the door. "Let's do what?"

"Barkley set it up. I want to begin learning what Rompart does, how it does it, and where I can become involved. My father's reputation also needs to be cleared. I thought for a long time that the answers are within the company records." She smiled as she straightened her back in the soft chair she sat in. "Jeremy, I'm sure you have the names of some worthy investigators. We can start amassing employees for Finders Keepers Agency."

She grinned at the look of astonishment that dominated Jeremy's facial features. "Wow. I like a decisive woman but ..." He shrugged his shoulders. "Yeah, Yeah. Later. Klippenstein is the person who has what we need for Wednesday night. Let's go get the stuff and drop by the office. I'll follow up on this case for Dad and you can research the Mexico deal. Right?"

Chief slowly lifted his head. He reclined on his side seemingly not in any hurry to leave. Barkley stepped closer and bent to rub the dog's belly. "Looks like you're leaving again boy." He chuckled as the animal stretched his legs out in front of his reclining body.

Christine stood. Chief rolled over and hopped to his feet in one smooth motion. He sauntered toward his mistress and brushed against her leg. Her hand automatically reached for her friend. "Come on boy. You can sleep the afternoon away while I search for answers." She followed Jeremy out the door.

Chapter Six

Christine scrolled through one article after another as she scanned the information about the Mennonites They settled a long time ago in Mexico. She glanced at Chief as he lay beside her desk. "The people from these colonies originally come from Canada in 1922. Several families left because the Canadian government wanted their kids educated in public schools. The people believed that to protect their heritage and their beliefs, they needed to move where they would be allowed to be separate, teaching their children in the Low German dialect." The dog's intelligent gaze studied her as he angled his head to one side. He wanted to understand what she was saying it seemed.

I can't imagine what the people who left experienced as they travelled to that part of Mexico. She looked on the map. The land surrounding Chihuahua, Mexico was primarily desert. *These people were farmers. I wonder how they lived without electricity or a way to irrigate their fields.* She dug further.

One article, with a video, portrayed a segment of the Mennonite population who chose to hook up to electricity, so became a more thriving community. The video, a National Geographic piece, told of how they still continued to keep their children and women subservient, though. The commentator told how the women weren't allowed to learn the Spanish language so couldn't converse with the local Mexican tradesmen and store owners. The children were only educated to eighth grade and the teachers used only the Bible as their textbook.

Wow! She sat back in her chair. *Some countries are a little backward compared to Canada and the US. But purposefully remaining in the early 19th century when all around them are modern conveniences they are forbidden to use ... I can't imagine.*

The next article tied the Mexican drug cartels to some of the Mennonites caught in Alberta smuggling cocaine. As she read further, Christine discovered that over the years, as the Mexican drug dealers cozied up to their Mennonite neighbours, the ensuing social problems, violence, and economic hardships drove some Mennonites north. A few immigrants brought the drug business across two borders as they travelled through the US to Canada.

Christine shook her head. *So Helen was telling the truth.* The Mennonite community in Mexico either adapted somewhat to the world around them or, she further discovered, they left for even more austere conditions in Belize. *I guess their elders couldn't agree on how they wanted to live. But the women aren't given a say at all in whether to stay or go.* The documentary portrayed one woman who acted as the local dentist. She was well respected by both male and female patients. They showed another family where the husband made all the decisions totally disregarding the hardships involved for his family.

What a way to live. We take so much for granted. Christine walked slowly toward her small coffee maker. She poured a hot cup of dark brown liquid and turned the machine off. She contemplated the plight of these poor people as she took a tentative sip. She walked back to her desk and set the cup down. "Chief, want some water?"

The dog wagged his tail thumping the floor with a happy rhythm. Christine picked up his bowl, tossed the warm fluid in the sink and let the faucet run until cold refreshing water poured out. She glanced at Chief. He was slowly rising on all fours as if he was too old to move very fast. She chuckled. "Come on, old man. Drink some cool water. You'll feel better,"

She set the bowl in front of him and the dog lapped contentedly.

I wonder if the Mennonites in Mexico own dogs. The picture of dusty conditions and cinder block buildings flashed across her brain. *Probably not. The kids were always clean, though, and the girls wore such cute dresses, at least for the documentary.* They smiled a lot. *I wonder if Helen is exaggerating about the conditions her kids are subjected to. Maybe ...* She jotted down another question to ask Helen Rempel the next time they met. *I still don't know how we're going to sneak into that community and spirit those kids out. There's no place to hide.*

Chapter Seven

Jeremy walked into the office, noisily slamming the outer door behind him. He dropped a couple of packages on the counter. Jenna looked up from the computer. "What're those?"

"Christine and I are planning to infiltrate the church where the pastor we caught with the judge preaches. If he's abused one kid, you can bet more exist. Irving wants us to find them. Right now all they can charge him with is aiding and abetting but we all know he's up to his ears in this business. The judge hasn't implicated him either, which is strange since he squealed fast enough on the Crown Attorney." Jeremy crossed his arms, a frown forming between his eyebrows.

"Maybe the judge is holding back in case he needs more leverage. I'll bet he's not doing too well at the Remand Centre while he waits for trial." Jenna ran her hand across the small of her back.

Jeremy was quick to notice. "You hurting?"

Jenna grinned. "Naw. Been in one position too long. Did Irving tell you whether the judge is in general population or secluded?"

"He's secluded. He'd never make it otherwise. He's made a lot of enemies over the years and now that the word travelled about his misdeeds, you can bet some want him dead. Serves him right. If it were me ..."

"You'd protect him, too. You aren't the vindictive type." Jenna stood and twisted from side to side to relieve the kinks.

Jeremy glanced toward Christine's closed door. "She been occupied since she got back?"

"I haven't seen her. She said she had some research to do so I don't expect her to stick her head out anytime soon." She returned to her desk. "A little more to do and I'm going home."

Jeremy's pensive stare seemed preoccupied. He shook his head and glanced toward his office assistant. "Go home. The filing can wait till tomorrow. As far as me being vindictive, I don't think it takes vindictiveness to punish someone who hurts, or in this case, kills little children. He's a monster."

Jenna pursed her lips. "He is, but the law will deal with him. He'll receive the punishment he deserves."

"He's actually denying he did anything to hurt the kid. Thankfully we recorded it. Irving wanted us to clarify what we saw, though, since he expects the defence attorney to accuse us of doctoring the video. As if we had time before the police showed up."

Jenna looked toward the packages. "If only you had some of that equipment when you tailed him to the house. Maybe the boy's death could have been prevented." She reached for her coat. "I will leave the rest of the invoicing till tomorrow." She slipped an arm into the sleeve of her jacket and then reached to turn off the computer. "I'll be in as soon as breakfast is done."

"Don't rush. I don't know where Christine and I will be and what time we'll arrive tomorrow. I'll keep you filled in though." He walked toward Christine's office. "See you in the morning sometime." As he continued his trek, his pensive gaze reflected his concern for his friend. *She is usually more committed to the work piling up. I wonder if she's not telling us something.*

He knocked on the closed door. "Christine. Can you take a break?" He turned the handle as soon as her voice invited him inside. "How's the research going?"

"I found out a lot regarding the people living in the area where Helen said she's from. I found several ..." She made quote marks with her fingers, "... campos in the area, some only thirty or so miles from the other. They travel by horse and buggy, though, so thirty miles is a long distance. They don't visit with each other except on Sunday's. I did a Google search of the landscape. Trees are scarce but along the river, a few places exist where we can hide if we need to. The school is also located near the river. That might be the best place to take the kids." She paused to take a breath. "Otherwise ..."

"Maybe we need to speak with a minister up here to find out if he has any suggestions. It would need to be someone who doesn't agree with their lifestyle, though." Jeremy plunked himself down on the only other chair in the room. "You need some more furniture in here."

"Why. I don't interview clients here."

"Yes, but no place to put your feet up. Research can become tedious sitting in a desk chair for hours. A sofa would be more comfortable." He glanced toward Chief, "I'll bet your dog would enjoy lying on a leather sofa once in a while."

Christine missed the slightly tender appearance of Jeremy's gaze. Her finger paused over the keyboard. "Maybe. Jeremy, we need to figure this out. These people live as they did in the early nineteenth century so anyone using modern conveniences of any sort will stand out. We couldn't even use older cars since most of these campos don't use any. One nearby town uses electricity and automobiles. Maybe we could use that town as a base and travel closer by horse ... Oh, I'm just thinking out loud." She crinkled her nose as she looked in Jeremy's direction.

"Let's wait until we talk to the Mennonite pastor. Then we can meet with Helen again and run some of our ideas past her. She'd know what will work better than we will. And she managed to escape without detection. There must be a way." He crossed one leg over the other. "Time to head home. Jenna left already. Want to stop someplace along the way to find a bite to eat?"

Christine closed the lid on her laptop computer. "I'm going to bring this home with me so I can check out a couple of other ideas." She fit it into her carrying case. Looping the strap over her arm, she stepped out from behind her desk. Her cell phone emitted the musical tone designated for her lawyer.

Christine grabbed the device and held it to her ear. "Hello, Barkley. What's up?"

Jeremy watched as Christine listened to his dad. He waited for her to speak.

"I see. Well, yes, I guess that could work. I gotta start sometime. Did they give you any indication about how long it would take to familiarize me with the client list?" She glanced at Jeremy. "What time?"

Jeremy glanced at his watch. He stuck his hand into his pocket.

Christine ended the call with, "I'll see you later" and looked at Jeremy. "Your Dad made arrangements for me to go over the client list at Rompart tomorrow morning. You'll be shadowing that person for your father anyway so I said it would work. Maybe we can sneak into the church later in the day to plant those bugs."

Jeremy relaxed his posture a little. "So dinner on the way or not?"

"Sounds good to me. Been a while since we had lunch." She wrapped the strap of her computer bag over her arm again and followed Jeremy to the door of her office. "You heard me tell your dad I might as well begin. I can do both jobs for now but I really think someday I might hire a person or two to run my investigation business. As soon as you provide me with that list of names. I'll miss it, though."

Jeremy reached the outside door first. "Yeah. The gratification comes when we can reunite some parents with their child. I wish we could prevent them from being kidnapped. They come back so damaged."

"Oh, that's something else I found out in my research. Do you know some father's in the Mennonite culture believe they have the right to break in their soon to be married daughters?"

Jeremy stopped in his tracks. "You mean ...?"

"Yes. Disgusting, isn't it? And apparently, it happens in this country as well. I wish I could wrap my hands around the necks of some of these religious fanatics ..." She opened the passenger door of Jeremy's truck and guided Chief inside. Christine followed and secured her seatbelt.

Jeremy glanced at her flushed face. "Repulsive." He shook his head and inserted his key into the ignition. "Where do you want to eat?"

"Any place is fine with me. You choose." She paused to look out the window as Jeremy steered the vehicle down the street. Then her gaze returned to the man beside her. "What makes your church so different from some of these Mennonite ones?"

"Not all Mennonite churches are perverse. Most of them are like ours, following Christ's teachings in their everyday lives. A few are off track, that's all." Jeremy glanced at the new believer sitting on the seat with him. "God gave us His Word to live by, instructions how to treat each other. If we follow Him, things work for our good and the people around us grow spiritually in their walk too. But sometimes, His Word is perverted when a group of people pursues their own agenda. They twist the truth of God's Word to suit their own needs and desires. It's called sin."

Christine remained silent for a few extra minutes. She swallowed. "There's a lot to learn, isn't there?"

Jeremy grinned. "Just take it one day at a time. By the way, are you using the devotional I gave you? My women friends think Beth Moore is a brilliant teacher and her devotionals will inspire you in the right direction."

Christine's face turned a little pink. "I've been too busy. When am I supposed to read it? In light of what I am finding out, I probably need some instruction."

Jeremy focused on traffic. He glanced at her but then fixed his gaze on a restaurant with a partially full parking lot. "This ok?"

"Looks good to me. Do you read a devotional?" She reached for her seatbelt as soon as Jeremy stopped the truck. "Chief, I'll bring you something when we leave. We won't be long."

Jeremy stepped out of the truck, clicked the lock button on his key fob, and walked around to the other side. "I read my devotional early each morning while I am having a cup of coffee. I read my Bible too. I begin my day with the right perspective."

Christine tried to match his footsteps but had to walk fast to keep up with his long stride. "I'll try it tomorrow morn-

ing. It might be what I need before going to Rompart with Barkley." She edged her way through the door that Jeremy held
open for her and sniffed the delicious aromas permeating the
air. "I'm hungry."

Chapter Eight

Christine slowly opened her eyes. She blinked once but a vision remained. The dream had visited her again. Her father's face, his horrified glimpse of her mother lying in a pool of blood, lingered in her memory. The dream dissipated just as her father's head exploded when he was shot a minute or two later. She sobbed, her tears causing Chief to scramble closer. His warm body drew her attention to the present need for a quick walk outside. *A run may be the order of the day. It'll clear my head.* She swiped at the moisture on her cheeks. "Let's get dressed."

Christine stumbled sleepily toward her bathroom, grabbed her sweats on the way, and tossed her night clothes in the hamper. She spotted the devotional sitting beside her lamp on her nightstand. *When I return*, she promised and looked skyward. *You understand, don't you Lord?* Chief followed her out the door a few minutes later.

Christine and Chief had forged a new running path since moving to her former neighbourhood. A security guard frequented the path she chose so she felt secure racing along the tree-lined street. The run brought back memories this morning. "Come on, Chief. Let's work the kinks out."

She raced, putting all her strength into the effort. Chief easily paced beside her but he would have to stop for his own purposes sooner or later. For now, she ran as if trying to outrun the demons that continued to haunt her sleep every so often. *Last night .... maybe my meeting at Rompart has something to do with it.* She inhaled slowly as she entered the area where the policeman had sheltered her from the attacker. Her parents' killer had tried to finish the job.

Christine stopped. Her breath came out in huffs and she rested her hands on her knees. Chief licked her hand as if to remind her she wasn't alone. She watched him move toward a clump of trees as she straightened her body and allowed her respiratory system to regulate. *I sure don't want to stop too long. The air is cold and my body is sweaty.* "Come on Chief. Let's head home."

The animal lumbered closer but then slowed to a walk scanning the area. Christine reached down and scratched his head near his ear. "You're such a good dog. I'll bet you're hungry." They walked in companionable silence.

Christine noticed the familiar jeep up ahead. "Scotty's making his rounds a little early this morning." She jogged along the edge of the roadway as the jeep approached.

The man inside opened his window and stuck his head out. "Good morning Miss Christine. You cut your run short this morning?"

"I did Scotty. You're early, though."

"I don't want my drive through the neighbourhood to become routine. Someone may count on that. After all, you've been shot and I aim to keep undesirables away from your house. Thankfully Chief runs with you. Otherwise ..." He shook his head and rolled the window back up.

Christine waved her thanks and continued toward her home. The sun was almost all the way up by now. *Coffee sounds good. I wonder if Jeremy is awake yet. Oh right. Need to spend time with God first.*

Chief kept his pace even with hers as they walked through the wrought iron gate in the stone wall surrounding her property. Most of the homes in the area had a wall of something edging their yards. *Privacy matters but ... maybe if the **neighbours** had known each other a little better, a killer wouldn't have been able to kill my parents and escape justice all these years. Someone would have seen something. The kill-*

er's dead now but the someone who killed him hired him to kill mom and dad. I want to know who and I intend to keep searching until I find out. I think Rompart is the key so ... She took her key out of the pocket of her sweat pants. Unlocking her front door, she stepped into the bright interior. *I wonder if I will ever stop missing them.*

Removing her running jacket, she dropped it over the back of a hall bench and continued to the kitchen. Gathering the can of coffee, she took the carafe over to the sink to fill. Chief let out a low bark. "Oh, okay. You want some water too." Christine set the coffee pot on the counter and reached for the dog's bowl.

Glancing at the clock on the kitchen wall, her coffee preparation complete, she sighed. She pressed the start button on the coffee maker and sauntered toward the staircase leading to the bedrooms. Her leaden legs carried her up to gather her devotional book before she sat down with her Bible. The Good Book always sat near her favourite chair in the living room. Chief remained by his water dish lapping contentedly.

Christine took the stairs one at a time, the exercise warming the muscles in her legs all over again. She sauntered into her bedroom and stripped off her damp jogging clothes. Inside her bathroom, she stepped under the hot spray of the shower. The water stung her cool skin as she soaped the morning's activities down the drain. A scant few minutes later, she descended the staircase, devotional in hand, and smelling extremely feminine.

Chapter Nine

An hour later, Christine pulled into the parking lot at Rompart Industries; the legacy her Father left her. Rompart was a successful holding company, according to Barkley Goodman, her Father's lawyer and now hers. He'd kept his eye on the company from a distance for the last twenty years, waiting until the day she could assume responsibility. Today was the day.

Her feelings about taking over the reins of the company were ambivalent. As she stepped out of her Jeep Grand Cherokee, she thought about what this day meant. *If her Father and Mother had lived, it would be a day of celebration.*

She walked toward the front door, outwardly confident but nervous nonetheless. *This is what they wanted, maybe.* She would assume control and in the process, clear their names, she hoped. Before her hand could grab hold of the large brass handle, the plate glass door opened as if by magic. She walked through, plastering a smile on her face expecting Richard Belcher, the CEO, to greet her. Instead, Jason Mitchell, the firm's attorney stepped forward with Barkley close behind. "Good Morning, Miss Rompart. May I call you Melissa?"

"Of course." She accepted his offered hand. "Where's Richard?"

"He's waiting for you upstairs. Your office is all ready for you. This has been a long time coming and your Father, although I didn't work for him, would be proud today." Jason led the way toward the large bank of elevators. "Your office is on the top floor, the same one your father occupied."

Christine swallowed. She glanced at Barkley. His nod of approval went a long way in stemming the battle of butterflies in her stomach. She smiled her thanks and then gazed at the door, waiting for it to open.

Her silence seemed to give Jason permission to prattle on some more. "The files you requested are ready for your perusal. Richard has the answers to any questions about the various businesses we own ... er ... should I say, you own. Anyhow, it's all straight forward."

"Jason. I plan to operate this company as my Dad did with Barkley's help, I'll be up to snuff very quickly I'm sure. I also want to check all the personnel files so I can become better acquainted with the people who work for me." The large steel elevator doors slid open to reveal the mirrored and brass interior. Christine was the first to step inside.

Barkley stood by her side as Jason entered. "Barkley, are you familiar with the inner workings of Rompart? I thought you only made sure everything was active and above board, looking after Miss Rompart ... er ... Melissa's interests."

"Oh, I kept a lot more control over the years than that. I kept my distance but I also checked on each of the companies, who operates them, and what they do. As Melissa's lawyer, I could have stopped any and all acquisitions at any time. Parker's will gave me the legal right to do so." He nodded toward Christine. "Melissa is my only full-time client now so I have all the time we'll need to make the transition."

Jason took a couple of steps away from the duo as they reached the top floor. He cleared his throat and was the first to step out, barring the door for Barkley and Melissa to exit.

Richard Belcher stood quietly outside the elevator. He smiled and then reached his hand toward his new boss. "Melissa, welcome to Rompart. As the new Chairman ... er ... Chairwoman of the Board, I hope you'll find your office space satisfactory." He led the way toward the wall of offices overlooking Portage Avenue in downtown Winnipeg. Several staff members watched the procession with interest.

Christine walked confidently, her posture erect and her head held high. The butterflies continued to do somersaults but no one watching would be aware of that. Richard Belcher appeared unfazed by her presence. *I wonder if he's aware of the accusations his brother's made against him.* Although the police had not acted on them, Irving had filled her in. *Now we'll see.* She stepped into the plush office space. "Did you redecorate this room since my father's death?"

"I did." Richard stepped aside to allow her a complete view of the landscape outside the Windows. "I hope you don't mind but this was my office for the last twenty years and I wanted to make it my own. You can do the same if that pleases you."

"I may hire some company to repaint it. Something a little more feminine." She glanced toward the bank of windows. "You sure can't beat the view." She reached down with her left hand and then remembered. Chief was with Jenna at the office. *I miss him. He gives me confidence.*

Richard walked nonchalantly toward her desk. "This desk was your Dad's. I had it brought up from storage. There are a few other pieces down there as well if you'd care to check it out."

Christine took a seat in the large swivel office chair. It cushioned her body with support. Sitting where her father had brought a catch to her voice. "I-I'd like to g-get to work." She cleared her throat.

Richard pointed to the pile of file folders sitting near her right hand. "Those should contain the information about each company that you need. If Barkley can't answer your questions, just keep a list and when I get back from my meeting after lunch, we can discuss them."

Christine glanced from the files to his face. "Is this a meeting I should be attending?"

Richard swallowed. "No. No. I'll handle any meetings till you're up to snuff. I wouldn't want anyone to lose confidence in our company just because we're changing leadership. I'll introduce you to them one at a time later in the month. Okay, Miss Rompart?"

"I guess that'll work. The sooner the better, though. My intentions are to do what my Dad did and the clients need to get acquainted with me so they can be confident I intend to do the best I can for them. If they want to purchase anything, whatever it is, we'll handle it as always, right?"

Richard cleared his throat. "Of course." He walked toward the door. "I'll stop by later." Jason followed him out the door.

Christine looked at Barkley. "Using my real name is confusing. I wonder, now that they understand I'm taking over if I should just use Melissa all the time. It won't matter to my investigations and you and Jeremy are already familiar with my birth name."

"It would sure simplify matters. How do you want to handle those files?" Barkley moved closer to her desk.

Chapter Ten

Jeremy walked into the bank at the corner of Portage and Hargrave. His hair was neatly combed and the collar of his charcoal grey suit was turned up slightly. He walked to the information desk with the confidence of one who owned a great deal of money. "Can I meet with your branch manager? My name is Albert Decapoulis."

The young woman raised her eyebrows at the mention of the Decapoulis name. "You are the owner of the airline that amalgamated with Air Canada, right? I read your name in the newspaper."

"I am. Now about that meeting."

"Oh, of course." She stood. "Why don't you take a seat over there? I'll check if Mr. Barker is available." She left her station and walked toward the last office in the far right corner of the immense first floor of the building.

Jeremy picked up a financial report he found lying on the table beside him. *This bank is pretty open about their finances. I wonder if Barker is as crooked as dad thinks he is. Someone certainly thinks so. I wonder if this document is doctored.*

He read through the first two pages, understanding most if not all of it. This place had a lot of investors. He took a notepad from his inside coat pocket. Just as he was about to jot down some information, the young receptionist returned. "Mr. Barker will be happy to visit with you. Follow me." Jeremy pocketed the document.

She led the way toward the office she'd come from. Knocking gently on the door, she waited for her invitation to enter, and then opened the door. "Mr. Barker, this is Mr. Decapoulis. Shall I bring you some coffee, Mr. Decapoulis?"

"No. Thank you. Mr. Barker, my time is limited. I'd like to go over the business I intend to bring your **way,** if your bank meets my criteria." He hoped he sounded as intentional as he expected most extremely rich people to act.

Mr. Barker held out his hand. After accepting the sturdy grip, Jeremy took a seat at Mr. Barker's invitation. Then he began questioning the manager of one of Winnipeg's largest banks.

Thomas Barker swallowed. His answers were to the point and totally unexpected. Jeremy frowned. *Someone's been giving this guy a bad rap.* Barker even provided all the paperwork that his intended client asked for and he deferred to the Decapoulis' name as someone who deserved to ask questions before depositing his money in this bank. *The man is a professional. I wonder who asked Dad to check him out.*

Jeremy spent the better part of an hour going over all the paperwork, asking for and receiving copies of some before standing, ready to leave. He held out his right hand and, removing his left hand from his jacket pocket, he slipped a listening device under the edge of Barker's desk. "Mr. Barker, it has been a pleasure. I'll bring this information back to my board of directors and will have an answer for you by tomorrow. Thank you for the time you've spent with me."

Barker stood. He shook Albert Decapoulis' hand and then escorted him to the door. "I'll be waiting for your decision. I can assure you we will do everything we can to protect your interests."

Jeremy strode toward the doors leading to the street outside the bank. *Now we'll find out who he contacts, if anyone. I can't see anything wrong here. Either he's very good at hiding illegal intentions or truly innocent.*

He walked around the corner. His truck had been swapped for a rented Mercedes. The silver-grey vehicle glistened in the sun. Jeremy walked to the driver's side door, used his key fob and unlocked the expensive machine. He folded his long frame into the driver's seat and was about to close the door when he heard the sound of a gunshot echoed from a nearby alley. *That was close.*

Exiting the vehicle, he surveyed the nearby streets and alleyways. No one else seemed to have noticed. Pedestrians continued toward unknown destinations and automobiles, trucks and buses flowed with the traffic patterns. *I wonder.*

He stepped quickly across the street and entered a nearby passage. He picked up speed as he neared the end, a recessed doorway now visible. A body, folded up like a pretzel, lay propped against the door frame.

Jeremy wandered hesitantly closer. He looked around to see if anyone else was nearby. The assailant might come back. His thoughts careened all over themselves as he remembered his handgun was in the armrest of his truck. He pulled his cell phone from its holster. Dialing 911, he took a closer look at the young woman in front of him. *There is something familiar about ... wait a minute. This is the girl Christine helped the other morning. Oh man.* "Yes, I heard gunshots and found a young girl, maybe twenty or so slumped in a doorway." He paused as the operator asked another question. "No, she looks dead. A pool of blood surrounds the body."

Jeremy hung up after giving the dispatcher his location. He knelt beside the body. Without touching anything, he scrutinized the bruises evident on the girl's face. *She obviously was beaten to a pulp before the assailant killed her.* He looked at the twisted limbs. *It won't surprise me if her arms and legs are broken as well.*

Sirens blared in the distance but sounded as if they were descending on his location. Their screeching echoed off the walls in the alley before they turned them off. Flashing lights illuminated the dark recesses as men dressed in paramedic gear approached. One dragged a gurney behind, loaded with medical equipment. "You the guy who called this in?"

"I am." Jeremy lowered his gaze. "She's been tortured by the looks of her."

The paramedic knelt beside the body. He felt for a pulse and shook his head. "No need to hurry." He looked toward his partner. "We'll have to wait for the forensic pathologist before we can take the body. There's Doc Belmont now."

An agile man of about 50 years of age exited a large black hearse. He carried his camera and a few other pieces of equipment with him. His driver grabbed a large case and followed. Dr Belmont was the coroner and had been on the job for almost a year. Jeremy knew his reputation but had not had many dealings with him. He stepped aside as the man briskly pushed his way toward the corpse. "Did anybody touch anything?"

Jeremy blinked. "No." He grimaced, his furrowed brows drawn close together as he watched the doctor take pictures from this angle and that. "I found her that way."

Chapter Eleven

Melissa Rompart, aka Christine Finder, carefully perused each file from the pile near her elbow. She glanced at Barkley. "Everything seems to be above board, so far. I wonder if his brother just wanted to take the focus off him."

"It's early yet. The pile doesn't seem to be getting any lower. Have you considered some of these files may not be accurate? I mean, Belcher could have cooked the books, so to speak. There may be a second more accurate set of files for some of these companies locked away somewhere." Barkley continued to read the file Melissa and he had worked on for the last ten minutes. "Ever considered having an audit done?"

"What would that prove? If we can't find something shady here ..."

"An audit will show whether the financial statements are accurate. We would be able to trace where the money transactions come from and which company is responsible for which transaction." He glanced out the window and then back at Melissa. "How long do you want to spend on this today?"

Melissa glanced at her wristwatch. "I can spare a couple more hours but then I need to meet with Helen Rempel. She's the woman who wants us to bring her kids out of Mexico."

Barkley frowned. "I think you may be out of your league. You and Jeremy haven't needed international contacts. A passport won't help if you plan to spirit those children away from their abusive father. If, as Helen says, he is connected with the drug cartels, you can bet they are well protected from outside sources."

"I know. I've given this a lot of thought, done a ton of research. I can't find a way around those obstacles. I plan to tell Helen she needs to hire someone else," Melissa hung her head. "I hate this. According to her, those kids need rescuing."

"If you're going to make your meeting, we'd better continue checking these files. So far I found nine names of companies with home offices anywhere but Canada. All your clients are foreign entities. I hope the background checks are done as soon as possible so you can move forward with the takeover." Barkley spotted the name of the next client as Melissa opened the file. He jotted it down on his notepad along with any pertinent contact information. "I'll pass this list onto Sergeant Irving for the police investigation. The cops aren't making any progress. After all these years they've failed to come up with any motive for your father's death. They can't affirm he was laundering money or show reason to clear his name. According to Irving, no evidence has surfaced to obtain search warrants. You being here should speed up their investigation, I should think."

"Irving said he would engage the right agency once I hand over the list of names. I'm not sure, if these transactions are all above board, why Belcher would withhold these names." Melissa looked at the file in front of her. "Look here. This company, Donaview Holdings, is out of Chihuahua, Mexico. Isn't that just south of the US-Mexico border? I found some information in that regard when I did the research for Helen Rempel's case."

Barkley looked more closely at the file. "There are drug cartels all over that part of Mexico. Maybe we've finally got something to connect the dots with what Richard Belcher's brother told the sergeant."

Melissa looked at the date of the first entry in the folder. "This company's been doing business with Rompart for thirty years. How long has Richard Belcher been associated with Rompart?"

"I think thirty-one or thirty-two years. That's one question we'll ask him. I also want to find out how much of what his brother accused him of is true. He shouldn't find a problem disclosing information about his relationship or lack thereof." Barkley continued to jot down potential questions to find answers to. "Our work is cut out for us. I'm glad you're not going to be taking any trips abroad anytime soon."

Melissa let the statement hang in the air. Her eyes ached from all the reading they'd already done. *I wonder if I could take these files home.* She glanced at her watch again. *I could do this at a more thorough and a more leisurely pace and still make my meeting with Helen on time.* She glanced at Barkley. *I'm glad he's on my side. The man is thorough to a fault.* "Barkley, let's call it a day. I know Richard isn't back from his meeting yet but I'm taking these files home where I can search through them later. I'll take notes and pass them on. If any questions pop up, I'll call. Does that work for you?"

"It does. Clare and I planned an early dinner. Besides, I want to talk to Jeremy to see what he found out about the person I asked him to investigate." He paused for a moment and watched a few clouds roll slowly past the window. "We've been focused on Richard Belcher as the man behind all the criminal activity. But what if he's an innocent party? What if someone else is behind the illegalities, if there is any at all?"

Melissa grimaced. "I guess we need to keep an open mind. I hate to think that my Dad may not be so innocent, but I suppose I should consider the idea in passing." She stood and straightened the pile of folders in readiness for departure. "I intend to find out who killed them or ordered that sleaze ball to kill them, no matter what we find out."

Melissa led the way toward the office door. "From now on, I'm Melissa Rompart, here and on the street. Can you get used to that?"

Barkley chuckled, "It took me awhile to stop thinking of you as Melissa and now I need to reverse my thinking. Jeremy will take a little longer, I think."

Melissa crossed the threshold, walked toward the person assigned to her as an office assistant, and left instructions that she would be out of the office the rest of the day. "Tell Mr. Belcher I'll be in first thing tomorrow morning."

"Will do, Miss Rompart. Is there anything specific you'd like me to do for you?" The young woman looked eager to please.

"Find a decorating company and set up a meeting for the morning. I want to redecorate as soon as possible and have the rest of my Father's office furnishings brought up from storage. I'll decide with the decorator which pieces to keep and which to get rid of tomorrow." She smiled as a means to soften her commands and then walked with Barkley toward the elevator.

Chapter Twelve

Jeremy walked into the downtown office of Winnipeg police headquarters. *I'm beginning to feel as if I live here.* He stepped toward the sergeant's desk and asked to speak with Sergeant Irving. While he waited, he scanned the room. As usual, an officer occupied each desk with some working on a computer and others interviewing a suspect or witness of a crime. *This city has gun control laws but the murder rate per capita had risen. Harrumph. Gun control disarms the good people. Criminals will find their weapon of choice no matter what laws are on the books.* His frown deepened. He lowered his head. *Someone needs to repeal those stupid laws.*

Someone nearby cleared his throat. Jeremy glanced up. Sergeant Irving stood patiently tapping his foot. "Seemed you were a long distance away, Goodman."

"You guys are so busy. I thought the gun control laws were supposed to prevent crime. They aren't making a lot of difference." Jeremy followed the sergeant toward his cubicle.

"You got that right. There are some of us think the laws are redundant." He waved his hand around the room before sitting in the well-worn chair behind his desk. "Nothing has changed except for the crime rate. It's gone up." He straightened a few papers. "What can I do for you?"

Jeremy took the seat facing the desk. "I reported a murder about two hours ago. Doc Belmont ... boy, Christine nailed it. He is one disgruntled human being. Anyway, I found the woman Christine tried to help this morning. Someone tortured and shot her by all appearances. Did they send you the particulars for identification yet?"

"Let me check with forensics." He picked up his phone. "Put me through to Belmont's office." He stared unseeing in Jeremy's direction and then looked toward the ceiling as he waited. "Sergeant Irving here. What can you tell me about the girl brought in?"

Jeremy listened unashamedly. He saw the frown on Irving's face. The sergeant sat straighter in his chair. His foot started tapping the tile floor. Jeremy leaned back, his eyes never leaving Irving's face.

"Okay, thanks. We'll get on it." Sergeant Irving dropped the phone on his desk a little too firmly. "That girl's name appeared in the registry. She was reported missing ten years ago. Guess where she went missing?"

Jeremy blinked. "I don't have a clue."

Irving grimaced before answering. "Chihuahua, Mexico from Campos Tinades or something like that. She was only five years old when the report was submitted but nothing surfaced till now. This smacks of human trafficking."

"From the condition of her body, someone decided she was no longer worth keeping around. How come a report of a missing kid in Mexico made it to this precinct?"

"Her family originally settled near here before moving to Mexico. They were Canadians so they sent the information here as well as distributing all the particulars throughout Mexico. I don't think the Mexican authorities take anything like this seriously though." Irving leaned back in his chair.

Jeremy closed his eyes for a few seconds. "For just one day I'd like to forget human trafficking exists. We can't seem to move away from it. I need to contact Christine. She'll want to be told." Jeremy pulled his cell phone from his pocket. "Did the coroner give you a name?"

"Yeah. She's Jessica Penner. Only fifteen but the Doc said her body was abused in every way and showed signs of a botched abortion. Do you remember what the fellow looked like who knocked her around this morning? I can bring you mug shots of known pimps to look at. The sooner we catch this guy, the better."

Jeremy nodded as he spoke into the phone. "Hi, Christine. Do you have time to come by Irving's office? The girl you helped this morning turned up dead and we need you to help identify her attacker." He listened for a moment. "When you meet with her, ask about a place called Campos Tinades. Someone reported this kid missing from there ten years ago." He heard the gasp that **travelled** between their phones. "Really? Wow! Okay, just stop by when you can. I'll give Irving all the information I can, from what I remember of the incident. Call me later."

The conversation ended and Jeremy looked at Irving. "This Helen Rempel comes from Campos Tinades. Christine … oh by the way, she's using her birth name from now on. Anyway, Melissa is going to ask her about Jessica when they meet in a few minutes. She's on her way there now."

Irving folded his arms and leaned on his desktop. "I hope she doesn't get offended when I forget what to call her." He chuckled but then his face sobered. "I thought you guys had decided not to take the case."

"We did and Chris …. er …. Melissa planned to tell the woman when they meet but now ..." Jeremy shook his head. "If kids are being stolen or sold from that village, we need to re-think that decision."

"Is Melissa coming by afterward?"

Chapter Thirteen

Melissa walked through the door and almost bumped into a woman standing directly in front of the counter line-up. "Sorry." She looked into the face of Helen Rempel. "Oh, hi Helen. I almost knocked you over. You ordered yet?"

"No. I just got here myself." The older woman looked haggard. Creases framed her mouth. Dark circles shadowed her eyes.

Melissa hoped her smile would send a message of encouragement but she suspected that by the end of their conversation, the woman would leave more discouraged than ever. I wish I had another answer for her. "Why don't you find us a seat and I'll order something to drink and a snack, unless you skipped lunch."

The woman glanced around the room. Before she headed toward the booth she'd spotted, she thanked Melissa and asked for a coffee. Melissa took a step toward the counter as Helen ambled toward the booth.

The line moved quickly at this time of day. Before a few minutes had passed, Melissa had their coffees along with a couple of apple pies. She zigzagged through the tables toward the woman waiting for her. As she set the tray on the table, she glanced out the window. The traffic was light, the parking lot half empty, but the rushed feeling persisted. She had a lot on her mind today.

She returned her gaze to her table companion. "How has your day gone so far?" Melissa pushed one mug of coffee toward the woman and handed her one of the apple pies. "By the way, I'm using my real name from now on ... Melissa Rompart. The other was a cover until I took over at Rompart."

"I try to remember. I'm used to Christine." She smiled tentatively. "I've not been sleeping too well. I feel so cut off from everything known to me. The noise bothers me and the traffic. It never stops." Helen sighed. She pushed a strand of hair off her forehead and secured the scarf over the rest of it.

"I imagine things are really different from where you've come. I did some research about the campos in Mexico. Why are your people so adamant about maintaining their lifestyle?" Melissa understood the answer but wanted to probe Helen's opinions on the subject.

"The elders thought they were losing control of our young people. Many were leaving for more exciting places and leaving the faith along the way. We ... the elders wanted to pre-vent this from happening." She hung her head. "They control everything. Even the bad stuff, I think."

"Helen, are you familiar with a girl by the name of Jes-sica Penner?" Melissa decided to stay away from the reason Helen had contacted them in the first place, for a little while.

Helen stared at the table. She tapped her index finger on the wood surface. Slowly she raised her head. "Why do you ask such a thing? No one knows me here?"

"This girl grew up in Campos Tinades. Isn't that where you said your children are?" Melissa scanned the woman's face closely. *She seems scared. I wonder why.*

Helen sat quietly for a few minutes. She glanced around the room and then turned her gaze toward the street. She shifted her focus back to Melissa. "I know her or used to. She went missing many years ago. She was only five. The talk in the village suggested her parents ... well ... they sold her. In any case, no one went looking for her." A lone tear trickled down the woman's face.

"Someone is looking. Someone filed a missing child report. Otherwise, we would not know who she was. Someone cared that she went missing, Helen. Do you think it's true? About her being sold, I mean?"

Helen stared at Melissa. Her nervousness caused her to revert to her broken English. "Ve don't go to de authorities for any reason. Who told dem about her? I don't know about selling. Ve just hear of such things. De men do all the handling of anything to do wit decisions."

Melissa tried hard not to look disgusted. "Well someone reported her missing. Her body was found this morning. She was badly beaten."

"Ohhh." Helen lowered her head and silently allowed tears to flow across her folded hands. "She was only a b-b-baby. My girl is not much older."

Melissa reached across the table. She placed her hands on those of the distraught woman. "Do you think the same thing could happen to your daughter? Is this a common occurrence in your village? How can they get away with something like this?"

Helen's tear filled eyes stared at Melissa in disbelief. She straightened in her seat and cleared her throat. "I will speak better English, maybe." She hesitated. "I told you. The elders make all the decisions with the other men. They don't tell us why they do what they do. The Mexican authorities leave us alone. They promise us that when we settle there. Only the men have authority. They do what they want. There's no one to stop them."

"So maybe her mother managed to find a way to inform the authorities. The report says nothing about the kid being sold, though." Melissa's heart ached at the terror in the mother's eyes. She couldn't imagine what she would do if she suspected her community was capable of such a thing. Telling this woman she couldn't find a way to rescue her daughter is going to be hard.

Helen sniffed. She reached into her handbag to retrieve a tissue. She wiped her eyes as she glanced around to see who watched them. Then she blew her nose. Stuffing the tissue back in her purse, she stared hard at Melissa. "The mother sure. We have no say but when ve go to the next village for supplies, de vimen can sometimes get away with some tings. I knew de mother. She was a good woman."

Melissa sat up straighter. "Would you be willing to tell the police how to get in touch with her?"

Helen shook her head, the terror clearly visible. Her speak reverted again. "Dere's no vay. Mail is picked up by de men. Dey read it all since mostly de women receive nothing for demselves. I don't vant to become involved anyhow. I don't vant to risk my children. Dey can't discipline me since I run but dey take it out on dem."

Melissa thought for a moment. "Would someone in the next town be able to deliver a message to her when she comes for supplies?"

Helen's frown lines deepened. "She might not be alone. She gave a report to the police but maybe dey would notify de family ... no dat would never do. Den dey would find out she reported. She would tell de police to make no contact."

Melissa pounded her fist lightly on the table. "Helen, this is so unbelievable in this day and age. How these people can so control your lives is beyond anything imaginable. There must be a way. The child needs to be given a proper burial. With family, people who love her. Help us?"

Tears accumulated in Helen's eyes again. Melissa reached for her hands trying to still the trembling. Fear radiated from her. Helen sucked in a deep breath and then coughed. "My children. What will dey do to dem if I help wit this child? You have to rescue dem and den I help. Ok?"

Melissa pulled her hands back and placed them in her lap. "Helen we haven't found a way to rescue them. The terrain surrounding the village is flat and desolate. Only a few places to hide. The kids will fear anyone trying to snatch them. Without you there with us, they would have no incentive to go with complete strangers. There are so many obstacles ..."

"You have to. You can't abandon my children. Please." The quiet mouse of a woman had become a roaring lion. Her voice quivered with determination. "Please."

"You abandoned your children. You left them defenceless so you could look after yourself. Now you want us to risk a Mexican prison to bring your kids to you but when we ask for your help ..." Melissa glared at the distraught woman. "I understand you have been raised without defences against the men in your life. Your culture's subservient attitude places roadblocks where none should be. The elders knew what they were doing when they kept you all so controlled. There's no way we can sneak in there unnoticed." A thought popped into her head. "Unless ..."

Melissa looked out the window. Her brain was working overtime. *I wonder.* Her silent stare gave her mind a few minutes to process the idea. Then she looked at Helen. "What would happen if complete strangers brought Jessica's body home for burial?"

Chapter Fourteen

Jeremy flipped one page after another, methodically searching for the man who'd abused the young girl that morning. His eyes blurred and began to tear. One face began to look like another. He rubbed his eyes. He snuck a peek at the clock on the wall. *Half an hour. I never thought there were this many sex offenders in the city.* He sighed and turned another page. *There.*

He opened the door with the toe of his boot. "Sergeant, I found him." The police officer nearby scowled but turned toward the cubicle where Sergeant Irving leaned over a stack of file folders. He nodded his head in Jeremy's direction before resuming the report he was working on.

Sergeant Irving strode toward Jeremy. "You find something?"

"I did." He pointed to the mug shot of a man who looked to be no more than a teenager. "This is the guy we saw smacking the girl around this morning. He seemed to think he had every right to do what he did and that we were interfering where we didn't belong." Jeremy looked up at the large man standing nearby

"That's Mongrel. He runs a few girls but is mostly into drug trafficking. He's never been convicted but not for lack of trying. We've had our eye on him for a long time, but the last time we had enough evidence to put him away, he disappeared before we could nab him. This is the first I heard he was back in the city." The sergeant leaned a little closer. "Are you sure you recognize him. This was taken a few years back."

"He does look a little older and his hair is longer. He's also a lot skinnier. I'll bet he doesn't just sell drugs, right?" Jeremy leaned back, the chair creaking in protest.

Bill Irving stood straighter. He placed his hand on his back just above the waist and rubbed. "Bones are getting old." He beckoned for Jeremy to follow him as he picked up the photo album. "It's a good thing you're a trained observer. With the changes you described, no one else would have picked him out. Like I said, he's slippery." He led the way back to his desk. "I need to put an APB out on him. He's not going to get away this time."

Jeremy stood beside the sergeant's desk for a few seconds before his cell phone vibrated from its holster. He placed it next to his ear. "Hi, Chr ... Er ... Melissa. What's up?"

Sergeant Irving watched and listened as Jeremy remained silent for a few seconds. Jeremy looked at the sergeant as Melissa reiterated a string of information. "How can we do that? We don't have permission to move the body and if the mother doesn't come forward, I'm not sure the coroner will release her to us." He scowled. "I agree. It would be a way in but ... Melissa, don't tell her we'll do it, yet. Let's do some checking first. Let's not get her hopes up." He listened as Melissa offered a few possibilities. "That might work. But let's give this some thought before we jump in with both feet. It'd have to be soon, I think."

Jeremy said good-bye after agreeing to meet Melissa at the office in an hour. He looked toward Irving. "Melissa thinks we might be able to deliver Jessica's body home and rescue those kids at the same time." He shook his head. "The Rempel woman is scared spit-less about going back, but Melissa thinks she can be persuaded. Otherwise, they'll charge us with kidnapping."

"You might be charged anyway if the Mexicans don't recognize her as their Mom; if the father has sole custody. How closely do these people work with the authorities?" Irving placed his hands over his ample stomach before leaning back in his chair. "A Mexican jail would not be a good destination."

"I know. I told Melissa to hold off making a decision until we worked out the logistics. I don't intend to be caught." He stood again. "Let me know if you catch this guy."

"Oh, I will. You can do the line-up when we bring him in. Keep me posted about your case." The sergeant fingered the next file folder in the stack he worked on.

Jeremy lifted his hand in a casual wave and strode toward the front door. He planned to sit outside the bank where Barker worked to catch the man in anything incriminating. *I think the man is clean, though. Time will tell.*

Chapter Fifteen

Melissa walked toward the nondescript vehicle parked near the light standard in the parking lot. Helen Rempel opened the door and turned to look into the investigator's face. "I am so scared. Your plan might work but I wish I didn't need to be involved." She swiped at a tear that leaked from her lowered lids. "If it's de only way ...."

Melissa placed her hand on the woman's shoulder. "I think this may be the answer to getting your kids out of there. Jeremy and I will go over the plan, check everything out, and get back to you, okay?" She took a step back before Helen closed her car door. The woman waved as she drove slowly toward the street, circling a few of the parked cars.

Melissa walked toward her vehicle. *Chief must be wondering where I am. Jenna, too, I'll bet.* She unlocked her door and slid inside. *Jeremy said an hour. That was ten minutes ago. I need some groceries.* She placed her car in drive and headed toward the exit.

Traffic had increased with people heading home at the end of their work day. Daylight had given way to street lights and headlights. Melissa glanced at the pile of folders sitting on her passenger seat. *The night's going to be a long one.*

She pressed the on-button for the radio, selected a Christian channel and relaxed into her seat cushions as the News Boys latest song of praise flowed through the vehicle. *Lord, I don't know what You want us to do about Helen's kids. I believe You put us in this place to find kids, but this is so much more complicated than any of my other cases. You helped us in the past. I ask for Your help now. Please point us in the right direction and Father, please protect those kids. Thank You.* Melissa lowered her eyelids for a second before concentrating, once again, on the traffic surrounding her.

The idea of beginning their search with prayer flitted across her brain. She glanced skyward. "The planning too. Right, Lord?" The music floated inside the Jeep as if in answer to her prayer. Her mind wanted to panic. She thought about their plans for the next night when they would infiltrate a church led by a paedophile for a pastor. *We have too many irons in the fire.* The phrase brought back memories of growing up on a Texas ranch.

"I'd better call Jenna." She picked up her phone but thought better of it. *I'll wait till I'm in the parking lot of the grocery store.* Just as she thought about her next stop, the sign for Sobey's caught her attention. "This'll do." She chuckled. "I'm so used to travelling with Chief and talking to him as if he understands everything; I'm now talking to myself." She turned her car off and once again reached for her phone. She punched in the number for the office she shared with Jeremy. "Hi Jenna. Wondering where I am?"

She listened as Jenna told her about the day she had with Chief as her sole office companion. Melissa chuckled. "He's good company. I swear he knows what I'm saying most of the time. Jeremy and I agreed to meet at the office in ..." She glanced at her watch. "... about half an hour from now. Sorry for keeping you at the office so long. How are you feeling?"

Melissa doubted that Jenna was being totally honest when she said she was fine but she let the retort on the end of her tongue slide. "You can leave as soon as one of us gets there. Have you heard from Jeremy?"

Jenna replied in the negative. "I know he wanted to check on something to do with the case his Father handed him. Anyway, see you soon." Melissa pressed the end button and slipped out of the vehicle. She began making a mental list of the items she needed.

Chapter Sixteen

Jeremy opened his computer to the program that listened to the device planted in Barker's office. He relaxed into the seat cushions as the voice of the bank manager rang out loud and clear. The man was obviously clearing his desk to leave for the day. "Sharon, put that call through." Jeremy's ears tingled.

"Duval, thanks for calling me back." Jeremy wondered who Duval was. Barker continued speaking. "I made the decision to head to that resort after all. My wife and kids will really enjoy themselves there. Do I need to send a deposit?" Jeremy's heightened interest dropped a few notches. *He's talking to a travel agent or someone like that.* He continued to listen as Barker requested a car as well. *I wonder where this vacation rental is.* The name Mexico drove his senses into overdrive. Barker was talking about meeting someone there. "Is there enough room for the family?" he asked. Apparently, the response was positive. Barker continued. "It'll need to be well stocked. I assume that service is one you provide?"

Jeremy continued to listen as Barker went over his plans to leave by the weekend. *I'll need to make a phone call before heading to the office.* He listened as the bank manager ended the call and then silence. Finally the disembodied voice spoke again. "Barker here. The arrangements are made. We'll meet on Monday at the address I gave you. We'll conclude our business then. This is the last time. Understand?"

Jeremy sensed some conflict in the man's voice. *Conclude what business?* Then, "I don't care. I'm done." The call ended abruptly and Jeremy furrowed his brows. Scattered thoughts raced across his brain. *Maybe this guy is not so innocent after all. This might mean I'll need to tail him down to Mexico. Why does everything end up in Mexico all of a sudden?* He checked his notes and found the bank manager's home address. *I wonder if he is even taking the wife and kids or was that a sham for the realtor's sake. I guess I'll find out.*

He turned his ignition on again and pulled into traffic. *Life is getting way too busy. Lord, help me to focus on one case at a time.* He drove as fast as the busy streets allowed which was well under the speed limit. *Good thing I don't have far to go.*

Ten minutes later, Jeremy stopped in front of the building that housed the office of Goodman Investigations. He noticed Melissa's Jeep was in the parking space. His stomach growled. *When was the last time I had anything to eat? We'll order a pizza or something.*

He marched up the steps and through the front door. "Hi, Jenna. Oh, you're not Jenna. Hi Melissa."

"I sent her home. The poor woman was exhausted but she wouldn't admit it." Melissa rubbed the back of Chief's neck. The dog's tail wagged in greeting. "Chief missed you."

Jeremy walked over to give Chief a pat on his head. "Hi boy. I missed you, too." He shifted his gaze to Melissa. "You eat anything yet? Wanna order something?"

Melissa chuckled. "Until you mentioned it, I hadn't thought much about food. I did get a snack when I met with Helen. I always feel obligated to buy something when we meet at a coffee shop."

"Yeah, I hear yah. Are you hungry enough for some pizza?"

"I could eat a slice or two. Go ahead and order. Then we need to focus on a course of action for the next few days and maybe a trip to Mexico. I can't believe how busy we've gotten. Now I have to make time for Rompart as well." She sighed and moved toward her office. "Let me know when the pizza gets here."

"I will. Can I help with anything?" Jeremy stood taller as Chief brushed against his leg to follow Melissa.

She glanced over her shoulder. "I thought I'd spend the time on some of these folders I brought from Rompart. I'm trying to get acquainted with their customer base, to find if anything suspicious is going on. I need to prove my Father had nothing to do with it if laundering mob money was ... is something Rompart is involved in. It would be easy enough, I suppose, since buying large properties and reselling them is what they do. Barkley found one client with a Mexican address in Chihuahua if you can believe it."

Jeremy strode toward the woman who'd become a close friend in a very short time. "I'll work with you on some of it but I need to make a call to dad before I start. My bank manager is planning a trip to Mexico to meet someone whom he's told will be the last time. I think I'm going to Mexico this weekend." He continued toward his office. "I won't be long."

Jeremy moved quickly toward his desk and sat, taking his cell out of its holster. He punched in the number for his dad and waited. Seconds felt like minutes as the phone eventually went to voice mail. He pressed end call but as soon as he did, it rang with the familiar ring programmed for his Father. "Hi, Dad, sorry if I interrupted something."

The chuckle on the other end of the call clearly told Jeremy his Father was not too busy, just involved. "How is Clare? You two making more decisions about the big day?" He couldn't help but tease a little. "Maybe you're spending too much alone time. Need to take a break from intimate dinners till you're all legal. Maybe?" He erupted in a belly laugh at the indignant tones travelling the airwaves.

Waiting for the older Goodman to recover, he chuckled some more. "Dad, I have some news about this case you handed me ... if you can concentrate, that is." He was satisfied with the loud harrumph he heard before he continued. "Barker is planning a trip to Mexico, with wife and kids, to meet someone he adamantly told would be their last visit. Whatever he's into, he wants out, but the person he's meeting doesn't seem to agree. What do you want me to do?"

Jeremy's frown lines increased. "I thought you would. I'll go over to his house and see what I can find out tonight yet and then tail him when he leaves for the airport. I hope to find out what flight he's taking and where." He listened as his Dad reminded him of the contact he had at the airport. "If you can find out, Dad, I would appreciate it. Text me later."

Jeremy hung up and retraced his steps to Melissa's office. "Chris ... er ... Melissa, it looks like I'm going to Mexico. Dad's looking into when and which flight. You know, it's hard to think of you as Melissa. The change is timely, though. No more hiding who you are."

Melissa looked up from the pile of folders in front of her. "Did you order the pizza yet? My tummy's rumbling."

"No. Hold on." He took his phone in hand again and speed-dialled his favourite pizza restaurant. Completing the order, he took the vacant chair in front of Melissa's desk.

"I'm having almost as hard a time getting used to being Melissa as you are. When the Finders took me in, they felt it was appropriate to change my name to Melissa Finder. You're right, though. I was born Melissa Rompart and since I intend to run the company my father started, I need to use my legal name. Every time someone calls me Melissa, though, I want to look over my shoulder to find out who they're talking to." She chuckled. "So Mexico, eh?"

"Yeah. Dad wants me to tail this guy. His connections at the airport will find out which flight. If I can't book the same one, I'll be right behind him. He's not meeting anyone till Monday." He sighed. "That may mean that I won't be able to help you with this stuff very much. I think we're juggling too many balls in the air."

"I agree. I'm a little overwhelmed right now, especially after talking to Helen. Speaking of her, what do you think about transporting Jessica Penner's body home to her mother? According to Helen, who remembers the kid when she went missing ten years ago, no one is looking for her. The rumour in the village is that her parents sold her. But someone reported her missing. We think it was her mother." She studied Jeremy's reaction.

Jeremy flinched. "Sold. How could they?" He shook his head. "Hold that thought for a minute. I've given this church thing some consideration. The pastor can identify us. I think I should tell Irving to put two under covers on it and leave us out of it. His knowledge about the case and what he needs to convict is within his purview. He can handle it without us. What do you think?"

"I hadn't **thought along** those lines but I like the idea. I hate to leave a case unfinished. You're right, though. Irving can handle it." She sliced the air with her hand over the files. "I need to concentrate on this too. What are you going to do with the equipment you rented to bug the church?"

"I'll hand it over to Irving for his guys to use." He smacked his hands against each other. "Okay, that's settled. Now, the Helen Rempel case. Transporting the body will sure give us a reason to be there. Will Helen go with us?" Jeremy opened the file folder he snatched from the top of the pile. He glanced surreptitiously at the information but he waited for Melissa's response instead.

"She will ... reluctantly. That woman is terrified of going back. Whatever the man did to her, he controls her even with all these miles between them. I explained that we would be jailed if we take those kids away from a custodial parent whereas she could make it easier for them to leave without making a fuss if she's with us. She doesn't think her husband applied for legal guardianship. Their sect doesn't recognize government authority." Melissa leaned back in her chair. "She brought the kids birth certificates or at least copies with her. It seems when the women go shopping in a **neighbouring** town, they gain some freedom. She copied the certificates the last time she went for supplies before she ran. We'd deliver Jessica to that town if we can find a way to get word to the mother without her husband finding out." Melissa took a deep breath. "Surely God never intended people to live this way. I mean, the women ... and the children ... are chattel." She threw up her hands in frustration.

Jeremy used the folder to fan himself. "The air is hot in here. I wonder if Jenna turned the temperature up." He stood to walk toward the thermostat in the hallway. "We take our freedoms for granted in this country." He turned the dial on the thermostat a little lower. "I thank all those soldiers who lost their lives and limbs for maintaining that freedom. Muslims move here and push their Sharia Law which is completely contrary to our way of life. We need to fight to maintain things as they are." His scowl deepened. "Some people shed the freedoms available all in the name of religious freedom, but I don't define what they do to their families as freedom. It's control, pure and simple. I guess when you've lived that way all your life, you aren't familiar with any other way. Helen is adjusting, though. She's making her own decisions now, driving a car, earning a living. Her fear comes from what he might do to her when he catches up with her, I think. It sounds like he's pretty brutal."

Melissa shuddered. "I could never live like that. Now that I'm a Christian, don't expect me to change a whole lot. I love my independence."

Jeremy chuckled. "I can't even imagine you bowing to some man or wearing a dress all the time. Do you own a dress?" He teased.

She swatted the air in front of him. "As a matter of fact, I own three." She stuck out her tongue and crossed her eyes.

"Wow, that's appealing." He grinned wickedly in her direction. "I'll take you out somewhere fancy one night to see what you look like in a dress. Maybe we'll double with Dad and Clare." He chuckled. "That could be interesting."

Melissa pretended to ponder the idea. "So that would mean you'd wear something other than a pair of jeans and cowboy boots?" She chuckled. "That might make it worth the trip."

Jeremy laughed out loud. "I see what you mean. Let's concentrate on these files so we can at least get something done before the pizza arrives." He pointed his finger over some of the typed information and bent his head to the task. Melissa did the same.

Chapter Seventeen

Erna Penner roamed the street, hoping to out-distance her companions. She wandered into one store after another but the three women she came to town with followed each twist and turn. "Vat are you looking for Erna? Ve are getting tired." Their German language was foreign to many in the commercial district so they could speak freely. "Ven can ve get some coffee?"

Erna glanced around. "There is nothing that resembles vat I am looking for. Vy don't you ladies go cross the street to dat restaurant and I meet you dere in a few minutes." She crossed her fingers.

"But we must stick together. The Elders ..."

"... are not here." Erna trembled a little as she said the words. Trust was a commodity she couldn't afford. "I von't be long."

Another lady spoke up. "Come on Bettel. She said she vill come shortly. My feet hurt."

"You always do dis. Ve must stay together but you always manage to go off on your own. Vat do you do alone? I wonder." Bettel shrugged her shoulders. "I am not de one who vill be in trouble. Don't be long. Ve order for you, ya?" The three walked toward the entrance to the restaurant never once glancing back to see if Erna followed.

She sighed. Watching the women, she glanced once or twice toward the back exit of the building behind her. The place she was seeking lay just beyond that door. Her gaze followed the women as they crossed the street filled with many types of transportation today. When the Mennonites came to town, some used wagons, some buggies but some also drove cars. They looked out for each other.

She stepped backward a few paces and then turned abruptly, entered the store and hurried through the back door. Erna crossed the alleyway and entered the street beyond. She spotted her target. The sign 'Policia' beckoned.

The mother's heart thundered in her chest. This place frightened her but they could also help ... maybe. Lifting her long skirt to step over the curb, she walked toward the door. Pulling the handle, she was almost knocked off balance as a uniformed officer barged through, his focus on some crime he was heading to, she supposed. She slid through after he left, walked to the nearest counter and asked for the detective.

Pointing toward a closed office door, the desk sergeant waved her through. Erna stood still for a moment but then the reminder to hurry crossed her brain. Her companions would be looking for her. She stepped confidently toward the door, knocked and when invited to enter, she grasped the doorknob in sweaty palms.

The man behind the desk recognized her. "Mrs. Penner. I was thinking about taking a ride out to your place. They found your daughter." He didn't smile.

Her stomach tumbled over itself or at least that's what it felt like. Erna waited for the bad news. The search had been long. Ten years.

"She was found dead, beaten to death." He made a slicing motion across his neck to supplement his poor knowledge of the German dialect. "They have her body in the morgue in Winnipeg, Canada." He stumbled over the word morgue.

Erna understood. The news she dreaded hearing had been spoken. A tear escaped but she quickly brushed it aside. Her Jessica was not to be spoken of but her husband needed money. The children are sometimes used to pay the bills. She hung her head. She looked at the man who had continued the futile search. "Yah." She nodded.

The detective leaned his forearms across his desk. "Come home." He gestured as best he could to help the women understand her daughter would be coming home. "Soon."

"Here?" Her eyes grew round. "Nien. Not here." She trembled at the implications of her daughter's body returning home. Her husband would know someone had reported the missing child to the Policia. *He will find out I'd done the unthinkable, disobeyed. The man will accuse me before the Elders.* Her breathing slowed. *So what? Dere punishment, when I tell truth is worth it.* She nodded toward the officer who'd watched the flood of emotions. "Yah. Ven?"

She knew the detective had always questioned her story. *A five-year-old runaway? Hardly.*

He looked **toward** her with his brow furrowed. "Soon as the autopsy is complete and transportation can be arranged, people are bringing her. Someone you know, I think."

"Ok. I **vait**." She stood. "You send dem to me **ven** dey comes." She lowered her head. "Tank you. For finding." She stepped out of his office. The noise in the precinct seemed louder than when she'd come in. Her head hurt. Her footsteps were drowned out by the din surrounding her. She hurried toward the exit. Another tear **escaped,** this time left to trail down her weather-beaten cheek. Her baby was coming home. She couldn't tell anyone.

Chapter Eighteen

Melissa woke early. Chief had climbed into her bed the night before. His warm body made it almost impossible to keep the sheets across her body. *He's like a furnace.* She didn't move. Her hand reached down her side to stroke his furry ribcage. *Why does he sleep with his butt toward my head?*

She stroked his fur. *Poor boy. He missed me yesterday.* The dog groaned, "You're awake. Wanna go for a run, Chief?"

The dog lifted his head but seeing no movement from his mistress, he lay it back down. He stretched his long legs almost hitting her in the face. "Come on, lazy bones. Let's do it." She pushed him over the side of the bed. The dog landed with a thump. "Now I can move."

Melissa rolled out the same side she'd ejected Chief. The animal looked at her, the end of his tail twitching as he stood there. "I'll grab my running gear and be right with you." Talking to her dog was second nature to Melissa. She chuckled. *Uncle Conrad would be quite amused since all animals belonged outside on the ranch.* "But it's too cold for you to stay outside all the time, isn't it Chief. This is not Texas."

She skipped a step toward the closet where her track suit hung. Slipping off pjs, she stepped into the loose fitting pants and then shrugged the fleece jacket over her head without

undoing the zipper. She laced up her running shoes.
"Let's go boy."

They raced each other toward the front door, stepped out into the early morning crispness and began to jog down the driveway toward the gate. Jeremy caught up to them just before they raced through, matching his pace to hers. "Good morning."

She glanced sideways. "To you too. You're up early."

"As are you. Couldn't sleep?" He sped up a little as her strides gained in momentum. Chief sniffed some taller blades of grass several paces behind.

Melissa slapped the side of her leg and Chief quickly obeyed her command to stay close. "I just feel so restless this morning, like I'm missing something. Those files we went through last night should have given us some clue as to who's laundering money at Rompart and we found nothing. I wonder if your Dad found anything with what he took home."

"Melissa," Jeremy huffed. "We never checked any further into that company that's located in Chihuahua. That may be something we can check on when we take Jessica Penner's body home. We'll figure this out, you'll see." He raced on ahead.

Melissa sped up. She couldn't match Jeremy's long legs no matter how hard she tried. She decided to jog in place for a few minutes to let Chief do what he needed to do. As soon as the dog indicated he wanted to run, she increased her speed to make a cursory attempt at catching Jeremy. He sat on a nearby bench by the time she caught up. His smile added to her sense of competition. She sped past.

"Oh come on. Haven't you had enough for today?" Jeremy jumped to his feet and raced after her. With a little effort, he steadied his pace beside her again. "I need to ..." He huffed, "... check on Barker this morning. Gotta head back for a shower." He turned toward home.

Melissa raced after him. "Beat you home." The adrenaline kicked in and she raced past him. "You're not a long distance runner, are you? Great in the take-off but no endurance." She laughed into the cool morning air.

Jeremy sucked in a lungful of air and raced toward the closed gate. "We'll find out who has stamina." His footsteps pounded the pavement, close on her heels.

Melissa and Chief were at their limit, so when Jeremy crossed the opening to their shared yard space ahead of her, she was not surprised. She watched him round the corner of the house before she heard a loud horse laugh letting her know he'd won ... *This time. I'll show him.*

She dipped her head toward her running companion. "We'll need to train harder, Chief. That man is not going to beat me next time." She unlatched the door, walked into her foyer, and slipped off her runners. Bending at the waist, she inhaled a large **lungful** of air. It took a while to get her breathing under control. *Nothing like an early morning race to clear the cobwebs. Next time Goodman, next time.* Her chest rose and fell with each breath as she walked toward her bedroom and a nice hot shower.

Chapter Nineteen

Jeremy parked outside the address for the bank manager's home. The large stone structure appeared peaceful in the early morning sunshine. The crisp cool air had warmed since his run that morning but the evident onset of winter was in the air.

Trees lined the driveway directing visitors toward the front door. As Jeremy focused on the surroundings bordering the Barker's residence, the front door opened. The vehicle the man had left with the night before stood facing the street this morning.

Barker emerged from the house, followed closely by a smaller version of him, and a little girl. Barker carried the larger bags but each child had a smaller tote bag to add to the suitcases already in the trunk. Jeremy slid farther down in the seat of his black Dodge truck. A woman stepped into the early morning daylight. "Thomas, did you cancel the mail?"

Barker lifted his head out of the trunk. "I did, yesterday from the office. We'll only be gone a week, anyway."

The woman laughed. "I'm not able to persuade you to go away often. I may be able to talk you into a longer stay."

Barker's grimace spoke clearly to Jeremy. "Marcia, leave it alone. I promised a week, nothing more. Be satisfied." He grabbed the suitcase she handed him and then motioned for her to get in the car. His body language spoke volumes as he walked to the driver's side. Thomas Barker was not happily heading out for a family vacation.

Jeremy surmised the banker expected resistance from the man on Monday. *The wife sure seems to be clueless about her husband's plans, though. I wonder if she really knows the man she's married to.* He sunk even lower in the truck's cab as the Barker's vehicle drove down the driveway and turned left, toward the **centre** of town and the airport beyond.

He followed at a discrete distance. The traffic this morning was more congested than yesterday. *I guess the resort in Mexico is going to receive a call regarding a change of plans. It sounded to me as if he planned to leave on Friday. Today is only Wednesday.*

Jeremy picked up his cell phone from where he dropped it on the passenger seat. He connected it by Bluetooth to his vehicle's communication system and spoke clearly. "Call my Dad's office."

Ringing quickly ended as soon as Clare, his Dad's office assistant and future **wife,** answered. "Hi, Jeremy. Want to speak to Barkley?"

"I do." A few seconds later, his father's deep bass voice greeted him. "Good morning son. You're out and about pretty early."

"My instincts are sharp this morning. Barker is leaving town this morning, with his wife and children. It looked to me like they packed for a lot longer, though. What do you want me to do?" Jeremy made the turn at King Edward toward the airport.

"Just follow to make sure they are heading to Mexico. I may have you leave on Sunday to stake out that meeting on Monday. Keep me posted." The older man hung up. Jeremy knew he hated talking to his son when he was in the middle of traffic.

The light up ahead had turned yellow so Jeremy prepared to stop. However, the Barker vehicle made a quick turn. He's heading toward the tarmac for private planes. *I wonder.*

Jeremy signalled and followed just before the traffic from the cross street began to flow toward him. He cautiously stayed a few car lengths back but was able to spot the target vehicle as it turned into the private landing strip. He inched toward the gate. The Barkers vehicle stopped beside a large Lear Jet. *Wow, the man travels in style.*

The occupants of the banker's car stepped into the warm air surrounding the sleek aircraft. One man who appeared to be a baggage handler unpacked the trunk of the car as family members climbed the steps toward the interior. The baggage man gave instructions to load the bags into the baggage compartment. Then he, too, boarded the plane. *I wish I could hear what was being said.* He grimaced as he thought about the bug he placed in the man's office. It was not where it should be.

The plane's engines began to roar. The door shut. The aircraft began to taxi toward a designated runway. Jeremy shook his head. *I have no way of knowing ... wait. The pilot would have to file a flight plan.* He turned his truck toward the gate, entered slowly and parked at the side of the building used for such a purpose. He headed inside.

Jeremy faced the counter, walked toward a woman in uniform and asked if he could speak to the person who was responsible for the planes leaving this part of the airport. She smiled, asked what she could help him with, and then smiled again. Jeremy produced his investigator's license. "I need to know where that plane is headed." He pointed toward the runway.

"Which one?" She tucked her smile behind her efficiency.

Jeremy frowned. "The one that just left the taxiway." He heard the roar of its engines as it prepared to take off. "Where is it going?"

"Oh. They are headed to Chihuahua Mexico."

Yeah, assuming they filed the correct flight plan. "Fine. Thanks. That's all I needed." He retraced his steps to the door and walked briskly to his truck. Sitting down on the driver's seat, he instructed his system to call his Dad again. When the older man answered, Jeremy informed him Chihuahua was the destination. "Thanks, Son. I'll get back to you after I talk to my client."

"There's a resort down there Barker had his travel agent book for him. I'll see if I can find out which agency he used, probably one he's used before by the sounds of it. Maybe Mr. Decapoulis wants to take a trip and, since he's new in town, will ask Barker's secretary whom he should contact as an agent. Might work."

Barkley laughed. "I can't say I raised a stupid son. God go with you. Talk later." The man ended the call with a click and Jeremy started his vehicle. "I'll need to change."

Chapter Twenty

Melissa Rompart, aka Melissa Smith, barged through the doors of Rompart Industries, dressed in a grey pinstripe pantsuit with black five-inch heels. She'd arranged her hair into a knot on top of her head. Chief strode confidently beside her, ready to strike if anyone approached unannounced. Melissa stroked his head to calm him.

She nodded her head at the security desk before marching toward the elevators. *They aren't expecting Chief but since I own the company, they'd better not object to his presence.* She pressed the button for the eleventh floor. The briefcase she carried contained the files she'd worked on at home.

When the elevator opened, she almost ran into Richard Belcher. "Oh, hi Richard. How did your meeting go yesterday?"

"Interesting, as usual. What happened to you? I came by your office but you'd already left." He straightened his back hoping to intimidate her.

She returned his scowl. "I chose to work at home." She continued into the elevator. "I'm curious about some of these clients of ours."

Richard ignored her invitation. "I see you brought you pet to work. I'm not sure ..."

"Chief is a service dog. He goes where I go." Her firm facial expression told him the choice belonged to her. "Now, about those files."

"I am scheduled for another meeting. I'm just heading out." He scurried toward the door he held open. "Maybe later. You will be here later, won't you?"

"I haven't decided how long I will be in today. I want to see that my office is arranged as per the instructions I left yesterday and then I may spend some time going over the company's financial records. I assume you've told that department to expect me."

Richard swallowed before answering. He dropped his head but quickly glanced up. "Of course. There shouldn't be any problem." He stepped toward the lobby as the elevator door began to close. "Later?" He waved.

"Sure." Melissa leaned against the back wall as the momentum of the small room lifted her skyward. *Another meeting without the owner of the company. I'm going to insist that I be present at all meetings in the future, I think.* She glanced at Chief. The dog had stood in front of her during her conversation with Belcher. *I wonder why.*

As soon as the elevator doors opened, Melissa emerged into the early morning bustle. She led the way with Chief just behind her heels toward her office. "Good morning Courtney. Where can I find a cup of coffee?"

"Oh, Miss Rompart. I'll bring you some." The young woman acted as if caught doing something she shouldn't but Melissa suspected it was probably just nervousness.

"Show me where." She smiled. "And, please, when we're alone, call me Melissa."

"Oh ... er ... sure. Melissa." She returned the smile. "Come this way." Courtney led the way toward a small break room located near the large photocopier. "I had your father's furniture delivered last night. Your office looks rather cramped, I'm afraid."

"When will the decorator arrive?" Melissa walked over to the coffee maker. "Does everyone bring their own cup or can I use one of them?"

"I took the initiative of getting you a new cup. Yours is the bright red one." She glanced at Chief. "I should also obtain a dog dish for him."

"Chief will be coming to work with me every day. Today, we improvise but tomorrow I'll bring a dish. I should have thought of that myself." She poured a cup of hot, steamy liquid and grabbed one of the plastic cups she located on a shelf above the coffee maker. "This will do for today. I'll fill it from the sink in the bathroom."

Courtney reached toward the animal but quickly drew her hand back. "Is he friendly?"

"He is but he's a service dog, one trained to protect me." Melissa decided that his interaction with found children was not relevant to her job at Rompart. "He'll let you pet him. In fact, he thrives on a few pets every once in a while. Now about that decorator."

Courtney led the way toward Melissa's office. "Jennifer Watson's reputation for tasteful office décor is her trademark and she'll be here ..." She glanced at her watch. "... in about ten minutes." She opened Melissa's door and stepped aside.

Melissa gasped. "Wow. You weren't kidding about the amount of furniture." She looked around the room.
"There seems to be enough here for two or three offices." She wound her way past one desk, placing her hand on the dusty top. I wonder which one my father used most of the time. Her heart felt heavy. I never had a chance to visit him at work. I guess I was too young but ... "Courtney, did you happen to find out why he had two ..." She spotted another one. "... no. three desks?"

"I spoke with one of the older employees. Your father had just redecorated before he ... well ... before he was killed. He never threw anything away, but liked to change his surroundings often." She pointed to the most modern piece. "This was his last one although he never used it for long before ... well ... you know."

"That's the one I want then, like a springboard into the future of Rompart." She slowly walked by each piece of furniture. Chief followed, shifted, and walked on. Melissa's thoughts vibrated as she made some attempt to picture her father seated in one chair after another. She ran her hands over the desk that held her father's interest near the end.

Sitting in the chair positioned nearby, she opened one drawer at the side. The clean interior gave credence to Courtney's research. It looked brand new. She ran her hand along the bottom of the middle drawer. The texture was rough but had no evidence of wear and tear. Pulling the chair close, she rested her elbows on the desktop. It feels right.

Her reflections were interrupted by a slight cough. Melissa looked toward the door. Courtney stood there with another woman, one younger than she was. "Miss Rompart. This is Jennifer Watson of Watson and Devries."

The young woman marched forward with her hand extended. "Nice to meet you, Miss Rompart. I take it you own this company. Kinda young aren't you?"

The woman seemed pushy, almost intimidating. Melissa ignored the offered hand. "Long story. You seem young to be an established decorator." Chief stood silently aside, his eyes never leaving the stranger moving in Melissa's direction.

Jennifer took a step back as soon as she noticed him. "Unusual. A guard dog, eh?"

"Only if he's needed. Show me your references?"

"Shall we sit and I can give them to you. I assure you I can make this place look exactly as you envision it." Jennifer glanced around the room. "My, there is a lot to choose from." She parked herself in one of the easy chairs with a coffee table in the foreground.

Courtney looked in Melissa's direction and back toward Jennifer. "Would you like some coffee, Miss Watson?"

"No thank you." She pulled a bottle of water from her valise and motioned for Melissa to join her. "Shall we begin?"

Melissa sighed. This woman is sure a take charge sort. She grabbed her cup of coffee and walked toward the vacant chair beside Jennifer to sit down. Her smile had disappeared when the woman arrived but she decided to give her a chance. "I'm sorry. You caught me in a moment of introspection. My father used all this furniture and I was imagining him sitting at that desk. I decided to keep it."

Jennifer chuckled. "Please don't think you should apologize. I tend to barrel my way into a new situation." She handed Melissa several letters of recommendation. "My ideas have decorated many of the offices you see in the Portage and Main towers. The letters are from those clients."

Melissa glanced at each one, all glowing with praise for the artistic woman. Jennifer kept quiet to allow the paperwork to speak for her. Melissa decided she was the right fit for this job. "I think we can proceed. I want to use any of these pieces as will work in your design but that desk and chair are not negotiable. This space needs to be functional but with a slight feminine flair. No frills but softer." She looked around the room. "Most of these pieces are overly masculine but ..."

"We can work with that. Let me peruse the collection, Can you work around this mess for today. Tomorrow morning, I'll come by with the design. If you approve, we can begin to move some of this out." Jennifer stood, took a swig from her water bottle, and went to work studying the lines and workings of each piece of furniture. She took notes as she worked.

Melissa stood also. *I want to check out all this stuff. I might want to keep a few other items.* She ran her hands over this chair, that credenza, and another chair. *I think I want to thoroughly check out each of them before deciding one way of the other.* "Jennifer, can you give me a day or two. I want to investigate each piece. I was very young when my father died and never visited him here. It'll give me a chance to reflect on him a little better."

"Oh, of course. If you can handle this hodgepodge, so can I. I'll be back day after tomorrow, say about the same time of day and we can go over my ideas. In the meantime, if you decide to keep any other pieces, I can incorporate them into the design, no problem." Jennifer continued to look down the sides and over the front of the each piece. She pointed to the desk Melissa and Barkley had used the day before. "What about this one?"

"That one goes. Not one of my father's. The CEO said it was but while I worked at that desk yesterday, it didn't feel right. My father's stuff was still in storage." She glanced at Chief, rubbed the top of his head, and strolled back toward the desk she felt was the best one. "This was his last desk."

She sat again and pulled out the centre drawer. This time, she took it all the way out to make sure that some of the joints had not dried out in storage, that it was strong. Chief lunged underneath, grabbed a piece of paper that had slipped to the floor, and backed out. He lifted his head toward Melissa. "What did you find, boy?"

Chapter Twenty One

Jeremy, dressed as Mr. Decapoulis, walked intentionally toward the large glass doors and into the quiet business-like interior. He spotted the woman who acted as office assistant for Thomas Barker. He strode toward her.

The woman smiled, stood beside her desk and held out her hand. "Mr. Decapoulis. Back so soon. Mr. Barker left for a week's vacation."

"This is a coincidence. I came to ask who Mr. Barker would recommend as a travel agent. Since I am new to this city, I hoped he would help me." He turned to leave.

"No Wait. Jenson Duval handles all Mr. Barker's trips." She rummaged around on her desk. "I looked at this card yesterday when Mr. Barker asked me to call and change the date for his arrival at the resort." She handed him a business card.

Jeremy scanned the name and address. "Can I take this with me?"

"Sure. I keep another one in my card index." She walked around her desk to escort this potential client to the door.

Jeremy stopped her. "No need to bother you. Thanks for this. I will contact Mr. Barker when he gets back. A week, you say?"

"Yes. He should be at his desk next Wednesday or Thursday. Call before you come and we will be prepared to meet with you."

She remained as Jeremy waved and strode toward the exit. *Now for a visit to Duval Travel.* He left the building, walked to his rental vehicle and slid inside. Deciding to return the vehicle first, he remained parked till he called his office. "Jenna, how are things this morning? Do you need me to make an appearance anytime soon?"

His office receptionist gave him the all-clear and said she felt stronger today when he asked about her health. He hung up, pulled into traffic and headed to the Pervis Rentals office. Handing in the keys and paying the bill took no time at all. He walked casually toward his truck and loosened his tie.

The temperature had climbed already. Jeremy took off his suit jacket to lie over the passenger seat. He unbuttoned the top button of his shirt as soon as he sat down. *I wish we had some down time away from all these problems .... maybe I should call Melissa.* He picked up his cell phone again. He punched in the speed dial for his colleague. "Hi, Melissa. Are you still at Rompart? I wondered if you were available this afternoon for a short break."

He listened as Melissa said she had something to show him. She planned to leave the office in a few minutes. Jeremy's mind roamed around a few ideas and he inserted one into the conversation. "We've not taken time off for a few days so I thought, maybe some paintball would be fun with dinner afterward. It could be like getting some shooting practice but a lot more fun."

Melissa liked the idea but asked about Chief. "Bring him along. The game will be good practice for him too." They arranged where and when to meet while Jeremy made a mental note to change. "See you later." He hung up and pulled into traffic. *If Lawson Travel is able to book a flight for me, I'll be away for a couple of days.*

The trip to the travel agent took no time at all. Jeremy parked and walked to the front door. He checked the card for the travel agent's name. Stepping inside, he looked around the office. No man in sight. "I'm looking for Jenson Duval. Thomas Barker's assistant referred him to me."

The older of the two women looked up and stood, ready to help. "Mr. Duval is out for lunch. Can I help you?"

"Maybe." He walked toward the polished woman admiring the dress she wore. He decided to turn on the charm. "I decided to take a trip and Thomas Barker expounded on all the benefits of a resort in Mexico. Do you ... but of course, you do ..." He smiled, knowing his bright smile added softness to his otherwise rugged features.

He sat in the chair she offered. "Mr. Barker ..." He glanced around the office before continuing. "Mr. Barker, Mr. Thomas Barker left for a resort in Mexico but he never mentioned which one. Can you find the information for me? I'd like to leave tonight. Is that enough notice?"

"Of course. Do you have your identification with you?" The woman looked all business.

Jeremy smiled again. "I am Mr. Albert Decapoulis. Call Mr. Barker's office assistant and she will tell you I stopped by this morning. She gave me the name of your agency."

The agent made the call. She smiled. "The Barkers are staying at a high-end resort in Chihuahua, about a little over fourteen miles from the airport. Sheraton Chihuahua Soberano provides a restaurant on site, a large outdoor swimming pool and a fitness centre. Rooms start at $146 US per night. Would you like me to book a room for you?"

"Let's book an airline before we book the hotel." Jeremy's mind swirled with things needing his attention before he left the country. *Maybe our plan to relax this afternoon won't work.*

The agent checked the flight schedule on her computer. "I found a flight at 8 pm. Will that work for you?"

He paused only a second. "It will" Jeremy pulled out his false credentials including a credit card in the name of Decapoulis. She booked his flight and scrolled back to the resort site. *Maybe Melissa would like to go as well to explore the terrain near Campos Tinades.* "Book two rooms. A friend will come with me."

The woman plugged in the numbers but said nothing else until she finished. "All done. Oh, we'll need to book a flight for your friend too. Right?"

"Oh, for sure." The agent repeated the steps to acquire another ticket. *I hope she sees the value in coming with me. More importantly, I hope she will take the time.* When the agent completed the transactions, he stood. "Thank you for all your help. Does the resort provide a shuttle to meet us at the airport ... no, forget that. We'll rent a car."

He gave a casual wave as he left the office. *It may take some talking to persuade Melissa to come with me. I'll dangle the carrot of being near the village.* He headed toward his home, the apartment Melissa had constructed when she renovated her parents' address. Switching the radio on, he **tuned** it to some Hispanic music. Humming along, he thought about his attire for the trip and other particulars. *Do I go in disguise or act as if I planned to relax? This resort sounds wonderful. Hum -m-m-m.*

Chapter Twenty Two

Melissa read the slip of paper carefully. Her father's signature appeared genuine based on the files she'd opened recently. *Barkley will be able to confirm the signature's authenticity.* She slipped her cell phone from her pocket and called. "Barkley, do you have some time this afternoon. I found something I want you to look at."

Her lawyer said he'd be available about three o'clock. "That'll work. See you later." She glanced at the scrap again. Chief's saliva stained one corner but the words were legible. *They're closing in. Have to protect my family. Can't involve the police yet. Need more proof. It's all there, in the financials. I didn't do this. Parker Rompart.*

I wonder where there is. Melissa's eyes glistened with tears. *He was aware someone followed him and he had information someone didn't want him to divulge to the police. Why didn't he go to them?* She tossed her head. *That's what I intend to find out. I won't be so slow to involve the authorities. Not this time.*

She opened her handbag and grabbed a tissue. Blotting her face and putting the edge of the tissue near her eyes, she avoided the task of redoing her makeup. She looked around the office. *Time to leave.* She motioned for Chief to follow and stepped toward her assistant's desk. "Courtney, the decorator will return day after tomorrow. Please place her on my calendar. Also, make an appointment for tomorrow with the accountant Rompart uses. Who takes care of all the financial records besides the accountant?"

"Oh, That's Pierce. Pierce Smalley. His office is on the third floor. Do you want me to schedule a meeting with him?" She added notes to her scratch pad.

"No. I just wanted to know who did that job. I'll be back tomorrow." She closed her office door behind her and walked slowly beside Chief toward the elevator. Lifting her wrist, she noticed it was already 1:30. *No lunch yet either. After that, I'll head to Goodman and Associates to meet with Barkley.*

Just as she reached her Jeep sitting in the parking lot, her cell phone rang. "Hi, Jeremy. What's up?" She listened as the excited voice on the other end of the line fed her the details of the trip to Mexico. "I can't leave town, Jeremy. I have ... He interrupted her with information about how close they would be to Campos Tinades. *Jeremy presents a possibility,* she thought

"I'll clear my calendar for the next few days. When do we leave? I'm on my way to your Dad's office for a short meeting before we connect later." Jeremy informed her of their travel plans. "This evening. Wow. Amazing how you obtained plane tickets on such short notice? Maybe Barkley would look after Chief." She took a deep breath. *The trip could be fun and informative at the same time.* "I'll make things work." She fastened her seatbelt and glanced at her watch again.

"I'll quickly go home, pack a few things and call your father for permission to drop off Chief." The dog's ears lifted up when she spoke his name. "I'll meet you at the airport. Jeremy this is crazy." She giggled as she ended the call. "Chief, were you listening?. I'm going to Mexico with Jeremy." Her heart did a funny little thump. When she looked in the rear view mirror her grinning face peered back. *What is that about?*

Fortunately, the traffic pattern flowed sporadically this time of day. Melissa arrived home in record time, planted her foot on the brake and turned off the ignition. Slipping out of the driver's door, she helped Chief land on the ground and skip-walked to the house. *What do I need for three or four days in the tropics?*

She stopped just inside her front door. *Jeremy said the plane would leave at eight. That means I should be at the airport at seven. I have time. Almost two and I really need to visit with Barkley.* She fingered **the scrap** of paper in her pocket. *This could be the proof we need to clear Dad's name. I'd better hurry.*

An hour later, with her suitcase in hand, Melissa grabbed a bag of Chief's supplies and headed back out her front door. The dog never left her side the entire time she packed. "Come on Chief. You like Barkley and he likes you. Think of this as a vacation from me. I'd take you to Denny's ranch if time allowed." The animal lifted his face toward her as they walked rapidly to her still-warm vehicle.

Her stomach growled. *I hope we're able to grab a bite to eat before we board the plane. I'm starved.* She glanced at Chief as she fastened her seatbelt. "You thirsty, boy? I'll fill your bowl with some water at Barkley's, I promise." She turned the ignition on and accelerated down her driveway. "The traffic had better not slow me down."

As expected, the increased number of vehicles kept the flow steady. She arrived at Barkley Goodman and Associates Law Offices with time to spare. Grabbing Chief's leash and his bag of supplies, she strode hurriedly toward the office door. Once inside, she greeted Clare, Barkley's office assistant and headed toward his inner sanctum.

Clare stopped her. "He's on a conference call. Can I help you?"

"I am here for my three o'clock appointment. I assumed he would be free. Sorry for not checking." She retraced her steps and took one of the vacant chairs in the reception area. "Clare, do you and he have any plans for the next three or four days?"

The older woman smiled in Melissa's direction. "Not anything we can't change. Why?"

"I wondered if you would take care of Chief." The dog's tail wagged as he received his usual pat on the head from Clare. "Oh, I promised him some water. The day has been crazy."

Clare grabbed the water dish from Melissa. "We can certainly take care of him. What's up?" She walked toward the tiny restroom and filled Chief's bowl with cold water. On her return, she looked with interest at Melissa. "Oh, I'll bet you're going with Jeremy, aren't you?" Her eyes began to twinkle.

"Yes. Business. Close to a place where I might need to go next week. We thought we could scope out the landscape nearby." Melissa felt her cheeks begin to glow. She placed her hands along her jawline.

"Yes, well, you may want to believe that but I think ... Oh, never mind." Clare chuckled. "You'll find out soon enough." As she spoke the last words, footsteps announced Barkley's appearance. Clare's eyes gave away the personal nature of their relationship.

Barkley grinned back at her. "I thought I heard voices. Hello, Melissa. Hello to you, too, Chief. What's so important that you needed to interrupt your day with a visit to an old man?" He rubbed Chief's head when the dog crossed the room to lick his hand.

Melissa reached into her pocket. "This."

Barkley looked toward Clare. "No phone calls."

Clare smiled and informed Barkley about their dog-sitting commitment. "Melissa and Jeremy are going to Mexico. He called a few minutes before Melissa got here." She grinned. "It's time these two enjoyed some down time."

Barkley's eyes lifted just a little. "I guess he found out where Barker went." He turned to Melissa. "So you're going with him?"

"It turns out that the resort is only a few miles from Campos Tinades where Helen Rempel's kids are living. So, we thought ..."

"Yeah I hear ya." His eyes twinkled. "Good place to spend some quality time and enjoy the Lord's Creation a little as well. You could get to know Jeremy a little better, don't you think?" He looked toward Clare who sported a silly grin on her face.

"You two are awful. This is business, nothing more. Jeremy and I are working on a common case with the Rempel woman and since we found out the fifteen-year-old murder victim also came from that village ... well, we are thinking we'll escort the body home as a cover for getting those kids out of there. But we need to explore the lay of the land and so we thought ..." Their expressions hadn't changed any. She threw up her hands and stalked toward Barkley's office. "You're incorrigible."

Barkley's deep chuckle followed her into the spacious room where he looked after her affairs and had since her parents' death. She handed him the scrap of paper found earlier that day. "This was hidden under a desk used by my dad before he died. I figure it might be the last desk he used since this was found underneath. Man, he sure changed his furnishings often. Several pieces won't be needed once the decorator makes her selection. She's working on sketches as we speak."

Barkley motioned for her to sit in a chair in front of his desk. He turned the paper over in his hands a couple of times before he read the message. "This is definitely Parker's signature. I'd recognize it anywhere. Where did you say you found it?"

"Actually Chief found it. Those are his teeth marks on the corner. I was inspecting each piece of furniture my assistant brought up from storage to make my selection. When I came to this desk, I opened the middle drawer. This must have fallen under the desk. The paper wasn't on the floor before that. What do you think?" Melissa's face held concern but also hope. Her heart fluttered at the thought that her suspicions were correct in proving her father's innocence.

Barkley laid the paper on his desk. "I want to talk to the detectives who've worked this case all these years. Maybe this is the incentive they need to look elsewhere for the culprit behind the money laundering. All along they believed someone shot him for that reason, but now we can point them in a different direction. They killed him because he planned to blow the whistle on them but he wasn't the bad guy as we've known all along."

Melissa leaned back in the chair. "I need to go but can you find out what's going on? Maybe they discovered some new evidence that we aren't aware of yet. When I return, I want to visit with Rompart's accountant and someone named Pierce Smiley who looks after the books. Maybe he will tell us something. The Mexico connection is interesting as well. Did you find out where that company is located?"

"Apparently, the company is doing business near Chihuahua as well. I gave Jeremy the address but I don't want either of you getting in hot water down there. They tend to frown on visitors to their country breaking the law. Be careful, will you."

Melissa stood. "We will. Jeremy hasn't filled me in on all he's planned for this trip. Barker is one target. I'm sure he'll tell me all the rest when we're seated on the plane." Her stomach rumbled again. "Gotta go. I'm meeting him at the airport. I hope you're okay about Chief staying with you. Not enough time to take him to Denny's."

"Chief will be fine with us. We both love animals." He walked with her to the exit door. Giving her a big hug, he added, "Try to find some time for a little fun, will you? That son of mine could use a break, too.' He slapped her on the shoulder as she stepped outside. "Keep me posted."

Chapter Twenty Three

Jeremy stood near the main entryway to Winnipeg's James Armstrong Richardson International Airport. He spotted Melissa as soon as she stepped out of the parking garage. She stopped before crossing the line of cars dropping off passengers. Setting her one travel bag at her feet, she lifted her cell to her ear and talked for a few seconds. Her head swivelled from side to side as she tucked her phone back in her purse.

He waved as soon as she saw him. His heart did a summersault. *I'll need to keep that under contr*ol. He smiled as she approached. *I wish we were really taking a vacation. We need time to relate away from work.* He opened the door. "Hi, Melissa."

Her smile almost matched his. "Hi, yourself. I'm looking forward to this. It's been awhile since I **travelled** anywhere."

"I was thinking the same thing. This could be dangerous if my suspicions about this Barker character are correct. If he is in bed with some shady characters we'll need to keep on our toes. He will recognize me but not you so ..." Jeremy reached for her suitcase.

"So, you need me. This isn't just an opportunity to check out Campos Tinades." She walked confidently beside him as they headed to the ticket counter to check in. "I also have something to tell you once we're settled in the lounge area. By the way, I'm so hungry I could eat my way through an extra-large pizza. Will there be an opportunity to find some food before we board?"

"I'll ask." He stepped up to the counter and returned the smile waiting for him in the airline's uniform. "Miss." He handed her their tickets.

The attendant motioned for him to place their luggage on the scale as she prepared their boarding passes. "Enjoy your flight." She handed the passes to him.

"Will we be able to get something to eat after we go through security or should we find something first?" Jeremy handed Melissa her ticket and boarding pass. He watched as she slipped the documents into her handbag.

"You'll have plenty of time to eat after you go through security, Sir. Gate number three is in that direction." She smiled and pointed them in the right direction before looking to help the next person in line.

Jeremy placed his hand on Melissa's elbow to guide her toward the right gateway. "I hope you brought your passport."

"Of course. I may not travel often but I do remember what's needed, especially with us going to Mexico." She left her handbag on the conveyor belt. "Next year, I'll need to renew it, though."

She stepped through the security scanner and retrieved her purse on the other side. Jeremy followed in the same manner with no issues. "Let's find you some food. What are you hungry for?"

"I haven't had any lunch so a bowl of soup or sandwich will work." She glanced around at the various shops to choose from. "What about Tim Horton's?"

"Sounds good. We have forty-five minutes before we need to board." They walked swiftly toward the counter scanning the food choices on the menu behind the cashier. Jeremy ordered coffee and an apple fritter while Melissa added a bowl of soup to her coffee order.

Once they were seated, Jeremy bowed his head to say grace. "Lord, thank you for this opportunity to go someplace warm for a couple of days. Thank You, Lord. Melissa was able to make her way clear to join me, and Lord, thank You for this food. Please protect us as we inspect Campos Tinades and check out who Barker plans to meet in Chihuahua. Lead us to the right place in order to find what we need. Amen." He bit into his fritter as his eyes scrutinized the woman sitting across the table. "You look pretty today."

Melissa blinked. She hesitated but recovered quickly. "You've never seemed to notice me in that way before. What gives?"

He reached for her hand. "I've always thought you were pretty ... beautiful as a matter of fact. I just ... it didn't seem appropriate before. But ... I want to get to know you better." Melissa's eyes appeared more round. Jeremy wondered if he'd been a bit premature. "I mean, if ... aw, heck, Melissa. We've known and worked with each other for almost two years. We share the same house, for crying out loud. The time is right for us to develop more of a friendship, don't you think?"

Melissa took another spoonful of soup. "Oh ... friendship. I can do that. Yes, I'd like a friendship with you. But I thought that's what we had." She grinned and then slurped more ladylike from the full spoon again.

Jeremy sighed and let his torso relax. "Good. What did you want to tell me, something about a piece of paper you found?"

She swallowed. "Chief found a scrap of paper under the desk I chose for my office. By the way, my dad had three desks in storage. I think I'll be having a garage sale soon. There were all kinds of pieces to choose from but this desk was the last one he utilized. I want to continue using it as my own. Anyhow, I was checking through the drawers when I pulled out the centre one, this paper landed on the floor."

"Those furniture pieces are already twenty or so years old. I wonder if an antique dealer might be able to assess their worth. I guess the staff didn't clean them thoroughly before storing them. What was on the paper?"

Melissa thought for a minute. "Your father has it. He said something about them closing in; he didn't do it, and needing to protect his family. It was signed by him and your father has authenticated the signature. My father is innocent and Barkley plans to talk to the detectives handling the case. He wants them to read the note, too."

Jeremy leaned back in the chair. "You always thought he didn't do what the police said he did. It must feel good to be vindicated."

"Yeah, except, there's still no proof he wasn't involved. I have a feeling the police are simply going to ignore this and keep on trying to implicate him once they can prove money laundering is what Rompart is about. Once they do connect the dots, will I even own a company to run afterward? Is there any legitimate business going on there at all?"

"Good question." Jeremy glanced at his watch. "You finished? We need to head toward our gate to board the plane." He wiped his sticky fingers on a napkin. "That hit the spot. Was the soup enough for you?"

"It was good. Filled a hole." She stood. "Do we ... oh, I'll dump these dirty dishes over there." She grabbed her bowl and cup, placed them on the tray with Jeremy's cup and carried them to the receptacle for dirty dishes. "I'm looking forward to this trip." She grinned in Jeremy's direction. "Friend."

Jeremy chuckled. "Yeah, me, too." He hurried through the doorway and began their trek toward gate number three again.

Chapter Twenty Four

Melissa lifted her carry-on bag over her head into the open compartment above her seat. Grabbing one of the available pillows, she sat in her designated seat. Jeremy stowed his luggage but before he sat down, he looked at Melissa. "Would you like the window seat?"

"No, I'm okay not knowing how high in the sky we are." She began to buckle her seat belt.

"Are you nervous about flying?"

"I only travelled by air once, and that was when I returned to Canada a little over two years ago. I guess I need to develop air legs." Her nervous chuckle seemed strained to her ears. "I'll be okay once we get in the air, I think."

Jeremy reached for her hand. "I never thought to ask. You always act so **fearless**. Are you sure you'll be okay?"

Her hand tingled with the warmth emanating from his long fingers. She studied her much more diminutive appendage. *It feels as if it belongs there.* She yanked her hand from his grasp. *What was I thinking?* She placed it in her lap and concentrated on the other passengers boarding and getting settled.

She peeked at Jeremy with her head bowed to keep her gaze hidden. He was studying the tarmac through the tiny window beside him. Her heart fluttered. *I do like him. He's a good friend. I can trust him.* As she thought the words, she knew them to be true.

She dropped her gaze as Jeremy turned toward her. "Did you bring a bathing suit? The resort has a wonderful pool area with a lazy river and a swim up bar. They also provide a spa for massages and a facial, if that's something that might interest you."

Melissa smiled. "It sounds like a ritzy place. How much is this costing us? I intend to pay my share, by the way."

"Don't worry about the cost. I'm on an expense account for this trip. Remember I was hired to find out all I can about this banker. You're along as my significant other. You know, my cover. If Barker sees me, and I'm sure he will, we're enjoying our own getaway. It'll look like a coincidence that we ended at the same place as far as he's concerned." Jeremy fastened his seatbelt. "It looks like we're about to take off. You okay?"

"I'm fine. By the way, did you happen to find out how far Campos Tinades is from the resort? Is that a trip I could do in one day there and back?"

Jeremy reached inside his briefcase. He pulled a map out and spread it across the table top he'd dropped onto his lap. "Check this out." He pointed to the resort's location on the enlarged map of the Mexican Province of Chihuahua. He traced along a highway and pointed to the Mennonite village that held their interest. "The distance is only about two hundred miles, or kilometers I think they use, from the resort. Actually, two hundred kilometers are less than two hundred miles. That shouldn't take you too long. You'll need to be careful, though. There are not many trees to hide behind in that area by the looks of it."

"I can pretend I'm a lost tourist if they catch me." She studied the map. A small river ran near the village which appeared larger than the description given to her by Helen.

Jeremy scowled. "That won't work. They'll remember you and when we deliver Jessica's body, they'll recognize you. We'll figure out some sort of disguise, maybe a wig or something." He leaned back as he refolded the map. The flight attendant walked slowly past them making sure they had their seatbelts secured.

Melissa leaned her head back against the seat cushion. "I am tired. I'm not sure why."

Jeremy chuckled. "Maybe because you're burning the candle at both ends, trying to get acclimated to Rompart and also trying to take on clients with missing kids. Didn't you once say you'd use Rompart funds to hire some more investigators for Finders Keepers?"

"I did but I'm not there yet. You do just as much as I do but you don't tire as I do."

"Yes, but I'm not recovering from a near-fatal gunshot. You've only been out of the hospital for a couple of weeks, remember." He glanced out the window. "Hey, look at those fluffy clouds. We're on top of them. The sun is brilliant up here."

Melissa blinked before she leaned across him to look where he pointed. *How'd we get here so fast?* She turned her head toward Jeremy. "I never realized we'd already taken off. You kept me absorbed with other things. Thank you." She glanced out the window again. "Wow! I'd forgotten how gorgeous it is up here." She took a deep breath allowing her body to relax for the first time since boarding the plane.

She directed her gaze back to Jeremy. "I've recovered from that wound. No red around the site anymore. But my sleep habits have been anything but peaceful the past two nights. I think of each of the board members at Rompart and I can't imagine **any one** of them being so vicious as to kill my dad. Besides, Belcher was the only one to be part of the company when he died but even he seems so sincere. Do you think the brother knows something?"

Jeremy looked around to check if anyone nearby could hear their conversation. The plane was only half full with most of the passengers sitting by themselves near windows. They could speak freely. "Irving doesn't trust anything out of the man's mouth. He's an addict and a known felon. But he may be speaking the truth about his brother. If the CEO of Rompart wanted to oust his boss so he could take over, that would sure be one way of accomplishing his goal. Your note says otherwise, though. According to that, your dad was killed to shut him up."

The airline attendant stopped by Melissa's shoulder. "Did either of you want anything to drink?"

Melissa looked at Jeremy and back at the attendant. "Do you have any coke?"

"We do. What about you, sir?" She turned back to the cart that Melissa hadn't noticed before. Grabbing a can of **Coca Cola** and a napkin, she handed the beverage to Melissa.

"I'll have the same," Jeremy added.

The young woman reached behind her for the second can of pop. "Are you two on vacation or is this a business trip?"

Melissa grinned. "A little of both. I can't wait to begin relaxing in Chihuahua."

Jeremy nodded his head in agreement. "The little business we need to conduct won't detract one bit from the enjoyment."

"Well, enjoy yourselves. Mexico can be hot this time of year but not as hot as during the summer." She wheeled her cart farther down the aisle.

Jeremy leaned closer to Melissa. "I can't wait to watch you hit the water in a bikini." He lowered and raised his eyebrows in **effort** to portray one of the Three Stooges.

Melissa slapped his arm and **flapped** her eyelashes, displaying an exaggerated grin. "What makes you think I wear bikinis?"

Chapter Twenty Five

Melissa stretched her arms across the king sized bed. The cool sheets encompassed her body, reminding her that the humidity in this part of the world was a force to be reckoned with. *When we'd stepped off the plane last night, it was like hitting a solid wall of air, dense enough to touch.* She chuckled as she stretched her arms sideways. *I could add two of me to this bed, she mused.* The light filtered through the double sliding doors leading to the patio. *I wonder if this area is private enough for me to enjoy my first cup of coffee outside.*

She sat up on the edge of the bed, stretched again, and stood. Walking over to the glass portal, she slapped her leg expectantly. *Oh. Right, Chief's at home. I'm in Mexico.* She held the drapery aside. The day promised to be a warm one. Melissa opened the door and stepped outside looking from side to side. She had the privacy she wanted.

Retracing her steps, she approached the coffee maker and began preparations for a hot morning wake-up. The aroma soon filled the room while she visited the bathroom and made her bed. *I could get dressed I suppose but I'm on vacation. No hurry, right.* Humming to herself, she filled the cup provided and stepped back onto her patio.

The view down to the pool and the desert beyond took her breath away. *I never expected the desert to be so beautiful.* Flowering cacti dotted the landscape. Colourful blooms from other plants nestled amongst well-placed sculptures giving the stark, barren surroundings their intended beauty. Melissa sighed. She turned toward a cushioned lounge chair and set her coffee on the table beside it. *What a way to start the day.*

A large bird drifted with the air currents just over her head. She sipped her coffee hoping nothing would come flying downward to add to the beverage's perfect **flavour**. Melissa glanced at her wristwatch. *Jeremy wants to meet in an hour for breakfast. What should I wear for the day ahead?*

A lone bird **dove** toward a patch of desert and swooped skyward again, his claws grasping some rodent unfortunate enough to be wandering around that time of morning. Her stomach rumbled. *I guess it's time for my breakfast, too.* She chuckled. *I wonder what Jeremy has planned for today.*

The next half-hour sped by as Melissa replaced her night clothes for a filmy pink and aqua sundress and the jewellery to go with it. This was the first time this particular outfit, purchased at a sale last fall, graced the outside of her closet. It made her feel feminine, she decided, as she turned this way and that in front of the bathroom mirror. *Today, I need some colour on my face. Hopefully, by tomorrow, the natural tones from the Mexican sunshine will assure I won't need anything more than a little moisturizer.*

Deciding she was ready, she stepped toward the door to her room just as a soft knock sounded from the other side. She grabbed the handle and stepped through almost knocking Jeremy off balance. Her smile let him know she was expecting him. "Good morning. What a beautiful day. How did you sleep?"

"Not too long. I decided to do some sleuthing after you retired so I settled down at a table in the bar to watch who might be entertaining guests." He placed his hand on her elbow to guide her toward the elevator. "The corner where I sat was secluded so when Thomas Barker walked in, he didn't spot me right away. He was with his wife. At least, I think she was his wife." He punched the button for the lobby.

"So ... Did you let him know you were here?"

"No, but I'll do that today. This place is too small for me to hide forever. Remember, you're my significant other."

She chuckled. "I hate that term but in this case, it fits. I hope you can convince him we are here for fun and nothing more."

Jeremy's eyes gleamed. "He'll never think anything else when he sees you in that dress. You look beautiful."

Melissa's face soon felt as if the sun had already warmed it. She ran one hand down the other arm wondering how to respond. "I ... I... thank you. I bought this a long time ago but never had a chance to wear it anywhere till now."

"The dress is pretty but you would be beautiful in anything. I've wanted to tell you for a long time." He led the way out of the elevator toward the restaurant. "Did you do your devotions this morning?"

Melissa shrugged. "I got carried away with the scenery around here, the view from my balcony. I guess I should always take some time for the Lord first, before I get distracted."

"Making decisions without the Holy Spirit's involvement can be dangerous. Foolish at best. But I was wondering if you wanted to do them together, after breakfast. It might be a great way to begin each day we're here, letting God guide us where he wants us to go. What do you think?" Jeremy pointed out a booth in the corner near the large windows overlooking the pool area.

Melissa nodded in affirmation and followed his lead toward the table as she mulled over his suggestion. Do people do that? She slid into her spot across from Jeremy just as the waiter placed menus in front of them. Opening the folded list of breakfast items, she glanced at Jeremy. "I thought alone time with God meant alone. Do people do devotions together?"

"Sometimes. Do you remember Pastor Shultz telling us about when two or more are gathered in His name? Well, two people praying together and having a devotional works as well as time alone. I can show you how I do them and you can show me what you've been reading." He looked up as the waiter approached again. "Time to make a decision. Coffee?"

"Sure." She looked toward the young Mexican standing patiently beside their table. "Bring me like a glass of grapefruit juice, eggs benedict, and toast."

Jeremy proceeded to ask for coffee as well and chose the Rancher's special consisting of three eggs, toast, hash browns and a steak, medium rare. "Oh, and a large glass of orange juice."

The waiter wrote as fast as he could, read the order back to them, and sauntered away from the table. He disappeared through a swinging door emitting the sounds of clanging pots and pans. She chuckled. "You're hungry this morning."

"Always. Being a man of leisure makes me ravenous."

"A long walk might be called for after a meal that large. Would it be alright if we took our Bibles and found a quiet place of solitude to speak with the Lord?" Melissa folded her arms across her chest. "With all this beauty around us, I suspect there must be a rock or two we could find to sit on."

"Not with that dress on." He looked out the window. "The spot near the back wall of the pool area will be perfect? We could go there and you wouldn't need to change." His gaze rested on her face again.

"People will notice."

"So what?" His eyes travelled toward the terrace again. People were beginning to congregate around the pool but everyone seemed to be focused on their own agenda and not anyone else's. "No one is paying attention to what the others are doing. Think about it." He leaned back as the waiter placed his juice and Melissa's in front of them. Jeremy took a long sip. "Tasty."

Melissa did the same. "What did you plan for our day?"

Jeremy swallowed and tapped his index finger on the table top. "I need to find out what Barker is doing here. But he needs to think we're here on vacation so ..." He glanced up. "Speaking of Barker, he's here, wife and kids in tow."

Melissa glanced surreptitiously toward the door. A man of medium height stood contemplating which table to approach. She recognized as soon as his eyes landed on Jeremy. "He's spotted you." She smiled and placed her hand on Jeremy's.

Jeremy grasped hers a little tighter. "Remember, I'm Albert Decapoulis, new to Winnipeg. Maybe you should live where I used to." He swallowed and glanced casually around the room. "We should have given this a little more thought. Just follow my lead." He waved toward the banker.

The quarry led his family toward their table. "Mr. Decapoulis. What a surprise. Mina, this is a new customer of the bank's or at least, I hope will be one day. So nice to see you."

Jeremy stood, shook hands with Mina Barker and grinned at the kids jousting for position beside their father. "I'm not surprised you're here since your secretary gave me the name of your travel agent. Since I don't know anyone in Winnipeg, I thought this would be a good place for Melissa and me to get away for a few days." He turned toward his table companion. "Melissa Finder, this is Thomas Barker, the man who will soon be my banker." He glanced at Barker. "I made a decision in your **favour**."

"Well, good. We'll need to connect back in the city. I hope you enjoy your rest. Melissa, good to meet you? Do you also live in Winnipeg?"

"No, I still live in Kansas City. Albert decided to move to Canada so we are working out this long distance relationship." She eyed the waiter making his way toward them with loaded plates. "Albert, our food has arrived. Thomas and Mina, maybe we'll bump into you again. Enjoy your vacation." Her eyes took in the kids. "Lots to do for kids here, I guess."

The Barkers left for their table without responding but Melissa noticed the wife's shoulders stiffen. "I think she's not as happy to be here as he is. But then, what wife would be happy to tag along on a business vacation." She glanced at the plate set before her. "**Oh**-h that looks so good." She folded her hands in her lap waiting for Jeremy to bless the food.

Jeremy took a deep breath, inhaling the smell of perfectly

cooked steak and eggs. He grasped Melissa's arm.

She raised her hand to his and they bowed their head. Jeremy's voice was clear but quiet. "Lord, bless this food. Bless the hands who've prepared it and may our conversation **honour** and glorify You even though we need to lie about who we are. Amen."

Melissa raised her head and reached for the fork beside her plate. "That is a conundrum. We're supposed to speak honestly to people and yet, in this business, we lie all the time. I hope God understands."

Jeremy took a forkful of hash browned potatoes. "The Lord understood, long before we did, what type of business would hold our interest. Nothing surprises Him or disappoints Him." Jeremy put his fork down and studied her face. "Melissa, you remember when I asked you to rent space in my office? I couldn't ask you to be a partner at that time because the Bible is clear about being connected to someone whether in business or in marriage who is not a believer. However, you are a daughter of the King now so do you want to make our partnership official? We've been handling the same cases for a while now anyway."

Melissa leaned toward him, the look of surprise tingeing her cheeks a shade of pink. "Are you serious?"

"I am. The idea consumed my thoughts lately so you might want to think about it ... and please, pray about this decision. Take all the time you need. Now let's eat. Our food is getting cold." The waiter stepped close to refill their coffee cups.

I wonder how much he heard. Melissa couldn't help but think about the relationship she had with Jeremy. As she chewed on a slice of toast, she wondered how close they would become if she took him up on the offer of partner. Her heart skipped a beat as she envisioned them as a couple one day. She discovered she liked the idea. *Hmmmm!*

Chapter Twenty Six

Wiping the last trace of steak and eggs from his mouth, Jeremy stood. He held out his hand to Melissa as she also rose from the table to leave the restaurant. "Get your bathing suit. Let's take advantage of this hot weather. After all, we are supposed to be on vacation. Bring your devotional as well."

"I'd sure like to get some colour while we're here. I wonder if the gift shop has any sunscreen. I brought some but the tube is almost done and so old, it may be ineffective." She walked beside him into the lobby, her skirt swaying with each step.

"Let's take a look." Jeremy led the way down the short hallway to the shop where they would be able to find anything they needed. He glanced at the clerk who was busy with another customer. The shelves were stocked with toiletries of all kinds, mostly name brand, and even some snack foods. The shop had jewellery, shirts, dresses, and other resort wear.

Melissa held up a tube of sunscreen. "Found some." She glanced at the dresses but quickly looked away.

"Melissa, you would look good in this." Jeremy held up a green and white dress similar to the one she had on.

"The dress is pretty but there's no place at home to wear these clothes." She continued toward the counter where the clerk was more than happy to take her money. "This'll fit the bill," she tossed over her shoulder toward Jeremy.

They walked out of the shop, hand in hand. Jeremy felt Melissa's reticence but decided the situation warranted an opportunity for hand-holding. He chuckled. "Relax. We're supposed to be very good friends, remember?"

She dropped her hand as soon as they were safely inside the elevator. "Holding hands is out of character for me. We've never had to pretend a more serious relationship before." She lowered her head and seemed to study the floor. "I've never had a boyfriend so this is out of my comfort zone."

"Now that I would never guess." The slight jerk of the elevator indicated their stop. "Weren't there any good looking fellows in Texas?"

Melissa stepped off the elevator first. "The Finders never encouraged me to date. They always reminded me that my home was in Canada. I never found anyone who made me rethink their position, either." She stopped in front of her door. "I'll be ready in about fifteen minutes, okay?"

Jeremy nodded as she opened her door and slipped inside. He continued on to his room thinking about the naïve young woman that Melissa was. *No wonder she finds any intimacy between us strange. I'll go slowly.* He opened his own door. His heart was involved and he decided not to fight his emotions any longer. Pretending would suffice for now but getting familiar with the real Melissa Rompart would be his objective during the next few days. *I can't wait.*

Jeremy opened his suitcase, extracted the dark blue bathing trunks and stepped into the bathroom. He stripped of his street clothes, slipped the suit over his long legs and reached for the shirt he had hung on the back of the door. *I hope they provide towels down by the pool.* Grabbing a book and his Bible, he inserted his key card into the pocket of his trunks, zipped the opening closed, and sauntered down the hall toward Melissa's door.

He reached to knock as her door opened and she stepped out. His breath caught in his throat. She was wearing a modest two-piece that showed off her figure in all the right places. The cover-up only added to the intrigue that this woman presented.

Jeremy watched the pink creep up her neck as he studied her. He cleared his throat. "Sorry. Didn't mean to stare. You do look scrumptious." He walked beside her back to the elevator. "Did you bring enough sunscreen for me? I forgot mine in my room." He chuckled. "I was too much in a hurry to find the right spot in the sun."

Melissa giggled. "I concur. Having a few days to do absolutely nothing seems too good to be true." She waved a novel in his direction. "I borrowed this from the church library to read but never found the time till now."

The elevator ride was a quiet one as each focused on their own thoughts. Jeremy sensed Melissa's discomfort so he resisted the urge to tease her about her skimpy attire. Inside, his heart was whistling, though. *She's definitely a woman to treasure,* he decided.

The rest of the morning sped by. Jeremy and Melissa spent a little time with their Lord, swam, relaxed on a lounge chair, soaked up the sun, and made plans for Monday. "Maybe we could go together to Campos Tinades tomorrow morning," she suggested.

"That would work. We could remain by the pool for the rest of the afternoon." He closed his eyes. "I'll arrange for a rental at the front desk. We can go exploring as touristas, eh?" The warm sun baked his skin. "Some more sunscreen, please. Don't want to burn." *Besides, I like her hands rubbing my back.*

Melissa handed him the tube. "I wonder if we can ..." She spotted some tables nearby. "We could eat lunch at one of those tables, maybe."

Jeremy slathered on the lotion as he perused the area she pointed at. He studied the attendants for a few seconds. "The staff will bring our food out here by the looks of it. We might be able to stay right here. We'll order a simple sandwich and something to drink brought to us right here." He motioned for the waiter who had brought them each a soft drink earlier.

As the waiter made his way toward them, Jeremy noticed the Barker family near the children's pool and the hot tub. "They look like a happy family. What do you think?"

Before she answered, the waiter approached. "Can I help you, sir?"

Jeremy indicated the tables nearby. "Do you serve lunch out here at those tables or is it okay to eat right here?"

"Either would work sir. Whatever you wish." The young man had deeply tanned skin and appeared to be in his late teens. "Would you like to order something now?"

"No, later, I think." He looked at Melissa. "How about you, sweetheart? Are you hungry yet?"

"No darling. We ate breakfast not too long ago." She smiled sweetly in his direction and at the waiter. "Is that okay. How long do they serve lunch?"

"Any time is alright, miss." The waiter glanced toward the other side of the pool where someone else needed his attention. "Tell me when you are ready to order." He stalked off in the direction of other patrons.

Jeremy leaned back against the lounge cushions. "Oh, I could make a habit of getting away like this every week." He sighed.

"The Barkers are enjoying themselves as well." Melissa picked up her book again but changed her mind. "I'm going for a dip."

Chapter Twenty Seven

Melissa drained her coffee cup and leaned back in the lounge chair. Mist rose from the desert confirming a cooler day than yesterday. She sighed. *I wonder how I can build an oasis like this at home*. Her Bible lay open beside her. *Lord, I need to rely on you for decision making, but Father, how do I recognize that it's You?* She sighed again. *There's so much to learn.*

The phone beside her bed jangled. She stood, stepped through the sliding doors into her bedroom and grabbed the receiver. "Good Morning." She suspected Jeremy was hungry after his workout last evening. Her suspicions were confirmed when he chuckled and then asked how soon she could meet him in the restaurant. He'd been swimming for the last hour.

"You got up early this morning. I'm enjoying a leisurely cup of coffee on the balcony. Man, I feel lazy." Her stomach rumbled. "I guess I'm hungry as well although I do like sitting here and talking to the Lord. I want to practice sharing my confessions and concerns with Him each day before I ask the Holy Spirit to fill me. I'll meet you in half an hour, okay?"

Jeremy groaned in her ear but acquiesced, grousing about his lack of choice. She chuckled. "You really are hungry. I'll hurry."

She replaced the phone, walked back to the open door and slid it shut. She knew the cleaning staff would clear the used cup from her balcony when her room was tidied for the day. Stepping into the shower, she rinsed her body off, picked out another sundress to wear and some sandals, and stood ready to go in record time.

As she stepped from the elevator, Melissa fell in behind the Barker family also heading for the dining room. She smiled as she passed them to head for the table where Jeremy sat waiting. He stood as she approached, a smile highlighting his features. "Good morning."

"Good morning to you." Melissa took the seat he offered. "Did you notice the Barkers? That woman does not look happy."

"She seems to be putting a good face on now, though." He poured her a fresh cup of coffee from the carafe the waiter left on their table. "What makes you think she's not happy?"

"He tried to guide her by taking her arm and she reefed it out of reach. That was before they noticed me behind them. I wonder if I should try to worm my way into a friendship when they are poolside again. I might learn something useful." She dropped the subject as the waiter approached.

"Are you ready to order Mr. Decapoulis?" The young man was the same one who served them the day before. He waited patiently for Jeremy and Melissa to scan the menu.

"I'm not so hungry this morning. I'd like some dry toast, a fruit salad, and some orange juice." Melissa smiled in his direction.

Jeremy grunted before telling the young man to bring the same as the day before. "I am ravenous." He chuckled when Melissa's eyebrows rose upwards. "Well, I wasn't sitting around all morning."

The waiter left and Jeremy reached across the table for her hand. "Just to make it look good. I arranged for a rental car to be delivered about ten this morning so we don't have a lot of time to dally." The waiter returned with their juice. Jeremy continued the minute he was out of earshot. "Bring a camera. The photos will give us some idea of the location when Helen checks them out after we arrive home. Besides, that'll make us more believable if we are forced to use the tourist excuse for being in the area."

"I hope we don't, but this trip will give us some information about terrain, and maybe provide an escape route after we take the kids. It'll also tell us how tight their security is." She leaned back as the waiter placed their breakfast in front of them.

He waited until they had taken their first bite before asking if they needed anything else. "No thanks, Carlos." Jeremy watched the young man leave and then bowed his head to thank the Lord for their food. He filled his fork with a piece of the tender steak. "Melissa, did you want to check out the company that Rompart is doing business with down here?"

"I actually hadn't given it any thought since Barkley said he gave you the name. We could add the address to the GPS if it doesn't take too long. I know the address is around Chihuahua somewhere." She used her fork to poke a slice of melon from the dish of fruit she'd ordered. "This is delicious."

"I hope the car has a GPS system but if it doesn't, my phone does. Once we've inserted it, we can decide if time will allow for a visit today or we can do it another day." He remained silent for a few minutes while he assuaged his rumbling stomach.

Melissa did the same, interspersing each bite with a glance at the pool just outside their window. It looked so refreshing and the pool looked crowded with people enjoying the warm sunshine. "Is the water a little cooler today? Mist floated across the desert this morning."

Jeremy swallowed. "Not so much. The air was a bit chilly, but I stayed in the water doing laps so it never bothered me. According to the desk clerk, the temperature is only going to be 85 degrees today instead of the 90 from yesterday." He rubbed his arms with both hands crossed in front of him. "Giving our skin a rest from the intense sun today is a good thing. I think I got a little red yesterday. By the way, what was all that on the phone about confessions and concerns for the Lord?"

Melissa slid the piece of grapefruit she was eating to the side of her mouth. "I listened to a video where a woman taught about starting our day with a filling of the Holy Spirit. She said to open our line of communication with the Lord we should confess anything he brings to mind so we can keep short accounts with Him. Then we leave our concerns in His lap before we ask the Holy Spirit to fill us for the day. I thought it made sense and certainly coincided with what the pastor was teaching last Sunday about making decisions with the guidance of the Holy Spirit."

Jeremy sat there grinning. "I am amazed at how far you've come since accepting Jesus into your life. God is showing you how to rely on Him every day and it took me until I was out of my teens to learn that. Dad will be pleased, I'm sure. Thought any more about my suggestion we become partners?"

Melissa felt warmth creep up her neck as if he could read her thoughts. She was afraid they'd reveal more than she was willing to let on at this juncture in their relationship. She studied his face. "I thought about it. I guess I've considered us partners in a lot of ways. We spend a lot of time working the same cases so, yes, a partnership makes sense. How much money would I need to inject?"

"I don't know. I'll need to contact my accountant to give us a complete assets list to determine worth and we'll go from there. No hurry." He swallowed another mouthful and then sipped his coffee. "Let's finish breakfast so we can explore the desert, eh?"

Melissa wiped her mouth and set her napkin on an empty plate. "I'm done. I'll go fetch my handbag and my camera. I'll meet you in the lobby in about fifteen minutes. Does that work?"

"It does. I won't be long." He bent his head to the task of

cleaning his plate as Melissa slipped out of the restaurant.

Chapter Twenty Eight

A few minutes later, Jeremy steered the car through the portico where Melissa met him, and out onto the street heading northwest on Calle Barrancas del Cobre toward Calle Juan María Salvatierra.

Melissa fastened her seatbelt. "Where are we going? I assume you didn't tell the rental agency that we were heading toward a Mennonite Campos."

"No, I asked them how to get to Ciudad Juarez, the only other major city in this state. I checked the map last night and this will take us in the general direction but we'll take a few side roads along the way. Campos Tinades is not listed on any map but from what Helen told you, it should be off the highway." He turned left and took the first right onto Calle Barranca La Bufa. They continued to zig-zag through the streets of Chihuahua until eventually open desert greeted them again.

"Wow, those streets were sure congested. The resort grounds are pretty secluded giving an impression of open desert beyond. Many of the people around here appear impoverished. Their living conditions leave a lot to be desired." Melissa leaned back in the comfortable interior, the air conditioning cooling where the sun's intense rays warmed her skin. "The sun warms things up out here really fast."

"It does." Jeremy glanced at the GPS again and shifted his gaze for a few seconds to Melissa. "You're measuring the standards here by our own. Maybe for these people, what they have works for them and is an improvement from their former way of life. I find it hard to remember that things are not always what they seem when I travel to other countries."

"I guess you're right. What we consider basic necessities might be different than their needs." She glanced out the window to watch the rugged terrain slip past. "Let's stop and take some shots. If we're going to look like tourists, we'd better act the part. Besides a stop here and there will help us get our bear-ings." Melissa waved her camera to make her point.

"I need to turn right at the next fork in the road. We'll stop there, okay?" Jeremy checked the rear view mirror. The highway was empty, a sharp contrast from the bumper to bumper traffic in the city. "I'm glad I programed our hotel in the GPS as home. All these directional changes have me confused about exactly where we are." He made the turn, found a wide shoulder and pulled over.

Melissa stepped out of the car first. She motioned for Jeremy to stand along the side of the road with the scrub brush in the background. She was about to take his picture when a car crept past travelling well under the speed limit. She twisted around to wave but stopped when she saw the angry stares from the men inside the car. She moved closer to Jeremy. "We must be doing something wrong."

Jeremy noticed the missing chrome and the nondescript auto-mobile. The men were wearing straw hats as well. "I think those are some Mennonites. At least they look like the images we've seen and their car is uncommonly plain."

"Really?" Melissa twisted around to get a better look.

"Don't stare. I don't plan on getting into a battle with these people. But when they pass, let's follow. Find out where they go. They may be from the village we're looking for and since they've seen us taking photographs, they won't be surprised when we accidently stumble onto their turf." He posed for another shot as the car disappeared down the road and around another bend. "Let's go."

Melissa quickly hopped into the passenger seat, attached her seatbelt and waited while Jeremy put the car in gear and steered back onto the pavement. "They're gone."

"I know but there are so many twists and turns to this highway, they could be around the next corner." He revved the engine a little as he got up to speed and pointed. "There they are."

Melissa stared out the windshield. "You'd better slow down so we don't overtake them. Maybe another stop, when the road is a little straighter so we don't lose them. That should cement our persona in their minds." She looked out the side window this time. "I never thought Mexico could be so filled with bush and look, that creek winds its way through the ravine. The humidity is high with all this heat but the landscape is pretty."

Jeremy kept his eye on their target. "It is beautiful. From my reading, there are a lot of flat areas like our plains as well. Why don't you take some more images from the car as we drive? If they're watching us, they might catch you taking pictures and relax their vigilance." Jeremy slowed down so Melissa could open the window for her next photo opportunity.

They travelled in silence for a few kilometres, enjoying the trip but keeping their eyes on the car ahead. Are they staying on this road because of us? Melissa pressed the camera button for another picture and took one of Jeremy's pensive expressions as he contemplated the next direction change. "You look so serious."

"A turn is coming up if we are, in fact, going to Ciudad Juarez. I wonder if they'll turn that way as well."

The car in front slowed as the comment left Jeremy's mouth. "I guess they decided to go home another way, wherever that may be. We need to follow but not so we make them nervous. I think I'll drive past their turn off and turn back to head down the road. Act like we're having fun in case they ambush us up there."

Melissa let out a loud laugh and then leaned toward Jeremy. She snapped another shot of a few trees surrounded by cacti and flowers, and then set her device on the seat beside her. She brushed her hand across Jeremy's jawline.

"Hey, you're getting good at this clandestine stuff. Those strict Mennonites will think we're lovers or something." He chuckled. "If they only knew."

"Knew what?" Melissa batted her eyelashes at him.

"Never mind, Vixen. Let's concentrate on where these guys are headed." He chuckled as he turned the vehicle down the road where he guessed their quarry was headed. As they travelled over a short bridge, the countryside changed from rugged to grassy in under a couple of miles. Trees became scarce but the grasslands now contained a few animals. Cattle dotted the landscape as did sheep with a few horses here and there. Jeremy stopped the car as soon as he spotted the black car ahead of them. "Use your camera."

Melissa slid out of the car as it hummed by the roadside. She shot a photo of the terrain behind them and in front noting the marked contrast. "I may be only pretending to be a tourist but this place sure contains a variety of God's creative talents. Could that be why the Mennonites decided to settle here? It gives them options as far as what type of farming they do, don't you think?"

Jeremy put the car in drive as soon as she slid across the seat and closed the door again. "Who knows why they settled here. The area is close enough to the US that crossing the border should only be a short day trip but those ravines and streams aren't good for farming anything I know of. Maybe the cattle like those areas. Not being familiar with the business ...."

"I know my uncle used to use the ravines and arroyos as shelter when a storm threatened to dump on us. The cowboys herded the animals toward those places before the skies opened." She pointed to the vehicle that was almost out of sight. "If we don't catch up they're going to disappear."

"I don't want to spook them." He pressed a little harder on the gas pedal anyway. The Impala zoomed forward careening over ruts and bumps in the road. "Whoa. This road is not made for speed. If we're not careful, we'll lose some nuts and bolts off this car and then have to pay for some expensive repairs."

Melissa's hand began to ache as she hung onto the handle located above her door. "Those guys are familiar with this section of road. They're moving right along."

Jeremy's hands gripped the steering wheel. He swerved to miss another pothole, and added a little pressure to the gas pedal again. Trees lined the rough track but the ploughed fields beyond could be seen through the brush. An array of grain crops spread out before them, a definite sign of civilization.

Melissa turned the knob for the air-conditioning a little higher. She grabbed a tissue from her handbag. "I guess the heat is more intense in these flat places."

"Getting in and out of the car doesn't help."

"Jeremy, it's also the middle of the day, almost high noon. Were you planning on stopping for something to eat?"

"You're hungry so soon? It feels like we just had breakfast." Jeremy steered their car around a curve in the road. He slammed on the brakes. "Wow. Would you look at that?"

Melissa stared at the primitive village in front of them. "Boy, if this is the campos that Helen spoke of, it sure isn't far from civilization. How could all those things be going on so near the city and law enforcement?"

"I guess we're going to find out if this is Campos Tinades or not." He nodded his head toward the three men walking toward them. "They don't look very friendly." Jeremy drove carefully toward the main street. "This must be the main street. Not much in the way of businesses, though."

Melissa watched the men stop as they pulled closer. She studied the area in front and around them. The houses were unpainted, log huts with a couple of windows and a door. Curtains did not cover the windows and, in some cases, the door was left wide open. I guess they don't have to worry about bugs here. One woman emerged from her home and threw some water into the roadway. She hustled back inside. Some children, young ones, played in the dirt. "Jeremy."

He opened his door and swung his feet to the ground. Making sure his smile was firmly in place, he waved toward the men. "Can you tell me where we are? We seemed to have made a wrong turn or something."

Chapter Twenty Nine

Derek Penner looked at the man to his right. "These people followed us here. We do not recognize dem."

The man took his straw hat from his head and wiped the back of his hand across his glistening forehead. "They tourists, nothing more. Get rid of dem."

"Jason, they could cause trouble. If dey find..."

"Dey won't. Make dem leave. I go make sure de stuff stay hidden until dey out of sight." He walked toward a large barn located near the centre of the village.

Derek strode purposefully toward the strangers. His scowl was intended to make sure they knew he meant business. "What you want?" He looked **toward** the man and then at the woman who'd just emerged from the passenger side of their vehicle. She was fanning her skin with a scarf.

"Hi. Good afternoon. We followed the wrong people, I guess. We are trying to travel to Cuidad. We thought that car was heading in the right direction." The man pointed toward the vehicle Derek and Henry had driven from Chihuahua.

Derek shrugged his shoulders. *Dumb touristas.* "You go back. You can't stay here. No place to stay anyway. Ve provide no places for people to eat or sleep. You don't own map or GPS?"

The man grinned sheepishly. "I don't understand how to read a map, I guess. I also can't figure out how the GPS works." He glanced over his shoulder at his companion. "Honey, did you need a restroom?"

The girl stepped around the front of the car. "I do." She spotted an outhouse behind the nearest building. "Can I use that outhouse, do you think?" She smiled toward Derek.

Derek scowled. His grumpy demeanour wasn't working. *Maybe dey leave if she relieve herself. Women. Harrumph.* "Hurry up." The woman skipped across the road and wound her way toward the back of the house and into the privy. He looked toward the young incompetent. "Where's map?"

He reached inside the car and pulled out a wrinkled map that looked as if it had been twisted this way and that in an attempt to find where they were. A section was ripped apart. He handed it to Derek who slapped it on the hood of the car.

Derek smoothed the paper as it flapped in the breeze. He pointed to a dot not too far from Chihuahua. "That where you are." He pointed to another dot much farther away. "Dat where you want to go. Not hard. Take road back where you come until you hit pavement. Turn northwest. Easy." He sneered at this tourista's ineptness. "You shouldn't be driving around places where you not familiar."

The man smiled and held his hand out. "Thanks, man. I appreciate the help. My honey says I never ask for directions." When Derek ignored his hand, he waved it around the village. "What's the name of this place? It looks very quaint. Rustic."

"Campos Tin ..." Derek stopped before completing the name. "Why you want to know?"

"I was just wondering. No conveniences like electricity or anything. I didn't think people lived like this these days. I mean ... no electricity. How do you manage?"

"We don't need." The woman made her way back to the car. She smiled in his direction. "I was thinking that maybe some of your women made crafts that are from this town or region. Do you have a gift shop or something where I can buy a souvenir?"

"No. Nothing. Now leave. Go back the way you come. Ve don't like strangers around here." He raised his hand and swept it toward the road the strangers entered town on.

"But ..." A shot rang out from the barn. It zinged over the man's head.

"Leave. Now." Derek checked the door to the barn and spotted the barrel of a gun sticking out. "Ve like privacy and this is private property.

The man scrambled into the car. "All right. All right." His friend was already in her seat. He turned on the ignition and swung the car in an arc to retreat the way they'd come. Their dust followed them as they left in a greater hurry than when they arrived. Derek chuckled. *Some people need to be persuaded.*

Chapter Thirty

Jeremy pulled the car over to the side of the road as soon as they were out of sight. "Those guys were sure in a hurry to get rid of us. I wonder what goes on in that barn. The shot came from that direction, I think."

Melissa wrapped her arms around her torso. "The bullets might have hit their mark."

"But they didn't. They wanted to scare us. I wish it was closer to dusk. My curiosity about that barn is in overdrive."

"Jeremy, that's not why we took this trip. What's going on in the barn is none of our business. Did you find out if that is Campos Tinades?" Melissa sank further into the cushions of the front seat.

"I think it is. The guy almost told me the name before he caught himself. He said Campos Tin and then changed his mind about answering my question." Jeremy pulled back onto the road. "You're right, though. If they are hiding a drug operation, the law can deal with them. We just want those kids." Jeremy continued cautiously, making sure their car avoided the worse ruts and pot holes.

Melissa studied the landscape, viewing it differently than she had before. "Sneaking those kids out of this place is not going to be easy. But the ravines and arroyos would hide us. We need to hide someone out here so we can escape faster than they can drive over these roads. What about ATVs?"

Jeremy stopped the car. He turned toward Melissa. "We

could find some place to hide and spy on them. How hungry are you?"

"I'm fine. The village is pretty wide open. Where could we hide so they wouldn't catch us?" She ran her hand over the sundress she was wearing. "I'm not exactly dressed for trekking through the bush."

"Another chance to garner information about their routine and where the school building is might not present itself." He wrinkled his brow as he contemplated their options. "Didn't Helen say something about a town nearby where they travelled when they needed groceries?"

"She did. What are you thinking?"

"We might find a restaurant. In fact ...."

"There is. Helen told me the women eat there when they're in town." Melissa looked back over her shoulder at the road behind them. "Do you think those guys will tell us where it is?"

"They might. A return visit gives us an excuse to catch them doing something." Jeremy put the car in drive and began to turn the vehicle around.

"Yeah, and it might land us in trouble, too." She checked to make sure her seatbelt was secure. "Don't take the car out of gear in case we need to make a run for it."

Jeremy glanced at her. "I think they travel these roads so much, they'd be faster no matter how quickly we move if they decide to chase us. Anyway, let's give it a shot."

Melissa chuckled. "Honey, I think your stomach's talking, not your head." She looked at the trees along the road as they slipped by in a blur. "Maybe we should ask the Lord for protection. By the way, how can these people call themselves Christian? We've discussed this before but the difference between the teachings of Jesus and the behaviour of these guys is remarkable. They act nothing like the Bible describes a follower of Jesus."

Jeremy spotted the outlying buildings that indicated the village was around the next bend in the road. He pointed in that direction as he answered Melissa's question. "Many, according to the Bible, claim to be Christian, but will arrive in heaven and Jesus will say I never knew you."

People milled about in front of several houses. The women wore similar clothing. Their dresses were long enough to cover the calves of their legs and they wore a head covering that looked like a small bonnet. The men also dressed plain with black pants held up by suspenders, and a plain white shirt. Their heads were protected from the hot sun by straw hats.

The entire village looked suspiciously in their direction. They drove near the centre where the large barn dominated the space.

Two men, different than the ones they talked to before, strode quickly toward them, not waiting for their vehicle to stop. Jeremy slammed on the brakes. He stuck his head out the open window. "Please tell us where the nearest town is so we can find something to eat?" *I wonder if scowling is taught here.*

"Vat you say?" The first man to reach them placed his hand on the door frame. "Food. You want food?"

Jeremy smiled, as friendly as he could under the circumstances. "Yes, my girlfriend is hungry. We didn't come across anyone else to ask so we decided to come back here." He scanned the area without taking his eyes off the faces of the two men beside the car. *I hope Melissa is doing the same.*

"Dere's a town dat vay, not too many miles." He pointed at the opposite end of the village. "From dere, you can find highway to Cuidad. Don't come back here. This is private ..."

"Yeah private property. Thanks." Jeremy took his foot off the brake and accelerated through the village. "Melissa, did you notice anything out of the ordinary?"

"Everything here is out of the ordinary as far as I'm concerned, but no, nothing of a criminal nature." She let out the breath she'd not realized she was holding. "My stomach is rumbling but I can't distinguish between fright or hunger."

Jeremy nodded. "I think the idea is to scare people so they'll stay away from their domain. We can ask some questions about Tinades from the people in this town while we eat lunch. Maybe we'll be able to buy you some more appropriate clothing for staking out that village."

"You still want to do that, eh?" Melissa ran her hand over her warm face. She reached over to turn the knob for the air conditioner up a notch but discovered it was already as high as it would go. "Opening the window sure heated it up in here."

"Yeah, even at this time of year, the temperature is plenty warm. The car will cool off soon enough though. I wish I'd asked how far the town was."

"I guess we'll arrive in due course. Jeremy, how can we make sure we never represent Christianity falsely?" She slid her body, as much as the seatbelt allowed, so she could study his face.

"The Lord is clear about us needing to stay in His word daily. He knew we would mess up otherwise." He settled back into his seat. "We also need to keep each other accountable. Our pastor suggested that we men begin an accountability group at church. I think, especially for the men, accountability is important so we can be the leaders God called us to be." His words were met with silence. "Don't you agree?"

"I'm not sure how I feel about the role of men and women in

the church. Why wouldn't it be as important for women to be held accountable? I need some maturity in order to understand all the nuances of our roles as Jesus intended."

"Some people never figure all that out. I'm glad you are searching for answers. My faith is strong but each of us has to come to the place where we are comfortable with submission. Jesus himself was submissive to His Father. So it has nothing to do with stronger or lesser roles. They work together for the end result of bringing people into the kingdom."

Melissa straightened in her seat and peered out the front window. She reached for the button to turn on the radio. "We might as well enjoy the ride. After all, we are tourists." She chuckled and laid her hand on the seat beside her.

Jeremy placed his hand over hers, choosing to drive one handed. The atmosphere flowed with companionable silence. Her soft hand in his was right where it should be.

Chapter Thirty One

Jeremy wiped the residue left from the burrito he'd eaten from his upper lip. "People here are sure closed mouthed. I guess they are as suspicious of strangers as the people in Tinades."

Melissa focused her gaze on the fajita she was enjoying. "The food here is scrumptious. It's too bad we haven't been able to glean any worthwhile information though." She glanced carefully toward the couple sitting at the table nearby. Lowering her voice, she added, "At least I found some workable clothing, hotter than my sundress I think."

"And not so pretty, methinks." Jeremy chuckled. He reached across the table for her hand. He winked.

"You're taking advantage."

Jeremy gripped the hand she tried to pull away from him. "We have a persona to maintain."

"Yeah, right." She smiled anyway. "I might become accustomed to you holding my hand and then where would we be as business partners?" She made quote marks with her fingers for the word business.

Ignoring her remark, Jeremy let his eyes roam around the small restaurant. No one openly watched them but he felt conspicuous nonetheless. "Everyone here recognizes the others. There is no way they don't have any information about Tinades and its residents." He lowered his voice to a whisper. "I sense they're watching us as we speak." He stood. "Let's leave."

"I need to change."

"You can't here. That'll tip our hand. We'll find some brush along the way back to give you privacy away from prying eyes." He walked over to the cash register to pay the bill for their food.

Melissa followed closely behind. Her presence was noted by everyone who tried not to look conspicuous. *Boy, this is small town living at its worst. I wonder if we looked at strangers the same way when we went to town in Texas. I don't remember thinking who this person was or that person. These people sure seem curious, though.*

Jeremy finished paying the bill and led the way toward the screen door to exit the building. He waited for Melissa to walk through. "Is there anything else you need?"

Melissa took a quick inventory of her purchases. "Maybe some bottled water. We don't know how long we'll be out in the hot sun."

"Right. Good idea." Jeremy walked toward a nearby grocery store. "I hope they have cold stuff."

Melissa followed at first but caught up and grabbed his hand. "To keep up the charade, right?" She chuckled when she saw the surprised look on her companion's face.

"You're getting awful bold, aren't you? I mean, for a proper lady, that is."

Melissa let the comment pass. She studied the terrain on the short distance to the store and didn't miss the stares. "Strangers don't come here very often, I think."

"Yeah, I get that impression." He opened the door into the air-conditioning and headed straight for the nearest cooler. Grabbing several bottles of cold water, he noticed an insulated sack hanging from a hook near the cooler. Good idea. He grabbed one and proceeded to the cash register.

Melissa tossed a couple of apples next to his purchases. "We might become hungry before we arrive at Juarez Cuidad."

Jeremy nodded and pulled out his wallet. As soon as he paid for their purchases, he followed Melissa out the door toward their parked vehicle. Women in long dresses, children dressed the same as the adults, and barking dogs dotted the sidewalks as cars as plain as the one they followed to Tinades flowed along the street. *I wonder how many Mennonite communities there are in Mexico.* "Melissa, how extensive was your research on the Mennonites in Mexico?" He pressed the unlock button on his key fob.

Melissa opened her door, threw her packages into the backseat, and plunked down on the seat cushion. She waited until Jeremy had secured his seatbelt before answering his question. "I looked up information about Campos Tinades but when I couldn't find anything pertaining to that particular village, I did some general research. Why?"

He placed the car in drive and steered it toward the edge of town. "This town, like Campos Tinades, appears to be made up of all Mennonites. I didn't see anyone of any other ethnic group anywhere, did you? I mean, we are in Mexico so where are the Mexicans?"

Melissa focused on the streets they passed. "You're right. My research uncovered the reason why they moved here and about a great exodus from Canada but it didn't say anything about their isolationist attitude. That is what we sensed back there, wasn't it. They don't like anyone from outside their belief system to corrupt their values so they stay separate. I guess that means from Mexicans too."

The main thoroughfare soon gave way to gravel roads once again as Melissa and Jeremy headed back toward Tinades. Jeremy kept his eyes open for a place where Melissa could change from her dress to pants and runners. Mostly open fields filled their field of vision although he knew the woods were just ahead.

Melissa reflected on her last statement. She gazed out the window but kept any further comments to herself.

"Are you nervous about doing some surveillance?" He tilted his head in her direction for a split second before focusing on the road again.

"No, as long as we can keep our distance and stay out of sight. I've been a little worried about those guys recognizing us when we come back with Jessica's body. We might have to wear a disguise."

Jeremy pulled the car over to the side of the road. "Here's a good place for you to change. But, yes, we need to be discrete. I'd rather not wear a disguise when we come back but that may be necessary in light of the fact we intend to kidnap two kids. I wish we had another way of getting those kids to safety. And if they're in danger, how are the rest of the kids in that village. Are they all being mistreated?"

Melissa stepped out of the car, opened the back door, and took the pants and shirt from her bag. "I'll change my shoes when I finish dressing."

Chapter Thirty Two

Jeremy and Melissa parked their car in a dense area of brush near enough to Campos Tinades. They would have to walk a short distance to be able to observe anything. "I'll carry the cooler bag of water and the apples." Jeremy took the lead pushing away some low hanging branches for Melissa to be able to pass without getting snagged.

She followed close behind avoiding branches along the pathway. "This seems to be a well-travelled path. I wonder what they use it for."

"I hope we'll find out as we watch the activity from the village. I don't want any surprises when we come back and I don't want anyone to catch us out here either."

Melissa stumbled over another branch, compensated by taking a hasty step to one side, and then continued leading this time. "The harder I try to be quiet, the noisier I get." She trudged farther, side-stepped around a wet spot and almost stepped on a snake as it slithered into some brush on its way. She almost yelped but instead, placed a hand over her mouth.

Jeremy snickered, albeit quietly. "I remember. You don't like snakes. Say, do you keep in touch with little Jimmy's parents? How is he doing?"

She turned her head so she wouldn't talk too loud. "His nightmares are really bad. Apparently, his therapist is trying to convince his parents to use hypnosis. He thinks he can take the boogie man out of those nightmares. I don't think that'll work and I told them as much. But that's their call. If I was his mom, I'd love him and let God do the rest."

"Are they believers?" Jeremy slipped ahead to move some larger tree limbs aside.

Melissa stepped past him. "I don't know. He's been so traumatized by.... there's no word strong enough to describe how evil those men are."

The path began to widen. Jeremy took the lead again and slowly placed one foot in front of the other in case someone was close enough to hear them. He placed his index finger over his lips signalling for quiet. He pointed to his feet and the path indicating her need to step where he stepped. They had discussed the possibility of trip wires.

Two smaller buildings came into sight, one on either side of the path. Jeremy stopped. He looked around for some cover. Finding some brush a short distance from the building on the right, he walked in that direction with Melissa close on his heels.

Jeremy stashed the cooler under the branches. "We'll need to move closer so the village is visible from here but that cooler is too brightly coloured. It's too conspicuous." He stepped toward one of the cabins.

Melissa spotted a door opening before he did. She waved her hand and then scrunched down behind the trunk of one of the larger trees. Jeremy slipped behind a tree closer to him but not large enough to completely hide him. They held their breath.

Chapter Thirty Three

"Ramos, we gotta take delivery tomorrow night. One of the men is heading to Canada to visit relatives. He can take the shipment with him." A stocky man with dark hair, almost black, nodded toward the one holding the satchel of money. "You got your money as promised. If you want us to move your product, the deadline is tomorrow night."

The man called Ramos thought for a second or two. Then he smiled. "We can make that work. This business arrangement is good for us. We would not be able to move the stuff into Canada otherwise. I won't mess you up."

The stocky one placed his hand on the holstered gun at his side. He nodded toward the open door. "Make sure you don't. I don't have patience with someone who double-crosses me. You know that." He looked toward the wall where an example of his impatience was hanging limp, chained to some rings attached high off the floor. "You can take him with you when you leave. Bury him along the route back for all I care. Just make sure there are no more like him in your organization."

Ramos walked toward his near dead cohort, the self-professed leader of their cartel. He released him from the chains and let him fall to the floor. This man, his former boss, was not well liked so his loss would not affect their business dealings very much. "I can do better, señor. Your merchandise will be here before the supper hour tomorrow night. That'll give you time to pack it for delivery." He opened the door to the little cabin. Then he retraced his steps, grabbed the arms of his boss, and dragged him out the door.

Ramos made an attempt to take the body and the satchel. Señor interjected. "Leave the money. It'll be here when you arrive tomorrow night. Make sure you weed out anybody loyal to this idiot."

Ramos dropped the satchel. "That is not how we deal, señor. Always money first." He lingered in the doorway for another second or two. "But I'm not him. I'll trust you .... this time. Till tomorrow." He continued out the door with the body tossed over his shoulder. He walked down the path between the buildings back into the brush he'd walked through.

Señor stepped outside the cabin. He squinted in the early afternoon sunlight as Ramos disappeared. He turned in the opposite direction and headed back to town. He needed to prepare for the transport of more drugs in and out of the community. A few relatives remained strategically in the Canadian province of Ontario.

Chapter Thirty Four

Melissa held her breath. They were so close. Their path back to their vehicle was now occupied by a drug lord. She closed her eyes. *Thank You Father.* Carefully, she edged around the tree to find out if Jeremy had moved. He'd disappeared. She looked again. *Where is he?*

Using only her eyes, afraid a branch might snap and give away her location if she moved at all; she checked each tree within her line of sight. *Nothing. He's gone or ....* She jumped as soon as the hand touched her shoulder.

With a slight movement, her head swivelled. Her eyes took in his appearance. She let out a breath which escaped like a sigh. "Jeremy." Her whispered reaction could hardly be heard.

"That was close. You okay?" Jeremy stooped down behind the tree that kept her hidden, his eyes watching the trail toward town and back the way they'd come. "I guess we know what those guys are up to. Drugs. I didn't get a look at the man Ramos called Señor. Did you?"

"Yes I did. Briefly. He's not one of the men who stopped us in the village. But that doesn't mean anything." She stood, straightening her back to release tense muscles. "The village is small enough that I'll bet everyone knows what's going on. Did you notice the body the man was hauling out of here?"

Jeremy leaned against a tree and began to rub his thigh muscles. "I'm not in as good shape as I thought I was. My legs started cramping back there." He rubbed harder. "I didn't hear what happened but by the sound of the Señor, I'll bet he had something to do with it. Was he wearing a gun?"

"He was. It appears as if he's the one running things around here. He walked back to the village with a large satchel. I think it held money to pay for the drugs these guys are bringing tomorrow night. Maybe they were supposed to bring them today and that's why the one man was injured or killed. I couldn't tell which. The Señor said to bury him." She shuddered. "We'd better hope they don't find our car where we parked it."

"I agree. I think we found out what we came for. Let's go back."

"We can't yet. We could run into that drug dealer along the path. Besides, as long as we're here, let's check out the village. School should be out soon. I'd like to watch some of the kids and their inter-action with the adults around them." Melissa's eyes roamed the area once again to make sure no one was within earshot. She continued to whisper. "Helen told me the kids are treated as servants with chores before and after school. The children whose mothers have left or died are left to do all the household tasks she would be responsible for."

"What I will never understand is how a mother can leave her children knowing they would be treated that way?" He shook his head and took a step toward the nearest cabin. "Let's ascertain if things are as bad as she led us to believe."

Jeremy motioned for her to follow as he wound his way past a couple of larger trees and between the cabins. He stepped quickly toward the edge closest to the village and peeked around the corner of the cabin where Señor and Ramos had been. The village was only a stone's throw away. "We can stay here. We won't be able to listen to what is said but we will sure be able to perceive their body language."

Melissa and Jeremy found a bush to camouflage their pres-ence and settled down to wait. The air was warm, more than either of them were used to. Before long the temptation to ferret out their water supply overtook their need to remain hidden. Jeremy motioned for her to stay where she was and he went for the water.

Melissa kept her eyes peeled. At first, only one child was seen trudging up what appeared to be the main street but a few more filled the air with childish voices. However, the lack of laughter caught Melissa's attention as did the raised voices, anger spewing from little mouths who should not have known such words.

Jeremy slithered back to their hiding place with two cold bottles in his fists. He handed one to Melissa as he unscrewed the cap of a second. Simultaneously, each one took a long drink of the re-freshing liquid. "See anything?" He wiped the residue from his lips with his tongue.

"The kids are heading home from school but they don't sound like kids back home. I can't make out exactly why but they are sure angry with each other. No laughter or skipping, just shuffling feet as if they had the weight of the world on their shoulders. These kids act like no kids I've ever seen." Melissa stopped her words to observe one little girl as she walked slowly, head down, toward a homestead with a fence around it and a barn off to one side of the dusty yard. "Take a look at that one. She's not very happy with a day of school behind her."

"I see what you mean. Most kids are excited when school is over for the day." He studied the body language of the little girl. He looked toward a boy, a little older, who was following not too far behind. "I wonder if he's her brother. Ow! He threw a rock at her."

Jeremy began to rise but Melissa placed her hand on his arm. "There's nothing you can do. Let's find out what she does." They watched in silence as the young girl began to walk faster. Her hand wiped across her face as if removing tears that blinded her steps. Otherwise, she did nothing to defend herself except gain access to the house, slamming the door behind her. Melissa sucked in a breath. "She's used to that treatment."

Jeremy scowled. His hand, Melissa noticed, formed a tight fist. She placed hers over it. "I know. We've seen enough. Let's get out of here."

Chapter Thirty Five

Jeremy grabbed Melissa's arm. The afternoon sun penetrated the trees
making the trek toward their vehicle a hot one. They had only been
walking for ten minutes when the sound of a car igniting battled with
the crows and other birds that squawked overhead. He pulled her behind the nearest tree.

Melissa leaned into the bark, Jeremy's body blocking her.
They strained to hear. The sound grew faint till it disappeared in the
distance. She sighed, relief evident in every breath. "They've
left. That must have been the drug dealer who left the cabin back
there. I wonder what he did with the body" She shuddered.

"I didn't notice any place where the earth had been disturbed.
Did you?" Jeremy left the shelter of the tree and continued down the
path. "I'm sure glad we decided to hide the car a long way off. We
may have to walk a bit farther but that guy would have discovered it
otherwise."

Melissa glanced around spinning her body in a circle. "These
trees sure weren't dense enough to hide it." She doubled her pace. "I
look forward to some pool time when we return to the resort. This
heat is exhausting."

Jeremy picked up his pace also. "I need to find out where the
Barkers are and what they're up to. He plans to meet someone but I
don't know where. I think some eavesdropping is called for."

Melissa took a deep breath. She wiped her hand over her
damp brow. Off in the distance, a few birds continued to express their

impatience with the intruding humans. She caught sight of the tail of a snake as it slithered into some nearby brush. *Out of sight but not out of my mind.* She gazed at the ground beneath her feet. *I'd hate to step on one of those things.* "Jeremy, are snakes around here are poisonous?"

He chuckled. "Why? Are you afraid of them? Snakes never came up in my research. Obviously not yours either." He veered off the long used path. "Our car is this way."

Before long, Melissa spotted the **grey** paint through the trees. "It's a good thing they **didn't** assign us a vehicle with red or blue paint."

Jeremy reached it first and unlocked both doors with his key fob. He grabbed a fresh bottle of water for each of them before **stowing** the cooler bag in the back seat. "Want an apple?"

"That sounds like a good idea. I am getting pretty hungry." She took a swig from the water bottle. "Thirsty too, I guess." Melissa sat down on the cushioned seat. She sighed before making her request. "Turn on that air conditioning, please. I'm tired of feeling sweaty."

Jeremy turned on the ignition, put the car in gear and backed onto the road. "We'll go back through that town so we don't run into Señor or his henchmen at Tinades. They said we could travel to Cuidad from there so I'll bet we can also find the road back to Chihuahua as well." He held the bottle of water between his legs as he unscrewed the cap. He took a long swallow.

Melissa remained silent as she watched the trees speed by. Soon they were back in the town where their presence seemed to be noted by anyone along the sidewalk once again. "These people definitely don't see too many strangers."

"As long as they keep the information about where we came from quiet. We don't need those people in Tinades to become spooked about anything. When we bring Jessica's body back, they need to be concentrating on that event, not on our unexpected visit."

The gravel roadway turned to pavement just out of town with signs pointing to a few different cities. Jeremy checked the GPS. "It says we're only fifty miles from Chihuahua. That won't take us long. You'll be immersed in some cool, refreshing water, anticipating a wonderful dinner by candlelight in no time at all." He grinned in Melissa's direction and then focused on the highway.

Melissa didn't respond out loud but her thoughts zigzagged to a picture of the two of them enjoying a romantic dinner. "Hmmm." She smiled.

"What's the smile for?"

"Just thinking. A cool dip sounds good." She glanced out the window and shook her stray thoughts into the recesses of her mind.

What am I thinking? He's a friend. We're pretending here. Nothing more. She folded her arms across her chest. Uncrossing them, she leaned forward to turn up the air conditioning. *We **need** .... I need to put some distance between us. My imagination is on overdrive.* She laid her head back against the seat and closed her eyes. "Wake me when we arrive."

Chapter Thirty Six

The hotel sparkled in the hot Mexican sunshine as Jeremy pulled the vehicle into the parking lot a short hour later. Traffic had picked up since they'd left which had slowed them down a little. He glanced at Melissa. "I guess you were tired." He shook her. "Melissa, we're back at the hotel."

She stirred, slowly opened her eyes and sat up. "So soon?" She blinked. "Wow, lots of people coming and going. I hope that means we'll be able to enjoy the pool by ourselves."

"Probably not. But the pool is large." He pulled into a parking spot. "Don't forget your dress." He grabbed the cooler bag, locked the car and strode toward the front door.

Melissa matched his stride. Once in the lobby, they both walked with purpose toward the elevator. She chuckled. "I guess you're as eager as I am for some cool water. I don't think my hunger will allow me to be down there too long though. Lunch was a long time ago. I wonder if they provide snacks out there."

"If they don't we can order some." He waited while the door opened on their floor. "Meet you in ten."

He headed toward his door as speedily as Melissa did. She pulled the key card from her purse and walked inside. Dropping her package on the bed, she went to the bathroom, grabbed the swimsuit left drying over the shower rod and stepped out of her clothing. Slipping on a cover-up and some sandals, she was out the door before Jeremy knocked.

One other couple rode the elevator when it opened at their floor. Jeremy placed his hand proprietarily on Melissa's back and then wrapped an arm around her as soon as the door closed. The couple smiled in their direction. They were also dressed for the pool. "Cool water on my hot skin will take away this heat, I hope." The woman glanced at her husband.

He scowled at his companion. Melissa decided to ignore it. "I'm sure it will. We just got back from sightseeing. The weather is definitely hotter than back home."

The elevator door opened before any other word was spoken but Melissa got the impression that was perfect as far as the husband or whoever the woman's companion was. *Maybe they're having an affair. Or maybe they had a fight.* She gazed toward Jeremy who stood aside to let them pass. "Not too friendly," she whispered.

"Some people want to be by themselves, I guess. Let's find a spot to set our things down." He grabbed a couple of towels as he passed the cart outside the door.

Melissa spotted two vacant lounge chairs side by side and headed straight for them. She pulled the zipper for her cover-up all the way down. The azure blue of the water glistened in the sunlight. Laughter floated across the courtyard as waiters in festive colours attended to everyone's wishes.

Jeremy beat Melissa to the pool's edge. He sat down and plunged feet first over the side into chest high water. Melissa followed and soon they were over their heads in refreshing coolness. He leaned against the side as soon as a spot was vacated. "This feels wonderful." He made room for Melissa.

"Oh, boy, I could .... maybe we should install a pool in our backyard."

He leaned closer. "Yeah, for the whole three months the weather would let us use it. Remember, we live in Winnipeg or Winterpeg as some people like to call it. But this does make one think about living in a warmer climate." Jeremy splashed some water on his face. "The pool is too busy to do any laps but for standing around and visiting, there's plenty of room

"Well, maybe we'll build a pool house with a retractable roof for the few warm days we enjoy back home. Coming home after a long day and getting our exercise that way, would fit the bill, don't you think?" Melissa ducked down so her shoulders were under the water. She rolled her head back into the water as well.

Jeremy's grin greeted her when she straightened up. "Let's order a cold drink. Most of the adults are enjoying a beverage while the kids continue to play and splash."

Melissa leaned closer to him. "Frankly, I'd rather play like the kids. But people will begin to leave closer to dinner time.

Maybe we should have eaten first." She leaned her back against the pool and reached back with both hands to steady herself. "Hey, isn't that the Barkers?"

Jeremy's gaze followed hers. "Yeah, that looks like them although I've never seen them without clothes." The couple in question had their backs to them instilling some last minute instructions to two children. The man turned around. "Yep, that's him. We're supposed to be lovers so ...." He grabbed her by the shoulders and planted a lingering kiss on her lips.

Melissa sputtered but plastered a smile on her face, which felt as if she'd developed sunburn. She snuggled close to him trying hard to avoid touching his unclothed body underwater. "Let's order something to snack on and a drink." She looked up at him. "I'm uncomfortable with the intimacy." Melissa lowered her gaze and moved toward the stairs at the end opposite where the Barkers staked out their space.

Jeremy followed, his chuckle forced. A tiny cough cleared his throat. He placed his hand on Melissa's elbow to steady her when she stepped from the pool. He snatched it back when she stood on the pool deck.

Melissa grabbed a towel as soon as they reached their lounge chairs. She covered the front of her body and wiped water from her face and hair. She sat on the edge of the lounge and wriggled her way toward the back.

Jeremy sat next to her. He looked around for a waiter. Locating one, he raised his hand as a signal. "What are you in the mood for?"

"Some of the wonderful punch we had last night at dinner and some cheese and crackers should fill a hole until dinner." She continued to wipe the water from her legs and arms.

As soon as the waiter approached, Jeremy conveyed their choices. He leaned back and scanned the crowd of people.
"It seems to be thinning a bit. There are fewer kids. Some families decided to eat early, I guess."

"How do you plan to find out where that meeting is?"

"I'm not sure yet. I'll look for an opportunity as the evening progresses. Remember, though, you and I have got to be cosy. They can't think that we're here for any other reason than a romantic getaway. Remember, also, you don't come from Winnipeg. That was my mistake in the pool. Someone might overhear us, someone who knows the Barkers. Unless we're in our rooms, we need to be careful so even when we're at dinner tonight, we need to play our roles. Okay?"

"Sure. No problem." Melissa's face heated up again.

"That blush is a sure giveaway." Jeremy grimaced. "Can't

you pretend that you like me?"

"Jeremy, that's not the issue. Or maybe it is. I don't know. I can't help my reaction to you." She concentrated on her towel. *If only I didn't like him so much. Oh, brother. Why can't we behave toward each other as we used to? He was more business-like I think.* She glanced up and noticed the waiter approach with their refreshments. "What time is it, Jer .... er .... Albert?"

He glanced at the clock on the wall over the door leading to the lobby. "It's just five. We have a couple of hours before we need to go for dinner. Plenty of time to enjoy our surroundings." He moved the table between their chairs closer within reach. The waiter deposited two tall colourful glasses of frosty beverages down on the table and then one plate decoratively laid out with cheese and crackers and another with an assortment of fruit. Jeremy, a.k.a. Albert, signed for it. "This should keep us until dinner time, my love."

Melissa blushed but dropped her gaze so the waiter wouldn't notice. Darn. She reached for her drink. Taking a long pull on the straw, she swallowed the icy concoction. Out of the corner of her eye, she watched the waiter discretely melt into the background and make his way toward the bar area. "Jeremy, if I swim closer to the Barkers, I might overhear something of value."

"They'll see you." He took a bite of cheese.

"Not if I stay low in the water near the edge where they're sitting." She slipped off the lounge chair, lowered herself into the water and began to use her swimming skills as if doing laps.

She felt Jeremy's eyes on her. The cool water refreshed her warm skin. *It's good to be swimming.* She was soon on the opposite side of the pool near where she knew the Barkers were located.

"I don't understand why you brought us here." The woman's voice emitted a whine, her displeasure evident for all within hearing distance. "I thought this was to be a family vacation."

Her husband spoke, his voice a little quieter than hers had been. "Haven't I been at your beck and call since we arrived? This one meeting won't take long. You can enjoy dinner with the children and I'll be home shortly after you put them to bed. Just this once, I promise."

"Yeah, well."

Melissa splashed cool water on her face, her head above the water's edge but under the lip of the pool.

Mrs. Barker continued. "I certainly hope so. How did any of your customers find out that you're here? Did you leave your plans with your secretary? That woman will do anything to interfere with our home life."

"My dear, you are being paranoid. Now, I need to prepare for this meeting. The gentleman will be here in an hour. It won't take too long, I am sure." The lounge chair scraped against the tile of the deck floor.

Melissa ducked under the water and swam a few feet away from the edge of the pool. She took a quick breath and ducked under again. Once she reached the side of the pool where Jeremy waited, she motioned for him to join her. She waited while he slipped into the water. "Jeremy, Barker is meeting someone in an hour."

He looked around. Seeing no one nearby, he wrapped his arms around Melissa. "I'll dress and be ready to follow him. I'll use my phone to grab a picture if nothing else. I'm hoping to be within earshot but that may be impossible. Can you wait awhile for dinner?"

"I'll stay here and enjoy those snacks. The drink is delicious." She hoisted herself over the side of the pool and strode toward her lounge chair.

Jeremy followed, grabbed his towel, and made his way through the throng of people to the hotel lobby.

Melissa grabbed some cheese and a cracker with one hand and a piece of fruit with the other. *I was hungry before. Now I'm ravenous.* She munched on the titbits as she rested against the back of the plastic lounge. The crowd continued to thin. *Maybe I should head back to my room as well.*

Chapter Thirty Seven

Jeremy showered and slipped into a comfortable pair of slacks and a polo shirt. His skin felt warm and when he glanced into the mirror of his bathroom, his face was red. *I guess I'll be going home with a tan by the looks of it. It doesn't feel like I've spent all that much time in the sun.* He ran a comb through his moist hair.

He stepped into his bedroom area and stood near the window overlooking the scenery that flanked the hotel on two sides. *The scenery belies the fact that we're in the centre of town.* He glanced at his watch. *I'd better hustle if I want to beat Barker to the lobby.*

He slipped out of his room, marched toward the elevator, and pressed the button for the central hub. The restaurant, pool, bar and anything else could be accessed from the reception area. *Hotel guests don't need to go far to reach any one of their destinations here. Melissa and I should come back when we can fully appreciate the amenities.*

He walked through the doors as soon as they opened. A group of people were standing around, dressed for dinner but apparently in no hurry as they visited with new friends. He found a discrete location which had a clear view of the entire room. *I can keep my eyes on the elevator from here.*

He grabbed a newspaper from the table near his elbow. Pretending to read today's headlines in the Mexican missive, he scanned the room, checking for a recognizable face. *I wonder who Barker is meeting and why? Couldn't he conduct business at his bank? I wonder who initiated this out of the way rendezvous. So many unknowns. I hope they will meet some place where I can overhear their conversation. If they travel away from here, I don't know what I'll do. It'll take too long to access the car. Maybe I should park it in the outside lot, just in case.*

His thoughts formulated in that direction but before he acted upon them, his quarry appeared. Barker looked around the room. Spotting someone familiar, he strode in Jeremy's direction. "Decapoulis, nice to see you. I noticed you and your girlfriend enjoyed the pool this afternoon. Nice resort, eh?" Barker's eyes continued to roam never focusing on Jeremy's face for long.

"It is nice. I'm glad your travel agent was able to obtain a couple of rooms for us. How is your family enjoying themselves? There doesn't seem to be much for kids to do." Jeremy stood face to face with Thomas Barker. "You waiting for your wife?"

Barker blinked. "Um, no. I have an appointment. This is a business trip as well as a family vacation. Our bank looks after all our clients in a very professional manner. No matter where we are, when you partner with us we look after your assets." He smiled, the sentiment not reaching his eyes. "Now if you'll excuse me, have a great evening." He backed up a few steps and waved as he strode to the other side of the lobby.

Jeremy returned to his seat. He grabbed the newspaper again but, this time also took his phone from his pocket. Laying the paper on his lap, he pretended to make a call, pointing his device toward the man who approached Barker. He snapped a couple of pictures.

His instincts on alert, Jeremy was ready to stampede toward the parking garage if necessary. The two men glanced at a couple of different directions. They turned and walked down a short hall beside the reception desk.

I think there's a meeting room down there. Jeremy stood. He dropped the newspaper back on the table and worked his way across the room. He scanned the empty hallway before he followed his instincts. Sure enough. The meeting room was on the right. He walked closer. The door was shut tight. Not a sound emanated from anywhere nearby including the room. He glanced around the edge of the glass door.

Arms were swinging air-born as Jeremy witnessed the heated conversation inside the room. *Someone is not happy.* He ducked back toward the wall. *How can I ...* One of the hotel employees entered the hallway with an armload of table linens. Jeremy took a couple of steps toward the front desk. "Where's the restaurant?"

The staff member pointed in the direction of the lobby. "Down the right-hand hallway from the reception desk, Señor."

"Oh, thanks." Jeremy walked in that direction. *I might as well call Melissa for dinner since I can't hear what's going on in that room anyway.* He pulled his cell phone from his pocket and pressed the speed dial for Melissa's phone. "Hey, Melissa. How close are you to being ready for dinner?"

"I can be right down. Did you recognize the man Barker met?"

"No. We'll discuss it over dinner. I'm in the lobby." He ended the call and slipped his phone back in his pocket. Barker and his new friend walked across the lobby. Jeremy ducked behind a plant as they passed right by him.

"We'll handle whatever you deposit. Make sure the funds are untraceable." That was Barker's voice. His snarl left no doubt that he was in control of the situation.

"You'll not be sorry. We'll make it worth your while. No complications either. Right now the merchandise goes to Ontario but Winnipeg is not impossible to arrange." The other man had a raspy voice as if he'd spent many days smoking and it was ruining his health. Jeremy held his breath. The men continued to move toward the hotel entrance. Their conversation grew faint until he heard nothing. They'd left the building.

He only stepped from behind the large cactus when Melissa emerged from the elevator. He strode toward her. He wrapped his arms around her as he began to breathe a little easier again. "Boy, your timing is impeccable." He grabbed her elbow and escorted her toward the hallway where the restaurant was located. He stopped. "Why don't we ask at the front desk for a good steakhouse or maybe a Mexican restaurant nearby?"

Melissa chuckled. "I think all restaurants would be Mexican in Mexico."

"Oh, you know what I mean. What do ya think?" Jeremy studied her facial expressions. *Does she even like Mexican?*

"I'm game. We could explore this city a little too. Enjoy some of the nightlife." Melissa lifted her eyes in a mostly flirtatious manner. "After all, Mr. Decapoulis, we are on vacation."

Jeremy blinked. "Okay then. Let's go. We'll eat where the road leads us."

Chapter Thirty Eight

The night sky shone clearly with a myriad of stars glistening, once they travelled away from the city lights. The sky looked like one massive pattern of stars with hardly any space between them. He held the car door open for Melissa. "I wish we had the time to enjoy the country but the city had a lot to offer as well. I hope this restaurant is okay."

"Me, too, I'm famished." She checked the traffic and then made her way across the street.

Jeremy locked the car and followed close behind. He quickly stepped ahead of her to open the door into the well-appointed facility with a reputation for tasty cuisine. The hotel desk clerk had recommended the place and had, in fact, made the reservation for them. "The food here is supposed to be on a par with 'The Keg' back home by the sounds of it. It sure smells good."

"I may be hungry now but I wouldn't have done this meal justice an hour ago. It was fun checking out the city. There are some very historic sites it would be fun to explore if we had more time." Melissa allowed Jeremy to help her off with the wrap she'd worn.

He placed it over her arm as the maître d' led them toward their table in a secluded alcove near the stage. A sign outside promised live music tonight. Once they were seated, Jeremy picked up a menu and began to peruse their choices. "The filet is just the right size. Do you want an appetizer?"

Melissa's stomach rumbled once again. "I think some soup would hit the spot. The menu lists French Onion so I'll start with that but a steak and all the trimmings will round out this meal nicely."

"Sounds good." He closed his menu, crossed his hands and looked at his companion. "Melissa, I think we'll leave for home tomorrow. I got what I came for. We need to head home to make plans for Jessica's return to her parents."

"I agree. I still can't figure out how to take those kids without anyone seeing us?" She watched the waiter approach from their right.

Jeremy ordered their meals after assuring the waiter they weren't interested in an alcoholic beverage. "Just water with lemon for me." Melissa concurred.

The waiter left as Jeremy handed Melissa his phone. "This is the guy who met with Barker." He pointed to the picture taken earlier. "I hope the shot is clear enough so we can get his identity from somewhere."

Melissa gasped. "I don't believe it." She looked at Jeremy. "He's Richard Belcher, the CEO of Rompart." She leaned closer. Her hand landed on top of Jeremy's. "He is definitely looking more like the criminal in this scenario all the time." Her eyes glistened. The realization that some answers were finally falling into place left her breathless.

"Lets' make sure. Look again." Jeremy pointed to the second picture.

"I'm sure." Melissa's eyes glistened. "I've felt for some time that this man was the one but I'd hoped I was wrong." She hung her head. "By the way, your dad and I hired an accountant to go over the books at Rompart. Home is where I need to be, too."

The waiter returned with their meals. Jeremy studied his dinner companion's face as they waited for the man to leave. Melissa returned his gaze but also said nothing.

Jeremy offered to say grace as soon as the waiter left. Then picking up his fork, he began to make plans for their departure the next day. "Our tickets are open-ended so all I need to do is call the airport and book our flight. I'll do that now." He picked up the cell phone sitting on the table beside his plate.

Melissa glanced around the room, her mouth full of the delicious salad that came with her meal. She chewed slowly but her eyes took in the other patrons. *We look so normal, the same as everyone else, and we all have a different story.* She sighed.

Jeremy completed his call. "All done. Our flight leaves at seven in the morning. Will that work for you?"

"I'll pack tonight. Do you have to check out at the front desk?

Can we return the rented car at the airport?" Melissa took another bite of her steak.

Jeremy seemed to hum as he chewed, rolling his eyes heavenward. "Boy this food is so good. Either that or I was extremely ravenous." He swallowed and then leaned closer to Melissa. "The hotel will look after everything as soon as I tell them we're leaving. The rooms are paid for another two days so we're not running away with unpaid bills. I'll pay for the food we ordered but that won't take long. Do you want to enjoy the music in the bar tonight? There's no reason we can't .... "

A member of the wait staff stood beside them. "A call for you, Señor. Follow me, please."

Jeremy looked toward Melissa, worry etched across his face. She studied his hurried footsteps as he headed toward the reception desk. *I wonder who that could be. No one knows we're here except ... Barkley. I wonder.* The thought of something bad happening to her attorney and Jeremy's Dad caused a momentary sharp pain.

Jeremy's return ended her speculation. "That was Dad. He called the resort and they gave him this phone number when he told them of the emergency. Jenna took a turn for the worse, something she expected, I think, when she decided to stop her treatments. We've booked a flight already. That's a God thing, I guess." His eyes glistened. "This is going to be hard." He hung his head.

Melissa reached across the table and placed her hand over his. "I'm so sorry Jeremy. I haven't been acquainted with her for long but she's become a friend. Did he say how long the doctors had given her?"

"No, but doctors don't speculate anymore. It's all in God's hands, in His timing. Her faith is strong so we know where she'll be when she leaves us. The leaving and the missing are still hard for us, though."

"And for her. I'm sure she doesn't want to die any more than we want her to leave us." Melissa saw a drop of moisture fall on the tablecloth in front of her. She swiped another from following the first. "I guess the idea of not seeing her smiling face when we arrive at the office each day is affecting me as much as you." She shoved her half-finished plate of food away. "I can't eat anymore and listening to music doesn't appeal either. Is there anything I can do for you?"

Jeremy stared at his plate. "She knew. I remember when I told her about our trip she didn't seem as enthusiastic as she always does when I travel somewhere. She usually tells me about all the work she'll get done and how rested she'll be since she won't need to cater to my needs." His fingers made quote marks when he said cater. "This time, she just said good-bye with no sarcastic comments. She knew." He dropped his shoulders as he, too, pushed his plate away. "So much for good food. Instead of hungry, I feel sick."

"Will Barkley meet us at the airport to drive us directly to the hospital?" Melissa leaned back in her chair in preparation for their early departure from the restaurant.

"Jenna had the nurse call him as soon as she was settled in her room. He'll meet us." Jeremy stood to leave. "Funny how all this intrigue takes a back seat now. Nothing matters except getting to Jenna."

Melissa followed close beside. "Is she part of a large family?"

"No, she's alone. I think her parents died a few years back and she never married. She enjoys lots of friends, though, and a whole church family. They'll miss her as much as we will." Jeremy glanced at his watch. "I'm sorry we had to cut our evening short. Would you come to my room so we can pray for Jenna together?"

The question was left unanswered. As soon as they reached the resort, they related their intentions to the desk clerk. Their unhappy faces left no need for explanations. Jeremy and Melissa strode silently toward the elevator. Melissa reached for the button on the elevator panel. She pressed the one for their floor. "I'll drop my wrap in my room and come by in a few minutes. You can teach me more about how a Christian grieves and the heaven Jenna is looking forward to." She leaned against the back wall as the lift carried them upwards. "I've a lot to learn when it comes to dying and grieving."

Chapter Thirty Nine

Melissa quickly fastened her seatbelt in compliance to the sign illuminated overhead. She turned toward Jeremy, angling her body comfortably in the seat. "Were the hotel staff surprised we were leaving?"

"No." Jeremy leaned back, glanced out the window at the bustling efforts of airport personnel to ready the plane for take-off. He turned his head toward Melissa again as he clicked his seatbelt into place. "They figured we responded to the recent message we got. Barker just happened to be in the lobby when I checked out before you came down in the elevator. He also didn't seem surprised. Rumours run rampant in the hotel I guess. Anyway, he added his condolences when I told him a friend didn't have much time left." His eyes clouded. "I hate saying that."

Melissa's heart ached, reminiscent of her childhood. "I remember when my parents were killed. It was as if someone tore my insides out and left them to be trampled in the dirt. Running away from the killer was the hardest thing I ever had to do. I wanted to be with Mom and Dad. I understand how you feel. You want to hold onto Jenna as long as you can and it feels as if you need to be by her side to accomplish that."

Jeremy smiled tentatively. He patted her hand resting on the armrest between them. "Your experience has given you a spirit of empathy you wouldn't have otherwise. God uses all our trials in life to

reach out to others. Thank you for being here with me at this time."
He lowered his gaze and studied the final preparations on the tarmac
below them.

Melissa remained quietly introspective. *I'd never thought of
it that way. But I guess I wouldn't be able to relate as well if I didn't
experience loss myself.* The plane's engines became a little louder as
they taxied toward the runway for take-off.

She leaned back into the seat cushions as the plane began its
assent above the clouds, the sky overcast to match their moods. Closing her eyes, she willed her body to relax. The morning had begun very early. *There'd been no time for coffee, never mind breakfast.*
She hoped the flight attendant would offer them something soon.

She glanced at Jeremy also reclining with his eyes shut.
*Maybe a few winks of sleep will give me the needed energy for the rest
of the day.* Soft breathing next to her evoked a similar desire so she
closed her eyes again. Before long the hum of the engines faded as
she became lost in slumber.

****

"W-wh-what?" Melissa's eyes popped open. A flight attendant was standing beside her, a soft hand on her shoulder.

"We are about to land in Minneapolis. Please fasten your seat
belts again." The woman walked past them and stopped at another
dozing passenger.

"My goodness." Melissa couldn't remember unlocking her
safety harness *and here we are. Minneapolis.* "Jeremy?" She glanced
sideways.

Jeremy blinked his sleep swollen eyes. "I must be tired.
Some travelling companion I am."

"What about me. I nodded off as soon as we were airborne.
We're acting as if we're old, like your Dad. I didn't think we did
all that much in our short vacation." Melissa's stomach growled, reminding her about a missed breakfast. "Is there a layover in Minneapolis? I could sure use some coffee and a muffin or something. My
insides are touching."

Jeremy chortled. "I understand. I'm surprised you can't hear
my stomach protesting. I think we have an hour but,
for that airport, that's not enough time to find a restaurant. Maybe a
kiosk where we can grab something light will be nearby."

Melissa's insides recorded the bump as the plane landed
smoothly on the runway. She leaned forward to gaze out the window
beside Jeremy. "There seems to be a lot of planes on the ground. Do
we go through customs here as well as when we land in Winnipeg?"

"No, they'll transfer our luggage to the next plane for the
final leg of our journey. We go through customs in Canada. The seatbelt sign was off again. Time to move and find some food. Boy, I can

almost taste the coffee."

A short hike down the corridor after disembarking led them through some security gates and then into the hustle and bustle of the busy airport. A mechanical sidewalk scurried passengers from one gate to another. Jeremy glanced at his ticket. "We need to arrive at gate 31 in order to board our next flight. Let's head in that direction and keep our eyes peeled for a coffee station along the way."

Melissa followed his lead as he stepped on the moving conveyor belt. She held onto the back of his shirt to steady herself but soon found that the slow movement kept her balanced. "There's one." She pointed to their left.

Jeremy stepped off and held his hand to assist her. She matched him stride for stride as they rushed toward the small kiosk. The wafting scent of fresh baked goods tangled with the aroma of coffee brewing in the same location. "Yum-m-m." Her mouth watered. She reached into her handbag, extracted a couple of US bills, and smiled toward the attendant. "Coffee, please, regular, black, and oh, let's see. Give me one of those breakfast burritos. Make that two." She looked at the teasing expression on Jeremy's face. "Well, I'm hungry and who knows when we'll eat again." She tossed her head in rebuttal.

Jeremy took her place as soon as she completed her order and asked for the same selections. Melissa rolled her eyes heavenward. "I'm a guy. I'm supposed to eat like an army sergeant." He laughed out loud at the meek, apologetic expression she feigned. "Don't even try. You can put away food as good as I can."

Melissa grabbed her coffee in one hand and the sack with two burritos in the other. She looked around. "Now what?"

"We continue on the people mover until we find our gate. There'll be seats for us after we receive our boarding passes." He walked toward the moving sidewalk again.

Melissa followed, balancing her coffee with her sack and her handbag. "This is getting ridiculous. Here, hold this a minute." She handed him her coffee and then proceeded to sling her handbag over her shoulder. "You guys are lucky. All you carry is yourselves."

Jeremy handed the coffee cup back to Melissa. "Yeah, until we arrive at our destination and then I'll be carrying all the luggage, as gentlemen are expected to do." His expression was hidden from Melissa's perusal.

She sputtered. "Yeah like I made you do that when we left. I am perfectly capable ...." Then she noticed his cheeky grin. "Oh, you." She tilted her chin after sticking the tip of her tongue at him.

It didn't take long for them to find the gate they searched for. Leaving the people mover and stepping through security, they located the desk manned by an attendant to receive boarding passes. Jeremy located a couple of empty plastic chairs nearby and led the way toward them.

Melissa took a sip of her coffee before she sat down. "Oh, I needed that." She took a seat and reached into the sack for a burrito. Silence reigned as they polished off the first of their breakfast items. Melissa used the napkin to wipe her mouth. "That was quite good, even if a little cold. They should make these things really hot if they know we need to travel a distance before we can eat them."

Jeremy ran his tongue over his lips before gulping some of the tepid liquid in his coffee cup. "Yeah, it's cold or at least cooler than I would like but I'm so hungry, I don't care too much. It fills a hole."

Melissa took another bite from her second burrito. "Did your Father say when Jenna went to the hospital? Did she drive herself?" She waited while Jeremy cleared his mouth.

"He didn't say, just that the doctors figured she wouldn't last long. I'm just glad she called my Dad. Otherwise ...."

"Yeah. But we'd already decided to leave Mexico this morning. You think God had a hand in that decision?"

"He's more evident in our life than we sometimes give Him credit for. I hate the thought of breaking in someone new to run the office. Is that selfish?" He grimaced as the realization struck him. "I don't mean to be. I'll just miss her so much in so many ways."

"Yeah, I know. Me, too." Melissa crushed her sack with the remains of her meal. Looking around for a garbage receptacle, she walked to it and dropped in her trash. Deciding she'd been sitting too long and would be sitting again before long, she decided to walk the circumference of the waiting area. It felt good to be on her feet.

Why did I bring up Jenna? It sure puts a damper on our mood. Jeremy is hurting. He'll have a hard time letting go. "Lord, You understand better than anyone where Jeremy's heart is, where his faith is. Please comfort him and give me the right words to say." She closed her eyes for a second. *"Amen."*

Chapter Forty

The second leg of their journey dragged a little considering they slept through the first one. Melissa got up twice to use the lavatory and to stretch her legs. This time she occupied the window seat but she decided she enjoyed her vantage point less than Jeremy had. She stopped next to him waiting until he noticed. "Good article?" He was reading something from the airline magazine.

He stood to let her step past him. She dropped heavily into her seat as the plane hit an air pocket. Jeremy wavered on his feet as well before returning to his seat. "This is an article about sky-diving. Always wanted to do that."

Melisa twisted her body to give him an incredulous look. "Why would you want to jump out of a perfectly good airplane?"

"Looks like fun. I'm not in any hurry but I want to do it before age becomes a factor." He looked pensive. "I'm twenty-eight. There're just some things I want to do before my life gets complicated with a wife and kids."

Melissa glanced at her hands folded in her lap. "You think marriage would complicate your life?"

"Well, when I'm responsible for someone else, I don't think I'll take the same chances with my life as when I'm single." He studied her expression. "I take it you don't agree."

"I guess I don't enjoy the same sense of responsibility. The few times the idea of marriage crossed my mind, I've always thought

of responsibility as mutual, not greater for one than the other. But ...."
She looked introspective again. "I guess when I commit my life to
someone; I'll feel I should take better care of myself. It makes sense."
She glanced out the window and then back at Jeremy. "Who brought
this up anyway?" She frowned a little but decided to change the subject. "What are you going to do about Barker?"

Jeremy glanced at the man across the aisle. He lowered his
voice. "Not here. We'll talk later about all that." He looked around for
one of the flight attendants. "Do you want something to drink?"

"Might as well. What time did you say we're scheduled to
land?"

Jeremy motioned the attendant closer, requested a cold beverage for each of them, and turned again toward Melissa. "We should
arrive around 3 pm if we're on time. Dad is meeting us so it shouldn't
take long to get through customs and over to the hospital. Is that okay
with you? Going straight to the hospital, I mean."

"Of course. I can always flag a taxi from there. You can stay
as long as you want. I hope your Dad brings Chief with him. I miss
him." She smiled as she anticipated her reunion with her best friend
and service dog. "Did your Father mention anything about him when
you talked to him?"

"No, he was too consumed with filling me in about Jenna."
His voice dropped a little. "He didn't even ask what I discovered about
Barker," Jeremy spoke the last words hurriedly when he spotted the
flight attendant heading their way with the beverages.

Melissa took a sip from her diet soda as soon as she'd poured
some into the glass provided. She waited while Jeremy copied her
actions. "The lavatory is going to draw my attention again before we
land, I think. Oh, well. This is refreshing." She glanced out the window. "I never become accustomed to the sensation of floating on the
clouds up here. The sky sure looks pretty. I think I'm actually enjoying this trip home."

The plane lurched making both of them happy they'd only
chosen to fill their glasses half-full. "I think we've begun our descent."

Melissa glanced out the window again noticing that their
aircraft was indeed flying through the clouds in a downward trajecto-
ry. "It must be overcast in Winnipeg as well. Those clouds are pretty
thick."

"We're still a long way out. Things could clear up before we
land." He leaned back, angling his seat in a more reclined position. No
one sat in the seat behind him so he had no worries about landing in
someone's lap. He closed his eyes.

Melissa smiled. *He's going to need all the rest he can take.
I'll bet he stays at the hospital all night.* She relaxed against her seat
cushion and pulled a magazine from the pocket in front of her. Leaf-

ing through the pages, she scanned pictures of faraway places. *I'd like to visit some of these locations. They look so inviting.* She took another sip from her soda.

Quiet conversation resounded around her at the same time that mellow tunes flowed inside the cabin. She reached up to position the air stream flow in her direction. *I love this picture of green fields bordered by rock walls in Ireland. Someday.*

The plane's seatbelt lights flashed on. She reached over to Jeremy and shook his arm gently. "We need to fasten our seatbelts."

Jeremy's eyes opened slowly. He straightened his seat and reached for his harness. "That didn't take long." He clicked it in place.

"You've been sleeping for about a half-hour." She checked her watch. "Yep, it's almost three o'clock." The plane made a bump as it landed and rolled toward their gate. Melissa watched out the window as airport staff scurried here and there preparing flights for take-off. The pilot steered the plane in an expert fashion as they came to a complete stop. The flight attendant cautioned them to wait until the seatbelt light went off before standing to exit the plane.

Jeremy stood first, grabbed both of their carry-on bags from the overhead rack, and stepped into the aisle. He waited till Melissa stepped in front of him and followed her down the aisle toward the exit.

Melissa led the way down the ramp, signs pointing them in the direction of customs and their luggage. Jeremy's stride quickly brought him beside her as they stepped into the large area where drug-sniffing dogs and customs agents waited. They walked over to the conveyor belt where luggage was spit from a rectangular window.

Melissa scanned the crowd surmising that people meeting passengers were located somewhere else. She grabbed her bag as soon as it appeared and Jeremy did the same.

Jeremy walked toward the first available customs agent and right past one dog who acted as if he understood exactly what was expected of him.

Melissa wanted to reach her hand out to pet the dog but drew it back as she realized their working status. She headed after Jeremy but the dog behaved extremely agitated as soon as he walked past.

An agent stepped forward. "Sir, come with me." Jeremy was led toward a small room off to the side of the customs area. Melissa suppressed a desire to run after him and turned toward a table where an agent stood waiting.

"M'am." Another dog was sniffing her bag and as agitated as the first dog had been. "Come with me, please."

"What? Why?" She took a step backward. *What's going on here?*

Jeremy reeled his arm from the grasp of the agent. He, too,

appeared completely befuddled as to why he was being detained and when he spotted Melissa in the hands of a uniformed officer; he tried to reach her. The agent beside him stopped his retreat.

Melissa sensed danger. *Something is very wrong. Those dogs are trained to detect drugs. How?* She decided to comply with the officer guiding her. "We're together. I need to speak to Jeremy."

"No can do, Miss. Step in here. I'm sure it's a misunderstanding that we can clear up in a few minutes." He shut the door and dropped her bag on the table centred in the room. "Place you carry-on here as well."

"I just have my purse. Mr. Goodman has my carry-on." She stifled a sigh and laid her handbag on the wooden surface.

The agent unzipped her luggage, flipped it open and stared. Laying on her sundresses and lingerie was a package, wrapped in newspaper with the appearance of a large brick. The agent looked at her with accusation written all over his face.

She gasped. "That's not mine. I never saw it before. Someone put it there." Melissa's heart took a nosedive and her stomach felt as if she was going to throw up. "I don't do drugs. Test me."

The agent began to rifle through the rest of her belongings. "Come on. This is not mine." Melissa reached for her handbag and a cell phone. "I need to call my lawyer, I think."

The agent grabbed her bag. "Not so fast." He dumped the contents on the table. Moving this item and that, using a pen, he searched the contents intent on his task. "You brought enough here to sell. Is that what you planned to do or were you bringing this in for someone else?" He stared at Melissa.

"I don't know anything about this stuff." Her voice had risen high enough that she was sure Jeremy heard her in the next room. "I know my rights. I need my lawyer. Now."

"Fine. Call." He studied her face as she reached for her cell phone. Barkley was on speed dial so she pressed the appropriate button and he answered immediately. "Barkley, Jeremy and I are detained in customs. They found drugs in my luggage and, I assume, in Jeremy's." She relaxed when he said he'd join her momentarily. She ended the call and placed her phone back on the table. *Thank goodness he's already here.* "He'll be right here. He was picking us up."

"So. Maybe he's part of this." The agent seemed less surprised by that comment than she was.

"Don't be ridiculous. He's a well-respected member of the bar. Neither Mr. Goodman, nor I have a criminal history and Sergeant Irving, at police headquarters, can vouch for us. My lawyer is Mr. Goodman's Father." Melissa ended her diatribe. The agent wasn't convinced, she could tell.

"Take a seat. We're going to be here for a while." The agent motioned toward the hard metal chair located against the wall. He moved toward the door. "I'll be back when your lawyer ...." He spoke the words sarcastically. ".... arrives." He walked through the door. Melissa could hear the click as he locked her in.

She leaned forward placing her elbows on her knees. Her head felt as if it weighed a ton and the pressure behind her eyes was trying to escape. She laid her head in her hands. *How could this happen? Our luggage was with us the whole time until ....* She thought about her and Jeremy's actions prior to boarding. *That had to be when it happened. They accessed our luggage after we checked it at the airport. How did they know which bag was ours? Someone followed us from the hotel.*

Her head began to ache in earnest. Thoughts tumbled over themselves. *Who would have done this?* But as soon as the thought appeared she knew. *Those drug dealers must have seen us. Today ... yes, today is the day they planned to smuggle drugs into Ontario.*

Boy, what a mess. The door opened. The agent who'd detained her led the way with Barkley close behind. She jumped to her feet. Barkley embraced her. "Where's Jeremy?"

"Isn't he in the next room?" She looked at the man in uniform.

The stern-faced officer shook his head. "He's been taken to headquarters where the RCMP will take him into custody. I'm to transport you to that location as well but you called for your lawyer. Your partner didn't." He glanced at the older man in the room. "You have five minutes before I transport her downtown." He looked at Melissa. "You're in a lot of trouble."

The man walked out of the room leaving Melissa with her lawyer. Barkley spoke soothingly. "This is all a mistake. We'll get it cleared up, don't you worry." He hugged her again. "Say nothing. Someone framed you both. Now we have to prove it."

Chapter Forty One

Jeremy sat across the table from a large man in a black business suit. The room was small, typical of interrogation rooms at the police precinct. He knew the futility of trying to explain how drugs appeared in his luggage so he said nothing. A glimpse of his Father when the agents dragged him from the room reassured him. The stairwell led straight to the garage where official vehicles waited for just such a transport.

The man who sat across from him now had identified himself as a member of the Mounties. *We're being accused of transporting Heroin from Mexico for the purposes of selling so it's become a federal case.* He dropped his eyes lest the agent assumed more than he was willing to tell him. His thoughts flitted one way and then another. Like Melissa, he couldn't figure out who or how they'd done this. *Obviously we weren't as discrete as we thought. This is what happens when you make the assumption that criminals are stupid. Melissa must be in a complete state of panic. I'm glad Dad is with her.*

He looked at the man in black. "We didn't do this."

"Yeah, everybody's innocent. Tell me who your contact is in Mexico." The man displayed an intense expression with no hint that he found any of the proceedings funny.

In fact, Jeremy was convinced he had no sense of humour at all. "We have no idea where these drugs came from." Jeremy didn't want to reveal anything about their trip south, not yet. He needed to talk to Barkley. "I need a lawyer." It was the first time he pushed for his right to counsel

The federal agent shrugged. "Once you lawyer up, I can't help you. Help yourself by talking to me. You don't have a record and this is probably your first time. What made you do it? Financial problems?"

Jeremy grimaced but then quickly put on his poker face again. "I need to call my lawyer. Now." He folded his arms across his chest and leaned back in his chair, the cold from the metal working its way through his light shirt. He shivered but continued to stare at the agent.

"Fine. I'll retrieve your cell phone from the agents searching your data." He left the room letting the door shut behind him.

Jeremy tried to think about the calls he'd made recently. Would any of them further incriminate him? He didn't think so but ... *These guys can be so suspicious of the most innocent things, though. Man, we should have protected our luggage more, suspected something like this could happen. What was I thinking? Melissa should have stayed home?*

The officer barged through the door. He held Jeremy's cell phone toward him. "One call, no more."

Jeremy silently pressed the speed dial for his Dad. "Yeah I heard." Barkley spoke before Jeremy has a chance to say a word. He related his whereabouts and listened as he was assured his father would be right there. He was also told Melissa was at that location as well. "Thanks, Dad." He hung up.

The man in front of him grunted. "I thought you called your lawyer?" He crossed his arms and stood tall, his legs spread in an intimidating manner.

"That was my lawyer. He just happens to be my Father as well." Jeremy tried to hide the sneer on his face. No point in antagonizing the man.

The agent relaxed a little. "Goodman. Are you Barkley's son?" He turned the chair on his side of the table backward and straddled it. "He's a good man."

Jeremy face flushed, a feeling of gratitude for small things coursing its way through his psyche. "He is. Are you well-acquainted with him?"

"We've worked together a time or two. Don't you do investigations for him?" The agent was clearly in a more congenial mood now. "You did the research and ran down the whereabouts of Cody Longview a few years back. That was my case. You do good work. Very thorough. What happened to you?"

Just then the door opened. Barkley Goodman marched

through and headed straight for his son completely ignoring the agent in charge. "Hi, Boy. This will go away, you'll see." He turned toward the only other person in the room. "Elwood. Is this your case?"

Elwood reached his hand toward Barkley. The two men greeted each other as old friends. "I am. I just put two and two together. If I'd known this person was your son ...."

"You'd have done nothing different." He leaned on the table. "Jeremy and Melissa have been set up, Elwood. They're on a case."

The officer looked sceptical. "The crooks we catch tell us a similar story, every time. He used to work for you but ...."

"Still does. He was working for me when he went to Mexico. We .... Jeremy, tell him what you found out." The older man looked for a chair he could sit in.

Elwood surmised as much and left the room to find him one.

"Dad, there's no proof yet. I took a picture. We also overheard them talking about a drug shipment entering Canada through the Ontario border." He stopped talking as soon as the agent returned.

Barkley sat down and looked from one to the other. He paused, cleared his throat, and looked at Jeremy.

The younger man spent the time giving his intellect time to wrap itself around what they did know. "Okay, I can tell you this. I was hired to verify the credentials of a banker by the name of Thomas Barker. Dad was hired to find out if he had any criminal ties. When I found out he was going to Mexico to meet someone, I asked myself why would he need to go all the way there when he could meet the guy here at home? So, I followed him. Melissa came as part of my undercover story."

The agent excused himself without saying another word. Barkley and Jeremy looked at each other but only Jeremy seemed surprised by the move. "Another agent hired you, right? Dad, why didn't you tell me?"

"Cause. I know you don't like working with the RCMP. I think your reasoning is faulty but I figured there'd be less resistance if I kept you in the dark."

"I can't believe it." Jeremy made a sound close to disgust and scowled. "I don't ...."

The door opened. Elwood walked through with a folder about an inch thick in his hand. He waved it at Barkley. "You're working with Jennings."

"I am. Your office has been investigating Thomas Barker for some time. Jennings wanted me to weasel my way inside, find out who he was working with. Jeremy found that out when he was in Mexico. But, he and Melissa are also working another case. They did some scouting around for that case as well. Tell him, Jeremy."

Jeremy cleared his throat as he looked from one man to the

other. "Fine. Melissa and I were hired to find two children in Mexico and bring them here to their mother. We checked out the Mennonite community they live in where we overheard one of the 'Elders' I think they're called, telling a Mexican National, a drug lord, that a shipment was heading to Ontario today. We also watched the drug lord drag away a body. The Elder shot him."

Elwood broke into the story. "What makes you think you can take two kids out of Mexico? That's kidnapping no matter where they come from. How is the mother involved in all this?"

Jeremy knew how far-fetched the story sounded. As he said the words, the preposterousness of it surrounded him. He rubbed his hands over his eyes. "Melissa rescues children from **paedophiles** and human traffickers. She's worked several cases over for the last two years. This woman ran from the village when her husband threatened to sell her to another man. Apparently, this kind of thing goes on all the time. In fact, we planned to return the body of one of their victims in a few days. She worked as a prostitute. Someone murdered her but she also comes from that village."

Elwood hung his head. "We've been doing an investigation about the drugs coming into Canada to a Mennonite community in Southern Ontario from Mexico. It looks like you've gathered some evidence that could aid in our attempts to stop the flow of Heroin into our country **but** .... I can't overlook the fact that you brought the same with you." He glanced at Barkley. "The evidence is pretty conclusive."

Goodman, the lawyer, interjected. "Did you find Jeremy's or Melissa's prints on either of those packages?"

"Well, no, but ...."

"Right. How could they have gotten into their luggage without their fingerprints unless those packages were placed there by someone else?" Barkley sent a satisfied look in Jeremy's direction. He studied the agent's face.

"I see your point. But ....."

"No buts. Jeremy and Melissa are innocent. I'll vouch for them and so will Sergeant Irving at police headquarters who's been involved in this case from the beginning. Well, at least the case of the dead prostitute and her transportation to Mexico. I don't know how much he's involved in the Rempel story." Barkley looked to Jeremy for confirmation.

Jeremy nodded his head. "Sergeant Irving was the one who found the missing person report on this girl and confirmed her name as Jessica Penner from Campos Tinades, Mexico. He's releasing the body for us to return to the police department in a nearby town since the mother asked to be kept out of it. She filed the report but doesn't want any retaliation from her husband for doing so. They don't want the authorities involved for any reason in any part of their life, even for a runaway."

"Boy, you guys did a ton of research. Do you think you can sneak in there again? They'll recognize you now, won't they? How did you get away from them this time? They sound like some really dangerous religious nuts. I thought Mennonites presented themselves as pacifists."

"Yeah, well, there are Mennonites who follow their Christian faith and then there are Mennonites who pervert their faith to suit themselves. Drug trafficking is hardly pacifist. "Jeremy's face displayed the disappointment he felt over people who used his Lord for their own means.

Elwood grabbed the door knob. "I'll go find your girlfriend. We need to figure this out together, get us working on the same page."

Jeremy lifted a finger. "Uh, she's not my girl ...." The agent walked out the door never acknowledging that Jeremy had spoken. He glanced at his Dad. "They need to know ...."

"What?" He snickered. "You do care about her, don't you?"

"Well, yes but ...."

Barkley eyed his son. "I think it's more than that and, by the looks of it, so does Elwood, an investigator trained to read people. You could do a lot worse."

Jeremy frowned, the creases on his forehead deepening. "We're friends and colleagues, nothing more. Melissa has a long way to go in her faith. "

"Oh but her growth over the last few months is phenomenal. She ...." The door opened.

Melissa scanned the room. A smile ignited her face as soon as she spotted Jeremy and then Barkley. She sat down in the chair that agent Elwood brought with him. "This room is getting crowded. Anyone want a bottle of water before we begin?"

Melissa looked quizzically toward the Goodmans. "What's going on?"

Chapter Forty Two

Melissa and Jeremy locked glances. They studied each other as if extracting the right response before responding to Elwood's last question. For the past two hours, they discussed one scenario after another trying to figure out how someone discovered their presence in Mexico. "We stayed hidden the whole time. They gave us no indication that they knew we surveyed them. Their reactions when we posed as tourists did not lead us to believe they were suspicious." Melissa was adamant.

Jeremy nodded his concurrence. "Melissa wasn't even close enough to hear the exchange. Do you think their network is so far-reaching that someone in that town got word back to them? I mean, they behaved less than friendly but I assumed it was because they aren't used to people driving into such an out-of-the-way place."

Barkley sat back and listened as Elwood jumped in with his opinion. "From what we've gathered, these people went there in the first place to escape government involvement in their life. They wanted the freedom to teach their children their way of life, their religion, and their customs. They don't believe anyone can be a Christian who does not observe their customs. So they choose places that are off the beaten path but unfortunately so do the drug cartels. Now, years later, corrupt and criminal activity has become a way of life although what they do with their money is anyone's guess. They continue to live as if the past century of modern conveniences is a myth."

Barkley interjected. "My son and Melissa are a worm in their soup." He snapped his head toward Melissa as if he'd just had a revelation. "Could this woman ....Helen.... be using you to infiltrate this village so she can ...." He threw up his hands. "It all seems so nefarious. Maybe she's a plant. Jeremy, didn't you snap a picture of Richard Belcher meeting with Thomas Barker? Could he have hired Helen to occupy Melissa in a different direction?"

"Wait a minute." Elwood slapped his hands on the table top. "You took a giant leap. We don't have anything to prove a connection between Belcher and the drugs."

Jeremy glanced again at Melissa who nodded her head. "Melissa is digging into who ordered the hit on her parents. She suspects Belcher."

"What hit? What parents?" He stopped speaking and stared at Melissa. "Rompart. You're that Rompart? I've worked that case off and on for the last twenty years. Your Dad is suspected of money laundering and he was killed because of it."

Melissa sat up straighter. "Yeah, except he didn't do that. My Dad would never knowingly do anything to break the law. The man who killed them was himself killed but by whom? Who would benefit by getting rid of the hit man now all these years later? I believe he was a hired gun. I was there. I saw what he did. The nightmares about that afternoon still haunt me. Richard Belcher was working for my Dad back then. If Dad found out what his company was being used for, he would go to Richard. And he threatened to bring in the police according to a note I discovered hidden in his last desk. He was killed because he planned to involve the police, nothing more."

"But other than a note, concrete proof of wrong-doing is missing." Elwood's stern expression grew a little harder.

"N-no. But I just took over control of Rompart. I'll find the truth. I suspect the truth lies in those financial records, at least according to Dad's note." She crossed her arms and jutted her chin forward. "My parents need to be vindicated."

Jeremy patted her shoulder. "She's hired an accountant to go over the books, look for any discrepancies. The company's holdings are extensive so it may take a while. But in the meantime ..."

Barkley grew pensive. He tapped his right forefinger on the table. "Maybe Richard planted those drugs to move you out of the way? After all, he's had total control over this company for all these years and now you're stepping in to take over. If ...." He looked at Elwood. ".... and this is a big if, he is tied to the drug shipments coming into Canada, he could lose everything. Can we obtain his fingerprints?"

Elwood stood abruptly to his feet. "This is getting out of control. If what you're saying is true, all these things are tied together somehow. I'll check to see if our files show anything about any of these characters. In the meantime, I'm going to release you into the custody of your Father. I am well-acquainted with him but I don't know you." He pointed his finger in Jeremy's direction. "You wouldn't be the first son to disappoint his Dad." His gaze landed on Melissa next. "As for you, rethink your plan to rescue those kids. The Mexican authorities will toss you in jail so fast, your head will spin." He opened the door for the trio to leave. "Barkley, you got a minute?"

The lawyer looked at his charges. "Wait for me by the main door downstairs. I won't be long." He followed Elwood toward a small office. The door closed behind him.

Jeremy glanced at Melissa. The two of them had stepped into the hallway. Jeremy walked slowly toward the opposite side of the room, past some inquisitive stares, to the elevator. He pressed the down button just as Melissa stepped to his right. "You okay with this?"

"No." The single syllable was forced between clenched lips. She stepped into the elevator, pressed the number one button and folded her arms. "If Richard Belcher is involved in any way with this, he's toast. My instincts are definitely giving me that vibe." She stomped her foot." To think he would actually try to incriminate us when all this time he's been involved in criminal activity using Rompart as a cover. I won't be satisfied until he's stopped."

"Calm down, Melissa. Barker is dirty but how far he's connected to Belcher is anyone's guess. We need proof." He led the way to a grouping of chairs. An officer in uniform, the first they'd seen since they got here, guarded the double doors leading outside. "Barker and Belcher met to talk about something that irritated the heck out of them. They did not look like friends to me. Business associates, yes. I almost got the impression someone wanted to end the relationship."

Melissa listened, her mind racing. "Jeremy what if they planned to end their association? We'll never catch them." She slid closer to him. "We could continue our charade as if nothing happened at the airport. Neither Belcher nor Barker travelled on that flight so they don't know anything about us being taken into custody." She pursed her lips. "Unless they had someone else watching at customs and reporting to them. The look Barker gives Mr. Decapoulis when you walk into the bank will indicate how much he suspects."

The elevator doors swept open and Barkley walked through. "Let's get out of here. I don't know about you but I'm exhausted." He glanced at Melissa as he held the door for her. "Clare is watching Chief in case you're wondering.."

Jeremy grabbed the outside door as soon as the guard gave them the nod to leave. He held it while Barkley and Melissa walked through. "Dad we need to get to the hospital. Can you still drive us?"

"Right. Jenna. She'll be wondering where you are. I told her you'd come straight there." He led them toward his sleek, black sedan parked at the curb. "I'll call Clare to close the office and head home. She can take Chief with her."

Chapter Forty Three

Helen Rempel walked slowly along the sidewalk. Her neck muscles ached in the attempt to hold her head up. She dragged her feet, not in any hurry to get to the morgue. *I haven't seen her in so many years; how will I recognize her. But if she was my daughter ...* She remembered one of the few times her little girl smiled. *When her face lit up, then the sun shone brighter in that dark place.*

She never used to think of her home as a dark place. In the beginning, when her husband mentioned going to Mexico, a wonderful adventure awaited. *No more snow .... that couldn't be all bad.* Her heart ached. *Those dreams, all gone. Nothing but despair exists there now.*

Life was hard. *We worked hard to scrape a living from the soil of the dry, parched landscape. We worked side by side. I thought, and so did Henry, that the Lord wanted this. The Elders said we obey the Word. Ya, right.*

Their words we obeyed. She kicked a stone directly in her path. Her eyes roamed the area wondering how long this trek would take. Traffic hurtled past her, pedestrian and vehicular. *Everyone has someplace to go, something to do. I don't, so I go to the morgue.* She quickened her pace. Helen wrapped her arms around her thin body. *It's cold out here.*

She checked the address written on a scrap of paper. Her gaze landed on the nearest building to check the number stencilled on the plate glass window. She glanced across the street. *There.*

Helen craned her neck right and left. She darted into the street, quickstepped across to the other side and walked with purpose toward the edifice she searched for. *A deadly place. Full of bodies.* She shivered. Dread filled her, as well as the below zero temperature.

Warmth hit her as soon as she opened the door. Her bare legs sensed it first. Fingers tingled as she reached the elevator and pressed the button for the basement. She carried the letter Melissa gave her from the police. Jessica's mother gave them permission to transport the body back to Mexico.

Helen's heart lurched as if she might witness the demise of her own daughter. *It could be. If we don't hurry.* Evil resided in her husband for a few years now. He taught their son to do as he did. *The children need to be protected from him. Or they'd end up here, too.*

She skittered down the hall toward the coroner's office. Stepping inside, she held the paper for the doctor to check.

Doctor John Belmont pulled his glasses down the bridge of his nose. He slapped the paper he read onto his desk and glared. "What do you want?" The woman's eyes grew large, perturbed.

Helen hesitated, glanced toward the exit, and straightened her shoulders. I can do this. Melissa warned me. "I-I am here to view the body of Jessica Penner."

"You a relative?" The man grumbled something under his breath. He scowled as she thrust the paper toward him.

"I-I have permission." She hated the timidity that surfaced whenever she faced confrontation. I'll need to grow a backbone before this is over, I think. She stood as tall as her five feet five inches allowed.

The man towered over her. He shoved the paper back into her hands. "It'll take me a few minutes to prepare her for viewing. Why do ya want to put yourself through this anyway?" He strode toward the door. Helen began to follow. "Stay here. I'll tell you when you can see her."

The incorrigible man stomped through the door before she answered his question. His footsteps receded farther down the hallway. An identifying mark, a scar left over from a beating when the girl was about five years old, would reveal the child's true identity. Her father broke her ankle that time and the scar from a hurried surgery remained.

Do people live like this here? Are people who abuse their children and beat their wives living in this city? A gentle touch from her husband was uncommon. Believing people could be kind and gentle was hard for her. Even her kids tossed verbal abuse in her direction. *I must get them out before they are unredeemable.*

Do I believe in redemption? Melissa talked about that the last time we met. She certainly does. It has something to do with being born again. She'll explain that to me if I ask. Before .... The abrupt opening of the door scattered her thoughts.

"Come with me." The doctor's scowl preceded him into the room.

Helen stood. "I'm sorry I'm such a bother." She cowed before the grumpy coroner.

"Harrumph. No bother." He strode back through the door never looking behind to make sure she followed.

Arrogant man. Helen placed one hesitant footstep in front of the other. *I don't want to do this.* She reminded herself again that if this young girl was hers.... She followed the man through another door at the far end of the corridor.

"Over here. Quickly. My time is valuable." Dr Belmont stood in front of a window. The curtains were pulled aside revealing a gurney with a body lying rigid on its back. The doctor motioned to another young man behind the window and beside the gurney. "He'll pull back the sheet. Tell him what you're looking for."

Helen stared. Dread filtered through her arteries all the way to her heart, a hardened organ that very little emotion penetrated these days. The white sheet slide off a tender white face of one too young to be there. A bluish tinge gave evidence to a body with no life left in it.

Helen's hardened heart cracked a little as she imagined what this young girl experienced. Some of the abuse she witnessed, as it was no secret most adults treated their children as property and had no patience for them. "Can I - I s-see h-her ankle?"

Belmont poised his finger over the intercom button. He glared at Helen. "You sure?"

Helen nodded and studied the attendant as the doctor gave the instructions to reveal the body's ankle. She scowled at the doctor. "She's Jessica. Her name is Jessica." She scanned the identifying scar. "There it is. She's Jessica all right."

"When do you want the .... er .... Jessica?" The coroner waved his hand for the attendant to cover the corpse again. "I can provide a pine box for the journey. She'll need to be embalmed, though. That could take a while depending on which funeral home you choose and how busy they are."

"I'll let you know." *I better call Melissa.* Helen hurried from the room.

Dr Belmont was close on her heels. "You'd better decide soon. I need the space and we can't keep bodies here indefinitely. Now that the police released it .... er .... her, you can pick her up anytime." He made his way past her to his office door.

Helen remained pensive as she walked toward the exit. His 'harrumph' could be heard all the way down the hall. She stepped out of the building into bright sunlight. *Such a contrast from that gloomy place*. She sighed. *I wish I was feeling less gloomy.*

She retraced her steps along the sidewalk. *I'll call Melissa as soon as I get home. She'll suggest a funeral director. A cheap one I hope. There's no money.* She knew extracting money from the girl's family was impossible.

She wrapped her thin coat tightly over her slim frame. She missed the warmth of Mexico. *But that's all I miss.* She trudged on. Her memories kept her company as she dodged between pedestrians headed in the opposite direction. Her head rocked on her shoulders as the memory of the first slap invaded her subconscious. *He was so angry when he came home. Not because of anything I did but I was the brunt of his frustration anyway.* Her illusions of an apology kept her awake that night but none came. The slaps became punches. It was as if he gave himself permission to use her as a battering ram for his emotions.

Nothing made sense. *No rhyme nor reason existed. It was always worse when that man visited.* She stole a glance out the door one time when he arrived at their home. He was not like them, not Mennonite. She was sure. He was dressed so differently but he gave the orders. Henry was intimidated. She was not sorry when he was on the receiving end. But her turn would come. Later.

A broken cheek took her to the hospital the next day. Henry was too busy so she went with the woman next door. The Elders frowned upon friendships between the women so while they accompanied one another to town or for appointments, it was more to keep an eye out than be a friend. Stories always filtered back to the elders.

Helen stumbled. Her introspective journey helped her miss the chunk of ice in her path. A man right behind her, someone she didn't recognize, steadied her with his hand on her arm. She cringed and shrank away from his touch and toward the building next to her. *Where'd he come from?*

Chapter Forty Four

Jeremy walked slowly, his feet stepping over the tiles on the floor of the hospital corridor. *Jenna looks so bad. She's not in any pain according to the nurse but I saw her wince more than once. She wants to be aware of her visitors. Her smile, though. That lit up her face when she talked about the Lord. How can she be looking forward?* He swiped the tear he'd let escape.

Melissa placed a hand on his arm. She rubbed his forearm, her empathy clearly visible. "Jeremy, did your Dad say what time he wanted us to come for supper? Is there time to go home first?" Without waiting for an answer, she continued talking. "Jenna looked a lot better than I expected. I'll never forget her smile. She actually appears at peace. I don't understand that."

Jeremy hung his head. "As much as I understand the gift eternity is to us, I have a hard time accepting that someone can look forward to death. She's a wonderful example of that inner peace we read so much about in the Bible but ...." He pressed the button for the first floor. "I want to come back here after supper. I think I'll spend the night if they'll let me."

A rumble from deep in her abdomen reminded Melissa she hadn't had much to eat all day. "What about supper? When did your Dad say? I'd like to retrieve our vehicles from home first. I'll need my Jeep to bring Chief home anyway. I can't wait to see him."

Jeremy held the door open so they could exit the large glass enclosed foyer. A taxi stand outside beckoned. "There's time. Dad said Clare would have something ready no matter what time we arrive. I'll call." He pulled his cell phone out of his jacket pocket. "Our bags are in the trunk of Dad's car." The last words were spoken as if he was coming out of a fog.

Melissa listened as Jeremy explained their plans to his Dad before hanging up. She sighed. "It seems like we've been gone for more than three days with all that's happened since we got back. I'm tired, more so than when a case ends. Being accused of drug trafficking, when all I've ever wanted to do is help people, hurts big time. It's exhausting trying to explain yourself to people who don't believe a word you're saying." She leaned back against the seat cushions of the smoke infused cab. "I wish they had such a thing as smoke-free taxis."

Jeremy patted her knee. "I agree. Trying to explain your actions to a jaded police department is draining. They collar so many innocent-looking people who are felons."

"Life is disheartening." She lowered her voice when she spotted the cab driver staring at her in his rear-view mirror. "I mean, all I ever wanted to do was find kids who need rescuing. Now ...."

"Yeah, but I also believe this will all work out. Let's spend the next couple of hours with Dad and Clare catching up on their wedding plans. The big event is not too far away anymore." Jeremy sighed. "I don't want to dampen the mood at Clare's house just because .... " He nodded toward the cabbie.

Melissa smiled tentatively and matched his nod. She looked out the window on her side as Jeremy did the same. Traffic was at the height of rush hour. Streets slipped by and they sped west toward their suburb. *It will be good to be home.* He turned her head toward Melissa. "Maybe I'll let you .... no, never mind. I was going to suggest you stay home but Chief will be disappointed."

Melissa grinned. "Yeah, I'll come. Besides, I need to eat and it'll be good to be with people who trust us." She angled her body toward him. "Our alarm system is quite sensitive, right? I don't want any surprises when I open the door." She crossed her arms. "Later, Chief will protect me. Living next door to you is reassuring somehow but I feel spooked tonight." Melissa dropped the subject and returned to staring out the window. Then she glanced at Jeremy again. "What if Belcher wants me out of the way and tries again. Maybe he'll hire a hit man like he did for my Dad. Harrumph. My dad was blindsided. I'm on to him."

Chapter Forty Five

Paper flew everywhere. His voice rumbled through the room. "Those aren't them. I told you what to look for, you stupid, incompetent, bungling, idiot." He pulled a gun on the quivering mass of humanity standing near the door. "I oughta ...." He waved the pistol in the air.

"I looked boss. I really did. Them's all the papers they had, the two of them." He sniffed. "I did what you asked. I need a fix. Gimme some a that stuff you got hidden ...."

"Nothing. You get nothing. I'm not paying for a botched job." He marched around the room, the gun wiggling toward the face of the addict. "You smell. Leave and don't come back."

The emaciated bundle of tattered clothing opened the door. He slunk into the corridor before slamming the door behind him.

Good riddance. The man, his suit coat open, stuffed his gun back into the shoulder holster. He buttoned his jacket, tugged his shirt sleeves until they extended beyond the jacket sleeve and then ran a hand down the front of his pants.

He took several calming breaths before swiping a hand over his brow. Now what was he going to do? *Where could those accounts be hidden? I'll kill them. No one can do this to me. No one.* He fumed as he paced back and forth. *They'll pay for this, you wait and see.*

Chapter Forty Six

A couple of hours slipped by like a few minutes. Barkley and Clare had made tremendous progress for their December wedding. Melissa chuckled when she remembered the look of pure bliss on Clare's face. *The woman is behaving like a young bride instead of the middle-aged woman of the world that she is.*

Melissa, thankful that her property offered a peaceful homecoming, grabbed the door handle of her Jeep. She stepped to the pavement in her driveway and opened the back door to allow Chief to jump down, tail wagging his happiness to be home also. She snatched her luggage from the empty interior. "Come in Chief. We're home."

The dog walked very close to Melissa's side. She grabbed the bag of dog food and dishes, leftover from his stay with Barkley and led the way to her front door. She dropped the bags and fished around in her handbag for her key.

Melissa inserted the right one into the lock and stepped inside. *I've only been gone three days but it feels like a week.* Chief wagged his tail upon entering and waited while Melissa armed the security system again. "Let's unpack and we can head to bed. I'm exhausted."

Chief followed her, his tail causing a breeze across her legs. She entered the kitchen, placed his bowls on the special mat designed for that purpose, and stowed his bag of food in the utility closet. "I think you're glad to be home, too. Did Barkley play with you? I bet he did." She leaned forward and wrapped her arms around his neck. "I missed you, too."

She led the way to the staircase. Taking one step at a time, lugging her heavy suitcase, Melissa soon stood inside her bedroom. A gasp escaped. *Someone's been here.* "And obviously doesn't care that I know it."

Bedding was scattered on both sides of the bed and the mattress was tossed to one side. The closet door was opened and clothing hung haphazardly from one hanger and another. Her shelves were empty, with jewellery, handbags, and shoes thrown from one side of the walk-in to another. She sighed. *Whatever they searched for I hope they didn't find it. Robbery doesn't seem to be the motive because some of my jewels, the pieces I inherited from my mother are quite valuable. They're still here.*

Melissa exited the closet and located her cell phone. As soon as the police dispatcher answered, she reported the break-in. "Yes, the alarm was still active when I walked in. Whoever did this must have turned off the power somehow and then turned it back on." She listened as the police instructed her not to touch anything. "This neighbourhood has security. I wonder where they hid while this was happening." She added she'd wait downstairs and hung up. Then she called Jeremy.

As soon as he answered, she filled him in but wasn't surprised he decided not to come home right away. "Use the key to my place after the police arrives and see if they trashed it too. I don't have anything of value but if they couldn't find what they were after at your place, they may have thought I hid it. Are you okay?"

"I am but I'm so tired of all this. I thought when we moved here, break-ins would be a thing of the past but apparently, I'm as vulnerable here as I was at my little house. What I don't understand is where was the security company I pay every month for protection?"

She listened when Jeremy said he thought she should find out. "I think the police will want to know that answer as well, don't you? Anyway, you take care of Jenna. How is she?"

Jeremy told her the nurse had been in to give Jenna some more pain meds. "She's sleeping now. I'll call Sergeant Irving and fill him in on what's been going on. See you tomorrow."

Melissa hung up and sat down on the lower stair. Chief rested his head on her lap, his big sad eyes studying her face. "I know boy. We anticipated going to bed, didn't we?"

She popped up as soon as she the doorbell sounded, disengaged the alarm system and checked the peephole. A uniformed officer, flanked by Sergeant Irving, stood outside waiting. She opened the door. "Come in. Welcome to my home Sergeant. You, too, officer."

Chief added his welcome by nudging Sergeant Irving's hand. The Sergeant patted his head. "Hi, Melissa. Some homecoming. Where's the bedroom? You never saw anything out of place down here?"

"No. When we got upstairs, we discovered the mess." She pointed toward the staircase.

"Walk us through, Melissa. Tell us what's out of place and what might be missing." Irving stepped aside to let her pass.

Taking one stair tread at a time, Melissa led the way, careful not to touch the banister as she had the first time she ascended to the second floor. "I don't think anything is missing. I think someone was looking for something specific."

The officer and Irving spent the next hour going over everything out of place, dusting for fingerprints, and analysing the crime scene. Irving's phone rang as they walked out of the closet. "Hello. Sergeant Irving here. What can I do for you?" A second later, he added, "Oh, hi Jeremy." He glanced at Melissa. "Yes, I'm here at her place now." He bowed his head as he listened to the other side of the conversation.

Melissa tried to pull her mattress onto the box spring and had almost succeeded when the officer gave her a helping hand. Once she got it straightened out, she began to make the bed ready for the night. She managed to complete the task by the time Irving ended his call with Jeremy

Sergeant Irving walked to her side. "You didn't tell me about your security company. I think I'll pay their office a visit tomorrow to see if they noticed any strangers in the area. Of course, they would have stopped them you'd think, or at least checked them out. This guy was able to disable the security system and the cameras caught nothing. How did he know how to do that? Anyhow, they have some explaining to do." He paused. "I feel bad about Jenna. I never met the woman but talked to her many times when I called Jeremy's office. He'll miss her."

Melissa hung her head. "Yes, he will." She looked toward the other officer standing by the exit. "Did you find any clear prints?"

"We did. We'll have to obtain yours to eliminate them from the rest. Will we need Jeremy's too?"

"You mean, has Jeremy been in my bedroom?" She pretended to look indignant. Then she smiled. "He helped me move some of my stuff in here. So yes, his prints will be all over the place."

She led the way back downstairs. "Are you going to check his place now?" She turned toward the kitchen.

"That's the plan. He wanted me to go in there first just in case," Irving walked into her well-appointed kitchen. "You've done a good job bringing this house into the 21st century. Looks like you intend to become domesticated." He glanced at all the modern appliances decorating the room. "I'll bet Jeremy likes that side of you."

"Stop it. There's nothing going on between Jeremy and me. He's my tenant, nothing more." She reached for the key to open the adjoining door. "We each keep a key for this door should we need to .... well .... help each other with some case or other." She cleared her throat before wiping the dew from her face. *It's hot in here.* "I think I'll turn down the thermostat." Melissa handed the key to Irving.

Irving grinned toward the ceiling. "**Me** thinks she doth protest .... and all that." He chuckled.

"Harrumph. You're wrong." She followed him into Jeremy's apartment. Melissa slapped a hand over her mouth as soon as she spotted the complete disarray displayed everywhere. "Jeremy is a neatnik. He'd never leave his place like this. Why'd they trash his living area but leave mine alone?" She walked behind Irving into the living room. Cushions spilled their stuffing everywhere. Furniture was overturned and chair legs **broken**. Someone had painted graffiti all over the walls. "Oh, my."

Irving walked to one such graphic and ran his finger over it. He checked his finger. "The paint is still wet. This was done in the last half hour while we checked upstairs at your place, right under our noses. This guy is mocking us."

Melissa sucked in a deep breath. "Chief never reacted to a thing. She looked at her animal whose stance remained protective but calm. Slowly a low growl sounded deep in his throat. The dog looked toward the back door. "Someone is out there." She scooted toward the door grabbing a meat tenderizer on the way to use as a weapon, but Irving nudged her to one side. He stood on the other waiting. Chief angled his body in front of Melissa. "Sh-h-h." Melissa ran her hand over the dogs raised hackles. "Stay, boy."

The uniformed officer drew his gun as did Irving. Both policemen remained as far from the door as they could but still grab anyone who entered. A footstep sounded outside as a car door slammed. Chief growled again, a higher pitch this time. Melissa calmed him.

Oh my gosh. Was that a cough? Someone really is out there. Melissa's insides began to spit bile towards her throat. She swallowed and tried hard not to move a single muscle. Her legs decided to cramp but she held herself rigid, waiting. A click sounded as Irving chambered a round in his gun. She held her breath. *Who was out there and what did they want?*

Chapter Forty Seven

Melissa gripped the heavy mallet tightly. Its weight added security to an otherwise scary situation. The storm door creaked open and then the sound of a key inserted in the lock of the interior portal sent her heart racing for her throat. The door slowly opened.

Standing behind the police officers, Melissa raised the meat tenderizer ready to smash her weapon down on the unsuspecting intruder. Sergeant Irving hollered, "Stop. Police."

"Bill?" Jeremy took a giant step to the light switch and flipped it on. He glanced at Melissa. "I guess I should consider myself lucky you didn't dent my head or worse." He looked around the room. "Whoa. I guess I can understand why."

Sergeant Irving holstered his gun and motioned the other officer to do the same. "We're waiting for the crime scene boys to arrive. At first we thought it was just a simple break and enter, but now we think there's more to the story" He made way for Jeremy to inspect the damage.

Melissa replaced the kitchen tool as she set the container upright again. "Oops. Sorry. I guess I shouldn't touch things." She stepped toward the door connecting her living space to Jeremy's. "I'll wait inside for the officers to come. They'll be arriving at my door first since we thought it was the only crime scene."

"Melissa, wait." Jeremy rushed toward her. "What makes you think the crime is more than a break and enter?"

"Nothing is missing as far as I can tell. They were looking for something, but so far we haven't found what that was. Your place, though. The damage appears vindictive, a sense of rage out of control. Did you tick someone off recently? Who have you told where you live?" Melissa knew her concern was more personal than just as a landlord.

Jeremy's gaze roamed over the graffiti on the walls. He knelt to inspect the garbage scattered all over the kitchen. "I left this place clean and now look at it. Sergeant, this garbage is not from my trash can. Make sure the CSI guys pay special attention to the mess. Melissa, let's go to your living room and we'll wait together."

Melissa led the way toward the one room no one had tried to destroy and Jeremy followed her. "Jeremy, I thought this address would be safer ...."

"I know." He placed his arms around her. "How did they circumvent the security system? I think the company that installed it will have some explaining to do. Maybe one of their guys ...."

Melissa pushed away from him. "I wanted this place to be a sanctuary where we can safely enjoy down time after a search and rescue or whatever. After that gruelling interrogation this afternoon, all I wanted to do was sleep." She reached down to pat Chief between his ears. "Chief, too." She stood up. "I think better on my feet."

Jeremy sighed. "There's nothing we can accomplish until the police complete their scrutiny of the crime scene. As soon as they finish with your bedroom.... You told me that was the only room they touched. What could they be looking for and who are 'they'?" He relaxed against the cushions. His frown dominated the features on his face, though.

Melissa paced back and forth between the sofa and the window watching for any sign the detectives had arrived. She cranked her head from side to side as if releasing a few kinks. Her shoulders ached. "I was supposed to meet Helen tomorrow. She went to the morgue today to make sure the dead girl is really Jessica Penner. The mother sent a letter via the police departments in each location. She gave us permission to take the body across the border and the description of an identifying mark to guarantee her identity."

"I wonder how much Helen is aware of her husband's drug dealings. That may be something we want to ask her. She's told us she's deathly afraid of **him but if** she has information that'll help us stop his activities, she needs to come clean." Jeremy stood as soon as they heard a knock. "You stay here. I'll answer the door."

Melissa stood aside to let him pass. It felt good to let someone take over. She curled her legs under her as she returned to one corner of the sofa. She patted a spot beside her and Chief complied. He laid his head in her lap and whined.

He senses trouble even if he doesn't understand what. She

rubbed his ears. *I love his protective side. I'll have to thank Denny for raising him that way. I can hardly thank him enough sometimes. The sense of aloneness is gone when Chief is nearby.* "I love you, boy." Her hand scratched beside one of his ears.

Melissa closed her eyes. She tried to erase the images of someone violating her space but couldn't. *This house has too many bad memories. I thought when I renovated it, I wouldn't be reminded this was a crime scene once before. Now ....*

Jeremy walked back into the room. "The crime scene guys are starting with your bedroom. When they finish, why don't you go to bed with Chief and I'll ...."

"I don't think I can sleep here tonight. I was thinking about the last time this place was a crime scene. I thought I was over that but ...."

"I'll be right next door. We can't let whoever did this run you out of your home. Besides, as Irving said, it almost looks like they were after me. Your place appears to be a second thought. Someone tried to incriminate us and that wasn't expected either. I think we're dealing with something a lot more sinister than we suspect at this juncture. Even Dad is puzzled." Jeremy sat on the other end of the sofa.

Melissa stroked Chief's fur along his back. The dog moaned his pleasure and she chuckled. The smile died on her lips as quickly as it appeared. "My life is one big pile of trouble."

"Oh, that sounds like a pity party. The Bible says we will have trouble. Remember God says He will never leave nor forsake you. Let's pray about all this." Jeremy bowed his head slightly waiting for Melissa to place herself under God's control once again. "He understands Melissa. Do you believe that?"

"Yeah, I do. I guess I forgot for a minute He's much bigger than all this. Thanks for reminding me." She bowed her head. "Go ahead, Jeremy."

"Father, we need Your protection. Forgive both of us for not turning to You as soon as they found the drugs in our suitcases. You can identify who put them there just like You recognize who trashed our homes. It's so comforting to be able to turn all this over to You. Father, give us a good night tonight and help Melisa feel safe here again. Amen." He lifted his head and glanced at Melissa. "I know that made me more comfortable. Sometimes, when we stare at the issues, they seem humongous but when we see them through God's eyes, they become so much more manageable."

Melissa sighed. Then the smile from a little while ago came out in full force. "I like feeling small and insignificant when I envision myself alongside God. He's so much more able to handle this situation. Thank goodness." She looked heavenward. "I mean, thank You Father." She chuckled and then yawned. Chief caught the yawn and gave one back to her.

Jeremy followed with one of his own. "Like they say, yawning is contagious. Let's go find out if those detectives are done in your room."

Chapter Forty Eight

Melissa stretched, her arms reaching across her bed while her toes pressed toward the foot board. Chief grunted from his bed on the floor right beside hers. "Good morning, Chief." She looked toward the window. Although the curtains were drawn, the brightness shining through indicated morning had a head start already. "I wonder what time it is. Did we actually sleep in?"

Melissa flipped the covers away from her body, swung her feet to the floor, and sat there in silent contemplation. *I wonder how late the crime scene investigation team was here. I'll bet Jeremy is tired this morning.*

The jangling of her bedside telephone interrupted the peaceful reverie of her thoughts. She lifted the receiver. "Hello." An agitated voice on the other end of the line reminded her they had an appointment this morning. "I remembered or I would have as soon as I became fully awake. Remind me where we're meeting?"

She listened as Helen Rempel reiterated the place and time. "Is something wrong, Helen?"

"No. I.... well .... the visit to the morgue yesterday caused some painful memories to surface, things I worked hard to forget. They all came flooding back. I didn't sleep well last night." Melissa sensed the quiver in the woman's voice was a reminder of her past.

Melissa sighed. "Jeremy and I visited your village. I can understand why you don't want to go back there. But let's talk some more when we meet. I'll be there at ten." As she hung up, she glanced at the clock on her bedside table. "Yikes. I'd better move."

She jumped to her feet. "Chief, I'm gonna put you out while I shower. It's not too cold for you to be out for fifteen minutes or so." Melissa escorted the animal down the stairs toward her front door. "Don't go too far." She opened the door, her pjs a slim buffer against the cold air wafting around her.

"Hey, Melissa. You just waking up?" Jeremy stopped mid stride beyond her driveway.

Melissa eased back behind the door jamb. Sticking her head out, she spotted Chief prancing toward their neighbour. "We slept in. I gotta prepare to meet Helen at Tim Horton's on Portage Avenue, the one we stopped at once before. Do you have time to keep an eye on my buddy?"

Jeremy grinned. "I can do more. I can feed him once he's done with his constitutional. Want me to tag along with you? I have nothing else scheduled this morning. There are a couple of questions I want to ask Helen regarding the men we encountered. Maybe she knows who they are. We can bring Chief with us."

"Sure. We need to leave in thirty minutes, though. Does the timetable work for you? I won't be able to run today, obviously." She stepped back to close the door as soon as Jeremy headed for his own entrance. Taking the stairs two at a time, she stood huffing on the landing. *That's almost a workout.*

Her shower ended up as little more than a quick rinse off. Selecting jeans and a sweater, she dressed hurriedly; making sure her shoulder length hair was almost dry. Adding a dab of lipstick over her moisturizer, she dashed back downstairs. The rumble of Jeremy's truck outside her door speeded up her security procedures.

Grabbing her purse, she stopped and glanced around her home. *What am I forgetting? Anything?* She checked to make sure she had her keys and wallet as well as her cell phone and then armed the security system. *We need to add another stop to our list of things to accomplish today.*

Melissa strutted toward the black truck, opened the passenger door, and noticed Chief was happily ensconced in the back seat. "I'm glad you thought to bring him. Chief hates being left alone." She fastened her seatbelt.

"I figured." Jeremy put the truck in drive. They rolled down the short driveway. "How'd you sleep?"

"Better than I thought I would. Once my eyes closed, I dropped off. The Lord really took care of me. No nightmares." She grinned. "How about you? What time did the police get done?"

He pulled the truck out into traffic. "Are we meeting at the Timmies close to downtown?"

"We are. I'm hungry."

"The police didn't finish until after one. Sergeant Irving left after you called it a night. Those guys are sure thorough. If the intruders left any prints at all and if those prints are in the system, we'll find out before day's end who they are." He yawned. "I was hoping my run this morning would erase the cobwebs. I need coffee."

"I thought you'd be tired. You should have stayed home for a nap." She glanced out the window. "Life goes on, eh?"

"How do you mean?"

"Well, here we are dealing with the break-in and being suspected of drug trafficking but people go about their usual business...." She pointed to the pedestrian traffic. ".... seemingly without a care in the world. But then we must look like we don't have any worries either. Life goes on."

Jeremy pulled the truck into the parking lot of the restaurant. "Did Helen tell you about her visit at the morgue yesterday?"

"A little, but something's bothering her. I said we'd talk more when we got here. Her memories are almost as bad as mine. Helen needs the Lord." She stepped from the cab of the truck, tethered Chief to his leash, and took a step toward the door to the coffee shop.

"I thought she was raised Mennonite. Don't they consider themselves Christian?" Jeremy took a long stride to catch up. He pulled the door open and allowed Melissa and Chief to precede him. "I can't see Helen."

Melissa checked out the other patrons. "She's walking so she may be a few minutes late. I think she lives around here somewhere." Melissa stood behind the last man in line. She spoke softly over her shoulder to Jeremy. "These places always have a line-up."

"People like their Timmies. Now about my Mennonite question." Jeremy breathed in the satisfying aroma of fresh brewed coffee.

"Mennonite has become more of a tradition. It depicts a group of people who used to follow the teachings of Menno Siemens but, according to my research, many have strayed away from his doctrine. I don't think a lot of them believe the Bible to be the Word of God or that they need to be born again. Helen doesn't seem to have any confidence in her faith." She stepped forward and placed her order.

Jeremy ordered coffee and one of their delicious breakfast sandwiches. He stepped aside to let the next person in line order.

Melissa grabbed her breakfast and headed toward a table just as Helen walked through the door. Helen wove her way through the tables. "Don't you want to order anything?"

"I had an early breakfast." She removed her coat and laid it over the back of her chair.

Melissa felt guilty eating in front of her. She knew the woman had little cash to spare. "Let me buy you coffee. How about some pastry?"

Helen looked toward the line-up. "That'll take too long. Yours will be cold by then. Eat, eat. I'm okay."

Melissa looked toward Jeremy. He glanced at her and interpreted her motion for him to order another cup. She mouthed the word donut. "There, Jeremy will bring it."

"Oh. I didn't notice him." She dropped her gaze. "Hi Chief." Melissa gave the animal a plain donut which he demolished in a bite or two. "I try to keep him on his dog food but once in a while a treat doesn't hurt."

Helen fidgeted in her chair. "I identified Jessica. Boy, the doctor sure was grumpy." Helen made a point of speaking proper English.

"You've been practicing your language skills, I hear. Yes, I warned you. He's a curmudgeon." Melissa took another bite of her sandwich. "Were you able to confirm she's the Jessica from your village? The mom was pretty specific. She wrote about the scar as if it was one of many and an everyday occurrence. Can you explain that?"

Jeremy sat down and placed a double chocolate glazed donut in front of Helen. "I guessed, like most women, you like chocolate." He shoved the cup of coffee toward her. "Sorry, I didn't mean to interrupt."

Helen smiled shyly toward him. "You didn't. Melissa just asked me to explain the scar on Jessica's ankle. Thanks for the coffee and donut." She took a bite. "Hmmm. It is good." With her mouth half full, she began her story. "Children are beaten in my village for any number of reasons. They are property needing discipline, just like women. Jessica's father beat her so bad he broke her ankle and they had to bring the doctor to do surgery. It left a scar so we use that to verify her identity. I was there."

Melissa interrupted. "You went to the morgue?"

"That, too. But I watched her father beat her when he broke her ankle. She was six years old." Helen's distress over the remembered incident showed in the taut lines around her mouth and the creases across her forehead. "I don't want to remember anything about that place. I can't go back there." She shook her head slowly. "No way."

Melissa shared a look with Jeremy. She reached across the table and patted the shaking hand of the woman facing her. "Helen, for me, nightmares are a part of almost every night since my parents died. I told you the story. Anyway, when we got back from Mexico yesterday, someone sneaked drugs into our suitcases, and then when we got home last night, our homes had been broken into." She waved her hand back and forth between her and Jeremy. "Both of us. I knew, as sure as I'm sitting here, last night would be filled with bad dreams. It always happens when stress takes over my day. Jeremy prayed with me before I went to bed and I slept like a baby."

Helen glanced from one to the other. "I pray too but ...." She shrugged her shoulders.

Jeremy decided to jump into to the conversation. "Helen, who is Jesus Christ to you?"

Helen blinked. "He .... he's the son of god. I think. Right? The elders teach he's a good man but not much else. I leave their religion."

"Helen, Jesus is more than a good man or the Son of God although He is all of that. He's also God. Not a god but one of the personalities of God Almighty, the Creator of the Universe. As Jesus, God came to earth, was born to Mary, an innocent virgin, and when He completed His ministry among men, teaching them as much as He could about God, He obediently went to the cross of Calvary to atone, to pay for your sin and mine. What do you think about what I've just told you?" Melissa couldn't help the smile shining from her face.

"I don't know what to think. Why did He do all those things?" She sipped the hot beverage in front of her. "Why are you telling me this?"

"The Bible says we need to be born again in order to go to heaven for all eternity, to live side by side and worship Jesus face to face. Are you familiar with John 3:16?" Jeremy quoted, "For God so loved the world, you and me, Helen, He gave his only Son to die on a cross so whoever believes in Him will live in eternity with Him. Believing means acknowledging that because of our sin, we deserve the punishment God lays out in the Bible for disobedience. The punishment He sentenced us to is death. But Jesus was beaten, tortured, spit upon, and then nailed to a cross as a substitute for that punishment we deserve. He was innocent. Believing means letting God control our life, making decisions with Him, spending time with Him, and loving Him."

Helen dropped her gaze. She gulped another mouthful of coffee but said nothing for a few minutes. Finally, she slid her hand across the table and then back again to grip her coffee cup. She looked from Melissa to Jeremy and back to Melissa. "You give me a lot to think about. No one told me this before. Elders tell us the story of Jesus' birth but not the rest. They control our lives." She looked around the room. "I think about this."

Chapter Forty Nine

Helen studied the faces of the people in the room. The question of trust was a big one for her. She lowered her gaze. *Do I trust them? I ask them to go for my children. Do I trust them with this task? I think I do. Then .... but the elders. I trusted them for many years but they ordered us and controlled, not like these good people.* The sense of betrayal at the hands of all who were part of her life was overwhelming. *Did they lie to me or just embellish the truth to suit their own purposes. Is embellish the same as lying? How far do I trust these two? They seem to care .... a lot.*

Melissa returned from the washroom. "Do you guys want a refill? I'm getting one." She glanced at Jeremy, quietly typing in a text on his phone. "Jeremy, who's texting you now?"

He handed his phone across the table for Melissa to check it out but as he did so, the screen reverted to a photo he recently studied.

Helen gasped. She placed a hand over her mouth. Her body stiffened and she glanced around for a way out of the booth. Melissa hemmed her in on one side and Jeremy sat on the other. Her breathing grew rapid. She had a hard time catching a deep breath. "I-I c-can't breathe." She raised a hand to her throat.

"Helen, what's wrong?" Melissa sat down beside her.

The woman cringed, edged a few inches away so their bodies couldn't touch. She felt as if a scream had lodged itself in her throat. Helen glanced around the restaurant, her frantic need to escape almost overwhelming.

Melissa placed a hand on her arm. She repeated her question. "Helen, what happened? What's wrong?"

Helen looked from one to the other. "How .... Why do you have a picture of this man on your phone? I recognize him and he's not a good man. He's the reason my husband change many years ago."

Jeremy looked at his phone. "Oh. I hit the wrong button. This is a man we surveilled in Mexico when we were there. We ...."

"Jeremy, tell her the truth. If we want Helen to trust us when we tell her about Jesus' love for her, we must be honest with her about other things concerning her. This is important." She placed an arm around the trembling woman. "He's part of a case Jeremy is working on but he also happens to be the CEO of my company."

Jeremy blinked. "Yeah but she only recently became owner or at least took over as owner. This man runs the company she owns and has done so for the last twenty years. How are you familiar with him, Helen?"

Eyes like saucers, Helen studied their faces. *I've been so wrong for so many years. Thinking what was bad was good, and what was good was bad for me. The elders taught us education was bad and yet they keep us under their control because we aren't educated. They don't allow us to read the Bible so only they can say what it says. Now, these people say they care but they are acquainted with this man who is so bad.* Her frustration erupted in a sigh. "He's the man who my husband finds drugs for, the man who orders my husband, and the others, to bring them to Canada. He's mean. He makes my husband very angry sometimes and my husband beats me when he leaves."

Melissa and Jeremy listened, not saying a word. They waited for Helen to run out of words. Her fright was obvious. Melissa took a sip from her cup but realizing it was still empty, she stood. "I need some coffee now more than ever. How about the two of you?"

Jeremy and Helen nodded in unison. Melissa left. Jeremy placed a hand on Helen's arm and snatched it back before she misinterpreted his actions. "I'm sorry the picture scared you but I'm glad you saw it. We couldn't figure out how he fit into the picture of what's going on but now the pieces are beginning to make sense. Why does he scare you so bad? Since you're away from there, you're safe, aren't you?"

Helen stared at him as if his senses were impaired. *How can he believe the lie?* "You don't know this man as I do. Before I escaped, my husband threw me across the room and told me if I don't behave this man would kill me. Now you say he lives here, in this city. How he does things makes me afraid. He killed or ordered to be killed many that did not do exactly as he said."

"Helen, you need to come with us to the police. They need this information." Jeremy leaned his forearms on the table.

She could tell he was being sincere. But he was stupid if he thought she'd trust the police. "They don't believe people like me. This man, you say, runs a big company. My word against his will not be believed, I think." She inched closer to the edge of the booth Melissa had vacated. "I go now."

Jeremy held her arm and craned his neck to see if Melissa was on her way back to the table. "Helen, running from this will not rescue your kids from that place but helping put away the drug dealers will if we can prove your husband is one of them."

Melissa moved toward the other side of Helen to take her seat. "What's going on?"

"Helen wants to leave. I suggested she tell the police her story." Jeremy moved a few inches away from Helen so she could make room for Melissa. "I guess I spooked her." He looked at Helen. "We won't make you do anything you're not ready for but the sooner we stop these guys, the better for all of us."

Melissa set the three cups of coffee on the table and distributed them to each in turn. She also placed a bag of **TimBits** in the **centre** for a little energy pick-me-up. "Helen, how long have you lived in Canada?"

Helen blinked. *Now what?* "I come two years ago. Why?"

"Are you here legally? You'll understand in a minute." Melissa looked from one to the other. Jeremy's eyes reflected his confusion.

"I met with a woman who helped me obtain proper paperwork before I leave Mexico. She helps people who want to escape the Campos in Mexico, especially women. She says the paperwork is legal. Customs agent thinks so too. Now I am working on getting my citizenship back. I was born in Canada after all." She shrugged. "Why does that matter?"

Melissa glanced at Jeremy again and back at Helen. "You've been here over two years and this man hasn't come after you. I think your husband lied. I can't imagine why you would be of importance to them."

Helen slapped her hand on the table top. "Because I can tell you too much about their business. Henry did not find out but I used to sneak out and follow when he goes to meet this man or other ones. No names just **faces**. Anyway, I'm afraid Henry will find out so I leave. The beatings, they happen to everyone. Those I can deal with. I leave to protect myself from death, not beatings. So I left my kids." She glared at Jeremy. "I understand you think I'm a bad mother."

Jeremy dropped his gaze. His look of determination surfaced. "Helen, we need your trust here. What do we need to do to earn it?"

She shrugged her shoulders. "Trust is hard." She thought for a few minutes, the silence strained and thick. *I need to stop hiding if I want my kids. A decision. I need to decide.* "Okay. I trust you but if once you lie to me, I'll find another way to rescue my kids." Chief lay his head on her lap under the table. She slipped her hands down. His presence seemed to give her comfort.

Melissa spoke succinctly. "Are you safe where you live and work."

"Yes, I think so. There are so many Rempel's here I blend in. My name is common."

"If this man thinks you could identify him, he'll come after you." Melissa stared hard at Jeremy. "I think he's the one who put those drugs in our bags. Who else had any reason to suspect us?" She hesitated. "Or want us out of the way. Belcher has motive and opportunity."

Jeremy returned her intense gaze. "Yes but, I was careful. I'm sure no one noticed me."

"Someone did." Melissa turned back to Helen. "Would you be willing to give the police this information?"

Helen shrank back into the booth. Studying their faces, she pondered the question in light of her decision to trust these two. *They need me. They will look after me. They care that I'm safe.* She nodded her head as she straightened in her seat. "I do it. But then we go find my kids. Right?"

Jeremy patted the back of her trembling hand. "The Feds already agreed to help in that regard, as soon as we can pinpoint your village as the source of the drug traffic coming into Canada." He glanced at Melissa. "Didn't you and Da .... He hesitated. ".... your lawyer find a connection between Rompart and Mexico?"

"Yeah. We were supposed to check out that warehouse but when you got the call about Jenna, it slipped my mind." She finished the cold remains of her coffee. "We might need to make another trip or find a way to check that place out. Maybe the Feds will scrutinize any activity if we give them the address."

"Let's leave." Jeremy looked at Helen. "Did you give the coroner any timeline about picking up Jessica's body?"

"Oh, that's what I wanted to tell you. He said a mortician would need to take the body for embalming before we can transport her across the border. That could take a day or two. I don't have the funds for that. I don't think the parents can provide money either if the father would even consent to pay for it. They just bury fast and don't bother with that down there." Helen watched, her impotence felt across the table.

Jeremy answered before he gave the idea any consideration. "I'll pay for it. It's the least I can do since I might have saved that girl if we'd worked together more effectively."

Melissa interrupted. "You didn't know."

"But you did. You suspected she was in trouble but I didn't back you up. I feel bad about that." Jeremy lowered his gaze. "I won't make the same mistake again. These guys mean business. We will pull out all stops to protect you, Helen."

Melissa waved her hand in agreement. "Anyhow, let's get going. We need to talk to Elwood at RCMP headquarters. Did you, by any chance, find out his last name?"

Chapter Fifty

Richard Belcher rummaged through his desk drawer. *Where is that folder?* He pulled pencils, pens, a stapler, and some paper clips from the drawer and dropped them haphazardly on his desktop. *I need the file. How much do those meddling interlopers know. What are they up to? She doesn't have a clue what she's getting herself into. I can't stop things now. We're in too deep. Besides, my lifestyle requires I continue, all those gambling debts.* He continued rummaging, pushing this stack of papers aside and files to the right.

A knock sounded at his door. He scooped all the debris from his desktop into his top drawer and closed it firmly. "Come in."

"Richard." The younger version of himself walked through the door.

"Jason, I'm busy right now. Can't this wait?" Richard scowled. He pushed himself to his feet using the arm of his chair for support.

"I think you're going to want to hear this." Jason Mitchell was the firm's attorney but he also took other cases as a defence lawyer as well. He dropped into a chair facing the Chairman of the Board. "The body is being moved as we speak. Someone came forward who plans to take her back to Mexico."

Richard dropped into his chair again. "Who? There's no relatives here according to her father. In fact, until I told him she was dead, he had no idea anyone was looking for her. I expect his wife will be getting more than she deserves when he's finished with her."

He grinned. "I like the way they keep their women in line." A smile had erupted but he squelched the sentiment. "Did your contact at the morgue tell you who this person is?"

Jason crossed his right ankle over his left knee. "No. He only found out someone was taking the body when the coroner ordered him to get the stiff ready for transport. He didn't know who was picking it up for preparation or when."

"Well, keep on top of it. I want you to find out and quickly." He pounded his fist on his desk. "Are you listening to me?

Jason remained seated, his relaxed posture added insult to injury. "I told you you'd be interested in this. What's gotten you so fired up anyway? You were already hot and bothered before I came in."

Richard glared and then shifted his gaze to his desk top. "A file is missing, the one with the list of undocumented businesses we manage for Chihuahua. The drug cartel .... "

"Oh, you mean the file your assistant gave Miss Rompart when you weren't anywhere around last week. She came by and left with it but hasn't returned. When I asked, her assistant said she'd left for a short vacation. I sent someone to her house to find it but ...."

Richard sputtered. "The woman is fired. She had no business going through my desk."

Jason stood. "You've gotten sloppy. Why would this particular file be on your desk in the first place? Your girl just thought since Melissa owned ...."

"Yes, but." He leaned forward and placed his head in his hands, elbows propped on his desk. "Like I was saying, the cartel is getting nervous now she's running things. They want her taken care of." He stared at Jason. "Now is the time before she's had a chance to search out those companies. Use your contacts. Find someone to finish the job once and for all."

"What contacts? Who do you think I am? I won't jeopardize my position with the law board. If they catch me ...." Jason began to pace the room.

"You're already involved up to your armpits. Don't forget I hold the evidence of your extracurricular activities. Someone else may be running your prostitution ring but you're complicit and I can prove it." Richard leaned back in his chair. His smirk belied his lack of confidence. "Find someone reliable, okay?" He dismissed the man with a wave of his hand.

Jason grumbled all the way to the door. Before opening it, he turned toward Rompart Industries CEO. "One day you'll go too far, Richard. I wonder what the cartel would say about you leaving incriminating evidence where any yokel could find it." He grabbed the knob and pulled. "I'll keep you informed."

Richard watched Jason close the door behind him. He smashed his fist on the desktop. *That broad is just like her father. Nosy.* He growled. "Dead."

Chapter Fifty One

Elwood Frazier crossed his arms. He stared at the two detectives sitting across from him, amateurs in his estimation. "You guys are in over your heads on this one. How reliable is this woman?"

Jeremy glanced at Melissa. He returned his gaze to the Federal Officer who'd taken a chance on them the day before. "She's telling the truth. We saw some of what she told you when we visited the village two days ago. How she will hold up in court, your guess is as good as mine. She's scared."

Melissa nodded her head in concurrence. "We told her we'd protect her but now that she knows this man lives in this city ...." She shrugged. "If what we suspect about Richard Belcher is true and he's been informed that Jeremy and I travelled to Mexico, my life is probably in jeopardy as well. For me to act as her protector could just as easily cause her death."

Elwood shook his head. "So many unanswered questions. Other than this woman's word, the Belcher connection is vague. What exactly did you hear between Barker and him when they met? Anything?" He looked with scepticism at Jeremy. When the younger man shook his head, the officer continued. "Just as I thought. We need to tie up that loose end for sure. Any ideas?"

"I haven't thought much about it since we got back but yes, we need to search for proof of their complicity. Both of them. This whole thing, obviously, is much bigger than getting some kids back to their mother. By the way, someone broke into both our residences. My place was trashed. Sergeant Irving at City Police Headquarters thinks I am the target. I don't know what they thought they'd find since I don't keep any information about my cases at home." Jeremy paused while the Royal Canadian Mountie wrote that information in his notes.

The officer glanced at Melissa. "You didn't find anything missing either?"

"No, nothing. Just a mess. But nothing like Jeremy's." She shook her head. She glanced at Jeremy before her gaze slid back to the policeman. "It was almost as if someone was angry at him. I mean, the vandalism went beyond simple destruction. They wanted to hurt Jeremy." She studied Jeremy's face for concurrence. "Don't you think?"

"You might be right." Jeremy looked from her to Elwood. "It did appear personal. I can't think why or who."

"Parts of this case blend together, but some of it doesn't make any sense at all. For instance ...." Melissa looked long and hard at Elwood. "Why has it taken so long for you guys to discover who ordered the hit on my parents? I mean, twenty years. Come on." The officer was about to interject but Melissa continued, "Yeah, the killer is dead, but I also suspect he was simply a hired gun. If I can figure that out then why ...?"

"You were the only witness. We didn't want to compromise your safety by bringing you back here or by travelling to Texas. Too much information gets leaked around here. But, yes, now no tangible reason exists other than leads are in short supply. Proof never surfaced to implicate your father in criminal activity but the hit was an execution. Not a random killing. They had to be tied to organized crime. We did search Rompart business associates and everyone came through with a clean bill of health. No connections. Now ....." He lifted his hands in frustration. "We'll keep plugging away. Someone's going to slip up. Then we've got him."

Jeremy leaned forward. "In the meantime, Helen is in danger and so is Melissa." He glanced through the window in the door at the lonely woman sitting on a hard backed chair. "She's vulnerable. I can protect Melissa but not both women in two separate locations."

"I suppose she could stay with me. The house is big enough." Melissa's voice squeaked slightly. She bit her lip. "Oh. Whoa. Do I want that?" She stared at her feet and lifted her gaze to Jeremy. "I usually try to keep some distance between me and a client, you know that. But, the thought occurred to me that this might be the best solution only ...."

"Yeah, I know. Privacy." He placed his hand on hers.

Elwood decided to add his voice to the conversation. "Taking her into your home may increase her danger, not suppress it. Until you figure out how all this ties together, I'd suggest a safe house we've used from time to time. The place is actually a battered women's shelter. Their security is top-notch to protect their residents from abusive husbands."

Melissa's countenance brightened at the idea. "She is abused. They provide counselling in those places too, right? She could sure use some of that." She looked toward the hall. "Her self-esteem is non-existent although she becomes fierce when it comes to her kids."

Jeremy jumped to his feet. "Let's ask her." He opened the door and motioned Helen inside the small office. Her thin coat fluttered as she crossed the threshold.

Helen looked from one to the other. "I told you everything." She took another step forward. She stuffed her trembling hands into her pockets.

"We want to protect you." Melissa drew Helen to her side and sat her on the only vacant chair in the room. "A women's shelter that the RCMP use occasionally to protect female witnesses might have a spot for you, if you want it. The home sports a great security system. Would you be willing to hide out until we can work to clear all this up and ...."

"What would I do while I'm living with those women?" Helen seemed to be assessing the exchange of looks between the detectives in the room. Her trust issues surfaced. "Would they be told why I'm there?"

Elwood piped up. "No, not necessarily. They provide counsellors if you want to talk to someone, people trained to help battered women. You fit that description." He smiled, hoping to encourage the woman to accept their help.

"What about my job?"

Melissa blinked. "Right. Your job. I think that would not be allowed since it puts you in the public eye." She glanced at Officer Frazier. "Do they provide some sort of work at the centre?"

"Everyone volunteers to help defray the cost of food and housing. So, yes, she'd be working but not getting paid for it." He studied the distraught woman's body language. Tense could not begin to describe her. "What reason do you need money right now?"

Helen scowled before glancing at Melissa. She looked back at her interrogator. "I need to pay someone to bring my children back to me. I mean, I hired Miss Rompart here ...."

"This is now a Federal case. We'll retrieve your kids so paying someone is not necessary." He looked at Melissa. "Sorry."

"Oh, hey. That's okay." She patted Helen's hand. "See, God answers prayer. We weren't sure how to accomplish the task anyway. Now we can concentrate on putting the bad guys where they belong."

Chapter Fifty Two

Jason Mitchell walked purposefully through the door of the building that housed police headquarters and the coroner's office. He veered toward the bank of elevators that led to a variety of offices all connected to law enforcement in the city of Winnipeg. Stepping inside, he punched the button marked "B" for basement. The coroner's office.

The short ride left little time for reflection. He was here for one purpose, to find out who had arranged to move the body of Jessica Penner to a mortician's for embalming. Belcher insisted this person was of interest. The man was going to sic the police on his operation if he wasn't careful.

Jason walked down the hall toward the office for Dr John Belmont. A previous run-in with the man prepared him for the doctor' surliness if he ran into him. He hoped he didn't.

Jason pushed the door open. He walked toward the man wearing a white lab coat. "Where's Dr Belmont?"

"Er .... He's in the morgue examining a gunshot victim." The young assistant had been of help on more than one occasion when Jason had needed information.

The lawyer slipped a twenty dollar bill across the counter. "Did you obtain the information I asked for?"

The man slid a piece of paper toward Jason. "That's all I could find. I didn't ask for an address." He backed up a step or two.

Jason scowled. "I said I wanted an address. You couldn't find out when the funeral director picked up the body?"

"Not without drawing attention to myself. You got what you got. You don't pay me enough to cause me to be fired." A look of defiance dominated the man's features.

Jason shook his fist at him. He turned on his heel and stalked toward the door. "You'd better not become too cocky. Remember, I'm connected." He continued to grumble under his breath as he retreated to the elevator. *I wonder who works for this ghoul with the embalming fluid. I can't risk exposing myself.*

He walked back into the cool crisp winter air. His breath preceded him down the steps to street level. Plucking his cell phone from the holster on his belt, he speed dialled a trusted cohort. "Derrick, is there someone you trust at Mercy's Mortuary?"

He listened but continued walking. Derrick gave him a name. "Call him. Find out who hired them to take care of the body of Jessica Penner and find me an address." He heard a creative excuse why it would cost him more money. "Just get it done. Call me as soon as you garner the info." He hung up. *Everybody wants their pound of flesh. How's a guy to become rich in this darn city anyway.*

Jason checked the traffic and scurried across the street to his car, slipping a couple of times on patches of ice. He settled into the interior, turned on the ignition, and waited for the warm air to flow from the vents. He rubbed icy fingers together before slipping them into fur-lined leather gloves. He looked at his wristwatch. *Time for lunch.*

He placed his BMW in gear and drove into traffic. There was an Applebee's not too far up Portage Avenue so he headed in that direction. Just as he pulled into the parking lot, his phone rang. He parked and grabbed his cell. "Hello. Derrick. You got what I need?"

As he listened to the formation, Jason pounded the steering wheel. "Damn that man. How is he connected to Jessica Penner? Did the mortician say?" The informant said he had nothing else to offer. "Thanks. I owe ya." He hung up. *Why in the world would Jeremy Goodman pay for the travel preparation of a prostitute from Mexico? Every time I turn around his name or that woman's comes up.*

He turned the heat up in his car. Lifting the phone to his ear after pressing a speed dial, he listened. "Yeah, it's me. The name Helen Rempel mean anything to you? She's the dame who identified the body but, and get this, Jeremy Goodman hired the mortician. He's Barkley's son and a friend of Melissa's" The language on the other end of the call turned blue. "I don't know how they're connected or if at this point." Richard Belcher cursed in his ear again. "I know, she's a definite liability. I'll ask again. Does the name Rempel ring a bell?" The negative answer was spewed as if from the pit of hell. "Well, we need to find out, don't we?" He hung up, turned off his car's engine and stalked inside.

Chapter Fifty Three

Jeremy walked into the sterile hospital room where his office assistant lay among several pillows. Her bed was raised to allow for a better vantage point. A young man stood beside the bed, tears streaming down his face.

Matthew Cavanaugh glared, his hostile countenance in direct contrast to the distress Jeremy had witnessed a few seconds ago. The young man folded his arms as Jenna reached a shaking appendage toward him. "It's not his fault, Matthew."

"My fault? What's not my fault? What'd I do?" Jeremy leaned around Matthew to give Jenna a peck on the cheek. It felt cold and dry to his lips. "How are you friend? Melissa is waiting at the cop shop with Chief so this will be a short visit. I need to head back there to pick them up. The police are making arrangements to protect the Rempel woman."

Jenna forced a smile to belie her pain level. "That's okay. I'm doin' good. Isn't that right, Matthew? He's been here all day." She glanced from one to the other. "Matthew is having a hard time with all this. I told him that I'm ready for my real home but .... maybe you can tell him what the Bible says about heaven, Jeremy."

"I don't need nothin' from him." The boy-man scowled in Jeremy's direction. "You left her. You went off on a vacation when she needed you most. How could you?" Tears forced their way past his squinty eyes as he dared Jeremy to deny his neglect of their friend.

"Matt, Matthew, I didn't leave for a vacation. I was working." He looked pleadingly toward Jenna. "Jenna told me she approved and that, while the cancer had returned, she was okay for now. Otherwise .... I'm here now."

Jenna looked toward Matthew. "I think you owe Jeremy an explanation, don't you?"

Jeremy remained silent. His scrutiny of the boy's body language spoke of guilt and anger. Jeremy remembered that Matthew met Jenna while she volunteered at a homeless shelter. Matthew had been horrifically abused by a paedophile over a number of years, had escaped, and found his way to the shelter. Jenna had helped him find the Lord and they'd become as close as any mother and son. The young man frowned and planted his feet firmly apart, silence stretching from one male figure to the other.

"Come on, you two. Clear the air." Jenna emitted a shallow cough and then groaned. She held her hand over her chest. Reaching for her water bottle, she took a short sip. She closed her eyes.

Jeremy took a step closer. He looked at Matthew. "What is it you need to tell me?"

The boy looked contrite for the first time since Jeremy had interrupted his visit with Jenna. "I ...." He glanced at Jenna. She waved him on. "I .... well, I was so dog-gone mad at you for leaving when .... well, I trashed your place. The other guy did the woman's. Said he was looking for something."

Jeremy gasped. "You. But how did you get past our security system?"

Matthew dropped his gaze to the floor. "The other guy was one of the security guys who monitor the neighbourhood. He's one of those creeps who did business with ...." He looked from Jenna to Jeremy. "Well, you know. He told his boss some song and dance about needing to fix a leak so they ...."

"The security company was our next stop. Everything's happening all at once." He looked at Matthew. "You were pretty angry."

"Yeah. I couldn't understand, if you say you love Jenna, how you could put fun ahead of her when she's .... well you know." He hung his head. "Jenna told me how you are trying to rescue those kids. I-I'm so sorry." Tears cascaded down the boy's cheeks. "I'll fix it. I'll clean it up. I promise."

Jeremy punched the boy on his shoulder. "Matthew, I understand although I wish you hadn't teamed up with anyone else. Did the guy say what he was looking for? Melissa was really spooked. At least now the RCMP will have one less puzzle piece to solve."

"RCMP. Am I going to jail?" Matthew looked horrified at

the prospect.

"No, Matthew. Melissa and I won't press charges. But, I will need you to point out the security guard who searched Melissa's home. He's going to be fired at least but I am sure the city police will want to discuss his abuse activities as well. One more pervert off the streets." He smiled. "Thanks, Jenna, for helping Matthew clear this up for us. Can we pray together, thank God for His divine intervention in both of your lives?"

They bowed their heads and Jenna's smile grew bright while she visited with her Saviour.

Chapter Fifty Four

Melissa walked Chief to the parking lot, one step ahead of Jeremy. Helen remained inside the doors. She craned her neck to catch a glimpse of the frightened woman. "Jeremy, are we doing the right thing? I mean, getting her involved in this is scaring her to death."

"Melissa, she is involved. Sooner or later they'd consider her a threat and come after her. Those cartel guys don't like loose ends and she is one big loose end. At least this way she has a fighting chance." Jeremy stepped into the driver's seat as Melissa fastened her seat belt.

\The big truck circled the parking lot located behind the RCMP headquarters and stopped by the door. They checked to make sure no one else was within sight and motioned Helen outside. Melissa opened the back door from the inside.

Jeremy scrutinized the woman as she made herself comfortable. Once her seatbelt was in place, he took off. "Helen, after we drop Chief at our friend Clare's house, tell me the directions to your place. I'll circle the block to make sure no one is watching. Melissa and I will go inside with you to make sure you're safe. We'll help you pack."

"Do you think all this is necessary?" Helen looked outside before gazing at the two people in the front seat. "I should give notice at my job. I need to let my landlord ...."

"We'll handle all of that and, yes, we think this is necessary. We aren't sure how far reaching the criminal activity goes in this city or who's involved but they certainly don't want you telling anything to the cops. So far they are unaware of your existence and we want to keep it that way." Jeremy glanced out the window at the traffic surrounding them. *Rush hour.*

Melissa grinned. "You took so long visiting Jenna; we decided to find something to eat in the cafeteria. Helen prayed to accept Jesus into her heart, didn't you Helen?"

The woman nodded her head. "I think I need help from many sources and if you say I need Jesus, I ask. I'm not such a good person but you say that doesn't matter. I'm going to spend time at the shelter reading my Bible and studying about Him while I am prisoner in that place."

Melissa chuckled. "You're not a prisoner. You just can't move around outside as freely as you have been. I'll look after getting Jessica's body for the undercover agents to return to Campos Tinades. You will have done what you had to do to return her body home and now your testimony will remove all those from that village who are making life miserable for the families who live there."

Helen seemed unconvinced. "I accept. I've lost my freedom so I think I am a prisoner." They pulled up in front of Barkley Goodman's fiancée's house. Clare worked for him but their impending wedding was on everyone's mind these days. Melissa hopped out, grabbed Chief by the collar and led him inside.

Helen continued as if the conversation hadn't been interrupted. "At least I will have my things with me. I only have a few clothes and some pictures taken from the village when I left. Some food in the refrigerator and cupboards we can throw out. Packing won't take long." She sat back in the seat, her body relaxing for the first time all day.

Melissa waved toward the front door where Clare still stood. She yanked the passenger door open and slipped back into her seat. Jeremy smiled in her direction and quickly switched his gaze to Helen in his rear view mirror. "By the way, welcome to the family, Helen. The angels are dancing in heaven right now." He smiled at her reflection.

"Angels dancing? I never heard of that." Her smile was tentative. "What family do you talk about?"

"The family of God." Jeremy glanced at Melissa. "Speaking of family, I forgot to tell you about my visit with Jenna. She's failing, but always smiling. Oh, and she had a visitor. Remember that kid she found at the shelter where she used to volunteer?"

"I do. Matthew something or other." Melissa twisted her body to study his face. "Jenna has always been such an encouragement to me." She glanced at Helen. "Jenna is Jeremy's office assistant and friend. She's dying of cancer."

"I thought it. So sorry." Helen folded her hands in her lap.

"Well, the kid, Matthew, Cavanaugh is his last name, admitted to breaking into my home but someone was with him. That man ransacked your place."

Melissa gasped. "Why?"

"Matthew said he was angry I'd left with you on a vacation when Jenna needed me. He took his temper out on my place. I told him we wouldn't press charges. That kid's been through enough. He's become attached to Jenna apparently." Jeremy turned down the street where Helen lived. "The guy that did your place was looking for something specific according to Matthew. He worked for the security company so access to the house was not an issue." He ignored Melissa's angry pout and checked Helen in the rear view mirror again. "Which house Helen?"

She pointed to a small one story bungalow with siding that needed a paint job. "That one. The landlord said I could buy it maybe one day. Now I don't think so."

Jeremy drove past. Both he and Melissa scrutinized the neighbourhood to make sure no unsavoury characters lurked nearby. Jeremy steered his truck around the block so they ended up right in front of the little house. "Let's move fast. My truck kinda stands out on this street but there's no place to hide it.

Melissa stepped out. "I'm glad we took Chief back to Clare's house. This way we have room for all your stuff. He tends to take up a lot of space." Helen exited through the back door and the three of them proceeded to her front entry. She took out her key.

Using his body to shield the two women, Jeremy encouraged Helen to hurry. She glared at him for a second and then proceeded to open the door. She ushered her guests inside. They began throwing things into a large plastic garbage bag. She handed one to Melissa whom she directed toward the bedroom at the back of the building. "Grab everything."

Jeremy handed her some food items stored in a kitchen cupboard. Silence reigned. With the utmost speed, the task was accomplished in under fifteen minutes. Jeremy checked the street through the living room window. He grabbed a picture off a table as he walked back to the kitchen. "I think you'll want this."

Helen hugged the picture to her chest. "This is the only one I have of my kids. Thanks."

Melissa joined them with her plastic bag half full of clothes. She nodded at Jeremy who waved them toward the front door. "You ladies can sure complete a task quickly when you set your minds to it. It's all clear so let's leave."

He opened the front door, escorted the women to the truck

and stowed everything into the back seat. "Is there enough room for you, Helen?" He noticed a curtain move at a window across the street. "Are you acquainted with any of your neighbours?"

She slid up into the truck. "No. I pass them once in a while but we don't say anything."

Jeremy closed the door behind her and then sat down on the driver's seat beside Melissa. "Someone watched us loading the truck. I hope that doesn't prove to be a problem."

Melissa ducked her head and motioned for Helen to do the same. "Maybe they didn't catch sight of who was moving out. They won't be able to find out where she's going." She gazed at Jeremy as he drove the truck down the street and around the corner. "You have the address of the safe house, right?"

"I do. Fasten your seatbelts ladies. We'll be there in about a half hour." Jeremy leaned back after turning the radio to a local news station. The cab of the truck was filled with local happenings and reports of more gun violence. *The streets of Winnipeg are not as safe as when I was growing up.*

Melissa piped up. "It sounds like a story right out of the old west, gunfights and all." She sighed. "Living in the city is getting dangerous. Helen, it'll be much safer for you to be in the country."

"I like the country better. Quieter that's for sure. My street was not so bad but I didn't go out at night." She glanced out the window. "Days are getting shorter. Sun's going down already."

Jeremy checked his rear view mirror. A large black SUV caught his attention, just two cars back. The skin on the back of his neck felt as if a large spider was making itself at home. He nudged Melissa. "Keep your eyes peeled." He pointed to her side mirror. "SUV! Two car lengths back. Let's see what he'll do."

He steered his Dodge Ram toward the right lane and then down the first street. Melissa sat forward, keeping her eyes open for the black vehicle. "There it is. He turned but surely he knows we're on to him. No traffic to prevent us from seeing him now."

"Yeah but we could be paranoid. He may live here." Jeremy drove a couple of blocks and then turned left. Half a block later the SUV became visible again. "I guess that proves it." He speeded up. The car behind did the same. "Let's lose the creep."

Jeremy drove back toward Portage Avenue again, only this time he drove toward the centre of town. Traffic increased the closer they got to Main Street, commuters heading home after a long day at the office. He zigged one way, down one lane, and then zagged quickly into another lane and down a side street. Finding a parking spot, he'll pull in: shut off the engine and motioned for them to duck.

Melissa held her breath. Hardly daring to move, they waited. Jeremy was the first to pop his head up. "I think we lost them. This truck is hard to hide, though. Let's go switch with either Dad's or Clare's."

He took his cell from his jacket pocket. "Dad. We need something a little less conspicuous than my truck. Can we borrow your car?" Hearing a positive response, he ended the call. "Be there in a few."

Melissa straightened her back. "Were you surprised he'd be at Clare's?"

"He only goes home to sleep these days. He said he was just leaving now so we'll meet him at his house."

Helen remained silent. Melissa looked over her shoulder. The woman trembled. "How can you two be so blasé about what just happened. Someone was following us."

"This is nothing." Melissa grimaced hoping Helen was not even more spooked than before. She appeared scared to death. "I'm sorry Helen. We're so used to playing hide and seek with some of the criminals we try to put behind bars that this was just routine for us. We forget you're new to all this. When you search for missing kids who are being used by paedophiles and human traffickers, you expect to have them come after you once in a while. We'll be okay. Don't worry."

Helen visibly relaxed. "So .... you don't think they were following because of me?"

"Naw." Jeremy glanced in the rear view mirror again. "We didn't pick up that tail until we were well away from your neighbourhood. That was about one of us."

Melissa studied his profile. "I wonder who and why this time."

Chapter Fifty Five

Barkley Goodman perused the file folder Melissa had placed in his hands just four days ago. He'd done an item by item edit of its contents, but the conclusion was always the same. Rompart had assets beyond their yearly accounting for Revenue Canada. This file had names and dollar amounts missing from the accounting he received each year as the executor of Parker Rompart's estate.

I should hire someone to track down all these companies. Jeremy could do this but .... the doorbell interrupted his train of thought. He walked slowly to the door, surprised his son had arrived so soon. He checked the peep hole in the centre of his door. *That's him alright.*

He plastered a friendly expression over the frown he'd sported for the last twenty minutes. "Hi, Jeremy. Come on in." He peered past the taller man's shoulder. "Who's in the truck with you?"

"Melissa and I are taking Helen Rempel to a safe house for the RCMP. She's decided to cooperate with them. She knows some very incriminating details about what goes on in that village she's from. Anyway, we've picked up a tail." He closed the door behind as he stepped into his father's living room. "You left Clare's early tonight."

"With the wedding only a month away, Clare wanted to go through some of her stuff, pack some and throw some." Barkley pointed to the living room sofa. "Want to invite the women in?"

Jeremy grinned at his Dad. "Usually the two of you behave like a painting, she the picture and you the frame. Where one is so is the other." He watched his father hide a smirk of satisfaction with his bowed head. "The women are in a hurry. Melissa wants to relieve Clare of her dog-sitting duties and Helen is anxious to see where she will be a prisoner, as she calls it, for the next few weeks. My truck sticks out like a flashing light. We've lost whoever was following us but we don't want him to find us again."

"My car isn't exactly nondescript either. Bring Melissa back here when you return it. I have something to show her." He escorted Jeremy back to the door and handed him the keys to his Cadillac. "How is it going with you and Elwood? Are you going to be working closely with them on this case?"

Jeremy opened the door, stuck his head out to let the ladies know he was coming and then turned back to his father. "Elwood suggested, and we concur, that they would have an easier time getting Helen's kids out of Mexico than we would. So we are exchanging information. We both feel now since Helen recognized Belcher ...." He nodded when his father's eyes widened in surprise. "Yeah, she did. So Rompart is involved. Just how much is the question."

"I think I can supply some answers. We'll talk later." He leaned against the open door as Jeremy scrambled toward the truck. The women got out. Melissa waved in his direction and then they both walked to the back of the pick-up. Bag after plastic bag landed on the pavement before Jeremy opened the trunk to Barkley's pride and joy.

I hope they can avoid a high-speed chase and wrecking her. He stepped back through his door, shut it firmly, and sent a silent prayer to the Lord. *Protect them, Father.*

Chapter Fifty Six

Richard Belcher paced his office long after he'd hung up the phone. *Incompetents. Nothing but incompetents.* His face felt as if the sun had left its brand on him. The heat forced droplets to appear on his forehead. He swiped his hand angrily over his brow. *How could he have lost them?* A scream of pure rage began to build.

He pounded his desk as he passed it. *He has the description of both vehicles. Jason said he gave his hired fixer the addresses of their office and home. I thought Goodman sold that place years ago. This fixer had better find them and fast.* He ran his hand through his hair.

Things are unravelling. All these years. No mistakes. Now. The cartel will never let us end this partnership. They will come after me. Jason, too. His body dropped down in the chair that faced his desk. Laying his head on the cool surface, he let his mind wander.

His Cayman account had enough to make his defection easy. *I'll find a country where I can disappear for good. Then I'll conduct business as before.* He lifted his head. *Not if that dame isn't taken care of.*

He stood, walked over to the cupboard where his bar was located and yanked the door open. He poured a straight shot of Whiskey, and a second, half filling the glass. He gulped it down, the medicinal properties giving him a moment of calmness.

The moment passed. Richard pitched the glass across the room, shattering it. Shards of glass sprayed over the carpet with droplets of whiskey peppering the wall nearby. *She's not going to win. She may own Rompart but that is fixable. According to Jason anyway.*

He squatted down to gather splinters of glass. His heart burned with hatred. *If Parker had made me part owner of this company, I wouldn't need to go after his daughter.* He shook his fist heavenward and leaned back on his heels. Losing his balance, he landed with a thump on the floor.

Richard rolled over and stood slowly. His vision blurred as his brain told him the room was moving. He leaned forward on his hands, dropping his head to allow the moment to pass. He straightened. He stood tall and placed his hands on his hips with a new resolve. He dropped the glass into the trash can near his desk. *Tomorrow we win.*

Chapter Fifty Seven

Melissa wrapped her arms around the distraught woman. "You'll be okay here. The women's shelter was too easy for someone to break in so this is the next best thing. Lonelier but doable. You are a child of God's so He's here with you." She leaned back to gaze into Helen's eyes.

"I think I know that." Helen clutched her Bible close to her chest. Her attempt at a smile fell flat. Her heart thundered in her chest. Fear as thick as a blanket surrounded her. Her eyes roamed the room over Melissa's shoulder. She pulled from the younger woman's grasp. "This is nice. I'll be okay." She glanced at the two federal officers playing cards at the table across the room. "They take care of me?"

Melissa stepped closer to the door. "They will. Spend time reading your Bible and praying. God wants you to know Him better. Those guys won't mind. I've learned that when I am in trouble, God is always there to walk with me through it." She patted Helen's arm. "Settle in. Unpack. It may be a while before this case is wrapped up. Your testimony is going to speed things up, though."

Helen watched the door close behind her friend. She stepped farther into the room, grabbed her plastic bags and dragged them toward the bedroom she'd chosen. Her accommodations consisted of a small kitchen, a living room, one bathroom, and two bedrooms. Her protection detail would change every ten hours with three teams of two people taking turns. Helen shivered. She looked toward the two now on duty. "I'm going to unpack."

They waved and nodded their approval. Helen studied the floor all the way to her room. *What a way to live. But better .... how is this better.* She plopped the bags onto the bed. *I left Henry because I was so scared and now .... I run from another man.* She refolded items of clothing and placed them into a drawer of the dresser.

Within a few minutes, the task of settling in was accomplished as far as her bedroom was concerned. She bundled her toiletries and strode to the bathroom, stacked them on a nearby shelf above the toilet, and returned to her bedroom. The kitchen items were next. That plastic bag still sat near the door.

Helen stuck her head around the corner to see if the officers were still involved with their deck of cards. She remained silent as she sauntered past. Her protectors chattered to each other over the game that held their attention. One, the female, glanced at her and smiled. "There's food in the fridge if you're hungry."

"No, thanks. I unpack my dishes and ...."

"This place comes stocked. No need to unpack your personal items." The woman leaned her elbows on the table. "I'm Elena Fitzgerald, by the way. This is Tommy Felderman. We're one of the teams who will make sure no harm comes to you. You can relax. The TV's working. If you want to watch a movie or something go ahead."

Helen walked closer. She held her hand out. "I'm Helen Rempel. Nice to meet you." She also extended it toward the male officer. "Hi. Thank you for being here." Her small hand was engulfed by the man's larger one. She pulled back. "I'll store these in my room then." She pointed to the large plastic bag of household items.

Walking back to her room, she noticed an interesting look pass between the officers. *They are not happy to be here, I think.* Helen dropped her gaze. She continued to her room, stashed the bag in the closet and returned to the living room and the comfortable sofa where she'd left her Bible. Picking it up, she began to read the book of John as soon as she located it. *This book is not familiar to me but not for long.* She bowed her head, as Melissa had instructed, and asked the Holy Spirit to teach as she read.

Chapter Fifty Eight

Melissa and Jeremy kept their eyes peeled for anything suspicious as they drove back to Barkley's house. They wanted to make sure they didn't pick up an unexpected guest before changing vehicles again. "At least Helen is safely stashed for the duration, however long it takes. I hope it doesn't take too long, though."

"I agree. The longer it takes, the less diligent the officers will be, I assume. It would be hard to be on sharp alert for months at a time. The secret service does that for the president, but he isn't travelling every day. These guys need to be vigilant all the time. Her information will tie things together for the police. Elwood thinks they can obtain a search warrant from the Mexican authorities on her evidence alone." Jeremy made a left-hand turn unexpectedly.

Melissa looked around. "What's up?" She glanced through the rear window. "I can't see anything."

"I'm just being cautious. I figure that if anyone is following us, he'll be easier to spot on a less travelled street. Besides, we're almost at my Dad's house." Jeremy steered the Cadillac one more block and then made a right hand turn this time. No other vehicle gave evidence that they had been noticed. "I think we're okay." A few blocks farther, the large car made the final turn. Jeremy pulled over to the side of the road.

"Now why are we stopping? Barkley is expecting us, is he

not?" Melissa peered through the front window at the quiet street.

"I want to make sure." Jeremy studied the address where his Father had lived since his mother's death a few years ago. Darkened skies gave the street an eerie appearance. Trees bereft of leaves waved their branches as if signalling someone. Black trunks appeared capable of hiding almost anyone or anything. "We'll exit here and walk the rest of the way. Something's not right. My instincts are sizzling."

Melissa squelched a nervous giggle. She stepped from the car and inched the door closed. "What are you thinking?" she whispered as soon as she rounded the car's hood.

"I'm not sure I would recognize a strange vehicle if one was here but, if I was Chief, my hackles would be up. Caution doesn't hurt." He stepped behind a nearby tree.

Melissa found her own observation point. She remained as quiet as a falling snowflake waiting for Jeremy to signal all was well.

Jeremy perused the landscape. *Anyone could be entertaining at this time of night. Maybe if we move closer to Dad's.* He slipped past Melissa and walked a few paces closer, but across the street from his paternal parent.

He turned his head. Melissa remained where she was. In the distance, music blared from a well-appointed sound system. Jeremy turned in her direction and beckoned her forward. He watched as she walked ever so softly down the street to another hidden vantage point.

Shadows. Dad's not alone. Jeremy moved closer to Melissa. "Didn't Dad say Clare was staying home tonight?"

"You told me he did. There could be another visitor. Barkley didn't say he was planning to be alone all night, did he, and even if he did, unexpected company happens all the time." She stared at Jeremy. "I think you're getting paranoid."

"My instincts are usually spot on. Let's sneak around back and come in through the kitchen door. Dad keeps a spare key by the back door." Jeremy took a step toward the street.

Melissa grabbed his arm. "Jeremy, you'll scare him to death. Maybe we should phone." She shook her head. "No, that would give whoever's in there warning." She glanced toward a few of the neighbour's houses. "We'll do it your way."

Jeremy continued as quickly as he could across the street and on to the side yard toward the back of Barkley Goodman's house. He opened the gate to enter an inch at a time and held it for Melissa to pass through. "Dad hides a key under the big flowerpot near the door." An angry retort sounded from inside. "Whoever is in there is arguing with my Dad."

"You think. That definitely isn't your father's voice." She stepped aside to let Jeremy take the lead. "We didn't bring our weapons."

Jeremy's intense gaze was fixed on the back door. "Dad hides a loaded gun in a small nook behind the coats hanging by the back door. He believes in being prepared. As far as scaring him, he expects us to return." Jeremy slipped the key into the lock.

"I wish Chief was with us. He'd take anyone out who threatened Barkley." Her voice cracked a little in her attempt to speak in a whisper.

Jeremy inched the door open. *I hope he uses WD40 on this door's hinges.* He cautiously moved to one side to allow the door to open wide enough for access to the house. A slight creak forced him to stop. He listened. The heated argument continued inside.

Melissa followed, almost stepping on Jeremy's heel. He held his hand up for her to back up a little. He felt the heat of her body recede as he took another step forward. Inside the dark kitchen, Jeremy listened. Did he recognize the other voice?

Melissa stood beside him. He held his breathing to a minimum. She gasped and then slapped her hand over her mouth. "That's Jason. Jason Mitchell. Remember? Rompart's attorney?"

Jeremy turned his eyes toward her. His puzzled expression asked for an explanation. Melissa shrugged. He motioned for them to listen a little longer.

"You couldn't keep from meddling, could you? All these years you've let things alone and now, with that brat of his in the picture again, you think you need to snoop where you don't belong. Where's that file?" Jason's voice sounded unhinged.

"What file? I told you. No file." Barkley spoke with the control that had won numerous trial acquittals for his clients when his law practice was flourishing. "What are you talking about?"

Melissa and Jeremy heard a loud smack. Jason's voice raised another decibel. "Don't lie to me old man. She stole a file and gave it to you. Now where is it?"

Jeremy rushed into the living room without taking the time to see where Jason was standing. He ran right into the man's gun, knocking it to the floor. Melissa stepped forward, Barkley's spare gun in her hand pointed straight for Jason's heart. Jeremy sent the home invader to the floor with one blow from his powerful fist. "Keep your gun on him, Melissa. I'll be right back." Jeremy stooped to grab the thug's weapon on his way to the kitchen.

"Are you okay Barkley?" Melissa spoke without taking her eyes off Jason.

"I'm fine. I was hoping you guys would arrive in a timely manner."

Jeremy returned with some rope. He grabbed Jason's hands, twisted them behind his back, and tied him securely. "Now I'll untie you, Dad." Reaching behind the older man, he released his bindings and then looked intently at his Dad's face. "How many times did he hit you?" Several spots glowed as if someone had used a heavy instrument to break the skin.

"I'm okay, now that you're here. What took you so long?" His grin eased the harshness of his words. "Jason here seems to think we possess something that belongs to him."

Chapter Fifty Nine

Jeremy scowled toward Jason Mitchell. To impede the man's continu-
ous threats, Jeremy used Duct Tape to cover his mouth. Jason's hands
were tied behind the chair he sat on and his feet were bound to the
chair legs. The man struggled, his eyes blazing with hatred, anger
seeping from the snort of derision he sent toward his captors every
once in a while.

"Are you going to settle down?" Jeremy leaned closer. He
dropped his gaze when Jason tried, ineffectively, to lunge in his direction. Then he glanced at Melissa. "Let's find out what Dad discovered
in that file; give this guy time to cool off."

Melissa nodded. "Good plan." She frowned toward Jason.
"Your job at Rompart is over. We'll give you a few minutes to tell us
the information we want before we call the police. Think
about that while we check the file you're so on fire to locate." She
smirked. "By the way, thanks for telling us how important it is to you
and whoever you're working for. We'll take extra special care perus-
ing the contents."

Jason tried to stand again, the chair moving with him, but
was soon unbalanced by his restraints. He fell back against the chair.
Melissa tossed a shoulder in his direction as she passed by. Jeremy led
the way into Barkley's home office.

"Dad, what did you discover in that file?"

"Not a lot except there are some companies listed in this file but left out of the files sent to Revenue Canada. Yet they seem to be generating a bunch of cash for Rompart. I think the government would be interested in this stuff. I was also thinking we should research their existence before we report this." The older man glanced from Melissa to Jeremy. "What do you two want to do?"

Melissa scowled. "How far back do some of these companies go? Were they part of Rompart when my Dad was alive?"

"It seems so. Most of them anyway." Barkley picked up the file and pointed to one in particular. "This one, Escandeza, has been around since the seventies but who they are and what they do for Rompart except generate tons of money is a mystery."

Jeremy looked at the file Barkley had opened on his desk. "The list is extensive. When do we start finding out who they are and where they're located? I wonder if Jason has those facts." He turned his head toward the door. A faint scrapping sound filled the silence.

Melissa held her breath, listening. "That man is not going to give up. Getting him to tell us what is lodged in his brain is going to take some ingenuity." She stalked to the door and beyond. Jeremy followed.

As soon as they stepped into Barkley Goodman's living room, the scrapping stopped. Their prisoner had managed to work his way toward the kitchen door by then. "Going somewhere?" Jeremy grabbed the back of the chair and dragged it unceremoniously back to the centre of the room. Jason fell off once but Jeremy plunked him down on the seat with little consideration for the rope burns on his ankles that ensued.

Mitchell's eyes flashed his anger over being discovered. Jeremy picked a tiny edge of the tape covering his mouth and yanked it off. Jason Mitchell screamed, his voice pitched a little higher than a soprano's. "I'll sue. I'll make sure you rot in jail. I'll ...."

"You'll do what? You're the one who broke into my father's house illegally. When the police are finished with you, practicing law will be a long forgotten memory." Jeremy pulled a chair closer to their captive. "We'll pose some questions and you'd better be prepared to answer them."

Barkley and Melissa took their seats on the sofa. Content to allow Jeremy the opportunity to play bad cop, they leaned back and waited.

"I'm not telling you anything. You think that just because you got the drop on me that you can bully me into revealing .... I mean, disclosing company secrets, you're nuts." He glanced at Melissa. "You're not going to be around long enough to make a difference. Belcher ...."

"Yeah, right, what does your being here have to do with

Belcher?" Jeremy grabbed the knees of the man in front of him and squeezed. His large fingers, strong from years lifting weights, pressed into the sinews as he wrapped his hand around the kneecap of his victim.

Jason's face scrunched a little but he uttered nothing except a few curse words. "You'll find out." He hissed the words between clenched teeth.

Melissa blinked. She decided to stand as she moved closer to her employee. "I own Rompart. It doesn't matter what Richard Belcher wants or doesn't want. You work for me and I am privy to any information about Rompart. So what do you mean I won't be around long enough?" She placed a hand on Jeremy's silently asking him to ease his grip.

Jeremy complied. Jason glanced from one to the other. As Melissa guessed, he sensed her frailty as a woman. "What does a dame comprehend about running a business like Rompart? Richard Belcher has made more money than your Father ever could and he's not about to let go of the purse strings. He'll go before the board of directors and make sure you're voted out. Oh, you'll own the company but he'll run it." Jason's face brightened. It was as if the idea of a vote was a new one.

Melissa caught the lie. "But that's not what he plans to do, right?"

Jason dropped his gaze. He clamped his mouth shut. Jeremy moved back into position while Melissa walked to the kitchen. She moved to the sink and turned on the tap. Refreshing water flowed as she opened a cabinet door to retrieve a glass. Filling it, she retraced her steps. Taking a sip she watched Jeremy inch his chair close enough for his knees to touch Mitchell's. She took another sip. "Jeremy, do you want a drink of water?"

"I do." Jason's voice had softened to a plea.

Melissa kept drinking, one sip at a time. Jeremy shook his head. "I'm okay for now. Maybe later." He stared into Jason's eyes. "I can't picture you going to prison for someone else. In fact, I'll bet you have all kinds of damning information on every member of the Rompart board, don't you? Things you can use to protect yourself." He stood and walked behind Mitchell. Leaning forward, he spoke slowly into Jason's ear. "Now is the time. Protect yourself because no one else will." Jeremy rose up. He walked toward the kitchen, one step at a time, deliberate.

Jason wet his lips, his tongue sticking out of his very dry mouth. His eyes wandered around the room as he tried not to look at the homeowner or his boss. Just as he was about to speak, a shot from a high powered rifle pierced the front window and shattered a vase sitting on a side table. A puff of air passed by Jason's forehead. He rolled his body, chair included, to the floor.

Jeremy came running through the kitchen doorway as Melissa and Barkley also hit the floor. Jeremy flipped the light switch enveloping the room in the comfort of darkness. "Everyone okay?"

Melissa answered for both. "We are. I think Jason may have been hit"

"Not me. Whoever that is missed but not by much." He struggled with the ropes that held him fastened to the chair. "Untie me."

Jeremy crossed the room, and then sidled up to the window. His body melted into the curtains beside the panes of glass. He slid one panel aside to peer toward the street. It appeared empty. Nothing moved. Lights across the street flicked on or off in some cases. He supposed people were trying to figure out what they'd heard. "I'm going to check the back door. I don't think we locked it."

Melissa could just make out Jeremy's silhouette as he passed through the kitchen doorway on his way to the back door. As soon as he was out of sight, she followed his example and approached the front window. She made sure her shadow remained hidden. Peeking outside, she thought she saw something moved in the shadows. She looked toward the spot beside the house where a bush branch waved. The rest of the trees remained motionless.

Chapter Sixty

He plucked a cell phone from the front pocket of his black jacket. "It's me. He's inside. What do you want me to do?" The man listened, his eyes roaming left to right. Houses along both sides of the street glowed with light from within and a few had turned on outside illumination. He leaned back into the shadow of the tree.

His client screeched into his ear. "All right. All right. I'll do it. Want me to take out the girl as well. She's at the house with the lawyer. His son as well." He took a deep breath. "That'll cost you. I agreed to one hit and I agreed to follow Mitchell. Now you want me to eliminate all of them. I'll burn the house, lock them in." He thought about the can of kerosene he always kept in his trunk. *My car isn't too far. Sneaking back will take a few minutes but so what. I got all night.*

The disembodied voice on his cell phone growled his response. "Fine. The cost is one million. Nothing less." The agreement was made. He slapped his cell back into his pocket. *Gotta make sure those doors are locked up tight before I fetch the accelerant.* He slithered across the street like a dark spectre of someone's imagination. A nearby bush gave him a secure hiding place. He peered into the living room. He ducked. *The woman.*

He slowed his breathing as he inhaled and exhaled. Closing his eyes, he waited for a few seconds and opened them again. She'd disappeared. He crept from bush to bush under the bottom of the window until he crouched near the step to the front door. *I need something to wedge the door tight.*

He glanced around. He picked up a sturdy branch lying to the left of the concrete step. Being quiet was never one of his strengths but he tip-toed upwards. He placed the tree limb through the door handle, across the frame. *Even a strong person will never break that barrier.* He grinned. *Almost too easy.*

The thug stepped down and decided to skirt the right side of the house to the back yard. As he passed by, he grabbed another branch, this one almost as thick, and inched along the shadows to the back of the house. *They won't be trying to escape anyway. They know there's a killer out here.*

He made his way toward the back door. He saw the curtains at the door move and fall into place. He waited a few more seconds and inched toward the back entrance. Crouching, he wedged the stick of wood in place. *Now for the fuel.*

Chapter Sixty One

Jeremy flipped the dead bolt. The back door was secure. He peered through the slit in the curtain covering the back door window. Darkness covered the patio and the shadows beyond. He grabbed the door knob, rattled it to make sure it was secure and retraced his steps to the living room. He returned to his crouched position as soon as he entered.

Melissa stood beside the window. "Nothing unusual out there." Jeremy crouched beside their interloper. "We don't know who the target is either." Her eyes roamed the room. "Could be any one of us."

"Not me." Jason Mitchell spoke from his position on the floor, the chair still attached to his body as he lay on his side. "I don't have any enemies. You two, on the other hand ...."

"Shut up Mitchell." Jeremy crept toward the older gentleman. "You okay Dad?"

Barkley crouched behind the sofa. "Other than my knees giving me grief, I'm okay." He studied the hole through his front window and the damage the bullet had made as it travelled across the room. "How long are we going to wait before we call the police?"

Jeremy crawled closer. He kept his voice low, hoping Mitchell couldn't hear him. "I was hoping to gather some incriminating evidence from Mitchell either about himself or Belcher. But I think that sniper made the decision for us. We need to call them now."

He picked up his cell phone that had slipped from his pocket when he'd hit the floor initially.

"Wait. Jeremy." Melissa shook her head in Jason Mitchell's direction. "Jason, why would someone want to kill you? The shot was aimed at you. You were the only one in sight of the window. Who wants you dead?"

"N-n-no one. I ...." He closed his eyes and then stared at Melissa. "I .... well .... no one. I can't think of ...." He stopped mid-sentence. Fear then denial crossed his face. He glanced at her briefly and looked away. "No. Not me."

Melissa decided to pursue the idea. "So? Who is it, Jason? Why would anyone want you dead?" Jason remained silent. His frown revealed a lot. "Come on, Jason. Whoever is out there won't stop until you're dead." Her voice rose enough to let him know she meant business. "You've lost your job. Are you going to allow someone to get away with this, too? Who are you protecting?"

Jason's eyes travelled from Melissa to Jeremy and back again. "Lift me up, will ya? This is uncomfortable. Close those curtains. Whoever is out there won't be able make out where we are." He willed his captors into compliance. When none came, he whined, "Oh, come on. Fine. I'll tell you everything."

Melissa crouched below the window and pulled both panels toward the centre. Jeremy crawled toward Jason. He stood and bent to lift the fallen captive. Using every ounce of strength he had, his muscles strained as he lifted. "You're heavier than you look," he grunted.

Once Jason was upright, Melissa took a step toward him. "Out with it, Jason. Who wants you dead, besides me, that is? If you're part of the conspiracy to dirty my Father's reputation, you're going to be serving as a jailhouse lawyer for a long time. Now ...." An acrid odour wafted toward her. "What's that?"

Jeremy lifted his head. Taking a deep breath, he glanced at his father. "Does your furnace need cleaning?" He drew in a deep breath. "Smells like smoke."

Melissa eased her way toward the three pane picture window. She moved behind the right panel and glanced out at the street. "All appears quiet. I wonder where our attacker went."

"Jason, finish answering our question." Jeremy wrapped his hand around the intruder's shoulder and squeezed, hard.

"Take your hands off me. I said I'd tell you. Belcher forced me to hire a hit man, to kill Melissa." He glanced quickly around the room hoping his words rattled the owner of Rompart. Her stoic expression revealed nothing. He continued. "He really wants you out of the picture."

"What do you mean by forced? How could he force you to do something like that?" Melissa turned her head toward the kitchen. "That smell is getting stronger. It seems to be coming from the kitchen area."

Jeremy led the way. He crept toward the back door. An unusual light flickered from the kitchen window. Melissa leaned across the counter. "It's a good thing we never turned the lights back on. We'd be sitting ducks." Her comments were a way to disguise her tingling senses. "Those are flames!"

Jeremy rattled the door knob to make sure it was still locked before his attempt to unlock it. The door wouldn't budge. He pulled the handle with a measure of force and still it wouldn't open. "Something's wrong."

Melissa ran into the living room. Smoke poured into the room from the bottom of the front door. She grabbed the knob but yanked her hand away. She patted the red impression left on her open palm. No time for ice. "The house is on fire, Barkley. Call the police, fire department, everyone. We can't escape"

Jason's eyes popped as he began coughing. "What do you mean, we can't get out? Untie me." He coughed harder.

Melissa tried to take a deep breath but a choking cough erupted instead. "Barkley, do you own a fire extinguisher?" She snatched a small blanket from the sofa to protect her hands and returned to the front door. Using one corner, she grabbed the knob again and twisted the dead bolt open. The door wouldn't budge. She yanked it again and again. Nothing moved.

"Untie me. I'm stronger than you." Jason almost screeched his request. Red flickering lights danced across the closed curtains. "Hurry."

Jeremy collided with his father when he returned to the living room. "Where are you going, Dad?"

"Melissa asked for a fire extinguisher." The older man placed his hand over his mouth as a cough wracked his body. "I called the police."

"We need to concentrate on getting out of here. Let's look for a window large enough so we can climb through. The doors are obviously jammed."

"Let me lose." Jason shrieked, his panic reflected in his eyes.

Jeremy took the two steps necessary to gain access to the bound man. "I intend to keep you tied but I'll release you from the chair. You better not try getting away from us. The police will question you before they incarcerate you for ten to twenty. We're not through with you either. There are more questions than answers." He worked at the bindings the whole time he talked.

Once Jason was standing, Jeremy led him from room to room. The cracking fire had grown to a roar. Outside walls were fully engulfed and dense smoke filled each room. Jeremy searched for a way out while Melissa soaked some towels in the bathroom sink. Jeremy dragged Jason into the master bedroom. "In here. This window will work." He unlatched it and began to lift the bottom pane. A gunshot shattered the glass above his head. Jason ducked and Jeremy followed. "Stay down everyone. That shooter plans to make sure we never leave alive."

Melissa lay down on the floor of Barkley's bedroom. "The air is better down here." She threw a wet towel toward Jeremy. Barkley already had one over his nose and mouth.

Jason slapped a towel over his face as he crouched beside Jeremy. He sat with a thud. "Now what are we going to do. You can't just sit here. There's got to be a way out." He struggled to stand. "Let me out." His scream reverberated into the cold night air. Sirens sounded outside as well.

"The fire trucks are here. Keep calm." Jeremy emitted a choking sound. The smoke entered through the open window. "We must hurry or we'll never be able to use this window. The fire outside is growing." He stood beside Jason. No shots rang out. "I think he's left." Another bullet just missed his forehead. He ducked and pulled Jason down with him, again.

Melissa bowed her head. Lord. Please help us. Bring the firemen to this window first and let no one shoot them in the process. She glanced at Barkley. His laboured breathing was interspersed with coughing spasms. "Barkley, take shallow breaths. Keep the towel over your face. We'll figure something out."

The older man shook his head. His breathing grew shallow. He began to choke. Melissa patted his back and then looked frantically toward Jeremy. "Your Dad needs to get out of here."

The sirens grew increasingly louder. Flashing lights turned the neighbourhood into a fantasy of colour; flickering beams swaddled the trees in an orange glow. Jeremy peeked outside once again. He hollered through the window. "Hey. Over here."

Chapter Sixty Two

He stepped behind a tree. *Too many witnesses. I'll watch.* Maybe he got one. Disorganized bedlam reigned all up and down the street. Neighbours stuck their heads out of houses that had previously been put to bed. Unseen dogs barked. Fire roared, consuming, ravaging. People gasped and ran for their own hoses. Dousing sparks flying through the air became the order of the day. Water reigned down from fire hoses and water hoses alike.

He surveyed the scene. *The window is their only escape. I made sure no one tried it.* His hidden grin warmed his heart. He imagined where he would travel and how he would live with that much money. His reputation would be assured. His chest puffed. *Not many can eliminate four in one blow.*

A large red fire engine idled past the window, blocking his view. He looked around. He needed another vantage point. *I need to make sure.* The stench of burned wood, plastic and fabric wafted past his nose. He cleared his throat as he perused the small crowd across the street grow in size. *Maybe.*

He sauntered casually, hiding his rifle inside his calf length winter coat. His toque pulled low, revealed little that people would remember. He took his place amidst the onlookers, saying nothing, revealing nothing. Just a figure in the crowd. He focused on the chaos he'd created.

Chapter Sixty Three

Jeremy pounced on the opportunity as soon as the truck pulled in front of the window. "We can escape now. The gunman can't fire with so many people out there and that truck blocking his view of this window. This is our last chance. We can't go back. The house is fully engulfed by now."

Melissa moved closer to the window and peered outside. "He could be watching. Look at all those people. We may be able to climb though the window but what's to stop him from coming after us once we're outside?" She looked from Barkley to Jeremy. Barkley was barely moving. The older man had to leave.

Jeremy leaned closer. Her resolve reflected back at him. Lifting his Dad, he hollered again to the firemen nearby. A large man dressed in equipment intended to protect, reached upward to ease Barkley's descent to the ground. He escorted him, half dragging, toward the truck and returned once the EMT's had him.

Jeremy turned toward Melissa. He searched from his crouched position. He found her lying beside an unconscious Jason Mitchell. *What has she done?* "Melissa, Melissa." He shook her. No response.

He looked at Jason. The man's shallow breathing appeared non-existent. He checked Melissa. Her heartbeat appeared faint. Jeremy tugged Jason's dead weight toward the window. He went back to Melissa. His muscles ached and his lungs hurt from lack of oxygen. His eyes watered. The dense smoke made vision impossible. They had to escape.

A firefighter made his way into the room. He grabbed Jason and lifted him toward the opening. "That man is a criminal. Make sure .... police control him. Is he still alive?"

"Barely." The fireman grunted his response through his mask. "Come on."

"There's a .... gunman." He waved toward the window. ".... probably the person who set .... " He took a deep breath, his head leaning on the window frame. ".... house on fire. Shooting at us." He turned to the room, bent and clamped his hands around Melissa's torso. He yanked and pulled until he was almost at the fireman's elbow. He stared hard at the man's mask. "He needs to believe that the man you have and this woman are dead. Can .... do that?" Jeremy struggled to form words. He was becoming disoriented. He saw the fireman nod just before he collapsed.

Chapter Sixty Four

Jeremy felt his body scrap across the window ledge. He had no more strength left to aid in his rescue. He kept his eyes closed as the burly fireman did the job he was trained to do. His feet hit the ground first. He felt cold frozen grass under his torso. He coughed uncontrollably. Someone shoved an oxygen mask over his face. "Lie still." The EMT cradled the command in compassion.

The first responders slipped a board under him. Blankets draped his body. He breathed the pure clean air from the mask and coughed again. The fog rolled in slowly as it had before. His body went limp. The EMT shouted instructions but Jeremy didn't hear anything else.

****

Barkley stepped from his perch on the running board of the truck. The blankets wrapped around him fell to the ground as he walked wearily toward his son. He glanced at the mess. His house, the place he'd raised Jeremy, the home that held so many memories of his deceased wife Susan, sat dead in the night air, smoke drifting skyward. He sighed. *I can't lose Jeremy too.*

He knelt beside the inert man. Barkley stared at the caregiver. "Is he going to make it?"

"He's inhaled a lot of smoke. His lungs may be damaged but he'll be okay eventually. Right now we need to transfer him to the hospital." The young man continued his preparations for transporting Jeremy to the nearby facility where, Barkley assumed, the other two had been taken. "Are you okay, sir? Maybe you should go to the hospital as well to get checked out."

"I'm going, but to be with him. He's my son. How are the other two?" Barkley stood as the EMT raised the stretcher Jeremy lay on. He took a hesitant step toward the waiting ambulance, listening for the answer to his question.

"I don't know. The lights and sirens weren't flashing. Not a good sign." He pushed while a second responder pulled the heavy gurney over the frozen ground.

Barkley stumbled. He coughed, placing a hand over his mouth. He glanced again at the shell smouldering where his house used to stand. A tear formed at the corner of his eye. *The pictures, clothing, everything gone.* A water trail formed through the soot that coated his face. He glanced at Jeremy. *He's got to be okay.*

One by one, the fire trucks and the personnel they carried left the scene. One smaller vehicle remained, its owner sifting through the ashes. Barkley surmised, a fire inspector. *Where are the police I called?*

His eyes canvassed the area. The crowds began to disperse. Most wore coats over nightclothes. *What time is it anyway?* One man, a toque pulled low enough to cover his ears and the sides of his face, walked stiffly toward a line of cars parked halfway down the block.

Two police officers approached as Barkley leaned on the back door of the ambulance. "Sir, do you have a minute. Can you tell us what happened here tonight?"

The EMT urged him to enter the vehicle. He nodded and glanced at the officers. "We're going to the hospital. I'll talk to you there. I have some questions too. Like, where are the other two, the woman and our intruder. We tied the man up. He should be in police custody for break and enter, attempted murder and various other offences." He stepped up into the back of the ambulance. From his crouched position, before he sat down, he studied the faces of the officers. "Where's Sergeant Irving? I specifically asked he be informed of all this."

The officers shrugged. "We don't have answers for you right now, sir, but we'll find someone who does. See you at Health Sciences." They stalked off speaking quietly to each other, shaking their heads.

Barkley plunked his fatigued body down in the seat the EMT told him to use. The back door closed as the driver began his slow journey down the street and on to the medical facility closest to the scene. He coughed and bowed his head. *Father, you're aware of everything. Please keep Melissa safe wherever she is and protect my son from any further damage from all that inhaled smoke. Amen.* He closed his eyes. *What a night.*

The trip progressed a little faster as soon as the vehicle turned out of the residential area. As soon as they reached the emergency department of the largest hospital in Winnipeg, the back doors flew open and the EMTs wheeled their patient into the warm interior.

Someone forced Barkley unceremoniously into a wheelchair and pushed him behind Jeremy. The entourage moved through automatic doors into a brightly lit waiting area already filled to capacity. He perused several people waiting who appeared to be really sick. The staff ushered he and Jeremy into examining rooms ahead of them. *Must make them kinda angry.* Barkley coughed again.

Once the privacy curtain surrounded him, Barkley stood. A diminutive nurse helped him onto an examining table-like bed. His tired limbs could hardly hold him as he dropped onto the clean sheet covering the bed. It gave some semblance of comfort. "Where's my son?" He glared at the woman who slapped a blood pressure cuff in his arm.

"Did he come with you? I can go find him if you'd like. Waiting can seem long with no one to talk to." The nurse fussed with the buttons on his shirt.

"No, you don't understand. I accompanied him. They transported him unconscious." He slapped the nurse's hands away. "What are you doing?"

"You escaped a house fire, right? I need to check your lungs to see if oxygen is required. Now, let me unbutton your shirt, Mr. Goodman." The petite blond managed to appear stern.

"I need to know if my son is okay. Please. His name is Jeremy Goodman." Barkley continued the task of opening his shirt as soon as the nurse slipped through the curtain. Her compliance eased his distress considerably. Taking a deep breath, he began to cough in earnest. Something foreign had invaded his lungs.

The nurse stuck her head back in. "I heard that. Let me listen." She rubbed the end of the stethoscope between her hands and placed it on his chest. "Take a deep breath, Mr. Goodman."

His attempt to inhale deeply set off a coughing spell that began to choke the little air he had out of him. The nurse slapped a mask over his nose and twisted the knob on the oxygen tank beside the bed. "That'll help. Take short breaths for now but try deeper ones later." She spotted the objection before he uttered a word. "Mr. Goodman, your son is receiving expert care. You need to take care of you. Jeremy is conscious but his breathing is worse than yours. He'll be okay if he cooperates with the doctor. Right now, he's asking for Melissa and we don't have anyone out there by that name. We checked."

Barkley closed his eyes. He opened them again to stare at the ceiling. "She was trapped in that house with us. They took me out first, then her. But she wasn't moving. They put her in an ambulance right away and drove away. They treated Jason the same way. They must have come here."

The nurse shook her head. "I've been working since three. You two are the only ones transported here from a fire."

Barkley's eyes opened, alarm bells shrieking through his brain. He lifted the mask to one side. "I need to talk to the police. Now."

"Unless a crime ....."

"A crime did occur. Find Sergeant Irving ASAP. Someone deliberately set the fire and shot at us. I need to find where the woman and our prisoner are. Now. Their lives are in danger." He pushed his way to a sitting position using all the strength he had left. He immediately collapsed on the table, his breathing so laboured that his blood pressure cuff sent off alarm bells.

"Relax, please, Mr. Goodman. I'll look for the sergeant. I think I saw him outside in the waiting room." She patted her hand on Barkley's chest to calm him. After securing the oxygen mask, she slipped through the curtains again.

Barkley tried to relax. He knew he needed to remain calm but his mind had conjured several scenarios to explain the absence of Melissa and Jason. *None of them good. Someone is trying to kill one or both of them. Maybe all of us since he attempted to set us on fire.*

The curtain billowed, swept aside by the bulky frame of Sergeant Bill Irving, the commanding officer of the main police station downtown. The sergeant stared at Barkley for a minute as if he didn't recognize him. "I guess that is you under all that soot." He reached his hand toward the lawyer who had been a regular fixture around the precinct for a lot of years. He checked to make sure the nurse had left them alone. "How ya doin', Barkley? Bad business this. Jeremy okay?"

"The nurse said he's conscious but anxious about Melissa. Where is she? You know what's going on?"

"Some of it. Melissa called me as soon as she left the scene in an ambulance. After what she said, we decided to let the perp think she'd died. Jason too. By the way, he's in the hands of the Feds and talking a blue streak. He's madder than a hornet on steroids." Irving chuckled. "He doesn't even care that we got enough evidence about his extra-curricular activities to put him away for a long time. He doesn't plan to go down alone."

"We tried to force him to talk but until that gunman decided to shoot at him, he wasn't cooperating. Even when he denied it, he eventually had to admit the bullets were meant for him. But he also told us that Belcher wanted him to hire someone to eliminate Melissa. Before we found out who he hired, if he hired anyone, my place was set on fire." Barkley's breathing had begun to flow more easily.

"That's why Melissa initially agreed to allow the authorities to perpetrate her death. But, we're thinking that maybe she's not dead, just wounded. We may be able to flush this guy out if he tries to finish the job." Irving turned to leave. "You look after yourself. I'm going to talk to Jeremy. He's making quite a fuss, upsetting the nurses and everything. I think he's attached."

"I hope so. He could do a lot worse. They make a good team." Barkley closed his eyes. *Speaking of good team, I'd better call Clare. I don't want her hearing any of this from the TV or newspapers.*

Chapter Sixty Five

He stalked back and forth. The tiny hotel room felt like a prison cell. The phone crackled in his ear. The caller shouted abuses intended to cower the hearer. "I don't know. Maybe."

He listened to the threat. "We had a contract. They're dead one way or the other." But he was aware he couldn't prove the deed. *I need to rectify that if I want to get paid.* "I'll find out." He pressed the 'end call' button.

The man sat down at the desk. He spread a newspaper across the top and began to take apart his weapon of choice. While he cleaned, he schemed. He'd copied where his targets lived from the phone book. He also copied the address of the man who hired him. That person would never find out his identity, but he would pay.

He went over the events of the night before. The house was a pile of rubble when he left but he couldn't be sure who died and who lived. The old guy was taken to safety. The codger's face had scanned what remained of his home, his pain sending thrills of pleasure down the arsonist's spine. Even now, he hummed with satisfaction.

Things got dodgy after that. *Too many people.* He'd seen them take the bodies by ambulance, but dead or alive? The ambulance seemed not to hurry. *Maybe that's a good sign. Did they end up at the morgue or the hospital?*

The chair he sat on squeaked. He unfolded his lanky frame and walked slowly to the bathroom. Washing his hands, he glanced in the mirror. His eyes looked puffy this morning. *All the smoke*, he surmised. His skin appeared a little on the grey side. *A few lazy days on a quiet beach will fix things.* He grinned. *I quit after this.* He sighed. *Maybe.*

He returned to his seat at the desk. Crumpling the newspaper, he dropped it into the garbage can and then grabbed the phone book. *I wonder how many hospitals are in this city and to which one did they take the bodies. Let's see.*

He opened the book, found the listing for hospitals, and began taking notes. *I'll make the calls from a public phone in the library. That way, if they tried, they couldn't trace the call to his room. I'll find out if they are listed as a patient.* If so, he'd finish what he'd started.

Chapter Sixty Six

Jeremy yanked the oxygen mask off his face. Flat on his back all night, right now he wanted to hit someone. Irving just sent his blood pressure through the roof. "What do you mean? She's being used as a decoy." The heat from his face radiated toward the policeman.

The cop shrugged. "She's good at it. Besides it was her idea." The rotund sergeant grabbed a chair from outside the curtain and dragged it beside the gurney Jeremy sat on. "Put that mask back on. Your voice is a little raspy."

Jeremy stared incredulously at the sergeant. "You can't be serious. You're willing to risk her life?" He pushed the mask over his nose and took a deep breath. His lungs actually hurt. "Where is she?"

"I don't think I should tell you. She's pretty determined. You won't be able to change her mind. Besides, you need to take care of yourself." The sergeant rested his hands on his knees. "I saw your Dad. He's pretty devastated."

"Yeah, but he's getting married in a month and moving to Clare's anyway." He lowered his voice, forcing calm to reign over his anxious spirit. "I need to visit her."

"You're pretty blasé about your father's loss. Wasn't that the house where you were raised? His memories of your mother were all over the place, weren't they?" Irving closed his eyes for a moment before gazing out the window on the other side of the bed. "I know I'd feel pretty bad if I lost all my stuff."

Jeremy lay down, his head finding comfort in the pillow. He looked at the older man. "Dad will take his memories of Mom with him. The things, pictures and such, he'd planned to put into storage after the wedding. The Goodman's priorities are in order when it comes to material possessions." He dropped his gaze toward his feet. "Bill, I wanna talk to her. She was unconscious when I handed her to the fireman. What about Jason? Is he in custody?"

Bill Irving lifted his gaze to the distraught investigator. *I can't believe I'm going to tell him.* He lowered his voice to little more than a whisper. "She's in room 602. She's resting. She looks a lot worse than she really is. The nurses' covered her in bandages to make it look good. The newspapers will report that she is unconscious but expected to make a full recovery. A couple of the nurses are police women." He glanced at the crack in the curtain. "If you go traipsing up there, you could blow the whole thing."

Jeremy dropped his legs over the side of the bed. "What about Jason? He was about to give us some important information before the gunman missed his head by a breath. The Feds will be interested in his story, I think." He removed the mask again after inhaling as deeply as his lungs would allow.

Bill Irving placed a hand on Jeremy's leg. "Rest awhile. She's not going anywhere. As far as that Mitchell character, it doesn't surprise me that he's mixed up in all this. He's always seemed a little shady to me. He's squealing like a new-born pig, I hear. My detectives found out before the Feds took him he's tied to some of the human trafficking in this city as well. The RCMP is interrogating him as we speak."

Jeremy stood, his face a picture of defiance. Irving groused at him. "You're not going to listen, are you? Well let me take you. The police up there won't shoot you if I'm there. That guy will take another crack at Melissa if he thinks he missed. We'll catch him. By the way, Clare brought Chief with her this morning when she came to visit Barkley. Do you want to take him up to be with Melissa?"

A nurse bustled through the curtain. "Obviously you're breathing better than when they brought you in. The doctor should be here to release you in about an hour or so."

"I'm not waiting. I need to go visit a colleague on the sixth floor." He glared at the woman when she grabbed his wrist and shoved a thermometer in his mouth. He started to protest, but clamped his mouth shut when she scowled. Releasing his hand, she grabbed the blood pressure cuff and wrapped it around his upper arm. Her stethoscope fit under the edge.

Sergeant Irving squelched a chuckle as he witnessed the proceedings. Jeremy kept trying to leave and the nurse added another piece of information she needed to garner to fill the chart she'd brought with her. Jeremy sighed when she finished scratching numbers on the chart. "Are we done? Can I go now?"

The nurse scowled again. "The doctor won't like you leaving without his permission, but I can't stop you. You're free to go. Those lungs of yours took a beating so give them a rest, will ya." She slipped through the curtain while Jeremy laced up his boots. Her squeaky shoes took her to another patient.

Jeremy looked at Irving. "Let's go. I want to visit Dad as well so, yes, let's bring Chief to Melissa. She hasn't seen him since yesterday." He led the way through the curtain, but then stepped aside. Irving marched toward the spot where they put the older man.

Metal containers clanged. The hum of voices was constant as they walked to the other side of the nurse's station. Jeremy recognized his Father's voice long before they reached the cubical that hid him. He followed Irving to the second one from the door.

Jeremy stuck his head in first. "Hey, Dad. You okay."

"Jeremy, good to see you're up and about." Barkley was sitting on the edge of the bed. Clare, her hand holding Chief's leash, leaned forward in the only chair. She waved her greeting.

Chief's tail made a succession of beats against the fabric wall as soon as Jeremy appeared. His cold wet nose touched the younger man's hand as he reached to ruffle the dog's coat. "What a night, eh? You're sure you're ready to go home?"

Clare piped up. "I can look after him better at home than I can here. Besides, thanks to your intervention, he didn't inhale as much smoke as you did." She stood to give Jeremy a big hug. "Thanks for getting him out of that inferno on time."

"The smoke was doing a number on him." His affectionate gaze encompassed the two seniors. "I'm going to see Melissa. I'll take Chief with me. She hasn't seen him much lately and I'll give you my thanks for her, Clare. She appreciates how you care for the big fella." He scratched the dog between his ears. "Wanna go visit Melissa, huh?"

The dog's tail whipped the curtain to one side as the trio left, Sergeant Irving leading. "I'll be at Clare's." Barkley shouted to their backs.

The ebb and flow of the emergency room surrounded them as they headed toward the elevator. Chief walked beside Jeremy, held close with his leash. People gazed after them, curious about the dog. The doors opened, and all three moved inside at the same time. Jeremy pressed the button for the sixth floor. Another man and a woman joined them, each pressing their own destination button.

Glossy stainless steel walls reflected distorted images as the elevator transported them past a variety of floors. Jeremy and Bill Irving stepped off before the other two and headed to the nurses station. "Where is room 602?"

Following the nurse's direction, they marched down the hall checking room numbers. They soon found the one they wanted. Jeremy knocked on the door. "It's me and I brought Chief with me." They heard a faint invitation to enter.

Chief bounded toward the bed almost knocking Jeremy off his feet. He placed his front paws on the bed beside Melissa, his tail wagging like a spear slicing the air around it. "Oh, hi boy, I've missed you." Melissa had bandages covering her neck and lower jaw, which made talking a little difficult. She waved at Jeremy and the sergeant.

Jeremy pointed to one of the chairs for Sergeant Irving to occupy and he grabbed another. He pointed to the bandages covering both arms. "Did you receive some burns?" He had a hard time hiding his concern.

She grinned. "No. This is for affect. We want that creep to think I'm incapacitated." She reached under the blanket and pulled a Smith and Wesson out. "As you can see, I'm not." Melissa tucked it back into hiding. "How are you Jeremy? Once they pulled me out ...."

"You remember all that?" He leaned forward, his concern replaced with a frown.

"I'm sorry, Jeremy. Once the idea formulated, I thought it would be better if you thought I was dead or something. If that guy was watching, your face would convince him."

Jeremy grunted. "Thanks a heap. You scared me to death. I thought you were, at the very least, unconscious. They wouldn't tell me anything. I had to threaten Irving to tell me where you were." Sergeant Irving placed his hands on the arms of the chair. Jeremy chuckled. "Well, not exactly threaten. But he was tenacious. He cracked finally and here we are."

Irving's smile encompassed the bedside companions. "I tried to keep your secret. He practically begged me to tell him. It was all the nurse could do to record his vitals before he flew out of there." He chuckled. "By the way, Barkley sends his love, too."

Melissa smiled as best she could. "I'm glad he's okay. What a mess, though. Were they able to save anything?"

"No, it doesn't look like it although we'll know more when we check it out personally. I hope we can save some of Dad's pictures at least." Jeremy sat on the edge of his chair. "How are you, really? Any injuries at all?"

"No, just some smoke inhalation. Like you, I'll bet. The doctors said I could go home, but we want to keep this charade going. We leaked the story to all the media outlets."

Sergeant Irving stood to leave. "I'll give the two of you some alone time. My officers are ready. When that creep arrives, we'll **arrest** him. I wish we knew what he looked like." He moved toward the door. "Be cautious Melissa. Use that gun if the need arises"

"Don't worry. I will." She waved to his retreating back. Her eyes focused on Chief. "Hey, remember last time. Chief was here. He warned me. Maybe he should stay with me now, too."

"That might not be such a bad idea." His scowl deepened. "You seem to be filled with a ton of them these days. Why would you want to go through this again?" Jeremy placed his hand on her arm. "I was scared you'd been seriously hurt." He studied her face. "Melissa, I realized last night that I care a great deal about you, not just as a friend, I mean."

"I care about you, too. We make a good team." She patted his hand.

Jeremy swallowed. "No, I mean. I care .... Melissa, I'm in love with you. I guess it took this to make me understand that I want us to be more than friends. Is that possible?"

Melissa's eyes glistened. "Jeremy I realized a long time ago that I wanted a relationship with you, not just a working partner- ship but ...." She ducked her head but shifted her gaze back to him. In a tiny voice, she added, "I love you too."

Chapter Sixty Seven

Melissa relaxed against the cool sheets on the hospital bed. One hand casually ruffled the top of Chief's head as he sat beside her. He jumped upwards, placing his front paws on the bed again. "Wanta come cuddle, Chief." She patted the side of the bed. The animal didn't spend any time thinking about his decision. He leapt with ease to land beside her. Melissa hugged his neck. "I've missed you so much."

Chief laid his head on her torso and closed his eyes. His warmth invaded the sheets. Melissa scratched his ears gently, as if coaxing him into a deep slumber. Her mind went over the words between Jeremy and her before he left. *I wonder what this will mean for our working relationship.* She smiled. *I'm glad this is out in the open. I was so afraid my love struck puppy appearance would give me away.*

Jeremy had been reluctant to leave. *I hope he doesn't become overprotective now.* She remembered the worried frown that adorned his face and his retreating back with shoulders slumped. *I wonder how I'd feel if the roles were reversed. Does loving each other mean that we will always be worried? I guess I worried about him before anyway. But we aren't supposed to worry.* The Bible verse from her morning devotions came to mind. *God says that worry doesn't add a thing to one's day. He wants us to leave our worries on His shoulders. Well, I guess Jeremy and I will need to practice that.*

She closed her eyes. *Lord, please protect Jeremy. Please keep me safe, help the officers out there be alert and help us catch this killer. Amen.* Melissa looked around the room. She was supposed to be seriously injured, helpless. Chief wouldn't be allowed on the bed if that were so. She ruffled his fur. "Off the bed, Boy." She pushed him toward the edge of the bed. Chief grunted his disapproval. He easily landed on the floor and, as if understanding his role in the scene that could soon happen, he walked over toward the bathroom, and lay down on the cooler ceramic tile. His eyes remained focused on his mistress, however.

Melissa lay still. She allowed her mind to conjure up all kinds of scenarios regarding her and Jeremy, but then started thinking about the danger she was in. That man wanted her dead. According to Jason Mitchell, Richard Belcher had hired him to eliminate his competition for control of Rompart. *But Jason obviously has no knowledge of the drug activity. If Belcher finds out I figured out how Rompart fits into the local drug trade, he has another reason for wanting me dead. We need to coerce a confession out of this guy to go after Belcher.*

Something metal clanged outside her door. Melissa's insides tightened. *Maybe a bowl or bedpan dropped by a clumsy orderly,* she mused. She willed her body to relax again. Another sound forced her ears on hyper mode. *I wish I knew what was happening out there.*

The door opened, an inch or two at first and then wide enough to bathe the room in incandescent light. Melissa opened one eye. A young woman dressed in hospital scrubs walked a step at a time toward the bed. "Miss Rompart. I wanted to assure you that the situation is well in hand. That man will not surprise us." She folded her arms across her chest. "Are you sure you'll be able to handle your end?" The woman's scepticism was showing.

"I'm a trained investigator. Besides, my trusty steed is with me." She pointed to Chief, the animal standing inside the bathroom door, ready to pounce on the woman who approached Melissa.

He growled so deep that the woman backed up a step or two. "I wasn't told you had a dog in here. He sure didn't stop me, though."

"Oh, if Chief thinks you mean me harm, he'll be all over you, believe me. Chief can be vicious when he needs to be." His tail still wasn't wagging. She chuckled. "It's okay Chief."

Melissa glanced at the nurse. "I assume you're one of Irving's officers."

"I am, ten years to be exact." She backed up to the door and reached behind her for the handle. "I'll tell the other two you're protected inside here as well. What about the nurses? Are they aware of his presence?"

"Yes, Jeremy told them before he left. I thought he was going to tell you guys as well." She paused. "I mean, he probably forgot." She reached under the sheet. Her hand wrapped around the cold steel of the gun Sergeant Irving had left with her. She waited.

The woman glanced toward Chief. With her back to the edge of the door, she paused before opening it. Slowly, her arm moved bringing her hand into view. A small black pistol filled her palm. She quickly trained it on her target. A silencer added to the length of the barrel.

Melissa raised the angle of the gun she kept hidden. She fingered the trigger and pressed, sending a bullet into the shoulder of the assassin. Chief bounded out of the bathroom, a ferocious snarl accompanied his body's intent on reaching his target. He wrapped his powerful jaws over the hand holding the pistol just as the door burst open. It hit the assailant right between the shoulder blades and knocked her off balance. Chief tugged her the rest of the way to the floor. The woman who entered trained her gun on the assailant's head before showing Melissa her badge.

Melissa swivelled toward the side of the bed. Her gun pointed at the woman's head. "Who hired you?"

The woman cursed; her scream ignited the animal even more. "Take this mongrel off me." She wriggled in an attempt to free her arm from the dog's sharp teeth. Her pain-filled screech increased in volume. "Tell him to release me."

Another female burst through the door and grabbed the gun out of the would-be shooter's hand. Glancing at Melissa, the woman unveiled the badge she hid beneath her shirt.

Melissa blinked. "Chief, stand." She watched the dog release his victim. "Officers, I am so glad to see you. Her shoulder will need attending but she didn't get the chance to fire a corresponding shot."

"I think you were well protected." One of the officers nodded at Chief. "But this is not who we expected."

"No, the earlier gunman was a man. He hired her, I'll bet. She almost succeeded. I forgot to check her ID when she entered the room. I thought she was one of yours." Melissa hung her head. "We need to find out if she knows who hired her."

Chapter Sixty Eight

Jeremy walked into the house he shared with Melissa, turned on the lights and stared at the wall. Taking a deep breath, at least as deep as he could without coughing, he entered the refurbished kitchen. *Matthew did a good job of invading my privacy. That boy is going to hurt something awful when the Lord takes Jenna home. He'll need a friend.*

He entered the bedroom area. *The place is too quiet.* He turned on the clock radio by his bedside. Soft jazz filtered through the room; the mellow sound eased his disquiet. He looked at the state of his clothes. *These will need some extra soaking.*

Stripping, he turned on the shower in his attached bathroom, and stepped under the fine spray from the large shower head. He stood still letting the water flow over his tired muscles. His back ached and his chest hurt. Breathing was easier as water splashed the sides of the shower stall all around him. He let the flow wash away the surface dirt.

Jeremy's thoughts returned to Melissa. She loved him. Now, why was he surprised? *She's independent, strong, efficient, and above all else self-sufficient.* He didn't think she'd ever need him for anything but .... He tossed his head to one side. *She asked for help with the Rempel woman.*

We work well together. That's why I wanted her to be a partner in the agency. His heart skipped a beat. *She's in danger and I'm at home taking a shower. What am I thinking? I need to be there.* He soaped himself from head to toe. *As soon as I dress ....* His body sagged. *I can't remember when I slept last.*

He rinsed off, making sure the soap took all the soot from the fire with it down the drain. Stepping out, he grabbed one of the new fluffy towels purchased when he made the move to this address. He wrapped it around his body and rubbed, hoping to stimulate some energy. His towel covered hands removed the excess water from his scalp.

The phone shrieked by his bed. He walked toward it at a brisk pace. Picking it up, he pressed answer and listened. "Is she okay?" He breathed a sigh of relief. "I should be there." The voice on the other end assured him they were handling things. "I'm coming. Don't take the woman downtown until I've had a chance to question her."

He threw some clothes on and marched back to his exit and his truck. His regret was overwhelming. *The killer could have succeeded.* His heart hurt at the idea. *I can't lose her, not now.*

Traffic was light. The truck made good time getting to the Health Sciences Centre. Jeremy parked and raced toward the entrance. He was always amazed how many people waited in this emergency room. He walked past and into a corridor leading to a bank of elevators.

One door opened. He was about to step in when a tall, slim man stepped out almost knocking him over. The man rushed toward the exit. Jeremy gave him a cursory glance but remained intent on his desire to reach Melissa. He pressed the button for the sixth floor.

Getting off, he headed for room 602. The door was open and three other people, two women, and a man were inside. He zeroed in on Melissa, headed toward her bed and leaned down for a hug. "You okay?"

Melissa smiled. She pointed toward the culprit. "I'm okay, no thanks to that woman. I guess we didn't expect him to hire someone else." She leaned against the pillows. "We need to find out what she knows."

"Yeah, I told them I wanted to talk to her." He ran his hand down the side of Melissa's face. Before turning to the task at hand, he mouthed the words 'I Love You'.

Melissa grabbed his hand for a tight squeeze.

Jeremy walked over to the lady handcuffed in a chair. "Who hired you?"

She sneered at him. "Like I'm going to tell you." She looked at the two officers, one on either side. "Arrest me or let me go. You can't prove anything. Her word means nothing and you know it." She wriggled against her restraints and then kicked out at anyone within reach.

Jeremy nodded toward the officers who held up a plastic bag

with a gun in it. Then he led them to a corner. "We're not going to extract anything from her until we bring the Crown Attorney on board. Maybe if we can offer her a plea, she'll give up the one who orchestrated this hit." They uncuffed the woman and forced her to stand. Grabbing hold of her arms, the officers secured them behind the assailant's back and led her from the room.

"But Jeremy." Melissa waved her free hand in the air. "We need some information."

He strode to her bedside. "She's not going to give us what we want until we offer her something in exchange. We need the Crown Attorney to cooperate with us. We've got her on attempted murder so she'll be going away for a long time unless ...."

"Yeah, I understand. The whole ordeal is just so frustrating. That guy is still out there. As long as he's free, he'll keep coming after me." She hung her head. "I just want all of this to end." She lay back on the bed. "Has Helen called? What about Elwood?"

Jeremy shrugged. "The investigation is young yet. I think the plan was to record Helen's statement tomorrow, first thing." He yawned. "I was getting out of the shower when Irving called." He glanced at Chief. "How did she sneak past him?"

"He was following my lead. He growled, which should have given me a clue, but no one expected the hitman to hire a hitman. I assumed she was one of the cops. When their replacements arrive, I want to meet them so I'll recognize the good guys from the bad guys." She sighed. "Go on home. I'll be okay. You look bushed."

Ignoring her, Jeremy pulled a chair close to her bedside. "I'm not leaving till they show up. Even then ...."

"Go home." She scowled as best she could above the bandages covering the lower half of her face. "You're no good to me all zonkey from lack of sleep." She reached for his hand.

Jeremy grasped hers tightly. "Melissa, where our relationship goes from here is anyone's guess but I don't want to lose you. I won't sleep if I don't think you're safe. I want time to explore our feelings for each other." He leaned closer and kissed the back of her hand.

Melissa's face seemed infused with colour. Her eyes sparkled. "I want that too, but first things first. We need to catch this guy. I hope the Feds will be able to build a strong enough case against Belcher from Helen and, now Jason's testimony, one that exonerates my Dad." She dropped her gaze. "Jeremy, how am I going to separate the legitimate parts of Rompart from the illegal entities. I won't deal with drug lords."

"Yeah, the thought crossed my mind that making those guys mad isn't a good move. I hope Elwood can provide some answers when we talk to him again. Maybe they know how to separate the cartel from the company's legitimate business enterprises. Maybe

Rompart will be forced to close its doors. One way or the other, something needs to happen in that regard." He squeezed her hand. "Not tonight. We'll take one step at a time."

She closed her eyes briefly and opened them to study Jeremy's face. "Maybe your Dad will be able to answer some of those questions. Right now, I'm so tired I could nod off while you sit here."

"Why don't you. I'll wake you when the officers walk through that door." He watched as words of protest formed between her lips. He placed a finger over her mouth. "No use. I'm not leaving till you're protected. That guy may come back but he's now aware that we're guarding you. We can pray he leaves the country, but we want him to implicate Belcher, don't we?"

Melissa nodded sleepily. She closed her eyes and this time they stayed that way. Jeremy heard the soft rhythmic breathing of her slumber as he continued to hold her hand. *I want this woman to be my wife.* The thought astounded him. *Really? Already?* He grinned. *Yeah, as soon as possible.*

He tucked Melissa's hand beneath the sheet. Watching her sleep, he contemplated a lifetime with her. *I wonder if she wants kids one day. She's so good with them. The children whom she's rescued all come to trust her even though few adults in their lives are trustworthy. She's so gentle with them.* His heart warmed at the idea.

He chuckled softly so as not to wake Melissa. *Dad will be pleased. He's been trying to push the two of us together ever since she asked Jesus into her life.* He glanced heavenward. *You, too, Lord. I think this is what you want. Please tell me if I'm on the wrong track. Protect her Father, no matter what. Help me be the man she needs and help us work out the details to your honour and glory. Thank you, Father, for this woman.*

He slouched a little, relaxing his very tired back muscles. Then he straightened again. *Those guys will be here soon. I'm going to check out this floor, see where he might elude them and sneak past their security. I want all bases covered so we can catch this guy.* He stood. The door kept the noise from the hallway to a dull roar. Not wanting to disturb Melissa, he scooted through as quickly and as quietly as possible.

Chapter Sixty Nine

Morning sunshine warmed the room as Helen waited for Elwood Friesen to arrive. The Royal Canadian Mounted Police task force was amassing evidence to bring down the drug traffic trade coming into Canada from Mexico. Everyone assumed all Mennonites were Christian and therefore above illegal involvement. Helen's experience differed.

In the beginning, they toed the line taught by the elders but Helen had learned those men behaved no better than the Pharisees from Jesus day. They used rules to control the people, but faith, at least in her village, was not a part of anything they lived or believed.

When she returned to Manitoba, Bible-based teaching was available to her. The teachings of Jesus, filled with love and acceptance, guided every aspect of life. A desire to serve out of love replaced the harsh rules and forced labour. Melissa explained the way and Helen became a true Christian.

Oh, I want my kids to find out about this Jesus. I want them to experience the love and peace I am now familiar with. I hope the police can bring them safely to me. A tear made its lonely way down the side of her cheek toward her neck. She swiped at it but marvelled that her eyes actually watered. *To cried when my husband hurt me, gave him an excuse to use it against me every time, calling me weak. No more.*

The elders had arranged her marriage to Henry Rempel. He was farming with his father and brothers in rural Manitoba. *My par-*

ents thought it was a good match. It was at first, but they feared for her when he began to suggest they move to Mexico. Others left as well fearing government involvement in the raising of their children. The trouble started a few years after they settled in Chihuahua.

Helen wrapped her sweater around her thin body. The room was warm but her memories caused a chill to creep up her spine. She glanced toward the two plain clothes officers playing cards at the dining room table. Their coffee cups probably needed refilling. *I can do that.*

She walked to the kitchen, grabbed the coffee pot, and brought it to her protectors. "Want a refill?"

The female officer pushed her cup closer. "Are you okay, Helen?" She smiled. "Staff Sergeant Friesen will soon be here and then we can begin taking your statement."

"I'm just worried about my kids. I don't want them to be hurt when the police enter the village. All those years we lived down there, they told us to be afraid of the police." She retreated back to the kitchen.

The officer followed. She held out her hand. "Helen, I'm Officer Jenkins. I am not familiar with the Mexican authorities but here, the police work hard for your protection. They uphold the laws of the country and we try hard to be friendly and helpful. For those on the wrong side of the law, we tend to be less congenial but that's to be expected. Right?"

Helen looked at the sincerity emanating from the officer's face. "There's no evidence of anything to be afraid of on this side of the border, but I don't trust those people down there. The police don't ever come to our village, though." She shrugged her shoulders. "I guess I fear what I don't understand."

The police officer smiled again. She guided Helen back to the living room. Glancing out the window, she spotted her sergeant's automobile. "There he is." She headed toward the front door.

Helen returned to her seat near the window. She felt like a small dog they once owned, who followed the sun around the farmyard during the morning hours, looking for a warm place to lie down. Her spot in the sun chased away the clouds that pushed their way into her thoughts.

As soon as he entered the safe house, Elwood Friesen strolled toward her, his heavy boots leaving damp spots on the well-worn carpet. "Good morning, Helen." He held out his hand. "Are you ready to get to work?"

Helen's small hand was lost in his large one. She smiled tentatively but her heart fluttered. *Oh, where is my courage when I need it.* She returned to her seat when the sergeant indicated her warm sunny spot was perfect for their conversation.

He took out a notepad. Then he placed a tape recorder on the table in front of her. "We record everything you tell us so we can get the details right. We'll begin with your recollection about the village itself."

Over the next two hours, Helen replayed life in Campos Tinades, Chihuahua, Mexico. The sergeant listened intently, stopping her once in a while for more details. His questions helped her focus but when she started to recall the abuse, her eyes glistened. She crossed her arms over her body, wrapping the sweater tighter. "I don't want to talk about this. It has nothing to do with drugs or anything."

"It'll help us understand the culture a little better." Elwood added a few notes to his pad of paper.

"It's a culture of abuse. In my village, they treat children as mules, at least the boys. They use them when they cross the border. Customs agents don't tend to search kids and the dogs leave them alone because their handlers don't suspect kids." She dropped her gaze. "Girls are used as slave labour around the house. The kids are beaten when they don't jump at the chance to do what they're told."

Elwood shook his head. "I understand this is hard, Helen. But if you want us to go in there and bring your kids out, we don't want any surprises. Let's work on the men who visited your village. Tell me who and what they looked like."

"I don't know who. My husband never introduced me to any of his drug dealing buddies. I only saw one or two of them. I recognized that one guy because Jeremy had a picture on his phone. Jeremy and Melissa gave him a name." Helen stood and began to pace in front of the police officer. "How helpful I can be is the question."

"Things you take for granted may be a clue for us. Let's just sit down and begin with one tiny piece of the puzzle at a time." He motioned toward the sofa.

Helen returned to her seat. "Okay. I'm sorry. I'm just scared"

Chapter Seventy

Jeremy strode through the emergency room doors and headed in the direction of the elevators. *I spend as much time here as I do at the office. Harrumph.* His scowl was firmly plastered in place as he pressed the button for the sixth floor. *Maybe this guy will give up. He might not be aware that we caught his hireling. Maybe .... Yeah, right. If Jason is telling the truth, this guy will protect his reputation.*

He moved aside when the elevator stopped on the fourth floor. Two men entered; one dressed in hospital scrubs but the other wore street clothes. Jeremy dropped his gaze. He sighed. *Keeping this woman safe is becoming a full-time job. Maybe, when this is all over, she'll concentrate on Rompart and leave the detecting to me. Yeah, I wish.*

The elevator stopped on the sixth floor. Jeremy took his time, allowing the other passengers to step off first. One did, and then he exited. He decided to check on the guards. He glanced at his watch. *The second shift is probably on duty now.* He scanned the room to check if he recognized anyone.

Little blond nurses, intermingled with a few brunettes, scurried up and down the corridor, replacing equipment, entering rooms, and balancing trays of medications. A few male counterparts worked hard but he couldn't tell if they were nurses or orderlies. Everyone appeared busy with tasks they focused on. *Where are the cops?*

None stood out who might not belong. *Either they're good at their job or they've pulled the cops off this floor for some reason.* His heart raced. He quickened his pace to check on Melissa.

Striding toward room 602, he placed his fist on the door. Before he had a chance to knock, he was shoved inside. Two well-trained assailants had his hands behind his back and cuffs circling his wrists before he could utter a word of protest. They yanked his arms to one side rotating his body to face them. "Wh-what ...."

"What are you doing in this room?" The shortest woman to ever cross his path stood toe to toe with him and stared upwards, her eyes blazing with intent. Her right hand held a gun aimed for his lower abdomen. "Who are you?"

Laughter bubbled from their protected witness. "It's okay, Levinia. He's my partner, Jeremy." Melissa swiped at the bandages covering her lower jaw.

Jeremy scowled. He tried to raise his hands secured behind him. He heard the click when they released the cuffs. His upper arms relaxed. "You guys were well hidden. I couldn't spot you when I got off the elevator." He ambled over toward the bed.

His fist landed on Melissa. "You think that was funny, eh?" He grinned when she rubbed her upper arm.

"We're good at what we do. If you could spot us, we wouldn't be effective, now would we?" The short woman tucked her handcuffs into the pocket of her scrubs. She reached a hand toward Jeremy. "Hi. I'm Levinia Sharp. Joshua and I came on duty this morning. This is our specialty, laying a trap for some gun creep."

Jeremy accepted her hand shake and one from Joshua as well. "Wouldn't it be better, though, if you let the guy attempt to kill his target. I thought the police planned not to give him the option of saying he got the wrong room or something." He glanced around for Chief. "Where's the dog?"

Melissa's eyes roamed from one guardian to the other. "So you think they should let the guy shoot me before they arrest him? Thanks a lot." She pretended to cast a mean look in his direction. "Chief needed to go for a walk. There's a third undercover agent out there somewhere."

"Agents. What? From where?" Jeremy hands gravitated towards his waist.

The male nurse stood a little taller. "We're here with the FBI. We're working closely with the RCMP now since this case is crossing two borders and the drugs they manufacture are exported into the US as well as Canada." He deferred to the short one.

Jeremy pursed his lips. "So, you guys are protecting Melissa because ....?"

"She's a material witness." The woman walked across the room toward Melissa. "Not only does she own Rompart, but she was also raised on a ranch in Texas where some of the drugs are crossing onto American soil. We haven't made the connection as yet but the ranch is under surveillance."

"Wow. How long have you known about this? Are the Finders involved? I thought Conrad was genuinely concerned about Melissa." Jeremy's eyes betrayed the shock he felt over this latest piece of news.

"Whoa. Hold on, too many questions, not enough answers." The woman claimed the chair near the window. "All we found out so far is that the trail leads there. We haven't figured out who's involved so we're watching the place. We also planted someone undercover there as well."

Melissa shifted in the bed. "They told me all this when they came on duty. I can't think that I can be much help, though. I don't remember seeing anything suspicious."

The door sighed as it opened. Chief trotted toward his mistress.

"Boy, this animal possesses a one track mind. He let me know in no uncertain terms he wasn't interested in walking too far from this hospital." A larger man, also dressed in hospital garb, walked in right behind the dog.

Chief's tail expressed his greeting to Jeremy. "Hi, boy." Jeremy rubbed the animal's head between his ears. He glanced from one agent to the other. "So-o-o, how long are you planning to wait for this killer to make his move?"

"The information the police extracted from Mitchell about this thug is he's thorough. It appears he hired someone to reconnoitre how well she was protected, to force us to reveal ourselves, which we did. Now we go to plan B." The officer walked out of the room and came back before anyone said another word with three extra chairs.

As soon as he entered, Melissa piped up, "What's plan B?"

"We knew you had a partner so we wanted to wait until everyone was here but we think we can move you. He still thinks you're critical or near so. So we can do a well-publicized move to another facility which is better protected, tighter security. He'll be forced to make his move before then. Then we'll capture him." Levinia crossed her arms. "Chief and you can go home. We'll take it from here. You'll be protected there, of course, at least until we catch the guy but you don't need to put your life at further risk." Her feet swayed just above the floor under the chair she occupied.

Melissa yanked the bandages off her jaw line. "I can't say I'll be sad these are no longer necessary. How do you plan to let this guy think I'm on my way to the rehab facility when I'm really at home? Somehow, he seems to find out where I am at all times."

"Yeah, well. We found a mole inside your group of confidants." The man named Joshua twitched his finger in a circular fashion. "Jeremy, I believe you are familiar with Matthew Cavanaugh?"

"I do. Nice kid when he's not mad at you. What about him?"

"Do you discuss what's going on when you visit Jenna? When he's there?" Joshua grunted when he said the last three words.

Jeremy eyes grew wide. "No. Can't be. Melissa rescued that kid or at least we helped him escape from a paedophile .... You think he's involved? How?"

"He's been working for the drug cartel all along. He strung you along, telling you about some fictitious creeps who kidnapped him because he knew what you did for a living. He's actually in his twenties and looking to add to his riches. He's using Jenna to gain information. When you visit, you talk about stuff with her and she talks to him. He's dangerous. Don't give yourself away when you go visit your friend today." Levinia chuckled. "We'll use him to tell the people he works for where and when you'll be transported, Melissa, and leave the rest up to the hitman."

Jeremy plunked himself down in the edge of the bed. He grabbed Melissa's hand. "Some investigator I am. I missed all the clues." He shook his head; his eyes scanned the people in the room. "He had us all fooled."

Melisa rubbed the back of his hand. "You need to protect Jenna."

"No." Levinia almost shouted the word. "If you act as if anything changed, this won't work. He won't hurt her. He needs her to stay close to you."

Melissa glanced at the woman. She studied Jeremy's profile. "Didn't he commit his life to ....?"

"Yes he did." Jeremy frowned. He glanced at the agents. "He became a Christian ...." Jeremy's mind was having a hard time with all this. ".... so he could earn Jenna's confidence. He said all the right things, asked all the right questions." His frown became a scowl. "I guess some people just say what they think you want to hear. They ingratiate themselves into your life but are wolves in sheep's clothing." His eyes filled with dread. "One day he's going to understand how wrong he was."

"You still care about this kid; after all he's done to you and your friend? I'd want him behind bars where he can't hurt anyone else. Aside from what he's led you to believe, he's selling drugs on the streets of your city. He's ...." Joshua planted his feet apart and dropped his arms to his knees.

".... a sinner. Just like us." Melissa spoke almost in a whisper. She looked at Jeremy. "I hate to say it but I'll be glad when he's caught so he can't hurt Jenna anymore. She's going to be devastated."

Jeremy's eyes glistened as they always did when thinking of his friend. "Yes she is." He hung his head.

Chapter Seventy One

Matthew held the hand of the woman he pretended to care about. She was sleeping, her soft shallow breaths testifying to the effort it took her to breathe. *I really don't care.* He yanked his hand from her grasp.

His lean body slouched on the hard backed chair dragged beside her bed. Her insistence had placed him there, hadn't it? *I was perfectly happy sitting across the room.* He scowled. *This is getting monotonous.* He looked at her. *No one ever cared about whether he was in the room or not, whether he was alive or dead. People only cared when their business was affected.* He sniffed. She was different.

His walked toward the window. He rubbed his backside. *That chair is not built for someone to sit in for hours.* He scowled at the bright sunlight streaming into the room. He felt exposed. He checked if he could detect anyone outside who didn't look as if they belonged. *Why am I worried? I have them all fooled. They're dummies. They'll believe anything. Harrumph. Dumb fools.*

He remembered the tears this woman shed when he'd revealed his fake story. *It was so easy. And that dude. Another chump. The man had fallen for it hook, line, and sinker.* Matthew dropped his head. Jeremy loved Jenna too. *At least he says he does. But he did go away.*

He glanced at the bed again. *She looks so frail.* Would her death mean anything to him? *Yeah, like no more information.* He swallowed. There'd be no one who'd fight for him. He thought about that for a minute. *Fight for him. When has she ever done that?* He knew she would. *Why? I lied to her. She believes me.*

He leaned against the window casing, his eyes unseeing as his inner turmoil played itself out. The woman had tried to explain love to him. The other day, when it looked like she could die at any moment. She tried to tell him that without her he still had someone who loved him. *Yeah, right. This Jesus person again. She is one religious nut. She thought her religion solved all her problems. Fat chance. She's dying. No help there.*

He sucked in a breath. The thought paralyzed him. Why? He was playing a role ... To obtain information ... Nothing more. He sauntered toward the bed. He didn't want her to wake and not find him sitting by her side. That seemed important. *To her? No, to me. Why does it matter?* He returned to his seat. His eyes took in the slight rise to her chest. Her face was so grey. Wrinkles had appeared almost overnight when the weight fell off. He ran his hand over the thin sheet that covered her.

His eyes leaked. Was he crying? *I don't cry.* He swiped angrily at the moisture accumulating, blurring his vision. *Look what she's gone and done. She's made me soft.* A sob escaped but he sucked it back in. *I don't care. I don't.* A few more tears dripped past his nose. A fissure opened in his heart. He could feel it as if a physical breaking happened. He hiccoughed.

Tears streamed down his face. His eyes were closed but the anguish continued to direct his pain. A soft finger traced the back of his hand. Matthew's eyes flew open. Jenna smiled. He stood so abruptly that the chair hit the floor with a loud bang. He strode to the bathroom, cursing under his breath.

"Crying is okay Matthew." He heard the words as he entered the sterile, cold little room. He slammed the door. Yanking some tissues from the box provided, he swiped at his face. He couldn't remember ever crying before. *What's with this?* To admit it went against everything he believed. They couldn't hurt you if you didn't care.

He slid his foot across the threshold. Jenna was staring at him. She patted the bed beside her. Matthew pushed one foot in front of the other. He reached for the hand she extended. His torso hit the chair hard.

"I understand Matthew. Watching someone die is hard. You don't have to be here." Her voice was so weak. She coughed, her effort to speak a gargantuan task.

He scowled. "You don't want me here?"

Jenna smiled. He had to lean closer to hear. "I do. I love seeing your face when I wake up." She straightened her head on the pillow. "You don't care about people easily, do you?"

He blinked. How had she figured him out so quickly? "Not too many people in my life to care about, remember." He studied the sense of peace she conveyed. "You smile all the time. You aren't afraid, are you?"

Jenna took a shallow breath and then a second before answering. "Where I'm going, Matthew, Jesus is waiting for me." She shifted her gaze to the door.

Jeremy walked in. "Hi Jenna." He glanced briefly at Matthew before focusing on Jenna as he strode to her beside. "How's it going?"

Jenna opened her mouth but was cut off. Matthew cursed under his breath before responding out loud. "How da ya think she's doing? She's dying? She's in pain all the time and she has a hard time breathing." He stood, his confrontational stance barring Jeremy's access to his friend.

Jenna reached for his hand resting on her bed. She patted it and smiled apologetically toward Jeremy. Jeremy's body relaxed. He nodded and then walked to the other side of the bed. He gazed at Matthew for a few seconds. "I'll try to be here more often." He pulled the softer armchair closer to the bed. "I plan to stay for a while, Matthew, if you want to go to the cafeteria for something to eat."

Matthew returned to his seat. "No, that's okay. I might eat something a little later." His eyes dropped to the floor. "Sorry I jumped on you, man." He looked upward again. "How is Melissa?"

Jeremy glanced heavenward again but then looked at Jenna. His eyes spoke louder than his next words. "We're moving her to ...."

"You're. In. Love. With. The. Girl." Jenna grinned around each breath. "It's. About. Time."

Jeremy shifted his body uncomfortably. "I .... we ..... yes, we're in love. But ...."

"She. Told. You?" If it wasn't for the knowledge that Jenna had a few days left at most, Matthew thought she'd have jumped out of the bed to give Jeremy a hug. She looked as if a reprieve had been given to her.

Jeremy's heightened colour forced a giggle from the dying woman. His countenance sobered as he finished his sentence. "Her life is still in danger. We're moving her to a Rehab facility so we can better protect her." He tossed his head exuding confidence. "We'll catch that killer one way or the other."

Matthew rested his elbows on his knees. "When is this going to happen?" He tried not to appear too eager for the news. "What rehab?" He watched Jeremy for any sign of caution. There was none.

"We're taking her to Deer Lodge later today. She'll heal better with more individualized attention. Her room will be private, away from the other patients, so we won't jeopardize anyone else. The ambulance will take her. The cops are setting everything up at the facility as we speak." He leaned back in the chair. "Jenna, can I bring you something, water maybe?"

She shook her head. Then she grabbed her Bible from the bedside table. "Read." She handed it to Jeremy.

"I'll go find some food while you're reading to her." Matthew stood slowly. "Want anything, Jeremy? Coffee, maybe?" He turned toward the door.

"Coffee would be great. Thanks, Matthew." He opened the Bible to the book of John.

Matthew left the room, took a deep breath, and headed toward the phones near the elevator.

Chapter Seventy Two

Melissa raised her arm as the nurse cut away the bandages. She would not miss the restrictive pressure they caused. Her jaw moved easier, stripped of the restricting bandages. "I'll be glad to return home." Chief kept his eyes focused on his mistress. She reached for his head as soon as her arm was free. "You too, huh boy?"

The dog yipped. Melissa laughed along with Levinia, who stood by her side. "The decoy will leave this hospital in an hour. That'll give Jeremy time to come escort you home. Did he call yet?"

"No." Melissa reached for her phone. She checked to make sure it was turned on. As soon as she picked it up, the ringtone assigned to Jeremy sounded. She pressed the speaker button before answering. "Hello, Jeremy. How's Jenna?"

"Ask her yourself. She's right here."

"Hi Jenna. I wish I could come visit you but ...."

A weak version of the woman Melissa had come to respect spoke next. "I. Understand." She paused. "When. You're. All. Healed."

Melissa felt the moisture fill her eye socket before she spoke again. Keeping her voice light, she added. "Lord, give Jenna an extra measure of Your peace."

"Thanks. Melissa." Her raspy words left a different picture in Melissa's psyche. The woman was going home soon.

Jeremy spoke next. "I'm reading the Bible to Jenna while Matthew gets something to eat. Melissa, I told Jenna our plans before Matthew left."

"Oh, okay." She knew better than to spill what they suspected about Matthew. They saw no need to distress the woman farther. "We'll talk when you return. Take your time."

The phone went dead. Melissa ended the call as well. "So all we have to do is wait to hear how our subterfuge worked." She sat on the edge of the bed.

Levinia cleared her throat. "Yes and we'll arrest Matthew Cavanaugh momentarily. He has a lot to answer for and his information will be used to put another nail in the coffin of this drug gang."

"Do you think you'll be able to extract any information from him? If he could fool us into thinking he was a teenage victim, he is pretty hardened. He might be willing to protect those creeps at all costs." Melissa bowed her head. "I find it so hard to believe that the person you described is the man we're familiar with. He seems so credible."

"Yeah, well, he's been trained by professional criminals. It's anybody's guess how long they've been using him." Levinia rolled the sleeves of her shirt down to her wrists. She buttoned the cuffs. "I'm going to oversee the transfer of the pretend Melissa. You stay right here until Jeremy gets back."

Melissa watched the small woman leave the room. *She may be small but she's feisty and she has the experience.* The nurse continued to disconnect her from all the lines that had been inserted to further the appearance of critical when she was admitted. *One day and it feels like I was admitted more than a week ago.*

She glanced at Chief. *He'll be happy to be home.* Grabbing the outfit worn into the hospital, she removed her hospital gown and began getting dressed. *Yuck! These clothes smell of soot and smoke. They'll need a good washing.* Bending, she tied up her boots. Walking to the bathroom, she checked her reflection in the mirror. *I guess Jeremy will have to put up with the odour.*

She walked to the window and peered out at the sunshine. Then she ducked back behind the window frame. *I wouldn't want a watcher to notice me. That man needs to think I'm leaving in the ambulance.*

Melissa decided to sit on the softer chair in front of the window. She expected Jeremy to take his time. Reading to Jenna was the least he could do. The woman had kept his office running smoothly for the last five years. *Besides, he needs to make sure Matthew plays his part in this charade.*

She leaned back against the cushions. Closing her eyes, she

thought about the way her relationship with Jeremy had changed. She placed her hand over her heart. *Wow! Hearts actually can skip beats.* Her grin widened. *I like him .... a lot .... for a while now so why does he affect me differently now that he's told me he loves me?* She wanted to shout. *I feel vindicated. This thing is not one sided. He loves me.*

She giggled. *What will life be like now? Will we work together still or maybe, I can take Jenna's place as his assistant. No, that won't work. I'm committed to running Rompart. But ....*

The door whooshed open. Melissa, a smile of greeting in place, opened her eyes. Not Jeremy. The words registered before she recognized the man who stood inside the door with a gun pointed at her. She planted her backside firmly in the chair when she sat up, a gasp escaping through tight lips. "Richard, what's going on? Why do you have a gun?"

The man placed a foot forward. He wheeled around to the dog who growled menacingly at him. "Call him off or I'll kill him too." The gun was pointed at Chief but then swivelled toward Melissa. "Like you haven't figured out why I'm here. Nice scam this. You think I'm stupid?" He took another step toward her. "You couldn't leave things alone. You had to meddle. Your Dad was the same. He had to stick his nose where it didn't belong and we had to take care of him. Now you."

Melissa used her hand signals to quiet Chief. The dog walked toward the bathroom, turned and was about to jump toward Belcher when the man threw a piece of meat in his direction. Chief's jaws clamped on the food, something he missed for almost twenty-four hours and swallowed. His mouth opened exposing dangerous canines as he lunged toward the gunman. Belcher sidestepped just in time. The dog went down and stayed there.

"What did you do? Chief. Chief." Melissa began to rise but changed her mind when Belcher extended his arm toward her, the silencer almost touching her face. Her involuntary shudder exposed the lie her stiff posture tried to convey. "I don't understand. What did my Father uncover?"

Richard Belcher's face reddened. His eyes sparked with anger. His hand shook as it held the weapon waving it from floor to ceiling. "You Rompart's are all alike. Boy Scouts. The world doesn't operate that way. The person with connections and smarts becomes wealthy, not some do-gooder who only wants to house homeless people. I fought your Father every time he wanted to turn this warehouse or that building into some resort for old bums. My way, we made tons of money and no one was hurt in the process. Rompart exists today as one of Winnipeg's most successful enterprises because of me. The drug kingpins I do business with, need to launder their millions and I gave them a way to do that. Win, win. Then you come along." He pointed the gun at Melisa again.

Her body trembled. The memory of her Father and Mother lying in a pool of their blood washed over her. The nightmare that plagued her on and off for years was becoming real. She lifted her chin. With tearless eyes, she scowled at the man responsible for their deaths. "You left me without parents because of your greed. They were good people, and now I can prove it." She tossed her head, pretending a reassurance she was not experiencing.

"And what are you going to do about it, missy? You're as dead as they are. The nurse put a 'do not disturb' sign on your door so no one is going to interrupt us for a while. You think you and that nosy lawyer of yours can outsmart me? My organization will mourn your death as the owner of Rompart but I will continue to do business as usual." He shook the gun at her; his high-pitched voice screamed. "With no interference from you."

Melissa placed a smug expression on her face. He doesn't know the FBI is involved. "Everything has to come to an end sooner or later, Richard. For a good many years you've amassed the wealth you wanted. Now why don't you put down that gun and leave? I'll give you a head start before I call the RCMP."

"What can you tell them? You have no proof. Besides, I'm not ready to retire." His hand steadied the weapon as he pushed the centre of her forehead.

The click revealed his finger was about to squeeze the trigger. She closed her eyes slowly; dread filling every blood vessel and artery. A noise and then a grunt. Her eyes popped open with the sound of the gun sliding across the floor. Two men wrestled, each reaching for the runaway gun. *Jeremy.*

Melissa tucked her feet under her, away from the bodies hitting and gouging each other. Her heart skipped another beat, this time for the danger Jeremy was in. His fist landed on Richard Belcher's jaw. The bed crashed against the far wall and the wheeled table went spinning toward the bathroom. Chief was in the middle of it, his teeth bared as he snapped and snarled. Belcher had underestimated the dog's love for his mistress and his strength of character.

The racket brought a nurse who immediately closed the door again when she saw what was happening. Melissa hoped she was calling the police.

The fight between the two men suddenly ended. Chief stood over the assailant, his head bent with his mouth ready to tear the man apart. Jeremy lay panting on his side. He'd managed to grab the gun and had it pointed at Belcher's mid-section. He rolled to his knees and pushed his body off the floor. "Now, we'll wait until the police arrive."

Melissa swung her feet to the floor. She marched toward the CEO of Rompart Industries and swung her foot to kick him. "You hurt my dog." Her foot landed on the man's right kidney. His grunt was the most satisfying sound in the room. She looked at Jeremy. "He admitted he was the one who had my Father killed."

"I was listening at the door" He wrapped his arms around Melissa. "Are you alright?"

She laid her head on his shoulder. "I am now." Melissa looked upwards and then stepped back to inspect his face. "What about you? That was some fight." She reached her hand toward Chief but the dog was intent on making sure his prey was staying put.

"No broken bones." He strode toward Belcher. "Come on. Let's prepare you for transport to the city lockup if the Feds will leave you there. They have some very interesting questions for you. With the charge of attempted murder, drug trafficking and money laundering hanging over you, cooperating with the authorities might benefit you some. People who have drug cartel connections and end up in prison don't last long."

Belcher grunted but had no words for either of them. Melissa commanded Chief to release. Jeremy yanked the would-be assassin to his feet, and tied his hands with an electric cord he found in the bathroom.

Chief wobbled toward Melissa. She snarled at her former CEO. "What did you feed him?" She raised a hand to hit the man again.

Richard Belcher curled his lips, hatred spewing from a once refined vocabulary. "You witch. A sedative" was too good for him. I wish I'd blown his head off like I ordered for your good old parents. If my man had caught you that day we wouldn't be having this little conversation." He sneered, emitting a gleam of satisfaction over past deeds. "They got what they deserved."

Melissa opened her mouth to reply but clamped it shut. *Nothing I can say will bring them back or make him any nicer.* She leaned into Jeremy's side.

"Oomph." He winced. "Ah-h, honey, take it easy. I may have some cracked ribs after all."

Melissa glanced at his face. *Was he serious?* Then she rushed toward the door. As she reached it, the door opened almost hitting her in the face.

Sergeant Irving stepped into the room. "Where are you going, young lady, in such a hurry?"

"Jeremy needs a doctor. He's hurt." She rushed from the room.

Chapter Seventy Three

The sergeant examined the bindings holding Richard Belcher's hands. "I think some cuffs might be more reliable."

"I made do with what I had. I expected you'd bring some with you when you got here." Jeremy rubbed his side. "This case is going to take a long time to unravel. At least we know that Melissa's dad was unaware of the complete scope of his company's crooked dealings before he was killed. Belcher admitted to hiring their deaths because Parker Rompart wanted to turn his warehouses into homeless shelters. I heard that part before I interrupted his plan to kill Melissa."

The sergeant motioned toward a junior officer. "Take him downtown." He turned toward Jeremy. "You and Melissa will need to give a statement. Then we'll work out whose jurisdiction this case belongs to. With the FBI involved as well as the RCMP and the city police, this is one interesting case."

Jeremy's countenance changed suddenly. He smacked his side forgetting his injuries. "Jenna needs me. Matthew is still there with her and he is tied to the drug lords the FBI are after."

"We took him into custody already. We caught him when he was talking to Belcher on the phone about the decoy the FBI had in place."

"He phoned Belcher directly? I wondered why he never returned before I left Jenna."

Sergeant Irving walked toward the door. "He's spilling his guts. Evidently, he's not as loyal to those guys as even he thought, something about religion or Jenna. He's naming names and looking for a plea bargain."

Melissa rushed back into the room with a doctor right behind. She nodded at Bill Irving but continued on toward Jeremy. "This doctor will tell us whether your ribs are broken or not."

"Melissa, there's no time for this. I need to stay with Jenna. They've arrested Matthew so she's all alone." Jeremy took a second step toward the door.

"Sir, this won't take long." The doctor appeared at his side. He asked Jeremy to raise his shirt. Dark ugly bruises had already begun to form over his rib cage. As soon as the doctor placed his hand along Jeremy's right side, his groan of pain spoke volumes. "Let's get some ex-rays."

Jeremy tugged his shirt back in place. "I need ...."

"Jeremy, let them look after you. I'll go visit Jenna. I'll meet you there." She looked at the sergeant. "Can I finagle a ride to the Misericordia?"

"Sure. Right on our way." He looked at Jeremy. "Take care."

Melissa's eyes pleaded as she turned toward the first man she'd ever cared for since her Father. "Please, Jeremy. Do what the doctor says. Then come to Jenna. We'll be waiting."

He smiled. "So is this what life is going to be like from now on. I don't need a mother, Melissa." He put up his hands in a posture of surrender as soon as he saw the protest on her lips. "Fine. I'll go." He grinned. "I won't be too long, I hope.. Give Jenna a hug, gently."

Melissa walked out of the room ahead of him and the doctor. She marched toward the elevator, turning around once to make sure Jeremy was following doctor's orders.

Sergeant Irving was holding the elevator. "Sooo. Are those sparks I detect between you and Jeremy?" He pressed the button for the first floor.

Melissa grinned. "Something like that." She decided to change the subject. "Did you come in one car or two?"

"Two. Why?"

Melissa exited the elevator ahead of the robust police officer. "I've seen as much of Richard Belcher today as I ever want to. Riding with him would not be pleasant and I'm about ready for pleasant."

Sergeant Irving chuckled as they walked through the exterior doors of the hospital. "Your life is certainly **eventful** to say the least. How is Jenna anyway?"

"Only God knows how long we'll have her with us." She

hung her head. "Jeremy is going to miss that woman."

Chapter Seventy Four

Melissa placed one foot in front of the other. *It's been a long time since I witnessed someone die.* She shuddered. *I don't want to do it now.* She closed her eyes for a second. The hustle and bustle around her testified to the serious condition of the person she was about to see. *Lord, give me the right words.*

She walked into the room where Jenna Fisher would spend her last hours. Melissa plastered a smile on her face. "Hi Jenna." She reached her hand toward the woman who matched her smile for smile.

Jenna grabbed her hand and drew Melissa close to enable her to wrap her arms around the younger woman's neck. "Oh, Melissa. I am so ...." She took a shallow breath. ".... Glad to see you. How. Are. You. Doing?"

Melissa hugged the woman, her gentle touch controlled so she wouldn't harm her frail body. "I'm okay now that we have Richard Belcher in custody. Jeremy will be right over as soon as the doctor takes care of his sore ribs."

"He. Is? Belcher is. In custody? Tell. Me."

Melissa found herself taking a deep breath every time Jenna paused to inhale. "Let me tell you the whole story. Save your strength, okay." She patted Jenna's hand and checked the room for another chair. She suspected Jeremy would want to sit close as soon as he arrived.

"Jeremy told you about the ruse we planned to capture the hitman, right? Well, Mat ...." She caught herself just in time. "Belcher got a call from someone who told him about our plan but he figured we were playing him so he ended up at the hospital. He decided to do the job himself. He almost succeeded but Jeremy got there right before he pulled the trigger."

The older woman's hands fluttered as if wanting to know something. "Chief?" Jenna's one-word question spoke volumes.

"Yeah, he was there but Belcher anticipated that, brought some doctored meat that put him down really fast. But when Jeremy arrived, Chief pushed himself up and helped take that creep down." She did a fist bump in the air for Jenna's benefit.

"Like. That. Dog." Jenna coughed. She reached for a tissue from the box on her table.

Melissa handed one to her and went on with the story. "One of the nurses must have called the police because the FBI agents were gone according to plan. Anyway, Jeremy tied Belcher up before the cops could arrive. But my former CEO knows how to fight so before Chief jumped in to help, Jeremy ended up with some sore ribs. I went to find a doctor and we pushed him to attend to his ribs before he left."

Jenna grinned. "Chief?"

"He stayed with Jeremy who'll drop him home before he comes here. He's had enough excitement for one day. On the way over here, I phoned Denny to come and take him to his ranch for a rest." She leaned her forearms on the edge of the bed. "What about you? Can I do anything for you?

Jenna shook her head. She reached for the oxygen mask draped over the rail on the bed. Melissa helped settle the mask in place. Jenna's face relaxed. She closed her eyes. "Melissa. Read. Please."

Melissa picked up the Bible and turned to the gospel of John. The Apostle John had been loved by Jesus and he loved his Lord so his words infused confidence in the Majesty of Jesus. She began at verse one.

While she read, she watched for any sign that Jenna had nodded off. The woman smiled now and then with a sense of peace beyond understanding, at least to Melissa. Once in a while, her eyes popped open and she looked toward the bottom of the bed. The smile became brighter during those moments.

Melissa paused after the first chapter. Jenna turned her head toward her. She lifted the mask away from her face and flipped the bands holding it off her head. "You. And. Jeremy?"

Melissa felt the blush creep over her face before she had a chance to look away. Jenna's laugh sounded like the distant tinkling of a fairy bell. "You're incorrigible. Always the matchmaker." She shook a finger at her dying friend. She is a friend. I've been acquainted with her such a short time but ... "I'll tell you but don't you repeat a word to Jeremy. He and I .... well .... how do I describe our relationship?"

Jenna was the one to wag her finger this time. "Jeremy. Told. Me." She grinned. "About. Time. When's. The. Wedding?"

Melissa almost choked. "Wedding? Who said anything about a wedding? Did Jeremy? Only yesterday he told me he loved me."

Jenna's stern countenance evaporated into a smile. "Don't wait. He. Needs. Someone. He can. Count on." She paused and replaced the mask with Melissa's help.

"Who can count on?" Jeremy's masculine timber almost caused Melissa to fall off her chair. Jenna just stared at her friend and former boss. "I got here as soon as I could." He looked toward Melissa. "How's she doing?"

"Besides acting as Winnipeg's premier matchmaker, fine. She is using her oxygen more often, though."

"I noticed that when I was here earlier."

Jenna thumped her hand in the bed. "I'm. Still. Here."

Jeremy chuckled. He leaned toward the older woman and gave her body a squeeze. "Jenna. Did Melissa read to you a bit?"

She nodded her head. She took another breath as if she'd been holding it. "Fine. Job." She reached around Jeremy and patted Melissa's hand. She closed her eyes. Her head seemed to melt into the pillow. She reopened her eyes and gazed at the two of them. Her smile told them she was pleased with the way things had turned out. "Lord. Loves. You." She worked hard to speak through the mask. "Get. Married."

Jeremy glanced at Melissa and smiled. She grabbed his hand. She hoped the gesture demonstrated her compliance. Without another word spoken, Jeremy began to pray. "Lord, you know my friend Jenna very well. She is a servant for You. Please make her breathing easier and help her know that You are waiting to tell her 'well done, good and faithful servant'. Thank you for the example she's been to me and to Melissa. Amen."

As soon as Jeremy finished, Jenna took a shallow breath, exhaled slowly and deeply but never inhaled again. The alarm attached to her heart monitor began to buzz.

Two nurses rushed in, gently moved Melissa and Jeremy aside, and checked for a pulse. They shook their heads. "She's gone. I'm so sorry," one of them said. She patted Jeremy's forearm. "We'll leave the two of you alone with her for a few minutes. We need to prepare her for departure to the morgue and the funeral home she wanted us to notify." The woman bowed her head as did the other nurse and they quietly slipped out.

Jeremy didn't realize he was crying until his body shook with a great heaving sob. Melissa wrapped her arms around him but her vision was as blurred as his was. They both understood that Jenna was home now. The missing would be the hardest.

Melissa glanced upwards. Jeremy's tears were new to her. His eyes were raining and she wasn't sure what to say. Her body shook with his, both inconsolable for the moment. Jenna had been a wonderful woman.

Melissa was the first to gain control of her emotions. She eased out of Jeremy's grasp and grabbed the box of tissues from Jenna's bedside table. Handing a fistful to Jeremy, she used some herself to dry her eyes and face.

Jeremy walked toward the window and back to Jenna's side. "Goodbye old friend. We'll be seeing you." He moved back toward the window and pulled his cell phone out of his pocket. He pressed the speed dial for his Father. "Jenna's gone home to be with the Lord." He listened for a few seconds and glanced at Melissa. "She's here with me." Then, "Yes, she is. We'll talk later. Apparently, Jenna had made all ...." He paused to listen. "She did. Well, I guess we will be talking later." He replaced the phone and stared at Jenna. "Dad was her lawyer. That's news to me. The funeral is all planned out. All we have to do is show up."

Melissa walked to his side and wrapped her arm around his middle, careful to not squeeze too hard. "Why does that surprise you? She was an efficient woman who accepted she was dying. Let's go home and let the nurses do what they have to. I assume your Dad will provide the information about which church, etc."

Jeremy took a step toward the door and turned back to Jenna. He leaned down to give her a final hug. "I love you, Jenna." Tears began to flow again as he looked toward Melissa. Anguish covered his face as he swiped at his eyes again. "I'm gonna miss her."

Melissa led the way out of the room and toward the elevator. She reached for Jeremy's hand to give comfort but also as if it were a lifeline.

Epilogue

Melissa shoved the last of her belongings into the box. She carefully moved some papers aside to make room for the file folder containing all the details from her last case. *I thought the rest of my life would be spent looking for missing kids.* She hung her head.

Guilt, a new emotion for her, reared its ugly head. An image of a small child with pleading eyes floated through her psyche. *Get thee behind me*, she prayed, knowing her enemy was trying to move her away from God's plan.

Her determination firmly in place, she glanced toward the door to her office. Jeremy approached, his smile forced. "You are convinced God wants you to fund others to do the searching but ...." He glanced out the window. "I'm going to miss you. The picture of us working together took root in my brain some time ago."

"I thought along those lines as well. I've missed seeing you every day, too. I'll miss the satisfaction of knowing we put some twisted perverts away for a long time. I'm glad they found the kids from the creepy pastor's church to testify against him. I wish the law would force paedophiles to pay restitution. Their victims will never be the same and usually require many years of sometimes costly therapy." A grimace slid across her face just before she hugged him.

"Anyway, as comforting as all that is, I can't just leave my father's company unattended. Now that the FBI and the RCMP confiscated the illegal entities Belcher attached to Rompart, I am free to run the company as he wanted. Besides, I wasn't cut out for the sickness pervading human trafficking. I think my health was beginning to be affected. My sleep has improved since making this decision."

Jeremy sat on the corner of her desk. "The man I hired to find missing children should arrive tomorrow. He also recommended a woman who is an ex-US marine, trained to do search and rescue. Both are Christians and feel God wants them to stop the human trafficking in this province."

"I'm glad." Melissa reached toward Chief. She wriggled her fingers through the hair on his head. "Denny will use him whenever a kid needs a friend." She grabbed the box, setting it down on the floor near the door. "I'm happy that Helen is working out so well for you."

"Speaking of Helen, she phoned a few minutes ago. Her kids are enrolled in that school near the house she's renting. With her husband in jail, there's no reason to fear the drug cartel any longer. Her testimony put them permanently out of business. She also implicated several other members of that community. Now that the Mexican authorities put the bad elements in prison, Campos Tinades can once again be the safe Mennonite community the elders always wanted." Jeremy picked up the box and headed toward the front door.

Melissa followed with Chief by her side. The front door opened before Jeremy could place his hand on the door handle. Helen Rempel walked in. She grinned in Melissa's direction. "I was hoping I hadn't missed you." She walked toward Melissa and wrapped her arms around the younger woman. "I'm going to miss you."

"You do realize you're not getting rid of me completely. As Jeremy's wife, I'll be back often." Melissa glanced at Jeremy. "We need to make some decisions in that regard, by the way.
Now that Helen's here to answer the phone, can you spare the time for an early lunch?" She glanced at Helen. "Will that be okay with you? Your kids started school today, right?"

Helen grinned. "Yeah, they did. Samuel wasn't too happy about going back a grade but he'll get used to it. They are so far behind. Sarah is still afraid of everyone, but her **counselling** sessions are beginning to work." A tear escaped down her cheek before she could brush it away. "I think I need a Christian **counsellor**, too. When my little girl told me .... how can another human treat a little girl like that? Her father ...." Her face turned fierce. Her eyes flashed. "Prison is too good for him." Her hands clenched into fists.

Jeremy put the box down. "Make an appointment with the pastor. He'll help you understand forgiveness and then you'll be able to help Sarah when the time comes for her to release her own anger." He placed a comforting hand on the woman's shoulder. "Will you be okay here?"

Helen nodded her head. "I owe you guys so much. When the FBI brought my kids to me I thought all our troubles were over. But, they've just begun. I need this job to bring some normality to our lives. Answering the phone, filing paperwork, and, now that I understand it, Jenna's accounting program on the computer, I really enjoy the work. I'll be fine. Go. Make wedding plans."

Jeremy opened the door, grabbed Melissa's box of supplies, and stepped back to let his fiancée through into the early spring daylight. He drew in a deep breath as soon as he stepped outside. "Melissa, why don't I put these in your car, and we can take my truck to the Olive Garden for soup and salad?"

"I'll follow you. I want to travel to Rompart right after so I can deal with the people I still need to fire. The current board was so controlled by Richard Belcher, I need to clean house." She watched Jeremy drop her box on the back seat. "Besides, I have more room for Chief to lie down on my back seat than on that bench behind your front seat."

"Sure. Disrespect my truck. You know the restaurant I mean?"

Melissa nodded. "I'll be right behind you." She guided Chief into her back seat, slammed the door, and then climbed into her driver's seat. She waved toward Jeremy as she placed her car in gear.

Following mindlessly behind Jeremy's large Dodge Ram gave her time to think about the dress she'd found yesterday. *I felt like a princess when I tried it on. I hope Jeremy likes it.* She giggled. *I can't believe how comfortable I am with the idea of becoming his wife. It's as if. ....* She glanced heavenward before focusing on the street they travelled. *Lord, You did pick him out for me. Thank you.*

Melissa repeated her thank you as they turned into the parking lot for the restaurant. She found a space two over from Jeremy, parked, and studied her dog in the backseat. "I'll bring you some leftovers, boy. Be good." She patted his muzzle. "We won't be too long." She stepped out of her vehicle when Jeremy appeared beside her door.

Jeremy wrapped his arms around her. "This will never become old. Ever since Dad and Clare's wedding at Christmas, my craving for you is in overdrive. Are you aware of what you do to me?"

Melissa smiled, a secret knowing passing between them. Their decision to remain pure until their wedding night was forcing them to keep some distance between them but she knew it would be worth it. "I love your touch and began marking the days off on my calendar when we will truly be one in every way." She decided to put some space between them now. "Let's go. I'm hungry. Only three months. Not too long."

Jeremy emitted a grumble from deep in his throat. "An eternity, woman." He followed her inside. He groaned. "Three months seems like forever."

Dear Reader

If you liked Redemptive Justice, I would appreciate it if you would help others enjoy this book, too, by recommending to friends, family, and book clubs, and/or by writing a positive review for Amazon, Barnes and Nobles, Goodreads, and Smashwords.

Thank You

Finder's Keepers Mystery Series

BOOK ONE

An ominous shadow hangs over her, as Christine Finder, alias Melissa Rompart, visits the brutal slaying of her parents most nights in a dream. The threat of discovery propels her to search for the whereabouts of the killer to see the man brought to justice. In the meantime, the killer stalks her mind while she operates Finder's Keepers, an agency that searches for the people her clients hire her to find. Nathan Brent is only four years old and missing. Will she find him in time or will the killer find her first?

http://amzn.to/1io0CKR

BOOK TWO

Evil pursues Christine, in this the second book of the Finders Keepers Mystery Series. Retreat is not an option but her move forward makes her vulnerable to the very evil that took her parents' lives. Faced with yet another missing child, she embarks on a search that takes her out of her comfort zone to question her chosen career, her abilities, and her belief system as she helps stricken parents find closure. Christine finds herself confused about her growing interest in Jeremy but she is distracted by the essence of evil that surrounds her.

http://http:// amzn.to/1mdOQWa

BOOK THREE

Pedophiles and prostitutes, the last thing Christine Smith envisioned when she embarked on a career to find missing children. Will she end her work as an investigator and run the company left to her by her dead Father? Now she's been shot! How does her growing relationship with God change her outlook on life? Christine and Jeremy follow the clues in this, the third book in the Finders Keepers mystery series. In Wicked Disregard, they unravel a ring of vicious pedophiles while Christine continues to search for the identity of the man who ordered the death of her parents.

http://amzn.to/1VLthgB

More books by Barbara Ann Derksen
Wilton/Strait Murder Mystery series

Book 1

Vanished! That's what Andrea Wilton and Brian Strait discover when they come to visit their best friends one evening. Where could they be and does God answer prayers, two questions they find the answers to as they journey to another world of voodoo, murder, and more missing people. Andrea and Brian also discover each other as they learn to scuba, fight a common enemy, and search for the proverbial needle in a haystack.

http://amzn.to/VjW34a

Book 2

Andrea Wilton and Brian Strait, from *Shuster Detective Agency*, take on another case to find a missing person. This second book in the series introduces DJ Wiebe, a biker who rides with The Sons Riders, a Christian biker ministry. Another biker, a member of The Demons Raiders, is missing and presumed dead. DJ, his friend, hires *Shuster Detective Agency* to find him. He initiates Andrea and Brian into the biker culture, a world that encompasses motorcycles, leather, drugs and murder.

http://amzn.to/HO63y7;

Book 3

Brian Strait and Andrea Wilton discover that relationship and intrigue go together when they embark on their third adventure, back to the Caribbean. A visit cut short, the two sleuths uncover a plot that challenges their faith

when they search to clear a friend of murder. Their hunt for truth brings them head to head with the black market, human contraband, and culprits who will stop at nothing to line their pockets.

http://amzn.to/HHSfmB

Book 4

Brian Strait and Andrea Wilton leave behind a cruise ship at the Miami harbor for a short visit in the bustling metropolis. Their plans are to purchase wedding finery before flying to the Dominican Republic to marry.

A surprise awaits Andrea when she arrives at the bridal boutique. Trent and Diane Michner, best friends, are waiting to share their special day with them. Andrea believes everything is perfect.

Fate has other plans, however, when Diane and Andrea are kidnapped by Chechen mafia members who spirit women away to several other countries into slavery. Andrea fears for her friend's life when Diane is taken elsewhere. In captivity, she wonders if her wedding was just a pipe dream and where God is in all this. She also encounters a young girl who is hurting and in need of a Savior.

Brian, with the help of Trent and a young friend from the Dominican Republic, Troy, begins a frantic search for his bride-to-be, encountering drug addicts, dirty cops, and murder victims. His faith in God is stretched as he wonders why this has happened to them at this time in their life.

http://amzn.to/13WlYaW

More genres by
Barbara Ann Derksen

Children's Books
Shih-Tzu Puppy Adventures
Scruffles Finds a Home
Squirrels Are People, too

Devotionals
Straight Pipes
Two-Up, Riding with the Lord
Chrome, Shining Faith
Chaps
Road Trip
More Than Bells

Other
Dance With a Broom
Second to None, Warrior Voices

All books can be purchased and shipped
directly to you from
www.barbaraannderksen.com or email:
barbarawrites14@gmail.com to find out more

Acknowledgements

It takes a team to complete a book. I wish to thank my Lord for the gift of writing. Without it my imagination would remain tethered and frustrated. But above all, I thank Him for the ideas, the audience, and for the opportunity to learn new skills every day as I hone my craft and interact with other writers.

I wish to thank everyone who has ever read one of my books and for your diligence in placing a review where you purchased the book. Without you, my words would remain hidden and of no use to anyone.

I also wish to thank my husband for his patience. His input is important to the finished product as he helps me stay true to my male protagonist by making suggestions as he proofs the book.

Linda and LeRoy Collins are special friends who help me find missed typos, overworked words, and inconsistencies. I truly appreciate the time they expend on my behalf.

I also wish to thank a wonderful creative man who spent hours working on the perfect cover for this book. He is Howard Forte, company name **Infinite Skills Media**. If you wish, check out his website: www.infiniteskillsmedia.com or you can contact him about your project at admin@infiniteskillsmedia.com

I really do hope that you enjoy this latest attempt to give your imagination a workout as we delve into another world and step out of your comfort zone into Christian Suspense.

.

www.ingramcontent.com/pod-product-compliance
Lightning Source LLC
Chambersburg PA
CBHW060407260626
47160CB00006B/2464